GW00504126

Beyond
Downing Wood

Beyond Downing Wood

Connie Monk

PIATKUS

1253

Chapter One

She was with him again. The feeling of nearness was vivid, more overpowering than in real life. Where they were wasn't clear, only that it was somewhere by the seashore. Later, when she tried to rekindle these moments, she'd realise that this wasn't a flashback to something they'd shared in life; during the years she'd been with Jeremy any beaches they'd known had been out of bounds, cut off from the land by barbed wire to hinder Hitler's threatened invasion.

She felt no surprise that they should be together; the joy was familiar. The sun was warm, and it was only on her face that she felt a cool breeze. How natural it was to turn to each other! In dreams anything is believable, so there was nothing strange in the sudden change from running barefoot on the sand to lying among the dunes; she didn't wonder how it was they weren't restricted by clothes. In her warm bed she moved her head from side to side on the pillow. She strained to touch him but he remained just out of her reach. She wanted to cry out, to call his name, but her mouth was stiff; she heard herself shout yet couldn't form the words. In her dreaming mind for one brief moment she'd found him; desperately she tried to hold him, to draw him near.

When consciousness hit her, she found her cheeks were wet with tears and her heart was pounding. Joy had been stripped from her, leaving nothing but emptiness, hopelessness.

'Mum! Mum!'

The voice snatched away the last of the dream. There was enough light coming through the attic skylight for her to see Anna by the side of the single bed, her night-time nappy fallen around her ankles. She couldn't read the little girl's expression, but she knew from her tone she was frightened.

'What zat noise you do?'

1

Thankful for the darkness, Julie moved across to make room, then lifted Anna in beside her.

'I was dreaming. Did I shout?'

'Um. I awake.' She snuggled close, small arms and legs wrapping themselves around her mother. 'Mum?' Hearing her mother crying had shaken the security she took for granted.

'It's all right, darling. You stay cuddled in here.'

'Um.' Yes, she'd do that. Even so, her small hand touched Julie's face to check there were no more tears. Reassured, feeling warm and safe, she was soon drifting back into sleep.

Only Julie lay awake. If only she could bring his spirit close again. Her body was warm — from the sun-drenched beach or from the blankets? Across her face she could feel the cool breeze — a wind off the sea, or night air coming through the open window? Hearing Anna's even breathing she rubbed her chin against the light-brown curls. She was lucky, she told herself. Some women had been left with nothing. She had Anna, a meaning for her days.

Her eyes grew used to the darkness, the shaft of moonlight from the high window giving enough light for her to see the familiar surroundings. A large attic bed-sitting room, with Anna's low camp bed against the wall, her own single one only a foot or so from it. A table, one high chair, two wooden chairs, a gas cooker, a gas fire, a playpen and a second-hand desk where she worked at her typewriter completed the inventory.

For a moment self-pity took advantage of the stillness of night, caught her at her lowest ebb. The outlines of the poor furnishings of the home she had made would normally have made her feel proud of her independence, but the vivid memory of the dream temporarily stripped her of all hope. Her eyes felt like burning coals in her head as she held her jaw rigid. She cuddled the little body close, needing to feel the warmth and utter trust. She was lucky, again and again she told herself so.

And by morning she had herself in hand; once again she believed it. They were a team, she and Anna. At not quite three there were limits to the companionship the little girl could give. But that worked in both directions, even though Anna didn't realise what she was missing in having no other children to play with. So, with the coming of morning, the routine of the day took shape. At breakfast it was Anna's job to carry to the table the things Julie passed from the cupboard by the sink — plates, spoons, a packet of wheat flakes, a jar of marmalade — then it was her sole responsibility to put out her own bib and Julie's napkin. She was proud of her usefulness, although she was no angel and had her 'off' days the same as any

2

other child. Breakfast over, they had to take the typing Julie had done the night before to the agency and collect that day's work. In the afternoon there was the daily walk, stopping on the way home to buy the evening paper. After tea the attic had a special atmosphere of its own. Once Anna had bathed — sometimes in their own sink and sometimes she and Julie together downstairs in the bathroom shared by the other residents in the letting house — she would happily chatter herself to sleep over the nice friendly rattling noises that came from the typewriter. If Anna's life lacked anything, she wasn't aware of it; she didn't even know the importance of the evening paper and the column of Situations Vacant. For her, life was a very satisfactory affair.

The picture was the first thing Lydia Sutcliffe saw as she picked up the *Morning Herald*, the caption over it reading: 'Hollywood soon to welcome Britain's most recent export.' And there was Sebastian. Time and again during the day she reread the accompanying paragraph informing her when the play finished its run in New York Sebastian Sutcliffe, 'idol of the English theatre and screen', had agreed to play the lead role in the film version. Here in London she felt cut off, left out. Her mouth pouted petulantly as she remembered how adamantly he'd refused that she should drive him to Southampton when he sailed for America.

Once more a civilian when the war ended, he'd managed to divide his life neatly into two separate compartments: there was their home, and that included her and little Merrick; and there were the ever greater demands of his career. His real background was the legitimate theatre, but war service had put that out of the question, and it was the screen that had given him nationwide fame; he'd been granted leaves from the army for acting in films depicting him always as the gallant, uniformed patriot. On each occasion he'd found it irksome that so much had to be crammed into a few short weeks, depriving him of time to polish his performances. But none of that had been noticed by his adoring fans. Probably his greatest help to the war effort had been the number of starry-eyed recruits who'd rushed into the women's services after watching him on the screen. When the war had ended he'd been one of the first to be demobbed and had gone straight into rehearsal, the West End welcoming him back as a great actor and no less a conquering hero because he had not left the shores of his native land.

With a life so full there was little to spare for that other compartment, the one where he kept his wife and son.

The afternoon was half over. She'd read the announcement dozens

3

of times, looked at the photograph even more, and it became clear to her what she had to do. Life had been very dull lately; now, here she was being handed an introduction into all the glitter her adolescence in wartime England had lacked. She swooped her three-year-old son into her arms.

'Daddy's going to Hollywood.' She waltzed him around the room to be rewarded by shrieks of delight. 'Merry and me go too. We'll go to Hollywood, yes, that's what we'll do,' she sang.

He hadn't a clue what she was talking about, but she sounded pleased so it must be something good. He grinned his agreement.

'Shall we do that, shall we, Merry?'

'We do dat.' He jiggled in her arms, infected by her own excitement.

But what she needed was someone to tell her decision to, someone who'd understand. One by one she thought of her acquaintances here in London. Oh, of a sort they were friends, of course they were, but they all belonged to Sebastian's other compartment. They'd be thrilled for him − at least they'd make a pretence of it and hide their envy − but as far as *she* was concerned they wouldn't be interested. She was a mere wife, nothing to do with theatre. They might even consider that her going there, shadowing him around, would put a brake on his progress.

Lydia had first met Sebastian in Devon, where he'd been on release from wartime duty for filmmaking. It had been hardly surprising that, at eighteen, she'd fallen head over heels in love with him, an actor whose name was a household word, an actor whose pictures − although this was a secret she never shared with him − she used to cut out of magazines and stick in a scrapbook. She'd felt she'd tipped off the edge of reality into a golden world too wonderful to believe. It seemed incredible that Sebastian Sutcliffe, more than ten years her senior and used to the adulation that came with fame, should have felt the pull of her attraction. At eighteen she'd longed to be slinky and elegant but nature had had other ideas. Although no one could have called her fat, there had been a softness in her build, her face had been rounded, her cheeks plump; and how she'd hated her bosom and hips! Yet when she'd turned her wide-set eyes on the great Sebastian Sutcliffe, he'd found her unsophisticated charm irresistible − just as she'd meant him to.

All that had been four years ago. She was slimmer now, and as far as clothes coupons would stretch she was elegant too. But slinkiness would remain a dream.

For Lydia Harriday life had always been a very jolly affair; whatever she'd set her heart on, she'd had. In that spring of 1943

4

she'd set her heart on Sebastian. With a naivety more dangerous than she'd realised, and letting instinct be her guide to bring her what she wanted, she had been more the seducer than the seduced. He was older, he was experienced, he ought to have been wiser. At her first suspicion that she might be pregnant she'd told him, her eyes wide and trusting. Indeed, what could be better? But instinct had warned her it wouldn't be wise to voice thoughts along those lines, not to Sebastian nor yet to her parents. Right from the start she'd been uncomfortably conscious of her father's resentment of him. No wonder she'd hugged her pleasure to herself, sure in the knowledge that now there could be no obstacles put in the way of her marriage. Marrying Sebastian Sutcliffe!

The newspapers had delighted in the wedding, grasping at it as a relief from the war; Lydia had revelled in every moment of the occasion and the months that followed. With Sebastian back at his station she'd continued to live at home in Devon, indulging in the luxury of being pampered as her months of pregnancy went by. But she must have been growing up, for she'd learned enough understanding to know that when he had leave she should join him somewhere else. There had been a week in Gloucestershire, a weekend in Oxford. Only after Merrick came into the picture had Sebastian come to her family in Devon. Though Lydia was not the most sensitive person, she preferred now not to dwell on the unspoken atmosphere of those visits.

On discharge from the service Sebastian had taken a house in Grenville Place and brought his family to London, where she'd been received cordially enough by his colleagues but clearly considered to be of little interest.

Now her decision was made and she knew just to whom she needed to speak. Pulling the telephone towards her, she picked up the receiver, dialling 0 to call the operator.

'Long distance, please. I want Deremouth nine three two. Yes, Deremouth in Devon, that's right.' A wait while the receiver clicked; somewhere between London and Devon the number was repeated, then more clicks, another voice, before finally a distant ringing.

'Sorry to keep you ... trying to connect you ...'

Then a familiar voice telling her, 'Delbridge House.'

'Squire?' She knew her father's voice without the need to ask. 'It's me.'

So, apparently, did he know hers.

'Is everything all right? Nothing the matter, Poppet?' No one but her father ever called her Poppet. If they'd tried it, he would soon have made it clear they were trespassing on private ground. He knew

5

her so well, he must have been able to tell from her voice that she had a purpose for phoning. 'I see that husband of yours got his handsome face on the front page this morning.' His words didn't fool her, 'handsome' wasn't spoken as a compliment.

'Yes. It's about that – well, about him staying out there longer than we thought, going on to Hollywood. Look, Squire, I've made my mind up, I'm not going to let you talk me out of it.' She wished it had been her mother who'd answered the phone, for even at this distance the Squire could make her feel guilty. 'I've told Merry all about it, but I wanted to talk to a grown-up, someone who'd understand.'

'Understand? Then there *is* something wrong? You should be left to read his plans in the newspaper, he treats you like – '

'There's nothing wrong. Squire, I'm going to America.'

For a moment he didn't answer. Whatever he'd expected, it wasn't this. Sebastian must have sent for her. Philip Harriday gripped the earpiece of the telephone.

'You mean he'd told you this Hollywood business was coming up, he's sent for you?' She could almost feel his jealousy burning through the telephone wires.

'No, wait! Don't jump the gun. When I read about him making a film – that's when I decided. I don't know how soon he'll be leaving New York, but he'll make the arrangements for us. He'll be meeting a whole host of new people.' As she said it, she saw the way to a better approach. 'Squire, all through the war there was no time for any fun at all. I'll soon be twenty-three.' She heard her own voice as a plea for his understanding. 'Out there everyone will be making a fuss of him – and I'm his wife, I deserve some of the glory. You wouldn't grudge me, Squire. In America I shall buy the swishest clothes I can find. When I come home I'll make dull old London turn round and look at me. I'm going to be in the front line for all the fun that's going.'

Lydia's face broke into a smile as she pictured the scene, a smile made all the sunnier by the gap between her front teeth. Compared with the Hollywood brigade she had no glamour: the sandy freckles that peppered her short nose were the same colour as her curly hair, short as a boy's, just as she had worn it since she was a child. Her one real claim to beauty were her huge, velvety, brown eyes.

Her father could tell from her voice that those eyes were now shining with excitement. She couldn't mean to go away and leave him! What if it wasn't just one film, what if they stayed in Hollywood? But what could he say to stop her going? He felt incapable of answering at all.

6

'Squire? Are you still there?'

'I'm always here. But will he be, when he's got you thousands of miles from your own people? I've never heard such a damn-fool idea. Poppet, wait till he sends for you. *If* he wants you there among all these film people, then let him write and tell you so. Where's your pride, chasing him uninvited? You tell me it's not my business, I've no right to make you change your mind —'

'That's not what I said, you know it wasn't. I said you wouldn't be able to make me change it. It's where Merry and I ought to be, you must see that.'

'Give it time for letters to come through, see whether he gives any hint of wanting you there.'

'That's a mean thing to say. Of course he wants us.'

'How much of his life does he ever give you? Nothing but the scraps! And I'm supposed to throw my hat up with glee that my daughter means to chase across the world for that?'

'I wish I hadn't told you. If it had been you over there you'd have expected Mum and me to join you. Oh, but that's different. That's for *you*, so that *you* wouldn't be lonely.' Silence. She was hurt and angry. She knew why her father resented Sebastian. It wouldn't have made any difference whom she had married; he wouldn't have been able to accept any man but himself in her life. He loved her, yet purposely she was saying things to wound him. 'Squire?'

'Here's your mother.' His voice held no expression. 'You had better discuss your arrangements with her.'

If only she could have told her mother first, and left her to smooth things down with the Squire. Grace Harriday listened to her plan. But, to Lydia's surprise, from her too the reception of the news was guarded.

'Mum? I expected the Squire would niggle, but I was sure you'd think it's a good idea. Why don't you? Is it because you know he'll be difficult?'

'No, I can cope with that.' Grace brushed the idea aside. 'And you're wrong, I do think it's a good idea, you and Sebastian ought to be together — especially in a place like Hollywood, if one can believe half one reads. Anyway, you deserve a chance to live the high life for a while. It'll be very different there from London, you'll get a culture shock. No austerity. I doubt if they even know what the word means in that glittering city of make-believe. You go ahead and enjoy it, Lydia. It's Merry I'm worried for. I expect you'll only be away a few months, so why don't you leave him with us?'

'Leave him? As if you haven't enough to do without a toddler to

7

chase around after. Anyway, Sebastian would be furious. He would feel I was handing over my responsibilities.'

'If you're going to be free to share in the glitz, or whatever they call it, with Sebastian, then Merry will probably be left night after night with a nursemaid.'

'Well, that's different. Don't you see, that way it would be someone we'd employ. Sebastian is very possessive about doing everything that's best for Merrick.'

Grace bit back her words. As if some nursemaid would be better for the lad than being here at Delbridge House!

Lydia's mind was moving on, and in her imagination she could see herself as glamorous as any film star. The glitz, her mother had called it. Yes, that was what she meant her new life to be.

'Tell you what, Mum, if I leave him with you I must be able to tell Sebastian I've engaged a proper nursemaid for him.' He'd like that, a proper English nanny complete with uniform. The corners of her mouth turned upwards. 'Anyway, Mum, the paper doesn't say how soon he's going to Hollywood. I don't know when his play is coming off. I'll write to him and tell him I'm coming. He'll be pleased. It's just the Squire, he always tries to make me feel rotten about Seb. He's against the whole scheme. It's just plain silly. Tell him I deserve some fun, Mum. You can get round him.'

Her mind was already made up. Now she wanted to finish the phone call and get ahead to the next stage. As she replaced the receiver on its stand, she drew a pen and paper towards her.

It was sheer chance that Julie heard of a nanny being needed to look after Sebastian Sutcliffe's son. Reason told her it would be useless to apply. Who would engage an untrained young woman with a two-year-old daughter in tow? But listen to reason and she'd get nowhere. Perhaps fate had a purpose in bringing the advertisement to her attention. Queueing for a bus, she stood behind two girls who were looking through a weekly nursing magazine.

'Hey, Jen, listen to this. Sebastian Sutcliffe's got an ad in the vacancies.'

'For a nurse? I wonder what's wrong with him. I thought I read that he was in New York. Did you know he was ill?'

'Not for him, it's for his son. "To look after three-year-old son of actor. Apply Sebastian Sutcliffe" and then the address.'

'Pity. I'd quite fancy tending his every need. But a three-year-old – no, not even for the gorgeous Sebastian Sutcliffe. That's just not my line.'

8

'Anyway, they'll be looking for qualifications in nursery nursing. It was just that the name stood up and hit me.'

'Excuse me.' Julie tapped her on the shoulder. 'I couldn't help hearing. Would you mind if I jotted down the address – the Sutcliffe child?'

'Well, I'm blowed. You a children's nurse? Want a change from this one?' She nodded her head towards Anna's pushchair.

'This one's my own.' Julie didn't elaborate.

A famous name in the Situations Vacant column ensured one thing: a large selection of applicants. That was why Lydia had worded it the way she had, using Sebastian's name; if she was going to leave Merry in someone else's care, then it was vital she picked the right one. Yet, after interviewing one highly qualified and smartly uniformed nanny after another, her choice fell on Julie, whose only experience was in caring for her own child and who needed a home for them both.

The decision was made for her by the children. Lydia had started to ask Julie the usual questions, although she already had a mental short list of three that fitted her image of the British nanny.

'Where did you train, Mrs Freeman?'

Julie's clear hazel eyes met her squarely. She wasn't going to lie.

'Nowhere. Lectures, tests, practising on dolls, child psychology, all that sort of thing – I've not done any of it. Until I had Anna I'd never bathed a baby or even changed a nappy.'

'So, what work did you do?'

'Wartime?' Of course she had worked. 'As soon as I was old enough I joined the ATS. Secretarial. Now I work for a typing agency, collect work every day and do it in the evening when Anna is in bed.'

Lydia viewed her with new interest. She'd felt the other applicants had looked down on her as 'a mere mother', someone with no understanding of childcare. Moreover, because they'd been uniformed, their clothing had given no indication of their personality. Julie had on a brown tweed swagger coat and a fawn Robin Hood-style hat with a jaunty green feather in the band. Her clothes were practical, bought with an eye to making her clothing coupons cover all her needs, but she was well groomed, the colours suited her, her brown shoes were polished and there were no wrinkles in her stockings. Except for her wedding ring and a Royal Artillery brooch on the lapel of her coat, she wore no jewellery. Nice hands. Hands were important to Lydia. She thought of Julie's letter of application, imagining that smooth, capable-looking hand penning the

9

explanation that she could not attend for an interview unless she could bring her daughter with her.

'You are on your own, you and Anna?' No mention had been made of a man in Julie's life. The two young women were about the same age, and already Lydia sensed that they could be friends. She wished she hadn't asked; it only pointed up the difference in their situations. Quick to follow her question, so quick that Julie could easily have escaped answering, she indicated the children. They were rolling with complete abandon on the carpet, all their energy given to the sheer pleasure of kicking their legs into the air, revelling in having someone to play with. 'Just look at those two scallywags! Like a couple of puppies, full of life and no idea why. But go on, you were telling me about yourself. You were in the ATS, you said?

'I joined in 1942. Almost immediately I met Jeremy — my husband. My aunt — I'd lived with her as long as I can remember — said I was too young, but we persuaded her if I was old enough to join up I was old enough to be married. She wanted me to wait until after the war.'

'Sebastian and I got married during the war, too. I stayed in Otterton St Giles with my family, we met only on leaves.' Wanting to be friends, Lydia emphasised the commonality of their experiences. Talking to Julie made her realise how much she'd missed having her own kind to talk to. 'And Jeremy?' she prompted.

'We had leaves, too. We were so much luckier than many. He didn't go overseas until the invasion, just after I came out of the ATS because I was pregnant.'

'You mean he never saw Anna?' There was no need to spell out to Lydia that Jeremy had been killed.

'Just photos. I had photos taken. It was the following year, in April — you could sense it must be nearly over, they couldn't hold out much longer. Remember how in those last few weeks we began to relax, to let ourselves look forward without being scared we were tempting fate? It wasn't even a big battle, just a sniper's bullet.'

For a moment the room was full of silence. Even the children were still; like statues they knelt looking at each other, waiting for the next move. Nothing in Lydia's manner hinted that she'd already made her decision.

Julie was surprised that she could have talked so freely. Since she'd lost Jeremy, the things that meant most to her she'd learned to keep locked away. Determined not to look as though she wanted sympathy, she pulled her thoughts back to the present.

'So you see I've got none of the right qualifications. But I don't

10

think I'm making a bad job of things with Anna, she's a happy child. I've never bothered what the theorists say, I've just worked at each thing by instinct. It seems to me the most important thing one can do for children is make sure they know they're loved, see that they feel secure. Surely that's what matters, isn't it?' It was dangerously easy to talk to Lydia; Julie came close to forgetting that this was an interview for a job she wanted desperately. 'Mrs Sutcliffe, you must think I've got an awful cheek even applying to work here. I'm asking for a home for Anna as well as myself, and you must have had lots of much better-qualified applicants. I can't be what you had in mind. But if you give me the responsibility of looking after Merrick, he and Anna would learn to be friends and I promise you I'd treat them exactly the same.'

'We all call him Merry, not Merrick. It seems to me that, if Anna is anything to go on, merry he'll stay, too. So, when can you come to me?'

By the end of that same week Julie and Anna moved into the Sutcliffe's house in Grenville Place, taking over the rooms on the third floor. Julie's future suddenly held new and unknown promise.

She'd been at Grenville Place about four weeks when one day Lydia came to the nursery where the children were eating their tea, with jam on their faces to prove it. There was nothing unusual in her coming. Until she'd engaged Julie she had given Merry his tea herself, or sometimes left him with the housemaid. But all that was changed. In Julie she had a friend just as surely as Merry had one in Anna.

'I just rang my parents,' Lydia announced, drawing up a chair to join them at the table. Hardly a day went by without her talking either to her parents or to old friends back home. 'You know what we're going to do, Julie? We're going to Devon to see them — all of us. It's time you got to know them. When I hear from Sebastian about my arrangements, it may be to say he's booked my passage on one of the *Queens* — or perhaps he'll even want me to fly! Anyway, I'd like to see you and Merry settled at Delbridge House. We'll drive down. You'll like it there, I know you will.'

'When are we going?'

'No point in waiting, we'll go tomorrow.' Lydia beamed. 'There's nothing to do but throw a few things in a case. Mum and the Squire are over the moon that I'm coming home.'

'I must sort the children's clothes — '

11

Their wardrobes were sparse, since there were never clothes coupons to spare for anything but essentials.

'Doesn't matter if they have to be washed when we get there. No one stands on ceremony at home. Sebastian may tell me to join him in New York, but if he asks me to wait till he goes to California, I'd rather spend the time at Otterton than here. I can't imagine why I didn't think of it before — there's so much more happening there than here.'

More happening on the outskirts of some Devon village than here in London? Julie raised her eyebrows, her hazel eyes teasing.

'Oh, well, you're a Londoner, I'm not.' Lydia didn't mind being teased. Once Julie got to Otterton she'd understand. 'Lots of people, lots of noise and bustle, but in the streets here you'd be looked on as a nutcase if you wished people you didn't know "good morning". Anyway, in Otterton everyone *does* know me. I'll take you into the village — you wait till you see how pleased they are to see me. When I married Sebastian it caused a real flutter.' She didn't even try to keep the swagger out of her voice. 'Of course, you and my parents may hate the sight of each other.' She gave an infectious laugh that said how impossible she thought the idea. 'But if you get on, Mum is dead keen that you keep Merry there while I'm away. Anyway, whether I have to wait ages or go more or less straight away, I've promised the Squire I'll spend the time there. Much healthier for the children and much more fun in the country. And there's no reason for you to come back here while I'm away.' There was no love in the look she cast around the nursery; already she was into the next stage. Lydia thrived on excitement, and she knew Delbridge House would be buzzing with it at the thought of her coming. 'Bet you, by the time I go you won't want to leave Otterton.'

Julie concentrated on popping a piece of bread and jam into Merry's mouth.

The late-afternoon sunshine of a cold March day slanted in through the nursery window, not a rustle among the bare branches. After the fog of autumn and a winter of ice, snow and flood, today seemed to hint that spring must be in the wings. But during the night the wind started to howl, and through the atmospheric crackles on the nursery wireless next morning the newsreader told of blizzards in the north, gales already blowing into the West Country, winds expected to strengthen and cause structural damage.

Lydia wasn't a girl to let a puff of wind throw her plans, so, holding on to their hats, they stowed their luggage and set out. To start with, the children were fractious. It was cold in the car and they resented being confined to the back seat with Julie between them

12

ready to anchor them down if need be. But soon, without their realising it, they were infected by the air of excitement. It stemmed from Lydia. News travelled fast in Otterton, so by now the village would be abuzz with the word that she was coming. Those who made a weekly jaunt to Deremouth to the pictures felt she had been raised to the heights, and that through her they would share in some of Sebastian's fame.

'Bet you anything the Squire will have sorted out the pieces of music I can play and put them on the piano,' Lydia said and chuckled. 'And for supper tonight Mum's sure to have wangled pork chops from Mr Geary, the butcher. They're my favourite.' She couldn't think why she had wasted all those weeks in London without Sebastian.

Brought up by an aunt who had been killed by a V-2 rocket, Julie remembered her childhood as happy, but for her there could be no going back. Today was the start of an adventure, new places, new people. The trip to Devon might be a working holiday, but it was a holiday for all that, the first she and Anna had had together. Julie was young, the promise of a bright tomorrow was irresistible. She pulled off her halo hat and threw it onto the front passenger seat of the car, shaking her hair free. Quite straight, cut in the pageboy style of the day, it suited her personality; it suited her even features too. Catching Lydia's eye in the driving mirror, Julie laughed. Shedding her hat was symbolic of a new liberty.

Merry had memories of Delbridge House, maybe not clear memories but enough for him to know that he should be pleased as the car roared on its way out of London. Anna, six months younger and not used to car journeys, could only be sure that this was no ordinary day. There was a yellowy hint in the overcast, grey sky; to those who could read the signs it was a promise that the snow was moving south. Anna saw it only as part of the happiness she could feel all around her; the car was full up with it, making her mouth want to smile all the time. That must be why her mum and Merry's started singing as they went along. She liked it so much that she added her own contribution, la-la-ing out of tune and with no idea of the words.

'Miss Holly had a dolly who was sick, sick, sick ...', 'Ol' MacDonald Had a Farm', 'Hickory, Dickory, Dock' ... ah, now here was one she knew. Her smile turned into a beam as she looked along the seat toward Merry and chanted 'Hick'ry dick'ry hock, mousie up the dock ...' The way the branches of the trees waved at them as they went by added to the thrill of the adventure. This wasn't a bit like riding in a red bus in

13

London, where no one sang songs or smiled. Anna looked joyfully at Julie.

'Sing about sick dolly 'gen — shall we sing 'bout sick dolly?'

They did.

They had covered about eighty miles by the time they stopped for lunch. So far the journey had been easy and it seemed their luck was holding out. They were all hungry and had already decided to make for the first place they saw where they could take children.

'Look! Pansy's Pantry — half a mile.' It was Julie who saw the notice.

'Cross your fingers that it's not a lorry drivers' pull-in.' Lydia grinned. 'Although, come to think of it, with this little lot that might be the best place for us.'

Checked curtains, a jangling bell to announce their arrival, checked tablecloths and a welcoming, overlarge and far from young waitress wearing an apron of matching material. The effect of red and white squares was dazzling, but at least the place looked clean.

'Can we see the menu?' Lydia smiled, pleased with their luck.

'That I can't do.' The large chequered lady was poised ready to rush off and fetch food. 'Just the one meal. No choices. Managed to keep going all through the war like that, and as long as the scarcities last, it's the best way to make sure there's no waste.' She rested her folded arms on her plump bosom, pleased to have nice young women to chat to. Most of her customers were regulars. 'Today we've got a a good, warm stew with all the veg. Just the thing to keep the cold out in this wind. You leave it to me, I'll mash it small for the little 'uns. No high chairs, but there now, they'll be right as ninepence on your knees. Come a long way, have you? I see you parked a car outside.'

'From London. We're on our way to Devon.' Lydia took pity on her curiosity, which made her feel she was getting closer to home. Already people took an interest in strangers.

'Well, now. No one will ever be able to put the clock back to how things used to be — before the war, I mean. But fancy that! Two young ladies and their babies driving all that way. If we'd known twenty — ah, or even ten — years ago how women's lives would blossom, we'd never have believed it. Born too soon, that was my trouble.' Maybe she had been, but she sounded contented enough with her lot as she waddled kitchenwards to fetch their stew.

Good, wholesome home cooking. They were all hungry, even

the children opened their mouths wide with appreciation. The success of the meal fitted the pattern of their day, or so they believed. They had no way of guessing the chain of events it was to prompt.

Chapter Two

They'd been on the road again for about a quarter of an hour when Merry and his lunch parted company. From then on the mood of the journey changed. No one sang, and even Anna was restless. Every half-hour or so Lydia stopped the car and they all piled out to fill their lungs with bitingly cold fresh air. This was no ordinary gale; without being held the children could have been knocked from their feet. It was a relief when, as dusk started to fall, they finally slept.

'I thought we'd have been there ages before this.' Lydia frowned. 'I'm going to put my foot down now they're asleep. Warn me if he looks like waking.'

Julie looked fondly at the sleeping children, one cradled on each side of her, their legs outstretched along the leather of the seat.

So they came through Exeter, poor scarred Exeter. Julie had been there once before, years ago. Her memories of it were part of the holiday magic of childhood, something she'd taken for granted would stay unchanged. She saw reminders of war, sights accentuated by the dusk. In London she'd seen it all before and on a much greater scale, yet here it came as a shock. Cleared bomb sites; a row of houses with a gap in the middle, its neighbours still shored up for support; an area where rebuilding had already begun. As if to orchestrate the scene, the howling wind tunnelled through every gap and alleyway. Dust and grit, scraps of paper, discarded cigarette wrappers, anything light enough to move was pulled into the mad dance.

'One thing about Otterton St Giles' – Lydia's anticipation had bubbled back now that the journey was nearing its end – 'there's nothing there to have attracted friend Adolf.'

Julie's spirits rose too. A month ago she might have been frightened to look forward and trust in the future. But within hours of her arrival at Grenville Place, the drab period she and

16

Anna had lived in that attic room had slipped into the shadows. Oh, there had been good times, moments with Anna that would stay clear and bright for ever. And she had never allowed herself to stay downhearted. But she could not have envisaged an employer like Lydia, nor the friendship that had grown so naturally. If Lydia delighted in life at Delbridge House, then so would Julie. By the time they drove through the small coastal town of Deremouth she was ready for anything. The last of the buildings were left behind, and the lights of the car shone on a signpost that told them "Otterton St Giles 3 miles".

From then on the lanes were narrow and the hedges high.

'Here's Devon for you,' Lydia announced, as if she'd produced it all herself.

Another turning, another change of scenery in the fast-fading light. Sloping fields of farmland, the farmhouse and outbuildings edging the lane. Towards the summit was a spread of glasshouses.

'The Grants live here. Rowans is the name of the farm. Not the nursery, though, that belongs to Quintin.' To Lydia it seemed adequate explanation.

'Nursery? Oh, you mean all those greenhouses. You know the family, do you?'

'As long as I can remember I've known them. Mr and Mrs Grant — Peter and Tess they're called — are buddies of Mum and the Squire.'

'And Quintin, with the nursery? Is he a son?'

'Not a real son, but I think they've probably almost forgotten that he isn't. That's the way the Grants are. They had a son, Paul. He was super, when we were kids everything was fun if Paul was there. It was rotten, he got killed in North Africa.' The silence that followed told Julie just how rotten it had been. 'There's a daughter, a year or so older than us, she's called Trudie. Even when we were all young she never monkeyed around like the rest of us. Clever, serious' — that infectious giggle again — 'always made me feel boisterous and rough. When people are ultracorrect it does that to you, doesn't it? Makes you talk too loudly, laugh too much. It's different now we're grown up — me married to Sebastian, and Trudie a solicitor, would you believe — but when we were young I used to give her a wide berth whenever I could. If you wanted action, then Paul was your man.'

Lydia drove on in silence. Just beyond the boundary of the farm she turned right and they were almost immediately in near-night, the lights of the car beaming ahead through a tunnel of dark trees. This evening all the devils in hell seemed to have

17

been let loose in the wild gloom, snatching and tearing at the branches.

'This is Downing Wood.' From Lydia's tone she might have said, 'This is paradise.' 'We're almost home.'

A high, thin branch was ripped loose to fall with a sharp rap against the window. It did no damage, but the sound disturbed Merry. Half-awake he whimpered, his little body shuddering involuntarily.

'Stop, Lydia. He needs to get out.'

The brakes were jammed on, the door thrown open. Julie pulled Merry from the car and bumped Anna unceremoniously to lie along the seat. The action woke her to the fact she was being left behind.

'Me. Me tum too. Mum, an' me.'

'Can I leave her with you? It's awfully wild out here.'

'Sure. I'll pull off the lane, there's a way into the wood just along here,' Lydia shouted above the noise of the wind. 'We may need to give him a minute or two in the air. I'd hate us to arrive home just as he's sick again.' It was unlikely anyone else would be driving along here on a night like this, but the lane was narrow, barely more than the width of the car.

Merry whimpered. 'Wan' a wee.'

'An' me out. Mum, an' me.' Anna's little hands were beating against the rear window as Lydia drove off.

It was a good thing she'd left Anna in the car, Julie thought as she crouched, sitting on her heels to bring herself to Merry's level. She knew he was frightened, and who could wonder? From down here the dark shapes of the swaying trees were enormous, and even with her steadying hand it was as much as he could do to stand up in the force of the wind.

'What dat?' His scream would have drowned any answer. A gust caught Julie off guard, and she steadied herself by moving forward to kneel and grasped his little body against her. Was she trying to reassure him or was she drawing her own strength from his need of reassurance? Throughout the day the gale had buffeted ever more fiercely, each sharp thrust fading to gather its forces for the next. This time there was no easing, it was as if it meant to suck up everything in its track. Sharp twigs blew against them, scratching their faces, getting entangled in their hair; a tall bough was torn loose to force its way through the lower branches and land within feet of them as Julie protected Merry's head with her hands. All the force of nature tore at the wood, screaming through branches that waved and dipped. Julie's jaw was tight.

18

'Quick, Merry.' She tried to sound calm as she pulled his short trousers down and hoisted him from the ground. 'Then we'll go back to the car, back to find Mummy and Anna.'

This must surely be the crescendo; no storm could gather more force. But she was wrong. As she stood up, still holding Merry against her, the breath was knocked from her by a gust even more violent. She stood still, both feet planted firmly as she got her balance. Right then she heard a sound that made her blood run cold. With a triumphant screech the wind did its worst and tore one of the great beech trees from the ground. It was too dark to see which way it would fall, too dark to be sure how far into the wood it was; there was nothing but the eerie sound as it creaked and groaned its way earthwards, breaking everything in its path.

'Anna!' Julie heard herself shout, over Merry's piercing scream. Hugging him close, she started to run in the direction of the car, only to feel her ankle turning on the rutted ground. In pain, she shuffled to the edge of the grass, then onto the firmer surface of the lane. She'd seen how far down the lane Lydia had driven before she turned onto a track into the wood. But now there was no sign of car lights; all Julie could see near the start of the track was a dark mound where the tree had come to rest. Perhaps the car was beyond it, farther into the wood, perhaps that was why she couldn't see the lights.

She knew the uselessness of the hope even as she tried to clutch at it.

Please, please, she thought wildly, let it be just the top of the tree that's on the car, the small branches, those that won't have − won't have ... Her mind wouldn't go any further. 'Please help me to get her out,' she said under her breath. 'Anna! She'll be so frightened. Don't let her be hurt. I'll break the branches, that's what I'll do, then I'll open the door. Help me do the right thing. Don't let them be hurt, not either of them.'

As she came to the mound of branches she knew why the lights of the car had gone out. The great tree had crushed the front of the car, the main trunk falling across the windscreen and dashboard. At this time of year the branches were bare, but they were thick and spread out; from front to back of the car there was no way through them. Her eyes were used enough to the recently faded light to see that the back door must be buckled beyond opening even if she could have forced her way through to it.

'Anna! It's all right, Anna, I'll get you out,' she shouted. Oblivious to the cuts and scratches, she tried to reach through the jagged branches and twigs so that she could beat on the rear window. And in her other arm, propped against her hip, she held the crying baby – for that was what Merry had suddenly become. She hardly gave him a thought, with Anna there on the back seat of the car. And Lydia? One look at the front of the car and Julie's mind hit a black wall, her imagination came to a stop.

The rear window must be broken, there would be glass every-where, but if she could reach it she'd try and knock any remaining shards out and lift Anna free. Was that what she should do? She had to do *something*.

There was no movement from inside the car. Even a cry would have been better than this. Under the tent of branches it was too dark to see. They were thick, she would need a saw. She was helpless.

'Show me what to do. Help me, please, God, help me.' As if to taunt her the thought sprang into her mind that the storm was what people would call an 'act of God', so the crushed car must be an 'act of God' too. And she was calling for His help! What sort of a god was it who'd do this to a baby? And to Lydia – Julie knew that no one in the front of the car could be unhurt. Behind that thought came another, but she pushed it away before it could register: no one could be alive. An act of God! For a moment the wind had died, as if it had spent all its fury, the momentary stillness emphasising its triumphant progress. But the lull had been sent to trick her. A sudden harsh blast made last year's leaves leap to smack against her legs.

Even now, on her own she would have wasted time trying to tear away what small branches she could before she accepted she had no hope of reaching Anna and Lydia. 'Mum, Mum, where Mum?' It was only in mind she heard the small voice. From inside the car there was no sound at all.

In the distance surely that was a hint of light? A car must be coming. The beam of light was getting brighter, wider. 'Thank you.' She said it aloud, needing to hear her own voice as relief flooded through her. Standing out in the middle of the lane she started to wave, running towards what by this time was definitely car lights.

'I need a phone. I need help. Please help me.' Words poured out as the driver pulled to a standstill and wound down his window.

'Have you broken down? I'm not much good with engines, but I'll see if I can do anything for you. Where are you parked?'

'There – there's a track – tree down. Must get help . . .'

Now that someone else was there, the slim hold on her control snapped. She couldn't stop shaking; even her teeth chattered. The driver got out, then, shouting to her to sit inside and wait for him, ran on to where he could see the mound of branches enveloping the wrecked car. Just as she had, he expected to be able to break his way through. She sensed his confidence − in her first relief she almost believed in it.

In a state of numbed shock she lived through the next half-hour. Only later, remembering, would any of it register.

Back along the lane and out of the wood they drove, turning left at the junction, retracing the route she and Lydia had come such a little time before. In short sentences she told the man what had happened and where they'd been going; more often than she realised, she told him how frightened Anna must be.

'Where are we going? How far is it to a phone?'

'Almost there. I'm taking you home − the farm's just here. From there I'll call the police and the ambulance, then we'll go back to the wood. Aunt Tess will look after Merry.' Later, when her mind started to focus again, she'd realise that he'd known Merry's name without being told.

Then, too fast for safety, he swerved the car off the lane, braking to a sudden halt by the front door of the farmhouse.

'Rowans? Lydia pointed it out to me.' It seemed a lifetime ago.

'That's right. The Harridays, Lydia's people, they're old friends. Aunt Tess will keep Merry until either you or Mrs Harriday come back for him − or all night, if that's better.'

She accepted his word. In her present state she didn't even question.

It didn't turn out like that. Neither Tess nor Peter Grant was at home, only Trudie. Julie remembered what Lydia had said, though it didn't seem to fit the gentle kindness in Trudie's greeting. Later, thinking back to these moments, she'd see both Trudie and Quintin in her mind's eye, see them and really look. Now their appearance, and that of the rambling farmhouse, barely pierced her consciousness. All she could concentrate on was that Quintin was ringing for help and that Trudie took Merry from her as if they were already old friends.

Trudie, she realised later, was the loveliest creature she'd ever seen. Straight hair, pale and fair, cut in a fringe across her clearly defined dark brows; sweeping dark lashes that accentuated eyes of deep blue. And Quintin? An aristocratic face, but not a handsome one. His brown eyes were hidden behind thick-rimmed and shaded glasses; that was the only thing that initially impressed itself on Julie's awareness.

'Right, we will leave Trudie to look after Merry,' he said, rejoining them. 'That's all right, Trudie?'

'Of course. Let's go and find the toy box, Merry. Remember the toy box?'

Merry didn't. But there must have been something familiar in the atmosphere of the house, for he went off happily enough with his new friend. Then Julie and Quintin went back in the car, once again heading towards Downing Wood.

'You should have turned right there. That's the lane where they are. You're going to the wrong way!' What did he think he was doing?

'We'll have to approach from the other direction, through the village. If any rescue vehicles are there before us we shouldn't be able to get round them, then we'd be blocking the lane. There's another track beyond where Lydia turned off. We'll come up from the village, then we can pull right into the wood there and be out of the way. We'll have to give space enough for the police and ambulance to use the track to turn.'

The route through the village added a mile or so, but as they approached in the light of the headlamps they could see the lane was just as they'd left it. Quintin turned into the track and drove some way, putting the car right off the lane, then, without waiting for Julie, he got out and started towards the scene of the accident. She followed him. The gale had gathered up its strength again. He knew the path, while she had to feel her way, and the gap between them lengthened. It seemed as if he purposely put distance between them before he turned on his torch. By the time she'd shuffled her way along the uneven ground to reach the lane, he was already at the car, the beam of light shining between the mound of branches and through the broken rear window.

'Let me see!' she yelled, running now. 'Shine the light on me, let Anna see I'm here.'

He switched off the torch.

And at that moment the police car came towards them and they could hear another bell, either a fire engine or an ambulance, fast approaching.

'Phil, that was the phone.' Grace shouted up the stairs, as if he hadn't heard it. 'Phil, you'd better come.'

He was Squire to all of them, even his wife. It was seldom she gave him his real name and when she did he knew it was something important. One last look in the mirror, making sure that the red and white spotted handkerchief he wore around his neck was knotted with just the right jaunty grace, then he opened the bedroom door. He was always careful about his appearance, but especially today when, any minute, they'd be here. They? His mind didn't get beyond the one person, his Poppet.

'Was it her? What's been delaying her? I thought she would have been here in daylight. Didn't you tell — ?'

'Phil, it was Quintin phoning from Rowans. There's been an accident in Downing Wood.'

At the word 'accident' his heart seemed to miss a beat; but Downing Wood . . . a narrow lane like that, nothing worse than a scrape could happen there. Something she couldn't get round, probably, that would be why she'd gone back to Rowans.

'I'll get right over there. Don't waste time telling me, she can explain when I pick her up.'

Grace didn't move. It was something in the way she stood so still with her hand gripping the newel post, blocking his way at the foot of the stairs, that frightened him.

'Accident? For God's sake don't just stand there, woman! What sort of an accident?'

'A tree down.'

He ran his fingers through his iron-grey hair; his short, clipped beard seemed to bristle with irritation.

'Damned gale! What a day for the child to have to drive all that way and then find the lane blocked. So she's turned back to Rowans? That's what you're saying, isn't it?'

Grace shook her head. 'On the car.'

His hands gripped her shoulders like a vice. The piercing glare in his light-blue eyes held naked fear.

'For Christ's sake, the young fool must have told you more than that.' He might have been trying to shake the words from her. 'He's got her out? Why isn't he bringing her on home?' He dared not put into words the horror that painted a picture in his imagination.

'Don't look at me like that!' Grace rasped at him. 'She's *my* daughter as well as yours. I'll get our coats. We'll talk as we go. I'd better drive.'

Grace never let emotion get the better of her. In moments of crisis it was always she who stayed calm and pulled them through. One of them had to; little use it would be to depend on *him*. Her heart cried out, yet her expression said nothing. She hated herself for the familiar jealousy that tinged her anguish even at a moment like this. What if it had been *her* trapped in the car by a fallen tree? Would he be standing there like a cornered animal, terrified? She wouldn't let herself listen to the question, fearful of its answer. Instead she turned away to get their coats. Hang on to reason, don't let him see you're frightened too.

23

Fear in his eyes? In that moment it was more like hatred, for her and for everything that threatened the one person he truly loved. 'My daughter as well as yours ...' How dared she pretend there was nothing special between him and Poppet? Just look at her, cold as ice. My Poppet, what in God's name's happened to you? He put his arms into the sleeves of the duffel coat she held for him, then followed her out.

Before he'd slammed the car door she started the engine. That ought to have told him something of the turmoil within her, but he couldn't see far enough outside himself to notice.

'Where is she now, just tell me that?'

When she did tell him he sat hunched, arms folded across his chest as if he were in physical agony.

'Merry wasn't in the car. He's being looked after at Rowans. Just Lydia and Anna — Julie Freeman's little girl.'

She doubted if he'd even heard her.

'Is this the fastest you can drive? Hurry, can't you? She'll want to know we're there.' Time and again he said it as they cut through the windswept night, 'She'll want to know we've come for her.'

The firemen were already working with their lifting equipment, headlights of the rescue vehicles beaming on the path into the wood. Just outside the main orbit of light a group of men stood, waiting for the moment when they could play their part. Then Grace noticed the one solitary woman standing a little apart. That must be Julie Freeman. *Her* little girl was in there with Lydia. Leaving Philip — not that he noticed her going — she went to Julie's side.

'They're working fast, they'll soon get them out.' Still she managed to keep her low-pitched voice level and calm. In the gloomy shadows, as she and Julie looked at each other, both of them understood all that was left unsaid.

'You're her mother? Mrs Harriday?'

Grace nodded.

'So many branches, I couldn't even get near.' Julie talked more to herself.

An ambulance, turned ready for the journey to hospital, was waiting with its doors open. The wind tunnelled through the lane, howling as loudly as ever, but the sound was drowned out by the noise of the cutting equipment. Any second the lights beaming at the car would give the first glimpse of the two passengers. The last hour — hour? time had lost its meaning — had been a nightmare, leading to this moment. For Julie it was too late now to hold back the pictures that tormented her mind. The pressure of that hand on her arm was firm and reassuring.

24

For a second she turned to Grace; between them was the same unspoken fear.

'Now the stretcher ...' came the voice of one of the ambulance crew.

'Wait!' Grace's hold tightened as Julie instinctively moved forward. The stretcher was being carried to the rear part of the car. The cutters hadn't got through to the front yet. It must be Anna who was to be brought out.

It was too much for the Squire.

'For Christ's sake, get to the front! Get her out! Let me do it, let me get to her!' He couldn't keep still, his feet had been marking time on the spot, his clenched fists beating a tattoo on each other as if his sanity depended on movement. Now he pushed past the waiting stretcher. 'I can see her, let me get at her. Poppet, we're getting you – '

'Stand back, guv'nor, the chaps'll get through to her. They know best what to do.'

Then another voice, one of the ambulance attendants, 'Right, now lift.'

How tiny Anna looked on the stretcher! Grace must have let go of Julie's arm, for now it was one of the firemen who held it, guiding her to the step of the ambulance. Doors closed, the engine was switched on, and smoothly they started forwards through the tunnel of leafless trees. The clang of the bell had sounded comforting as it had approached; now, so loud and urgent, it sent a chill of dread through her. Anna's face was deathly pale, dark blood matted in her hair above her left ear, and her eyes were closed.

The time hadn't yet come when parents would be seen as helpful to a child's recovery. At the hospital Anna was transferred to a trolley and pushed away with a bustle of efficiency that held no place for Julie. She followed behind, along one long passage, round a corner and along another until, coming to swing doors, the trolley was wheeled through and she was told to wait on a wooden bench in the corridor. Someone wearing a white coat came to ask her Anna's details, gave her a form to sign authorising surgery if it was necessary. None of it seemed real. The only reality was the harsh green gloss paint on the walls and the heavy smell of disinfectant in the air.

'Miss Holly had a dolly who was sick, sick, sick ...' The words of the song echoed in her head. Oh, Anna, what have I done to us? I've brought you here, all my fault. None of this need have happened, we could have stayed in our room in Finchley, we were happy. I ought to have seen how happy we were. You could have been in bed, warm and safe. I ought to have been content, I ought to have been grateful. Now what have I done to you? You were safe . . . you were happy . . . Round and round it went in her mind.

'Are you the child's mother?'

Julie had been on the edge of losing the battle, tears had been very close. Now, at the sound of the nurse's voice, fear drove away every other emotion.

'What's happened? What are they doing to her? Can I see her?'

'This way' was the nearest she had to an answer.

One of the rules for the nurses was that they wore rubber-soled shoes; Julie had steel tips on her heels, that way they lasted longer. The clacking roused the attention of the inmates of the rows of beds as she was led the length of the long ward. One woman was plastered and bandaged so thoroughly she looked more like an Egyptian mummy than a live human; others had legs in traction or arms supported on frames. Julie scanned each bed for sight of the little figure she wanted. The curtains were still pulled around the last space and that was where she was taken. Anna had been cleaned up, a wound on her head stitched and bandaged. She was lying with her eyes almost closed. Only at the sight of Julie did she open them wide and start to cry.

'Mummee . . . up, Mummee . . .' She rolled over, ready to kneel and then stand. At home she'd given up using a cot, and now the sight of the imprisoning bars must have frightened her. She rattled the metal cot-side, her screams holding all the terror of the accident as well as the pain and frustration of the moment. When Julie leaned over the dividing barrier and held her shaking body, she fought to clamber into her mother's arms.

'Now, now, this won't do. You'll be waking up all my patients.' Authority in the person of Sister appeared through the opening in the curtain. 'Say good night to Mummy, Anna, you'll see her tomorrow. You settle her, Nurse Bryant. It's kinder to come away quickly, Mrs Freeman.'

It was swift but there was nothing kind about it. Julie knew she had to leave her, there was no arguing with hospital rules. Certain hours were set aside for visiting, those and no more. If only she could have stayed, held Anna in her arms until she'd fallen asleep. Instead she steeled herself to walk away, following the Sister as she indicated, to be given a chair facing her across the desk in her office and to hear the result of the examination the child had undergone in that inner sanctum beyond the swing doors.

'She has had a lucky escape, Mrs Freeman. We can't know exactly

26

what happened, but from the report of where she was lying I imagine she must have been thrown from the back seat when the force of the tree hit the car. In her fall she knocked her head, there is the one wound just above her left ear. It's been stitched. She must have lost consciousness immediately − a blessing, because with a car full of broken glass things would have been far worse had she been awake and fighting.' Sister was an austere-looking woman, the dread of many of the young student nurses. Now, unexpectedly, a smile lit her thin face. 'No bones broken, no lasting damage. The young are made of rubber.'

In her relief, Julie faced up to the sick dread of the last hours. Her arms and legs seemed to be made of cotton wool.

'Used to tumbles.' She forced an attempt at a laugh, doing her best to respond to Sister's effort. 'So when can I take her home?'

'We shall need to keep an eye on her for a few days.'

Home! But where was home? Where was Lydia? Long before this she must have been brought into the hospital. Was she still undergoing examination? In the front of the car, how could she have come off as lightly as Anna? Julie remembered the firm grip of Grace Harriday's hand on her arm, and heard again the agony in Lydia's father's voice as he had pushed his way towards the car. Where were they now?

'The accident ... the other person in the car?' If she'd been brought here, then surely the Sister would know.

'I'll see what I can find out for you. Wait outside in the corridor again while I go and make enquiries.'

When they came into the antiseptically clean corridor there was someone already waiting on the bench. It wasn't until she spoke that Julie recognised her.

'Merry's sound asleep, my parents are with him. I came to collect you.'

It was Trudie Grant.

That night Julie was taken back to Rowans. Lydia had told her the Grants were friends of the family, but how many people would extend friendship to include a newly engaged nursemaid, a complete stranger?

Inside the farmhouse the atmosphere was one of warmth and hospitality. It took every ounce of Julie's willpower to respond to it. All she wanted was to crawl away on her own, to keep mental vigil with Anna until morning came.

'We're back. Here's Julie,' Trudie sang out as she ushered her into the large, comfortable sitting room.

'Do you mind? Us calling you Julie, I mean?' The woman who stood up and held her hand out in welcome must be Trudie's mother.

'Of course I don't mind. It's so good of you to bring me back here . . . all that Quintin did, and now Trudie coming to fetch me. I haven't seen the others − Lydia, I mean. Trudie says she has to have surgery.' The scene in the wood was too clear in her memory. 'If only I hadn't shouted for her to stop so that I could get Merry out of the car, or if she'd waited in the lane instead of driving into the track − '

'If only − always one can say if only.' Even in that first meeting she was aware of the strength in the man. This must be Peter Grant. A farmer, a man of the country, but most of all a man who gave one confidence. It was as she looked at Peter that Julie recalled what Lydia had said about Paul, the son who'd been killed. 'If you wanted action, Paul was your man.' She sensed that much the same could be said of Peter. He was tall, broad-shouldered, with light-brown, curly hair that looked as vigorous as everything else about him. It was only March, so his tanned, weather-beaten complexion must have been with him all winter.

'Perhaps she might have parked the car a foot or two farther along the track,' Tess offered backing his remark, 'then it would have been the rear that would have sustained the major damage, not the bonnet and the engine; perhaps she might have set you down at that spot to get out with Merry, what chance then when the tree fell? Tonight we should be thankful that Anna hasn't been seriously hurt. And when Quintin gets home, let's hope he brings good news of Lydia too. Come by the fire while I go and dish up the supper.' Warmth and food were her way of giving sympathy and support, a way that seldom failed. 'Pour her a glass of something, Peter, I'm sure she needs it.'

Earlier Julie hadn't been able to concentrate on anything except the need to get back to Anna and Lydia. Now, as if in contrast, her senses were heightened. Affection seemed to radiate from Tess: it was in the glance that accompanied her words to Peter, in the smile she bestowed on Julie, in the way she scooped Henry, the black and white cat, off the armchair by the fireside so that Julie could sit there. Her pretty face looked untouched by strife, as if it still bore the innocence of childhood. Yet she had lost a son in the war − and tonight, with the fear she had felt while waiting at the hospital, Julie could understand something of what that must have meant. When Tess and Peter had first come to Rowans they had not been long married. In those days she had indeed been pretty, hair as fair as

28

Trudie's was today, and eyes of the same dark blue. Now the fair curls had faded into mouse, but her figure was as trim and her eyes as bright – even though these days she put on spectacles to read. The essence of her spirit was something far more deeply rooted than appearance; it stemmed from a deep trust in the ultimate rightness of things. This house had seen sadness, great sadness, and yet Julie had never been as concious as she was here of contentment. They weren't putting on a show for her; just as they were, this was the Grants. Already she knew they were her friends.

Later, as they sat at supper, Julie talked about the journey and the way they'd all sang.

'Lydia was so excited when we came through Deremouth and saw the sign that said "Otterton St Giles 3 miles".'

'You say *she* was excited, you should have seen the Squire,' Peter said. He frowned, his mind on his friend.

But Julie's thoughts were with Lydia. 'She is going to be all right, isn't she? Do you know what they're doing to her?' If only they could turn back the clock! She seemed to hear Lydia's voice as they drove, singing as if to defy the storm, 'Miss Holly had a dolly who was sick, sick, sick ...' Her mouth trembled, but she held her jaw firm.

'Quintin is with Grace and the Squire at the hospital. We'll know more when he gets home.'

That evening Julie could concentrate only on the things of paramount importance – Anna and her own thankfulness that soon she'd be well; Lydia and the uncertainty, the fear, that black wall that made it impossible for her to look into the future. Quintin was outside her tunnel vision, she felt no surprise that he should wait at the hospital for hours with the Harridays. She remembered the look of silent understanding that had passed between her and Grace. How must she feel now, waiting, frightened to imagine, sitting on the wooden bench, looking up expectantly as each soft-soled nurse rustled by, always hoping this would be the one to bring news ...?

' ... will fix you up with something for the night.'

She pulled her thoughts back to the room, making herself concentrate on what Tess was saying. Gratefully she let her take control of her wellbeing.

'You and Merry – and Anna, of course – are welcome to stay here while Grace and the Squire need to spend their time at the hospital. But it could be that by morning Lydia will be home sporting a plastered arm or leg or something. Let's wait and see what tomorrow brings.'

Chapter Three

It was five o'clock in the morning, too early for any hint of dawn. Quintin held Grace's arm as they came down the steps of the hospital.

'I wish he'd come home.' She talked as much to herself as to him. 'They know it's going to be morning before she opens her eyes again; she's bound to sleep like this for hours now she's safely been brought out of the anaesthetic. As if there isn't enough to worry about without − I know it's tough on him, but it's not going to help her if he lets himself go to pieces.' At the bottom of the steps she turned to him, and in the dim light from the hospital vestibule he could see her stricken expression. 'Oh, Quin, it's a bugger' − spoken quietly, but spoken from her heart 'that's what it is. A bugger.' She shut her eyes as if to hold off what she couldn't bear. To speak like that was out of character. Grace had made herself the family tower of strength, but words could not give her enough bravery to accept this.

Quintin tightened his hold on her arm. The shared fear stripped them of the normal conventions.

' ... helpless,' he muttered, ' ... would do anything ... just helpless.' He had never said it before, but Grace hadn't needed telling. Even as children he'd been Lydia's willing slave, there'd been no other star in his firmament.

She felt his need of comfort, and it gave her back some of the courage everyone had come to expect from her.

'I know, Quin. And she's going to need you, my dear, she's going to need all of us.'

A movement of the swing doors at the tops of the steps attracted them. The Squire! Something must have happened!

'What is it? Has she woken?' She couldn't ask that other question.

'I wanted to catch you before you left. Now listen — and do what I say. You're not to talk about this, start people gossiping about her. Not a word. You hear me.'

She not only heard him, she understood what he'd left unsaid.

'You mean you don't want me to get a message to Sebastian, is that it?' His hand was gripped in hers. A few hours ago Julie had felt strength and comfort in her touch. Now it had to be that and so much more, it had to convey to the Squire all the things that were impossible to put into words. If only he'd see that it was himself he was destroying by the possessive hold he tried to keep on Lydia. 'Squire, when she realises how things are, it may be Sebastian who can help her most.'

He shook himself free of her. Even in this shadowy light she could see the accusation in the look he turned on her. 'Can't understand you! Where's your fight? What's to say she won't prove that fool of a surgeon wrong? Dear God, if *we* can't have faith in her, it's asking for — for — ' He couldn't bring himself to say it. 'When she wakes she won't remember any of it, not the accident, not the operation. She'll expect to move, of course she'll expect — ' His last word was swallowed in a sob. From one to the other of them he glared, daring them to question his logic. 'She'll move, I tell you. Christ almighty, she's young, she's strong ...' Stifled by tears, his words were high-pitched and unnatural.

'Come home, Squire. Tomorrow she'll be awake. It's then she's going to need you.'

Quintin was forgotten. He didn't go with them to the car park, he watched them disappear into the darkness, Grace holding the Squire firmly by the arm, he muttering that his Poppet was all he had. As the distance between them lengthened, the words became less clearer, but Quintin knew there'd be no stopping them.

All the way home, as Grace drove, saying nothing, Philip let his tormented thoughts find voice. His little Poppet, that was what she'd always been, his, *his*. No more than a star-struck child when she'd let that conceited sod sweep her off her feet. Just an innocent child, beguiled by his attention, too naive to see him for what he was. She'd been nowhere, met no one — and that lusting swine had taken all she had to give, and left her pregnant.

'Not tonight, Squire.' Grace tried to stop him. It was like an old record, he played it over and over. As if any of that mattered after what they'd heard tonight. But she might as well not have spoken as Philip rambled on, his voice still tight and unnatural. That boy, you only had to look at him to see who his father was. Nothing of his mother in him, nothing of his Poppet. Sebastian Sutcliffe, the lecherous sod, he'd used her body to give him a son. Now look at him, swanning off, feted like some god. Conceited bugger!

All this time Grace said nothing; she tried to shut her mind to what he was saying, and think just of Lydia.

Whether or not she answered, or even whether or not she listened, would have made no difference to Philip. He had latched on to a new excuse for the hate that burned him. That boy, Sebastian's spawn — hadn't Quintin said it was because of him she'd had to stop the car? If she hadn't listened to his whining and grizzling, none of this would have happened. Where was the justice? She'd been just an innocent child herself until that fornicating swine had seduced her — bought her, blinded her with temptation, taken her freedom from her and tied her down with his child. 'Bloody brat, but for *him* Poppet would be here . . . ' So he went on, like a dog gnawing the last scrap of meat from a bone. Once home he seemed incapable of getting himself to bed. Still talking, still crying, he showed no interest in what Grace did as she undressed him.

Just once she spoke. She'd said it earlier, but this time there was no jealousy behind her words, only an aching loneliness.

'She's my daughter too.'

He looked at her as if she were a stranger talking a foreign language.

Ought she to find out the number of Sebastian's theatre in New York? What time would it be? Nearly one o'clock in the morning. He wouldn't be there. It surprised Grace how grateful she was for an excuse not to contact him tonight. Perhaps the Squire was right, perhaps by tomorrow when Lydia's soul came back they'd find that the surgeon who'd set her arm and stitched the cuts to her face had made a mistake. In the kitchen Grace dropped to sit on a chair by the wooden table. She ached with tiredness but tonight she was glad of physical pain, discomfort drew her closer to Lydia.

'Damn him,' she mumbled, 'damn him! *I* hurt too, but always he shuts me out. He won't share her. It's as if he hates me for loving her.'

The kitchen was very quiet. She must make herself go and lie down, tomorrow she'd be useless if she didn't rest. Switching off the light, she meant to go across the hall to the sitting room. She could lie on the sofa and be near the telephone in case a call came from the hospital. Instead her gaze was held by the uncurtained kitchen window. Tomorrow, had she said? Today. Already the first promise of dawn was painting the sky, grey giving way to smoky green, to silver and pink. In the last hour the wind had died; the trees in the garden were no more than shapes, their leafless branches quite still. The morning was silent, as if the world held its breath.

'Let her be well. Let her be a whole, proper person,' she whispered.

Reason reminded her she should be making herself rest. Instead, she sat again on the wooden chair, alone, elbows on the table, gazing at the promise of this new day. These minutes were her own, they belonged to the silence, to her need to find her way to the courage she lacked.

Tess Grant had said, 'Let's wait and see what morning brings.' Whatever they imagined that would be, none of them expected to see Sebastian Sutcliffe's picture on the front page of the *Morning Clarion* under the heading 'Tragedy in the wake of triumph'. His fame meant that a fallen tree in a Devon wood had caught the nation's attention within hours. Celebrities were few and far between in these rural areas, and yesterday evening's events had given the *Deremouth Post* a prize too good to miss, for Lydia belonged on its own home ground. Their keen young reporter had made his nightly enquiry at the police station and, on learning that there had been casualties from a fallen tree in Downing Wood, he'd gone to the hospital. There he had heard the name Lydia Sutcliffe. The weekly *Deremouth Post* was published on Friday morning, and this was only Tuesday. That meant that unless he could prevent it, the plum would go to the *Western Evening Gazette,* which covered the whole West Country and came out each day. Keeping one jump ahead, the Deremouth news-hound contacted the London papers. He was pleased with himself on three counts: he'd scored against his rival, for by the time tomorrow's *Western Evening Gazette* reached the paper stands the news would be cooling; when Friday's *Deremouth Post* came out he'd see it took credit for passing the story to London while it was red hot; and foremost in his mind was the hope that his own name might be noticed in places that mattered. Not for ever would he be reporting on council meetings, school plays, local foot-ball matches! He was delighted with the results of his evening's work when he checked the papers at the newsagent's next morning.

That first night after the accident Julie went to bed believing sleep impossible, her mind wide awake and jumping from one scene to the next as memory threw them at her. But as the wind rattled the windows and howled down the bedroom chimney, she burrowed deep, hugging the rubber hot-water bottle she'd found between the sheets and pulling the blankets to cover her ears. She meant to stay awake; she knew it was not rational but she felt in that way she would be keeping faith with Anna and Lydia. Nature was against her, however; she was more tired than she realised, and the hot-water bottle added that extra comfort that carried into a dreamless sleep.

As the night went on the storm abated. Unlike Grace a mile or so away at Delbridge House, Julie was oblivious of the dawn. By the time she woke, rain was falling steadily, beating on the slated roof and rolling in rivulets down the windowpanes. Her first thought was that she wanted to go to the hospital and see Anna. Her second, tumbling on top of the first, was of Lydia. Then a third, one that gave her a purpose. They'd come prepared to stay at Delbridge House for some time, with all their luggage in the car. Would the car still be in the wood or had it been towed away? If so, where? There is nothing better than a challenge to pull one's mind into order. Until Julie found the car she had nothing, not a penny. Even the pyjamas she wore belonged to Trudie. Ration books, clothing coupons, her Post Office Savings Book (which represented her worldy wealth) were all lying in the wrecked car on the woodland track or else — where?

Last night, in shock, Julie had accepted the Grants' kindness without question; this morning she was much more aware of it. She was a stranger, taken into their home out of sympathy for the trouble that had come to their friends, yet their acceptance of her was as natural as if she had a niche in their lives. It was Peter who drove her to the police station on the trail of the belongings that had been in the car; it was Quintin who took her to the hospital that first afternoon. Together they went to the accident ward, where they thought both the patients would be.

Enquiry told them otherwise.

'Anna Freeman?' the nurse repeated. 'The little girl brought in last night? She's been taken over to the childrens' ward. Follow the line painted red as you go through the door at the end of the corridor.'

'And Lydia Sutcliffe? Where can we find her?' This time it was Quintin. He spoke courteously, yet Julie sensed he was keeping a conscious rein on his expression.

'She's been transferred to Exeter.'

'You mean they'll be able to do something for her at Exeter? Last night they said — they said . . . '

Anyone would have asked the question with hope, but in Quintin's voice there was something more. Julie didn't look at him, indeed she had no need; she pretended not to have seen through the crack in his armour. Yesterday the impression he made had been of someone quiet and self-assured. This morning when she met him again her memory had been proved wrong. For olive complexion she now saw sallow skin; for proud bearing she now saw a nervous uncertainty. She noticed the way he fidgeted his long fingers, and the number of times he took off those dark-lensed glasses, polished them furiously and put them back on again. He was quiet, but certainly not self-assured. And in that moment she understood why.

'I'm sorry,' the nurse was telling him, 'that's all I know. She's to be in Mr Bonham-Miles's care.'

'I see. Well, thank you anyway.' The chink was closed. 'We'll meet back at the car, Julie. Don't rush, I've one or two things to do in town.'

It couldn't be said that Anna was happy in the childrens' ward, but the atmosphere was brighter and there were toys and coloured pictures. She was sitting in her cot, making a worn teddy bear dance on her lap while she sang out of tune. Seeing Julie, she threw away the toy and started to clamber to get out of bed, tears of frustration brimming over. Tess had sent her a doll from Greenaways' old toy box. With Julie sitting by the cot, playing 'families' with her with the bear and the doll, Anna almost smiled. But she was wary, she wasn't going to let anyone get the idea she was happy in this place. The slightest movement from her mother and she was ready to cling. Then came the dreaded moment. Standing in the doorway at the end of the ward, a nurse rang a loud handbell: visiting time was over. To Anna the sound was new, but there were plenty of occupants of other cots and beds who recognised the message of the bell. A chorus of screams was tuning up. Anna, quick to sense danger, shouted as loud as any. With one last hug Julie dumped her back behind her bars. What can 'I'm coming again tomorrow' mean to a frightened two-year-old?

'Mine's been in nearly three weeks,' an overweight woman, looking too old to be mother to any of the inmates of the childrens' ward, told Julie as they filed out. 'First off it used to worry me to death the way she cried. Elvira — that's her name — she's my eighth, you'd think I'd be hardened to the sound of crying by this time. Gets to you, though, no denying it. But, one thing I've learned: they're better once we're out of the way. I didn't believe that pretty little redhead nurse when she told me that was so, but one evening when Elvira had been a right monkey clinging onto me, I crept back and peeped after they'd been settled down again. True as eggs are eggs, not a blubber out of them, all sizing each other up, all kids together.'

35

The homely mother of eight did more to cheer Julie than the Sister's assurance that there was nothing to worry about with Anna's condition. Even so they meant to keep her in hospital until her stitches were out and her wound healed.

As for Lydia, no one dared ask how long it would be before she came home.

Grace's troubles were twofold: there was her natural grief and anxiety, and there was Philip. Lydia was their only child; they ought to be sharing their wretchedness, supporting each other. Was that more than she was entitled to expect? Her confused mind was filled with worries, fears that had been confirmed today when they'd talked to Mr Bonham-Miles; she tried not to acknowledge the resentment that was building up in her. Even the affectation of the name 'Squire' irritated her in a way it never had before. In her unconscious mind she attempted to hold on to the belief that her feelings for him were love and loyalty; if she let herself look into the hurt he was inflicting on her she knew it would be like lifting the lid of Pandora's box, there would be no turning back to the way things had been before.

That morning they'd gone to Deremouth Hospital, where they'd been told Lydia was already on her way to Exeter. Another journey, followed by a long wait. This time they were plied with cups of tea and told that Mr Bonham-Miles would see them when he had finished his examinations. Now they were home. They'd seen him, they knew the worst.

'I've found out the telephone number of Sebastian's theatre and booked a call to New York for three o'clock in the morning, our time.' Unflinchingly she faced the Squire as he came in from walking in the evening rain.

For a second she wondered if he'd heard her at all, then he seemed to collect his wits.

'Nothing he can do,' he mumbled like a sulky child. Until this afternoon he'd hung on to his illusions. They'd been stripped from him by the consultant, and there was nowhere now to hide from the truth: the damage to Lydia's spinal cord was irreversible. His Poppet would never walk – she'd never climb on the rocks, never dance, never stride across Dartmoor with him as they used to when she was a child, never ... A kaleidoscope of scenes was constantly before him, taunting him. Anger and frustration coursed through him, and the look he turned on Grace mirrored his bitterness.

'You'd better go on to bed,' she told him. 'There's no point in both of us sitting up half the night.' There was no emotion in her voice, neither pity nor love in her eyes. This way she could hang on to her courage.

'You think *I'd* want to speak to him?' Squire sneered. 'You suppose I'd want to see it's broken to him gently?' Screwing up his eyes he moved closer to her, defying her to look away. 'Remember how she was? Full of fun, full of innocence − till she was swept off her feet because the great bloody Sebastian Sutcliffe looked her way. What a hero he thought himself! Strutting in front of the cameras in uniform, winning the war with make-up on his face! And since then what sort of a life has she had alone there in London? *You* wouldn't know, you wouldn't hear the loneliness in her voice when she phones like I do − like I *did*. Now even that's over for her. And you say he has a right to be told!'

'He's her husband. Like it or not, it's Sebastian she'll want with her.' It shocked her that she could find pleasure in hurting him.

But had it hurt him? More likely he'd not even heard her.

'That's it, speak to him at the theatre.' Philip's sneer was aimed at Sebastian and her too. 'Perhaps you'll be able to catch him before the end of the play so that he can make something of it when he takes his curtain calls, a heaven-sent opportunity, a cry for sympathy. Ah yes, I can see it. He'll play it so that he has them weeping in the stalls.'

She heard the dangerous croak in his voice. Not again! She couldn't take any more. She turned her back on him.

'Go to bed. I'll stay down here on the couch.' Then, snatching at some restoration of normality, 'I drove over to Greenaways while you were out. I've arranged to fetch Julie − Mrs Freeman − and Merry in the morning.'

'My little Poppet . . .' He blundered out of the room, too absorbed in his grief to have listened to what she'd said. Where was the jaunty poseur who'd turned himself into 'the Squire'?

This was the first time Grace had made an international telephone call. When Sebastian had arrived in New York and phoned London, Lydia had said he'd sounded as near as if he'd been in the same country. So Grace was disconcerted to find that the crackles were louder than the American voice that answered her.

'I want to speak to Sebastian Sutcliffe. My name is Harriday.'

' . . .' The American's first words were lost in the depths of the Atlantic. ' . . . day too late.'

'Day too late for what?'

'Sorry, lady, line's bad this end.'

'This end too.' But she was getting more used to it, learning to hear through the interference to the voice beyond. 'It's important I speak to Sebastian Sutcliffe. Can you get him to the phone for me? This is an overseas call, I can't hang on long.'

'Sorry, lady. I just said – gone. Craig Dawkins has taken over. He's in the theatre still. Any use?'

'No. Of course not. Have you a forwarding address – studio number perhaps?'

'Wasting your time, little lady.' Only now Grace saw that he believed her to be some love-struck fan; probably he was used to shielding the stars from intrusions like this.

'Listen, this call is important. It's from England. I'm Sebastian Sutcliffe's mother-in-law. Just give me a number when I can contact him.' Instinctively she shouted against the increasing volume of crackle.

No reply. Perhaps he hadn't heard. She tried again.

'Hello, hello? It's about his wife.' Silence. The line was dead.

The letter was redirected from Grenville Place. Grace took it to the Exeter hospital when she and Squire visited the next afternoon.

Without a word, steeling herself not to imagine what Sebastian would have written, Lydia took it with her good hand and thrust it under the bedcovers. This would be his answer to her suggestion that she should join him. It wasn't so easy to thrust out of her mind how in London she'd watched each day for it to come. Now she was frightened to open it, frightened to think.

'Tess has made Julie and Merry very welcome,' Grace was saying, 'but the sooner they move in with us the better. After I drop Squire off at home, I'm going over to fetch them.'

'Before long we'll have you there, too, Poppet. Once the stitches are out you'll pick up quicker at home. Your mother and I can look after you.'

Lydia didn't answer. If she didn't talk, perhaps she could escape from thinking too. 'Pick up quicker', as if she were convalescing from an illness! It can't be true; someone must have made a mistake. Don't let it be real. Home, the Squire said, as if her life with Seb hadn't existed. Home, as if she were nothing more than their daughter. She was Seb's wife . . . no, don't think about it. Wife! What sort of a wife could she be? She shut her eyes, she tried to shut her mind. Still she was conscious that Grace and the Squire were looking at her. Watching over her – and thinking what? Had they talked to Mr Bonham-Miles? Had she spelled it out to them as he had to her: there would never be any life in her limbs; from the base of her spine all feeling was gone. Had he thought he was consoling

38

her when he'd told there was no reason to suppose her menstrual cycle would vary, in time her married life would adjust, she could still conceive and by Caesarean operation have another child. No movement, no feeling, no control, her body would function while she sat helpless and unaware. Sebastian's wife. She wouldn't think, she wouldn't let herself remember. God, don't let it be true, make it be a mistake. Closed eyelids were no hiding place.

'That's it, you have a sleep.' The Squire settled himself comfortably into the only armchair, prepared to keep guard.

'Before you sleep, Lydia, I must tell you about my phone call. I got through to the theatre, the line was atrocious — '

Lydia's eyes flew open. 'No, Mum! Don't tell him. Just look at me, the sight I am!'

'If he were hurt, wouldn't you expect to be told?'

The Squire crossed his legs, his whole attention seemingly on the mirror shine of his brogue shoe.

'I told your mother not to panic about getting in touch with him. There's nothing he can do, thousands of miles away, taken up with his own affairs.'

'I could get no sense out of the fool I spoke to. What with that and a bad line! Sebastian had already left New York. Your letter will probably tell you. If he doesn't give you an address we must ring the studio. You know who he's under contract to? Lydia, it's right that he's told.'

'Leave it alone, Mum. Don't interfere. I don't want him to know, not yet. Look at me, won't you!' This time her voice croaked. 'It's not like a face, more like a jigsaw puzzle.'

'Don't Poppet!' The Squire forgot his well-polished shoe. 'You'll soon be pretty as ever. You didn't even break a tooth.'

'Mum?' Lydia knew she'd get an honest answer from Grace.

'Your father's right. The bruises and swelling will soon go and the cuts are expected to heal well. When the stitches are taken out you'll have scars, but the Sister says that in time they'll fade considerably. And your arm was a simple fracture. None of those things are important.' She was tempted to stop at that. But Grace never took the easy way out. 'Mr Bonham-Miles has talked to you?'

'Yes. He's told me.' She couldn't talk about it, so she rushed on, 'But Mum, I look such a sight.' Bruised, swollen, stitched, her face presented a landscape in which only the freckled nose was familiar. 'Glad Seb can't see me,' she gulped. The threat of tears frightened her. If she cried, she'd be swamped in her misery; she mustn't let herself think, she must try and shut everything out. If only they would go, there'd be no need to look, she wouldn't have to watch their pity. It wasn't nearly as difficult with the nurses, nor even with Mr Bonham-Miles. To them she was a case, they were cheerful, brisk, efficient. Not like the Squire, looking at her with such sad love that she couldn't bear to meet his gaze. She let her fingers touch Sebastian's envelope. The letter she'd longed for, he'd be telling her how she was to travel, whether she had to get an air ticket or book a berth on a liner – or perhaps he'd already done it for her. She clenched her teeth tight together. With an effort she turned the corners of her mouth into a smile.

'If you're collecting Merry, then you ought to go.'

'Nonsense.' Squire folded his arms as a sign that he was here to stay.

'Please. Silly to be tired when I haven't done anything' – she tried to make a joke of it – 'but I'll sleep if I know you've gone. Seems a waste of time when you're here.'

'Come along, Squire.' Grace stood up. 'She's got her letter to read, and I've got Merry to collect.'

The Squire kissed the top of Lydia's head tenderly, letting his hand rest on her plastered arm. She knew he would willingly have sat silently at her bedside while she slept, but she couldn't bear it. Instead she held her good arm towards Grace.

'Thanks, Mum.'

For what? For coming? For bringing the letter? For going?

As the sound of their footsteps gave way to silence, she forced herself to open Sebastian's letter. Now she would have to face up to . . . to years and years, oh no, please make it be a mistake. Sitting here, being lifted about like a lump of . . . lump of –

She heard the door swing open and turned her head away from it. She wasn't going to let the nurse see her like this.

'They said I could come in.' Quintin! Always he'd been there for her. As a child he'd bandaged her knee with his handkerchief when she'd fallen off the ladder in the orchard, he'd taught her how to mend a puncture and how to put the chain back on her bicycle, he'd cheered her on when she'd ridden in the local gymkhanas.

Only a minute ago she'd been frightened to face what had to be faced; she'd tried to get rid of her parents so that she could sink into the numbness that was becoming her protection. But on hearing Quintin speak to her, she gave way.

'Don't know what to do,' she sobbed. 'Nothing I can do. Not even *me* any more, I'm just a thing, a lump. Look at me.' She turned her face towards him. 'See? Ugly – and I can't even move. Just a blob, not like a person. Wish I were dead!'

Quintin had no regard for himself, for what she might think of his actions. He cared for nothing except that somehow he had to share her road. When they'd been children the three years' difference in their age had been sufficient to make him look on her as on a younger sister. Three years was nothing now; for a long time it had been nothing. Perhaps it had been the appearance of Sebastian that had made Quintin realise just how important Lydia was to him. Too late — and in any case to her he was the boy next door, the brother she'd never had.

Now with easy grace he dropped to his knees by her bedside.

'No, Lydia, never wish that. Why you, though? I've been over and over it. There seems no reason, no purpose. I'd give all that I have to make it different.' In his quiet voice she heard suppressed emotion and knew this wasn't an empty expression of sympathy. Quintin cared; however rough her path, he travelled it with her.

'Don't tell Mum,' she gulped, her fingers gripping him. 'Promise you won't tell the Squire. About me crying, I mean.' She let go of his arm and gingerly dabbed under her eyes. Her face was too sore, tears would have to dry in their own time. 'They *look* at me — *he* does. Can't bear it. He's full of pity. Don't want pity, Quin. Just want to be *me* again.'

'You'll always be you, Lydia.' He took her hand in his. 'I'll never give you pity, but I hope I can help you to find courage. How's that for a bargain? You've got to make a bigger effort than most of us — but you will. You always had more than your share of pluck.'

His reward was a watery smile. He gave no sign of how it tore at his heart to see the way she looked. For a moment he'd forgotten Sebastian; now he remembered. It seemed to put a barrier between them.

'I'm glad you came, Quin. Been so frightened I'd cry. Tried not to. Then I thought of — did you know about me going to Hollywood?' she croaked. 'Glitter City, that's what Mum calls it. Well, I wanted it, I wanted every spark and glitter of it. Hadn't cried before. Mum brought this letter from Seb, though, it'll be the arrangements.'

'When he hears about what's happened he'll get something sorted out. Of course you want a share in the glamour.' He smiled at her, his face lit up. Then he took off his glasses, polished them furiously and put them on again, in the action somehow finding a strand of hope to hold out to her. His voice was firm and determined. 'You know how I see it? You'll hold court from some Beverley Hills mansion, you'll have them all dancing attendance on you. Sebastian Sutcliffe's wife will be someone far more special than she would if she were just the same as every other.'

41

Lydia caught her breath, a combination of a sob and a laugh. But for all that, just as he'd intended, Quintin had sowed the seed of a new thought.

It was after he'd gone that Lydia — this time without tears — opened the letter.

... in New York for a while yet. Perhaps when the run comes to an end you and Merry might join me for a week or so, not that this is an ideal place to holiday with a young child. Leaving him in London with a nurse is out of the question, as is sending him to your family. For the time being we'll leave things as they are. Between the play coming off and work starting on the film I had thought of coming back to England for a brief visit. We'll talk about it then.

The play continues to be well received and looks like running for some time ...

Still she didn't cry. Instead she screwed the short letter into a ball and hurled it across the room with her one good arm.

'When something happens suddenly, time plays tricks.' Julie voiced what both of them were feeling as she and Grace drove towards Delbridge House. 'Before an accident and after, before you're told the news and after. It may be only seconds or minutes, but it puts a sort of abyss, something impossible to cross, between what was and what is.'

Grace nodded. 'Not only events themselves' — she might have been thinking aloud — 'but sentiments that the suddenness of an accident can bring to the surface; sentiments that must have been there but you hadn't realised. Once they're out, there's no calling them back; no matter what else life has in store for you, you can never wipe them out. An abyss, as you call it, opening up and freeing things better kept buried.'

Whatever it was that Grace couldn't erase from the innermost recesses of her mind, Julie chose not to speculate on.

'Mrs Harriday, does Lydia know what Mr Bonham-Miles has said?'

Again Grace nodded. 'She's been told.' Quite unexpectedly she pulled off the road, to park by the gateway to a field. A cow ambled towards them, then stood gazing with a blank stare. Merry turned a beaming smile on his grandmother, convinced that she'd chosen her parking spot with the animal in mind.

'Look, cow coming to see us,' he said, giggling. 'How-d-do, Mrs Cow. Me get out?'

'Why not?' Grace approved.

Pulling clumps of grass from the verge, he put his podgy little fist between the bars of the gate to tempt his new friend. Julie watched him, ready to anchor him down if need be, while her listening mind belonged to Grace.

'Yes, Mr Bonham-Miles has talked to her, she said so this afternoon. But it's as if she hasn't taken it in. She grumbles that she can't use her plastered arm; worries dreadfully about her face, whether the stitches will leave scars. But the other thing — years and years ahead of her with no mobility . . .'

Her long, bony hand gripped the steering wheel.

'Perhaps it won't be like that. Medical people are learning all the time.'

'No. No, it's got to be faced. It won't change. It's no use running away from what you don't want to see. Julie, you must know that's true.'

Yes, Julie knew; she knew, too, that any road to acceptance had to be walked alone.

'Merry!' She used him as an excuse not to answer. 'Don't climb any higher, you can reach your hand through farther if you stand on the ground.' Probably not true, but the little boy hesitated a moment while he weighed her words, then decided she could be trusted. He clambered back to ground level.

'You've spoken to Sebastian?' she asked.

'He's already gone on to Hollywood.'

'Lydia knows the studio he'll be working for. We could send a cable to him, ask him to phone you. Deep down she must be so frightened — he's got to be the one to help her.'

'She doesn't want him told. Fearful of him seeing what she looks like. That's what worries me. They have to face it together. All so damnably silly, yet how can we even begin to know what she's feeling? It's as if she can't look ahead to anything until her face is her own again.'

She'd been told her face would heal, her appearance wouldn't be changed. No wonder that was the injury her mind could absorb.

'Listen, Julie, before we get home I want to try and make you understand something about how her father feels. She's talked about him, I'm sure?'

'Yes, often.' Julie added, a little less than truthfully, 'About both of you. You've always been Mum, but she calls him the Squire. The Grants did too.'

'I doubt if she knows how it all came about. When Philip and I were first married, things were pretty tough. We rented a mean

43

terraced house in Mitcham; I was a teacher, he did various things, we managed. I'm more than eight years older than he is. I'd been teaching since just after the war started – the Great War, as we thought of it. He'd been a Tommy in the trenches, straight from school into the army. I suppose you could say he'd been lucky, since he'd come through it in one piece, at least physically he had. I don't know what he'd been like as a child, but by the time I met him in 1919 he was ... was ...' She floundered, digging for a way of reliving those early days. ' ... was a mass of naked nerves.' Once started, she wanted to talk, Julie was no more than an excuse for rekindling memories, trying to find what it was that had tainted the tenderness she used to feel. 'I kept on with my teaching. We didn't have much money, Philip went from job to job – when he was lucky. I'd been on my own a long time, so he became my family. He needed everything I had to give, all the care, all the love. Don't misunderstand me' – she seemed suddenly to become aware that she was talking to a stranger – 'he gave, too. He was kind, loving, he filled every need I had. We'd already been married four years when I gave up work because I was pregnant. Things got more difficult then. Damned difficult, I can tell you. But Lydia made it all worth while. I think he worshipped her. Still does. Doubt if that surprises you.'

'Go on.'

'He'd fallen out with his family, I knew that. Probably because of me. His father had been in the colonial service in India for years. Philip had been sent back to England to boarding school. His only relative had been one difficult and cantankerous aunt. He wrote to her about me, but she didn't want to know. Can't blame her, I suppose. She must have been disappointed that he hadn't found himself someone younger – there were plenty of unattached women to choose from after the carnage of that dreadful war.'

'She must have changed her opinion when she saw that the marriage worked?'

'His aunt Hester wasn't a woman to change her opinion. When Philip got a job – I suppose Lydia was about a year old at the time – he started travelling around the farms with carboys of agricultural disinfectant. We moved away from our Mitcham home and rented rooms in Bristol. He was covering the southwest. I'd forgotten all about his aunt but in his travels he had visited her without telling me, staying with her when he was covering south Devon. One day from out of the blue – at least, so it seemed to me – he heard from his aunt's solicitor. She had died, and he was her sole beneficiary – Delbridge House was his. There was a letter for him in his

44

aunt's hand, lodged with the solicitor, telling him that it was never too late for a fresh start. Her legacy was to give him freedom and independence.'

'What a hateful way of putting it!'

'At the time we saw it as a joke. Life was one huge joke. From two rented rooms and mending our own shoes, we moved to Delbridge House. In those days, and right up until the war, there was even staff that came with the house and income enough to meet the bills. It was when we came to Delbridge House that he christened himself Squire. It was just a leg-pull at the time.'

Her face took on a closed-in look. Julie didn't probe.

'Look! Look! Comes more cows.' Merry eased the tension.

'Something else his aunt's legacy did for him — it put an end to his working. Life became very sweet for him and he was able to indulge his one hobby, painting. But more important than anything, he was able to worship at the shrine of Lydia.'

'Easily done.' Julie laughed, trying to ignore the bitterness in Grace's tone. 'I've only been with her a month or so, but nothing's ever dull with Lydia. She manages to make the most ordinary, everyday things special.'

'A trick he's taught her. I should be glad for them, I always was, truly I was. Only, after she was married, why couldn't he learn to let go? I said I wanted to explain to you how he felt. I suppose that's about the size of it. He can't let go — not to Sebastian, not even to Merry. That worries me most: it's not right to feel such spite for a little child.' She gave herself a mental shake. 'Time we got home. I'm glad you're going to be there with us, Julie. I hope you'll be happy.'

It was the next day. Fooled by the morning's hazy sunshine, Julie had promised Merry she'd take him out this afternoon. The word 'pushchair' hadn't been mentioned, but that was what she intended. She needed to walk, especially in unfamiliar surroundings, to shake off this feeling that she was a pawn in life's game. The shock of Anna being hurt had been replaced by a sense of being held in limbo. As a holiday, their stay here wouldn't have changed the pattern of their lives. But what now? Lydia could never live in Grenville Place, a house with three storeys. Her parents would want her to be here at least until Sebastian came back to England. And fast on that thought came another: Philip Harriday. She hadn't needed Grace to tell her how obsessive was his love for his daughter; she could see it after no more than a couple of hours in the house. He'd cling to Lydia, he'd use her helplessness as his trump card.

'There's wet on window.' Merry climbed onto a chair and pressed his button nose to the glass. 'Only bit, Julie. I got tackimosh.'

'Tackimosh and wellies.' Julie hugged him. 'Me too.'

But before the others set out for their afternoon trip to the hospital, the fine drizzle had turned to silver needles of solid rain. Grace had raided what she called the 'muddle box' for them and produced a packet of used Plasticine, and now, with the house to themselves and a newspaper spread over the kitchen table, they were engrossed in creating a fleet of cars. The fact that the wheels came off when he tried to push them annoyed Merry but at heart he was an optimist and each one that came off the production line he expected to do better than the last. They were at the back of the house — trodden-in Plasticine would do no good to the sitting-room carpet, but it couldn't harm the quarry-tiled floor out here. That was why Julie didn't hear a car coming up the gravel drive. The first she knew that they had a visitor was the clang of the bell set swinging high near the kitchen ceiling.

'What dat? Look!' Merry pointed to it, laughing with delight.

'Stay here, Merry. It's someone at the front door.'

'Come with you.' He clambered down to follow. But already she was out of the room and crossing the hall to see who the caller was. There must be lots of people in the village anxious for news of Lydia.

The visitor looked surprisingly familiar, yet in that first second she couldn't think where she'd met him.

'This Seb come!' Merry rushed at him excitedly.

'Come in.' Julie pulled her mind into order as the visitor lifted Merry into his arms. 'I recognise you now. Mr and Mrs Harriday are at the hospital. Have you been there yet? Come in.' Short sentences, one tumbling out after another.

'You'll be Julie. Lydia wrote to me about you and Anna.'

That deep, well-modulated voice she remembered from the cinema, a voice so distinctive that to turn the radio on and hear it people would say, 'Listen, that must be Sebastian Sutcliffe.' Yet meeting him face to face her feeling was of disappointment. She'd imagined him larger than life, more bronzed, more godlike. In the flesh he was a mere mortal. No taller than average, conservatively dressed in sports jacket and flannels. She'd not expected a matinee idol to be so ordinary.

'We were in the kitchen. Do you mind? It's better for Plasticine, you see.'

'No, I'd no means of knowing where she was,' he answered her original question. 'Spinal damage, that's what the New York paper said. I got the first flight I could, arrived at Croydon this morning, then hired a car.'

Julie had not considered that the newspapers on the other side of the Atlantic would also have carried the story of Sebastian Sutcliffe's wife's accident.

'Have you eaten? Or what about a drink first?'

'In a minute, some tea would be nice. But, Julie, tell me the rest. Spinal injuries? What does that mean? That's why I came. Is she . . . is she able to get about yet?'

Julie knew his question meant far more than that. She kept her back to him, busily filling the kettle.

'No.' She shook her head.

With the tap running she hadn't heard him cross the kitchen but there was no getting away from his hands on her shoulders turning her towards him.

'Tell me.'

So she did, her own reactions to Sebastian forgotten and her thoughts centred just on Lydia. No boosting him with hope, no pretence, just the plain unvarnished truth. There was no healing the damage done to the base of her spine; she would never walk.

'Poor little honey,' he whispered. 'God, but that's just awful for her.'

He sat down on the chair, staring unseeingly at the fleet of Plasticine cars lined up on the newspaper.

'Awful for both of you,' she said. 'I'm so dreadfully sorry.'

He looked up at her as if he didn't quite follow her meaning. When Merry tugged at his trouser leg he lifted him onto his knee.

'This man mine Seb,' the little lad announced in a voice gruff for one so small. 'My mum come soon, she doesn't going to be long.'

Julie felt a sting of tears.

'Before I decide what arrangements to make for her I must talk to the consultant,' Sebastian was saying. 'I'll phone him from here, make an appointment.'

First he drank his tea, dug into the biscuit tin and ate five biscuits, tasting none of them. Julie's first shock at his ordinariness had faded; perhaps it was his familiar voice that kindled the impression that she knew him already. Her paramount reaction was relief that he'd come when Lydia needed him. If the Squire looked for proof that she didn't play second fiddle to a career, then this must be it, she thought, as he went off to the sitting room to make his phone call to Mr Bonham-Miles.

'This evening at six o'clock at his home,' he announced, rejoining them in the kitchen.

'The fruits of fame!' she teased. Immediately her face was hot with embarrassment − Julie Freeman talking like that to Sebastian Sutcliffe! 'More tea?' she rushed on, as if that would wipe out her words.

He pushed his cup towards her. He had probably not even noticed what she said.

'This chap Bonham-Miles lives just outside Exeter, so I'll go into the city first and check in somewhere for the night.'

'A hotel? Won't the Harridays expect you to stay here?'

'The Squire, for one, would prefer I'd stayed in New York.'

She didn't answer. She was annoyed − at him and at the Squire too − and her expression must have said so.

'Why that look? You've not been here long. You'll learn, Julie.'

This time she forgot to be embarrassed. Why couldn't they put Lydia first?

'You behave like a pair of children. And what about Lydia, there in the middle being used like a rope in a tug of war? She doesn't have to stop loving her father because she has a husband.'

He must have heard her, but he gave no sign of it, concentrating on moulding a lump of Plasticine into an aeroplane.

'There you go, Merry, a plane just like the one that brought me. Hang on to it while you fly it or it'll fall to bits.' He dumped the child onto his feet to race around the room making what he believed to be aeroplane noises. 'Now, Julie, it's time you and I started to sort things out. I can't be away from the theatre longer than is essential, but before I go back I intend to have arrangements in hand for Lydia's future. From what you tell me, structural alterations must be made to the house; ramps, a lift, anything that will help her live as normally as she can. When she comes out of hospital she must be taken to her own home. You understand what I'm saying? If she comes here she'll be trapped, her independence gone. God knows she's been stripped of freedom enough, I'll not have her turned into the invalid daughter. You and she get on together, I know that from her letters. I want you to promise me you'll stay with her, take the responsibility of helping her to adjust and grow? Not the same thing at all as you anticipated when you came to look after Merry.'

'Wheee!' Merry screeched as he rushed past them.

They looked at each other. Between them lay the start of a future full of uncertainties; between them they also held the image of Lydia and the memory of her bright smile, her assurance that things always turned out the way she intended.

Julie was gripped by sudden panic. She felt the gates of freedom

48

close on her. In that moment she realised just how far she had come since her world had crumbled when she'd received the telegram from the War Office: 'It is with regret ...' Whatever she'd done, the decisions had been her own; she'd forged a path for herself and for Anna. Now Sebastian was asking her — asking? No, he was telling her, in a voice that expected to be obeyed — to commit her future. For this wouldn't be like any other job. This wouldn't be one where she could change her mind, hunt through the Situations Vacant to find something better. Yet she knew she couldn't leave Lydia, poor little honey, as he'd called her.

He held her gaze, willing her to promise. In those few seconds her mind sprang from Lydia to Anna then to Grace and the Squire with his possessive and greedy love, on to Quintin and the crack she'd seen in his reserve, and back to Lydia. Panic gave way to assurance. Julie had been in charge of her own canoe for too long to lose her grip on the paddle so easily.

Chapter Four

'It looks as though you have company.' Trudie drew up behind the vehicle already parked at the head of the drive at Delbridge House.

'That's the car Sebastian drove down from the airport in yesterday. You'll come in and say hello to him?' Julie opened the door and lifted Merry from her lap.

'No, I'll not wait. Something tells me things will be strained enough without a visitor. Tomorrow either Quin or one of my parents will collect you – Mum, I expect, the same as today. She'll hang on to Merry until I'm free so that you can be with Anna, then I'll bring you home.'

'Honestly, there's no need. If the Squire and Mrs Harriday are at Exeter, I'd be glad to leave Merry at the farm if your mother will keep an eye on him, but I can manage without transport. There's Lydia's bike I can use; I'll push Merry over on the saddle, then ride on into Deremouth. You don't need to hang around for me after you finish in the office. It's been kind of you, Trudie – all of you have been marvellous – but now Mrs Harriday has given me the bike to use I shall be fine.'

She appreciated just how kind the Grants and Quintin had been to her, but she wanted her freedom. At the crestfallen expression on Trudie's lovely face she felt trapped.

'I've enjoyed our drives back together. Let me meet you, Julie. We're becoming friends, aren't we? You don't know how much I look forward all day to collecting you. A few more days and Anna will be out of hospital. But we can go on seeing each other, can't we? A week ago we hadn't even met, yet I feel we know each other so well.'

Her large, deep-blue eyes pleaded. Julie got out of the car, concentrating on holding Merry up to say goodbye to Trudie.

'Of course we'll see each other, if Anna and I are still to be here. But as things are now, everything is so uncertain. Are you sure about tomorrow, Trudie? It'll take no time at all on the bike.'

'Humour me, won't you?'

And what could Julie say? She supposed that the Grants wanted to be involved in the tragedy that had hit their friends; for her to refuse their help would be churlish. So, holding Merry's hand, she waved Trudie goodbye and watched the car disappear down the drive.

'That looks like your daddy's car, Merry.'

'Daddy? Him's Seb. That's Seb come back.' He tugged at her restraining hand. 'C'mon, Julie, we go see Seb come back.' Then, his face puckering in a worried frown, 'When's Mum come?' Again his expression changed as a new thought struck him. 'Now?' It hurt to see the hope in his face. 'Mum wiv Seb? Will Mum be, Julie?'

'Let's go and find him. Your mummy won't be back just yet, Merry. But soon.' With a blind trust in tomorrow, she avoided telling him that the mum he knew, the girl who romped on the floor with him or played horses carrying him on her back, would never be the same. She would let the problems of each day be tackled when they must.

Voices led her to the sitting room where, after a light tap on the door, she ushered Merry in.

'How was she?' Surely there was relief in the way Grace turned to greet her.

'Almost as good as new. And Lydia?'

'The swelling's going down. Even in these few days she begins to look more like herself again.' Yet the atmosphere was alive with tension. 'She was very bright – too bright.' Lydia had told her parents nothing of Sebastian's visit except that he'd been to see her. Yet from the act she'd put on for their benefit this afternoon she might have been in bed recovering from a minor ailment. 'Sebastian has arranged that tomorrow she's to be transferred into Mr Bonham-Miles's private nursing home.'

The Squire, his face drawn and grey, had the expression of a sulky child.

'Now you've done what you came for, there'll be nothing to keep you.' He addressed himself to Sebastian. 'Every performance you miss you'll be disappointing people who've bought tickets.'

'I've hardly done all I came for. When I left New York I had no idea what I'd find. How can any of us do enough for her?' He must have been aware of the Squire's animosity, but he gave little indication of it. Then, sweeping Merry from his feet, he held him

51

high in the air. 'Hi there, Merry my son. How about you and Julie taking me for a walk before she throws you into the bath?'

A minute or two later Julie and Sebastian were walking through the walled kitchen garden to the gate that led to the lane. Merry was riding high on his father's shoulders, his small bottom bouncing up and down with delight.

'I brought us out purposely so that I could talk to you, Julie. You heard what Grace said about Lydia being moved tomorrow to Mr Bonham-Miles's nursing home. From him I've learned a good deal about her condition. There's no remedy. We knew that, of course, but I hung on to some semblance of senseless hope until I heard it from Bonham-Miles himself. She'll be so dreadfully dependent on assistance. Care like that must be harder to take from family than from a professional. So he's promised to take the responsibility of engaging a suitable residential nurse for when she can come home. One who can deal with daily sessions of physiotherapy. They can't cure her, but he says they can try to alleviate some of the pain. Just imagine, Julie, hour after hour, day after day, a prisoner in her own body.'

He said her name, but Julie had the feeling that he was doing little more than voice his thoughts aloud as if that way he'd come to terms.

'He took a lot of trouble explaining to me the things they can do to make her days as comfortable as possible, and the things that can't be altered no matter how much care she has. Do you know, if she were lifted into a bath with the water too hot, she wouldn't know she was being scalded.'

His mind was wandering, and Julie felt she was intruding.

'I can see her so clearly when she was expecting Merry. Humpty Dumpty, she called herself.' Memories, happy memories of a girl with all the world ahead of her. 'That young body ... now no feeling, no movement, no control, no life ... You could almost feel the optimism in her. You know what first attracted me to her? It was her boundless energy. God, it makes me so angry. Poor little honey! Just a child looking for fun.'

Julie felt that to answer would have been to trespass onto something that belonged just to Lydia and him. So for a while they walked in silence.

'Down. Me down now, Seb.' Merry broke the silence.

'Stay on the grass then, Merry, don't run in the road.'

'Want to see cows. They's in field. Julie see'd them 'efore.' From his high seat he'd caught sight of the herd he'd got acquainted with earlier.

'A nurse for Lydia would look after Merry too — she and Mrs Harriday between them. I expect you've talked about that to her?'

'Grace? I don't follow you. I thought I'd made it clear to you that Lydia *must* be taken back to her own home. You promised me you'd stay with her.'

'Yes. I know I did. But if there's a nurse — '

'A medical nurse isn't what I need for Merry. Neither is that enough for Lydia. She sees you as a friend, Julie. When I've gone back to New York I want you to put the necessary work in hand for alterations to the house. The stairwell is very wide, I think a lift could be — '

'No!' Just as he'd interrupted her, so now she did him. 'You can't do it to her! If she's to feel whole, to find a purpose in her life, then it must be where she knows she matters. Mr Sutcliffe — '

'Sebastian — even Merry manages Seb.'

'Sebastian, then. She's not like me. I belong to London, I always have. But Lydia loves it here; the people in Otterton St Giles are her friends. You should have seen how excited she was that we were coming to Devon.'

'I told you before, I'll not have her drawn back into his house, the beloved daughter, an invalid, a cripple, to be fawned over and given no space to find her way forward.'

'And you're right, I can see that. But not London, not back to Grenville Place. You say you want her to find her way forward, then let her be somewhere new. *You* have a meaning to your life in London. She deserves more than being on the edge of Sebastian Sutcliffe's world.' She heard herself say it, she had no power to stop herself. What drove her to speak that way to Lydia's husband? She'd never been told about those two compartments in Sebastian's life.

By now Merry had reached the gate and was climbing up to get a better view of his bovine friends. Exactly when Julie and Sebastian had stopped walking neither of them could say, only that now they were quite still, facing each other, both aware that they were on the edge of something important. Sudden panic gripped her. She was nursemaid to his son, just that and no more. What business had she to tell him what he must do?

When he spoke her panic died. He wasn't angry. Indeed there was a new warmth in his voice, as if they were two friends planning together for someone they cared about.

'Tomorrow we'll go to the estate agent in Deremouth. We'll go and look at all the houses for sale.' Had it been an hour or two earlier in the day he would have insisted they start here and then.

'Yes, we'll do that — and one thing more. You'll tell Lydia exactly

53

what we have in mind; we'll get details of houses and let the choice be hers. If we make all the decisions for her we're doing just what you're frightened of for her at home with her father.'

They both knew she was right. So why had some of the excitement gone from the scheme?

Optimism had always been part of Lydia's nature. It was the word picture Quintin created that gave her her latest hook on which to hang her dreams. The background of the image was Beverley Hills, a house such as she'd seen so often in photographs in her movie magazines; herself, her face made up so that there wasn't a hint of a scar, reclining in a wheelchair that somehow gave her more importance than she could have hoped for as Sebastian's able-bodied but ordinary wife. Female celebrities would throng around her, bring her their problems, lap up her advice; male stars (and if at this point her imagination was coloured by childhood scrapbooks she still hoarded in her bedroom cupboard at Delbridge House, she may be forgiven) would vie for her attention, would raise her to a pedestal, would envy Sebastian a wife who had such depth of character. She clutched greedily at this new dream, and wouldn't listen to an inner voice that told her she was building a house of straw.

That morning she'd been brought to Westerham House and established in a large and airy room very different from the hospital cubicle. Being the wife of Sebastian Sutcliffe gave her added prestige, particularly among the younger members of the staff. An emormous arrangement of flowers had already been delivered and was waiting by her bedside. No one actually told her but she was sure that the card bearing the words 'With my love, Sebastian' had been seen and admired by all of them. There was another flutter of excitement when, soon after lunch, he arrived.

'A photgrapher from the *Daily Clarion* was waiting for me outside. He wants to take a picture of us together. I said I'd have to see what you were up to first,' he teased.

'But I look such a sight!'

'Nonsense. Your face is healing wonderfully. If I come round to the other side of the bed, then you can turn that way and the swelling by your eye won't show.'

The reading public would be far more interested in their idol, rushed back from America to be at the bedside of his crippled wife. In truth, the more battered she looked, the higher he would be raised in their esteem. But he didn't point that out to her and, in the bright light of his reflected glory, she saw this as the first step towards her new dream.

'Then tell him he can come up. You're sure I look all right?'

Something in the way she said it touched him. Tenderly he rested a hand on her light-brown hair. 'My little honey.'

'If we'd known, you could have got Julie to bring Merry in, we could have had a proper family picture for the paper.'

'Not so sure,' he said with a grin. 'He'd steal our thunder. Never play with animals and children, that's what they tell actors. And when I see that young charmer I can understand the logic.'

'Does he miss me?'

'Of course. But he's fine with Julie. Let's ring the bell and get the nurse to fetch the reporter up. I've already talked to him, and he promised just to take the picture and go on his way.'

The photographer took several pictures. Sebastian posed on his knees by the bedside, holding Lydia's hand while she lay back against the pillows; next he was holding a book, presumably reading to her; he was sitting on the edge of the bed, holding her hand in both of his; he was arranging her pillows; in all of them the huge bouquet was evident. She'd wept to Quintin that she was just a blob. In those few minutes she felt beautiful and important. This was just a rehearsal for the way she'd be feted when Sebastian took her to Hollywood!

'We'd like to keep the story going, Mrs Sutcliffe,' the reporter told her. 'When you come out of the nursing home, when you move into the house we've been hearing about.'

Just for a second she was frightened. Here was something she didn't understand.

'I think we should finish,' Sebastian said quickly. 'By all means come and see my wife again, when she's stronger. I can see now, though, she's getting tired.'

'Not tired.' She sounded like a rebellious child, frightened of the tears that were only just beneath the surface. What a fragile thing her balloon of happiness turned out to be!

After the reporter had gone, the room seemed to echo his words.

'What did you tell him I was tired for? Just as if I'm some old lady! And what was he on about? Who's been talking to him about a house?'

'He ought not to have mentioned it. My fault, I hadn't warned him. See how I spent my morning: I've brought you three lots of details of houses to look at.'

He sounded so proud of his efforts, yet she couldn't raise a smile.

'You mean you don't want me to come and see you now this has happened? You said in your letter I might come for a holiday. I know it can't be New York now, but I could come to Hollywood, couldn't I?' She fought it, but she could feel the first warm tear roll down her face.

'My poor little honey.' Before the camera he'd taken up each pose so carefully; now there was no affectation in his concern. His tenderness was real as he cradled her against him, his lips on her short curls. 'You've got battles of our own to fight and win, difficult battles. But win them you will. To think of travelling to America at the moment would be impossible, you know it as surely as I do. Perhaps later on, but not yet.'

Silence.

'You know I'm right, Lydia.'

She nodded. 'S'pose so. Doesn't matter what I think anyway. Don't count any more.'

She sounded like a stranger — to him and to herself too.

'Stop it!' His voice was sharp; instinct told him this was the way to react. 'If you don't count, why do you think Julie and I spent the morning househunting with the chap from Meredith and Marshall, that agent in Deremouth?'

'For us? Deremouth? Don't understand. The Squire keeps talking about when he gets me home to Delbridge House — but, Seb, I don't live there any more. And I can't go back to Grenville Place, not like this. I can't! I won't!'

'I know. I wouldn't expect you to, my honey. I understand just how much it matters to you to be down here. I rather like the idea too. Devon is where we met, where I fell in love with you.'

Her smile might be watery, but it was a smile for all that, shining in her brown eyes and making her look almost pretty despite the crisscross of cuts on the left side of her face and the shining bruise on her forehead.

'Look' — he took the house descriptions from his inside pocket — 'the choice is yours. But this one, Mannerley Court, could be very pleasant. It's about ten miles inland, almost on the edge of the moor. Very spacious. We could have a lift installed, and the steps could be turned into ramps. Stabling, a gardener's cottage, really it's quite imposing or could be by the time we'd had work done. Or this, what do you think of this? Farther round the coast, a bit farther from Otterton, is Oyster Cottage. It was once a row of fisherman's houses, I should think, but someone had them converted into a single house. Very attractive, full of character. No garden worth mentioning, but a wonderful view from what at one time must have been about four rooms and has been turned into one. It's right on

56

the headland, a rocky path leads down to the beach. I admit that worried me – for Merry, I mean. I know Julie would watch out for him, but there's always a risk.'

She was busy reading the descriptions. His reminder of the time he'd fallen in love with her had worked the miracle, and she was ready again to fight her battle.

'And the third? You said you have details of three.'

'This one you probably know. Whiteways, only a mile or so along the coast from Delbridge House.'

'Of course I know it!' There was no mistaking her excitement. 'I remember when it was built. There's not another house like it. People were horrified, said it was out of place. As if that mattered! It looked so splendid there on the slope, all white and ...'

'Pretentious?' he teased. 'It was a 1930s folly, a bungalow that looked as though it must have believed itself in California. There was quite a spate of that sort of building in the Home Counties just before the war, but to have seen Whiteways in its heyday it must have taken the prize for unashamed ostentation.' He said it jokingly, his mind still on the alterations he'd have made to Mannerley Court.

'I never thought it ostentatious. So white and grand, it made the sea and the sky seem bluer. California, yes, or the Mediterranean. It suggested sunshine, freedom, being grown-up and part of the sort of life I imagined glamorous people led. I used to go along the beach and look at it. No one lived there all the time, just in the summer, I believe. But when they were staying there, there'd be lots of cars. It was sold when the war started.'

Her adolescent dreams had revolved around Whiteways. She'd never even seen the owner, but her imagination had run riot as she'd climbed on the rocks below the edge of the sloping gardens.

'It's fallen into disrepair,' Sebastian was telling her. 'I understand it was used during the war as a sort of rest home for workers from some factory in the Midlands. Not a window frame that isn't rusty and needing to be replaced. The whole thing looks as though it needs pulling down and starting again. They'll never find a buyer for it in that run-down state. I suppose the sensible thing would be to negotiate for Mannerley Court. Read the description, Lydia. You've got to be happy with what I decide.'

'I don't want to be stuck miles in the country. Might just as well live in beastly Grenville Place.' The pout was back in her voice; he detected it was a cover for her fright. 'If Whiteways is run down, why can't we get it done up again? We could make it really something! No one else has a house like it, it was never just boring and ordinary.'

Touched with tenderness for her, he felt it as a physical thing tugging at his gut, aching in his arms. If she wanted to turn what he considered a hideous folly into her idea of a film star's home, then how could he deprive her?

'If you buy Whiteways I won't need a lift, Seb. I could be the same as everyone else.'

He laughed, rumpling her curls. 'That's something you never have been, my little honey. You've always been special.'

Her new dream was born. Hadn't Sebastian said that Whiteways thought itself to belong to sunny California? And that was what she'd make it. The smile she turned on him was unnaturally bright, making him think of the way Merry had jumped with excitement when he'd given him a pink ice-cream cornet that morning. Her eyes shone with a happiness he saw as backed by terror. But for those few seconds she was fighting her battle and winning.

It took no longer than that for reality to hammer at her. The garden was a steep slope leading to the rocky shore. She pictured being confined to the house because it was too dangerous to steer herself outside in a wheelchair. No, just concentrate on the good things: it was near enough to Otterton for Julie to wheel her to the village, to Delbridge House or even to Rowans. Wheel her! No, don't think of it ... don't think of anything ... Oh, God, if you can make miracles, then why won't you help? Imagine if Mr Bonham-Miles came to tell her there was some new treatment. Imagine that when he came in the morning he said he wanted to examine her again, he thought there might have been a mistake ... Just dreaming, as she had about being in Hollywood with Seb. None of the things she'd pictured would ever happen. She'd never lie in bed waiting for Sebastian to come home, eager for his touch. What was the use of Mr Bonham-Miles telling her all that rot about having a married life? Had he told Seb that too? And had he told him about this beastly thing they called a catheter? She couldn't bear it if he saw her as she was. There was nothing ahead of her except each day being pummelled and massaged − and what for? None of it would make any difference. She'd just sit and get fat and old and ugly. No more playing with Merry, no more loving with Seb, no more ... no more ... She tried to escape behind closed eyes. She wished he'd go away and yet she was even more scared of being on her own with no one to act a part for.

Trudie was a practising solicitor, but not yet a partner in the Deremouth firm of Wilberforce and Woodburn. Sebastian went to see her about the purchase of Whiteways.

'Time is vital,' he explained to her. 'I must return to New York just as soon as I know everything possible is being done for Lydia and things going ahead with the house.'

'The house is empty, so there ought to be no delay in getting contracts drawn up and signed. It might be wiser, though, if you were to sign an affidavit, giving authority to someone else to act in your absence. What about Julie? I can easily take any papers over to her for signature?

'I was considering buying it in Lydia's name. The contract could be sent to her for signature.'

Only briefly disappointment clouded Trudie's expression, so briefly that he wondered if he'd imagined it.

'You'll be responsible for financing the purchase? And the work you want put in hand?'

'Naturally.'

'Then I'd still recommend that you give power of attorney to Julie. Bring her in to see me, we'll go over the formalities. I can deal with the bank, send them a specimen of her signature, save you wasting precious time. And after completion, much better to have it known that Julie is overseeing the work with your authority. She and I are very good friends, I'll give her all the support I can with local tradespeople.'

To Sebastian it sounded like an ideal arrangement. To Trudie it was the assurance that a common purpose would bind Julie and her closely.

Lydia had known that the people in Otterton St Giles were her friends, so she took it for granted that Jim Watts, the local builder, would gladly take on the work at Whiteways.

'I'll need to get a permit for the materials,' he explained to Sebastian and Julie. Even though she listened, her attention was more on Merry, who was outside in the builders' yard, chasing the tabby mouser around the piles of timber, drainpipes, tiles and other paraphernalia necessary to the trade.

'Surely there won't be any problems? The house is in a shocking state.'

'Leave it with me. I'll see it doesn't get tangled up in the red tape they want to strangle us with these days. War might be done, but makes you wonder sometimes whether we won it or lost it, damned if it doesn't. Just look at this load o' bumf I've got waiting to be filed away. Regulations, instructions, do's and don'ts – more don'ts than do's. Tie our hand every which way, buggered if they don't. Beg pardon, missie. But I'll give this job tip-top effort, put my best men on it; and if I hit against any hitches then I'll sort them out personally. Poor little lassie! I tell you, when we got the news of what had happened, my Lily – that's the missus – cried like it was one o' her own. Known her since she was riding her first bike. And what a merry little scamp she always was, too! How's the Squire taking it, eh?'

'It's a blow to both her parents. But there's only one person who matters, and that's Lydia. Having Whiteways – and as soon as possible – will help her. I intend to leave for America in a few days' time.'

He was oblivious of the way Jim Watts half closed his eyes, seeming to look beneath the surface of the matinee idol who'd put down shallow local roots.

'When I'm gone Mrs Freeman will have complete authority on my behalf. But before then I'd like us all three to go out to Whiteways, to check over the place thoroughly and decide what's to be done. Sliding doors would be easier for her, any steps replaced with ramps, a bathroom converted for her own use and leading from her bedroom. As we go round we'll talk it through.'

Jim Watts had his expression under control again. Lucky thing for poor little Lydia Harriday she'd found herself a husband with plenty of money. But a cold fish . . . or was that unfair? Sebastian was kind, thoughtful, sensitive to her needs . . . and yet . . . A bit of good old-fashioned anguish, that was what Jim would have appreciated. Married to a young girl who'd never be a proper wife to him – wouldn't you think he might have shown a sign of emotion? Too cool by half was his unspoken opinion. Even to his Lily he wouldn't say so, though, keeping his opinion to himself not for Sebastian's sake but for Lydia's. Never let it be said that Jim Watts put the knife in when a person was hurt. No, this evening when he called in at the Pig and Whistle for his nightly pint he looked forward to being the bearer of news that Sebastian Sutcliffe was taking that eyesore of a place along the coast and turning it into a home for poor young Lydia. In his own view it would be better by far to pull the place down, start again with a nice house in red stone, something that would sit happily in its background. Still, what could you expect from these stage people? Likely the very reason he was buying it was that it was conspicuous.

The beach was empty except for the man and woman who stood gazing across the tangled jungle of garden towards the long, flat-roofed, once white house. That morning Grace had taken charge of Merry so that Sebastian and Julie could give all their attention

60

to the plans for Whiteways. It was easier without him, yet even as Julie had accepted his grandmother's offer she'd been uneasy; the Squire made no secret of his resentment of the child. What a complex man he was! It was as if he idolised Lydia to the exclusion of all else, grudging even the affection she gave her own son.

'Going back, leaving so much to be done, I'm so glad to know you're here, Julie. Ideally I'd like to think that she can stay where she is until the house is ready for her. But, of course, once Mr Bonham-Miles thinks she's ready, and provided he's found the right physio-trained nurse for her, he may want her room for someone else.'

'He's not likely to ask her to leave!' Having some idea of what it was costing to keep her there, Julie spoke with confidence. 'But she ought to have a chance to see Whiteways while the men are working, to have *her* say about colour schemes for decorating. She can't do that from Westerham House. Mrs Harriday was talking last night about turning what originally was a housekeeper's sitting room into a bedroom for her. From Delbridge House I could push her along to Whiteways, so she could feel herself part of all that's going on.'

At Sebastian's expression she felt her anger rising.

'He *is* her father. Sebastian, if this happened one day to Merry — heaven forbid — don't you think you'd feel bitter and angry? Of course you would, and protective too.'

'Of course I should. Julie, you've only just come onto the scene, you don't know his insane jealousy. I don't think he hates me any more than he would have hated any other man Lydia had married. It's not healthy. I don't care what he thinks, but how Grace stands it is beyond my understanding.'

'Mrs Harriday's affections are generous and healthy. That's why Lydia needs her so much, it sort of balances out her father's possessiveness.'

'What complex animals humans are!'

They were sitting on the rocks at the back of the sand. He held a gold case towards Julie for her to take a cigarette, put one in his own mouth, then lit them both. The action immediately relaxed them, seeming to say that for ten minutes or so here they'd be, idly talking. Behind them the overgrown borders and one-time lawn that had turned itself into a hayfield sloped from Whiteways down to the shore. 'You'll have to sort out someone to landscape the garden, Julie.' He laughed as he went on, 'Just throw yourself on the mercy of Otterton St Giles, you'll be headed in the right direction. Someone there will "know a man" who "knows a man". Or the Grants — Quintin Murray may be able to recommend someone. I don't like being too beholden to them, though. They've always been close to the Harridays.'

'Now you're being childish. The Grants are a lovely family, and that includes Quintin. You don't have to be hand in hand with the devil because you're a friend of the Squire, you know.'

He laughed, shamefacedly. But immediately his mind moved on. He stood up, looking at the garden, thinking, imagining.

'Would it be Jim Watts or the landscape gardener who'd build a terrace? That's what we must do, Julie. Here, stand up. Look at the slope of that grass, she'd never control a wheelchair on that. If the window of the main sitting room was cut right out, replaced by sliding glass doors, then the land outside levelled and made into a terrace, she could get outside.'

'That's right! Not just a narrow one, but wide, as big as the room or bigger, somewhere where she could feel part of the garden.'

He came to stand behind her, tall enough to see over the top of her head. His hands were on her shoulders. When had he thrown away his cigarette? She was glad of hers and drew on it quickly, welcoming the familiar feeling of it between her fingers. Was he as aware as she was of the grip he had on her? He was so close that she could feel his nearness like a whisper.

'You won't leave her, Julie? I know you've promised me. But tell me again. Tell me that when I come back you'll still be here — still be with her.'

'I've said so. I don't break my word.'

'I know. I just want to hear you say it again. Humour me.'

'I won't leave her. When you come back I'll be here.'

By this evening he would have left and, suddenly, she was glad. For a week they'd been together for some part of each day. They'd walked in the untended garden of Whiteways trying to envisage how it would look when the work was done; they'd been allowed a key to the empty house so that they could measure and redesign. All of it had been done for Lydia, all their thoughts had been geared to making her life as bearable as they could. Once he'd gone she would be in charge of finalising the purchase, of arranging the work to be done by plumbers, electricians, the landscape gardener. Julie liked to be mistress of her own decisions. Eagerly she grabbed that as her reason she wanted him gone: it would put her at the helm.

And the next morning events swept him firmly into the background of her mind, for that was the day Anna came out of hospital.

Trudie pushed the purchase as fast as she could, but that was only as fast as the vendor's solicitor and the local authority. The weeks of spring were frustrating. Even when the house was officially Sebastian's, there followed the formalities of a building industry hidebound by bureaucracy. It was clear that when she left the nursing home Lydia and her nurse would be at Delbridge House for many months.

'I've a good mind to tell her to go!' The Squire gazed at Grace as though all his misery stemmed from her.

'Julie? No, Phil, I won't let you do it. It's not that I couldn't look after Merry — '

'Don't pretend you don't know who I mean. That officious, bloody nurse, that's who. Whose house is this? Tell me that. Does it belong to me or that conceited ponce, taking it on himself to engage staff? We looked after her all her life and, dear God, if ever she needed us it's now.'

'Now you're being ridiculous. She needs professional care. She needs the dignity of — '

'Paid help! You call that dignity?'

Grace looked up from the shopping list she was writing.

'Yes, Squire, I call that dignity. My dear, of course we would willingly wait on her as far as we're able. But she needs more than that, she needs trained care. Bad enough for her to have to be dependent, but at least Nurse Pepper is part of the way she has to make her life now. Could we cope with catheters, enema? No, of course we couldn't. And even if we could, how she'd hate it! The fetching and carrying we *could* manage would be a constant reminder to her of the freedom that's gone. Don't look like that.' She reached her capable hand towards him. 'Be grateful that Sebastian can buy her some sort of independence. And as for the other care Nurse Pepper gives her, well, be honest. Daily massaging — are we qualified for that? Of course not. Without someone here permanently Lydia would have visits from a district nurse, nothing more than that.'

The Squire ran his fingers through his wiry grey hair.

'What's the point of it, all this pummelling at her? Never going to make her any different.' He sat heavily as if his strength had gone, but his clenched fists beat with a steady rhythm against the upholstered arms of the chair in frustration. 'As if it wasn't enough to know she'd rather be with him than here where she'd always been happy — now, even the crumbs that were left to me are being taken.'

'Oh, for goodness sake pull yourself together! No wonder Nurse Pepper doesn't want you hanging around.' If he'd said 'left to *us*' instead of 'to *me*', would she have snapped like that? The sound of footsteps coming down the stairs heralded the approach of Julie and the children. Grace's face set in a smile of welcome.

'Is there anything I can get for you while we're out, Mrs Harriday? Just look at the sunshine! The first we've seen for ages. It's such a lovely morning I thought Merry and Anna could have their reins instead of going in that huge pushchair. That's too wide for the doorways and they do like to come into the shops and see what's happening.'

'Like a pair of young colts in harness.' Grace was glad to have her thoughts diverted from the sickroom. 'Just look at them, Squire, ready for their gallop.'

'While that poor child sits there, hour after hour, day after day . . .' The tattoo of the clenched fists speeded up.

'I was just talking to Nurse Pepper.' Julie pretended not to notice the ominous croak in his voice. In the weeks she'd been there, she'd learned how easily his control could be lost. 'She said the forecast is good, it'll stay dry. So this afternoon Lydia might go out.'

The Squire's head shot up. 'Out? You mean that gaoler will let her out of her sight? I'll push her to the village − or I'll take her to Rowans. Yes, that's where we'll go.' From anger to distress and now to elation, his moods could change in a second. The thought of pushing his disabled daughter bounced him from the depths to the heights. 'Remember how I used to push her when she was little, all her favourite places . . .'

'I've just written a list of groceries we want from Ken Brindley. Drop it in when you pass, will you, Julie? Nothing to bring − the lad will deliver it on his bike.' Grace concentrated on needlessly rechecking her list, confused by anger and pity for the Squire, while Julie bent down to adjust Anna's reins. No one had the right to see so clearly into another person's soul. A cloud seemed to have fallen over the prospect of Lydia's first outing.

'Julie ought to learn to drive.' It was Peter who suggested it on a Sunday morning when the Squire had pushed Lydia to Rowans. He often brought her there; he didn't even stand jealous guard over her if Quintin or Trudie took her off around the farm. The truth was it did him good to be able to talk to Peter or Tess, he felt they understood the special bond between him and his Poppet. On this particular Sunday it had been Quintin who had wheeled the chair away and from the window they watched as he steered it towards the path that led up to his nursery.

'Hope he's careful! That path's too steep. Suppose he can't hold it coming back down?' He sounded edgy. An hour with Peter and Tess, knowing that Lydia was safe with the young ones, always recharged his batteries. Having lost a son must give them some idea of what he was suffering. Their talk would be of other things — there was plenty to discuss in a world trying to sort itself out after the devastation of war, a country where the shortages of the last few years showed no sign of easing. New schemes for education, new schemes for health; a brave new world, some believed, others had less faith. Whatever they talked about, to the Squire a quiet chat with Tess and Peter, a tankard of ale in his hand, was a shot in the arm.

This morning it wasn't working out as he wanted. 'He ought to have more sense,' he said, still watching Quintin.

'Do you want Trudie to go after him?' Tess suggested.

'Nonsense!' Peter watched them too. 'You never have to worry about her with Quin.'

Trudie appeared to be engrossed in the Sunday paper, she didn't so much as glance up.

'Peter's right.' Tess went back to what was being said earlier. 'Julie ought to drive. Once they get to Whiteways they won't be able to depend on you and Grace.'

The Squire made an effort. He took the tankard Peter handed him and turned his back on the window.

'I suppose I could give her some lessons.' He sounded quite agreeable at the prospect until he added, 'As long as Grace would look after those children.'

'Those children ...' Tess mimicked his tone. She pretended to make a joke of it, but she was worried. With all the heartache of Lydia's problems, were Grace and the Squire finding it too much having two little ones in the house?

'Can't help it, Tess. It's that boy. I know what you're going to say — he's my grandson. I ought to have some sort of inbuilt affection for him. Well, don't waste your breath. I can't help it. There's nothing of Poppet in him, never was. He's his father through and through. A difficult child, too.'

'Oh, Squire, that's not worthy of you,' she said affectionately. 'He's just a little boy, confused that his mother isn't the same as she used to be.'

'Aren't we all! At his age memories are short. You'd think by now he'd be satisfied that Julie and young Anna are his companions.'

'He's had so much change to get used to — '

'I find him watching me. Just looks at me, you know.' From the way he cut in, she knew he needed to let off steam. 'Just the same expression as that strutting show-off of a father of his, as if he's too bloody superior for the rest of us.'

'Sometimes, Squire, you're a silly old chump. I wonder we love you at all.' She reached forward and planted a kiss on his cheek. 'You're as bristly as that face of yours.'

There was something about Tess that loosened the knot of hatred that was strangling him. He shut his eyes as if that way he'd cut himself off from his misery.

'Can't help it. Are we paid back for the wrongs we do? If so, I must have been a tool of the devil to have deserved this. We were always so close, you know that's true. It's as if she's frightened to be with me.' This Sunday wasn't following the usual pattern. For a moment he'd lost Tess. Was he talking about Grace or Lydia? 'And this nonsense about a home of her own. She has a home, she'll always have a home. Not that I want *him* in it when he does grace her with a visit. Whiteways was a tasteless monstrosity, it's never fitted into the scene down here any more than he ever could himself. We might have guessed that would be his choice.'

'He's having a lot of work done to make it as easy as he can for her there.' This time it was Peter who tried to bring him out of the trough he'd fallen into. But he didn't have any success; it seemed once started the Squire couldn't stop.

'Pay to have work done! Oh yes, he'll make a fine display of doing that. Buy her comfort just like he managed to buy her infatuation when she knew no better. I can't forgive him, I can't like him, can't even trust him. She's worth better than a husband who puts her a poor second in his life, and better than the sort of existence she's got to look forward to. Sometimes I don't know how I can bear it. I wake in the night and think of her. All I ask is to look after her, to give her back the happiness she had as a child.'

Grace would have recognised the warning signs; Tess put her hand on his arm, not aware that sympathy would be his undoing.

'My little girl ...' Digging for a handkerchief he wiped his eyes, turning his head away from her. 'Sorry,' he said, his voice still tight. 'Can't get a grip. Always there, just below the surface.' A sniff, a blow, another mop around his eyes, another sniff, then he turned her face again. 'And that brat, *his* son, all he wants is play.'

It shocked Grace to hear a grown man vent such venom on a child.

'He's a baby still, poor little boy!'

'If his mind isn't on romping and games, then he's grizzling to know "When Seb coming?"'

As if to remind him of her presence, Trudie made a show of folding the paper. She sensed the Squire was on the edge of a scene and decided it was time to take a hand in restoring calm.

66

'That's a good idea, Julie learning to drive, I mean. I could help. I'd like to. The evenings are long now, I could pick her up once she's got the children off to bed.'

Looking at her, the artist in Philip Harriday was struck by how lovely she was.

High summer: work going on apace at Whiteways, a small army of joiners, plasterers and plumbers labouring all the daylight hours. On that first day when Julie, Sebastian and Jim Watts had gone through the house they had planned much that should be done to make life easier for Lydia; as the work progressed Julie visited the place, trying to imagine what it would be like never to be taller than a sitting position, never to be able to stretch upwards. No use merely putting in new window frames; what was wanted was new and lower windows. In the kitchen there must be a shelf that was low; electric switches must be within Lydia's reach. Each time Julie went to Whiteways some other thought struck her. She had been given a free hand and she was determined that as far as was humanly possible Lydia was to find independence. Of course she wrote to Sebastian, brief and businesslike letters telling him of the progress. He didn't reply; she told herself she hadn't expected that he would. Outside the landscape gardeners transformed what had been a wilderness. The terrace was taking shape and this, at least, was just as Sebastian and Julie had envisaged.

'Let's go to Whiteways today, Squire,' Lydia said as they set off with him pushing her chair. 'I know all about the outside, Julie often takes me that far. But she's scared of pushing the chair nearer than the road, they haven't got the drive gravelled yet and it's full of potholes. But you're strong, you could manage.' Instinct told Lydia flattery was the best approach. Her father had never been able to refuse her when she'd turned to him with such trust in his ability.

It seemed today was the exception.

'Too good a day to spend in what's more like a builders' yard.' He turned the chair in the opposite direction. 'Not just a question of strength. It would hurt you, Poppet, bumping over uneven ground.'

He couldn't see her pout, but the set of her shoulders told him she was disappointed.

'Soon Sebastian will be home.' She clutched at the first thing to say to hit below the belt. 'And you're right not to take me. I want to see it first with *him* – and he'd be disappointed if he couldn't be the one to take me. Carry me over the threshold!' She wished she hadn't said the last sentence, for she didn't want

67

her father to hear the anger and hurt that to her own ears was so apparent.

'He's coming back soon, you say?' He tried to sound casual, then added what he meant as a throwaway remark, 'No mention of it in the *Movie Weekly* that came this morning. He looked happy enough escorting Marina Bessington to some nightspot. What was it it said under it? Something about the fabulous Marina's third marriage having just ended in divorce. You must have seen the picture. Or very likely Julie thought it more tactful not to tell you the magazine had come. But it's not fair to hide from you the way he behaves. Poppet, don't put your faith in him. He's not worth it, I've always told you so.'

'Stop it, Squire! Just because you've got me stuck here and I can't get away from what you say, that doesn't give you the right to be so beastly about him. And of course I saw the picture. If I'd been out there with him like we planned' (and just for a second she almost believed what she said) 'it would have been *me* with him. Marina Bessington isn't important. You don't understand anything about Seb and me. People like her don't make any difference to how he feels about Merry and me.'

She couldn't see his face but she knew from his step that she'd trumped his ace. It took every bit of her moral strength to sit straight and hold her chin high. Of course neither Marina Bessington nor any of the other retinue of glamour Seb mixed with touched his life with her and Merry, they never had. Ah, but that was 'before', whispered a demon of truth. What sort of a wife are you for him now? His little honey, to be humoured and amused. Think of the other times when he's come home after working away, you weren't his little honey then, you were a woman, a woman he wanted. You used to wear Chanel – now you wear surgical spirit. No, it's not Marina Bessington and her lot who make Seb feel differently about you. Bet that old fool Bonham-Miles wouldn't talk such rot if it happened to *his* wife!

Softly she started to hum, making her voice casual and relaxed. Who was she fooling, herself or him? The Squire, of all people, must never know the utter despair that could swamp her like this with no warning.

68

Chapter Five

At Rowans the harvest was almost finished. On this late September Saturday afternoon the last corn was being cut. By tonight all would be safely gathered in.

'Look that funny round and round it go, Mum.' Anna jumped with excitement as Peter drove the tractor down the field, the binder leaving the sheaves of corn in its wake. This was a very special sort of day, it even smelled different from any she'd known before. With her head between the wide bars of the field gate she watched, sniffing hard, not wanting to miss a single bit of the strange and exciting things that were happening. She hadn't bargained for the flying dust that tickled the back of her nose and made her sneeze — once, twice!

'Bless you!' Tess laughed, coming to join them. Tess and Julie were picking blackberries, reaching high on the straggling hedge that divided this field from the one where the work was going on; Merry was waiting hopefully, nowhere near able to reach the fruit. In the far distance a dog was barking, the sound almost lost in the sunny haze of afternoon.

'Merry! Quick, Merry!' Having sneezed the dust away, Anna drew her head back just long enough to shout. 'See, him come again. Round and round thing. See, big bunches it does.'

Tess reached for two ripe berries to pop one in each small mouth.

'I bet you they're having an afternoon that will stay with them all their days. Just sniff the air, Julie. Falling leaves, a hint of bonfires, ripe corn warmed by the sun ... you can smell each of them separately, can't you, yet put together they make a cocktail that's pure magic.'

'You have to make allowances for Mum.' Trudie laughed again. 'She always gets carried away with what she calls magic when Dad's

69

up to his eyes getting in the harvest.' Her blue eyes teased her mother.

'Mock if you like, my girl, but deep in your heart you know I'm right. Just look across there at the distant haze. Sniff it! It smells of everything we should be grateful for.' Hearing herself, she was embarrassed. 'I must get on, I've things to do. I just brought this bowl over to see if you want to empty your berries. This will be the last weekend for picking them.'

'There are plenty on the bushes still, Mrs Grant,' Julie told her. 'Lots of huge ones.'

'Don't encourage her!' Again Trudie was teasing. 'She believes the most awful tripe.'

'Never call country beliefs tripe. Once the month is out we mustn't take them, Julie, it'll bring bad luck. The witches spit on them.' Her blue eyes were solemn, so Julie knew she mustn't laugh.

'Then we'll have to get busy, Mrs Grant, make the most of this weekend.'

'Perhaps Julie wants to take her back to Aunt Grace.' Although not related, the Harridays had been Aunt Grace and the Squire as long as Trudie could remember.

'No, I make the jams and jellies for us both, I always have. When you get a chance to, Trudie, give Peter and the chaps these eats. I wouldn't mind betting it'll be dark by the time he gets done this evening.'

She dumped a picnic hamper on the ground, held out her container for them to empty their basins, selected two large berries to pop into the children's mouths, then set off back to the house. Somehow her visit had set the seal on the afternoon. For a while Julie and Trudie went on picking, but not with any sense of urgency. There was a timeless quality about the still afternoon. Perhaps Tess's words about the magic had made more impression than they realised.

'Just look at those two, Trudie.' Julie's gaze was on the children, both of them bent to lean through the bars of the gate, two small bottoms sticking out, four sturdy little legs unusually still. 'Do you suppose your mother's right and today is something they'll always remember?'

Trudie sat down on the ground, her arms clasped around her drawn-up knees.

'Will *you*, Julie? I know I will.'

Julie reached towards a high branch, picked a berry, then dropped it, rubbing her hand against her skirt.

'A wasp on that one!' It didn't need saying, it was the easiest way of ignoring something she didn't want to see.

70

But Trudie persisted. 'Will you want to remember it, Julie?'

'Of course I shall. I've never watched the corn being cut before. In fact, the only blackberries I've ever picked have been in Clifford Park at home and they were never fat and juicy like these. Why is it even brambles grow better in the country?'

It was Truddie's turn to ignore the question; she wasn't going to be sidetracked.

'I've known the harvest-time, blackberry-time, every autumn of my life. But I'll remember today. You being here – and the children, of course. Stop working, come and sit down.'

'Slacker!' Julie laughed. 'Look at your father and the men out there in the field, they don't take breaks.'

'All right then, I'll pick.' Then, laughing, 'Get them before the witches do their worst. It is good, though, isn't it, Julie? Us being friends, I mean?'

'You've been marvellous to me, teaching me to drive, helping with the things I had to do for Sebastian.'

'That was work. I'm talking about friendship, companionship. I looked forward to our driving lessons, you know I did.' For a minute or two they worked in silence, then she went on, 'You've never talked to me about your husband, only that he didn't come home from the war.'

Julie heard it as a question and felt herself recoil from it. She and Trudie were friends, she could talk to her about the years she lived with her aunt, about joining the ATS, about earning a living for herself and Anna and their bed-sitting room in London. But Jeremy wasn't someone to be shared – not with anyone.

'You must have been happy together,' Trudie probed. 'You had so little time. And during the war no relationships were normal. The periods of happiness were unnaturally perfect.'

'It wasn't like that. Of course they were perfect, but there was nothing unnatural.'

Trudie felt herself slapped down; she realised she'd trespassed on private ground. But it was important that Julie should realise that suffering was something they shared, that she, too, had known love and had lost it.

'That's what I believed about Jo and me. Jo Veasey was his name. It was the autumn of 1943. I'd just qualified and I went to Bath for the weekend; it was a sort of self-indulgence by way of celebration. I was on my own, but that didn't matter to me. I'd never had any real, close friends. Plenty of friendly acquaintance, but what I felt at that point was far too important to share with any of them. I'd worked terribly hard, it meant so much that I was making a proper

71

career. At home there were the three of us — well, almost as far back as I can remember there were three. Quintin came here when I was about four. He's two years older than me. Then there was Paul, my brother, he was two years younger.

In 1943 the boys were both in the forces, of course, but I knew that afterwards they would do what they'd grown up to: Paul had always been heart and soul in the farm, all he ever wanted to do was leave school and be on the farm. Quin, well, you've seen his nurseries. From school to horticultural college, he knew just where he was going. But me — I was a mere girl! But I was determined. I had a brain and I meant to prove myself. Mum had never wanted anything beyond the farm, taking care of Dad and us. That kind of life wasn't for me.' She fell silent, lost in her own thoughts.

'Well, you've certainly proved yourself! They must be proud of the career you're making.'

'Anyway,' Trudie brushed aside the interruption, 'I was telling you, I went to Bath for the weekend. That's when I met Jo. He was a sergeant in the US Army.' She laughed, remembering. 'It was a real GI pick-up. Nothing like it had ever happened to me before. And that's how everything was with Jo — sort of super natural, all our emotions larger than life. We saw each other every weekend, unless he couldn't get away. He even spent a leave here at Rowans. Then divine providence stepped in, he was sent to the South Hams, stationed less than twenty miles from Otterton. You've probably never heard about how the US military commandeered an area in the South Hams, evacuated everyone who lived there. They were getting ready for the Second Front, practising for the invasion. It was kept frightfully secret, the papers never printed anything about it. Jo was there for six months, right up until they went across for the D-Day landings. With him being so close I dare say I saw more of him in that time than you did of Jeremy even though you were married and we weren't.' Her deep blue eyes defied Julie to belittle what she and Jo had had. 'I didn't have a wedding ring, but I had all the rest.'

'Trudie, I'm sorry. Did it happen at the landing?' Julie gave up pretence of blackberrying and sat down, Trudie joining her. 'Remember the morning we heard the news on the wireless? It had really happened. Like a storm that breaks after the air has been heavy with the threat of it. We'd known it was coming, it *had* to happen, *had* to be got through before anything good could come. There was that — and there was the terror of what we should hear next, every ring on the bell or click of the letterbox turned us to jelly . . . Somehow we got through it, there was no choice.'

72

'You were a wife. You forget, I wasn't.' There was no mistaking the bitterness in her expression.

'So who told you? A colleague? How long did you have to wait?'

'There's no point in talking about it. I just didn't want you to think I'd not known about love, about being with a man.' Her voice was hard, she drummed her fingers on the hard autumn ground.

Julie covered Trudie's hand with her own in a brief, affectionate movement.

'You and Jo loved each other, but you mustn't live your life looking backwards. There's no point in doing that, Trudie, not for either of us. I'm lucky, I have Anna. I just pray the memories will never fade. I think that's the most frightening thing about looking ahead. Supposing memories get blurred. I want always to picture the things we shared, even things as everyday as a walk on the hills or sitting together in some frowsty tearoom. Not just picture them because I know that's what we did, but bring back the atmosphere, the spirit. The smell of that sort of disinfectant stuff they impregnated into the material of the khaki uniform is more evocative of those days than any other. Some little thing like the hiss from a hot-water urn hits unexpectedly and brings it all back. And I'm glad. I must never lose it.' The grip of Trudie's hand on hers pulled her back from where her mind had rambled. 'Things outside ourselves, and yet I know that as long as I can hang on to them then he hasn't quite gone. And that's what frightens me, Trudie. If you try too hard to remember, then you can chase away the spirit.'

'Like you just said, it's the future we both have to look to. You're frightened that you won't hang on to your memories; I'm frightened that they'll sneak up and catch me unawares. I trusted him, Julie. I was so eager to believe all his cunning, hateful lies, never for a moment doubted him.'

'You mean you never heard from him? But perhaps he couldn't help that. An official letter − next of kin − it couldn't have been *his* fault.'

'No, I didn't hear what happened to him. I imagine by this time he's safely back home in Maryland − unless that wasn't true either and he came from somewhere else − living happily ever after with his wife.'

'Wife? You mean he was married, he talked to you about his wife?' She knew plenty of girls had gone out with married men far from home, but the idea that Trudie was one of them shocked and disappointed her.

'It was during the winter after the invasion. I'd heard nothing from him since the landings. There was only one possible explanation; he must have been killed. Like a fool I'd gone to Bath to wallow in my misery. I was mooning around our old haunts in the teatime dusk when I met a comrade of his. He'd been sent back wounded but was almost fit again. I asked him to tell me how things had been for Jo. To be honest, I expected that he'd be wanting to tell me, give me some sort of comfort from knowing how Jo had met his end. Did he do that? Did he, heck! He was embarrassed, I could see that, so I said I'd rather know everything, even if it was hard to bear. My mind steeled itself: perhaps he'd stepped on a landmine, perhaps it had been a hand grenade or even a bayonet. But no.' Her voice was hard, full of hate. 'Jo was fine, thank you very much. "But I've never heard." What an innocent I must have sounded! That's when he told me about Rosie, his wife. Joe's friend — I never knew his name — made excuses, said he was sure Jo had had a real fondness for me, etc. A wife and two sons waiting at home. And me to work off his energy on in his bed here — or more often behind the hayrick, in the shelter of a barn, sometimes during the winter in a sleazy hotel where no questions were asked. Now you can understand why I don't want to remember.'

'Trudie, that's rotten! For you and for her too.'

'Oh, I don't waste any tears on her. If he came through, then she got him back. I don't expect Jo was different from any of the others. All of them the same, British, Canadian, American — Germans too, I wouldn't wonder. Not a jot of difference between any of them.' She needed to hurt Julie too. 'My regard for men isn't high. And with just cause.'

'Yes, Jo wasn't the only one. Some of the men were unfaithful, and so were some of the women they'd left behind. But not all. Don't let yourself be bitter, Trudie. You're too nice a person for that. One of these days there'll be someone else, someone you can trust.'

'I'll not be that sort of a fool a second time. Men! Who needs them? Come on.' Trudie stood up with new determination. 'Let's see how many blackberries we can get before Mum's witches fly over and spit on them! Like you say, it's the future that counts. And Julie, we'll make it a good one.'

While the others spent the afternoon at the farm, Lydia sat in her wheelchair on the grass in front of Delbridge House. It was a good many minutes since she'd turned the page of the book she was reading; it was rather something she could hide behind, putting up a pretence that she was enjoying herself. This being Pam Pepper's free half-day, she'd borrowed the bike and gone to Deremouth, where she'd leave it at the station and go by train to Exeter; the Squire had ambled off with his sketchpad; Grace had gone to the village.

'I'll take the car, then you won't be on your own many minutes,' she'd said.

'Mum, I'm a big girl now.' Lydia's voice had held a laugh. She wouldn't let them see how frightened she was by their concern. Even her mother couldn't seem to understand that she'd rather battle to do independently what was next to impossible than be watched over and protected. 'I can hardly run away. Once you've all cleared off I shall read my book so don't hurry.'

Even so she noticed that Grace took the car.

Minutes ticked by, the book lay open on her knee, her face took on that closed-in look that was becoming her natural protection while in her mind she recalled word for word the letter she'd had that morning from Sebastian. The sound of an engine suddenly warned her someone was turning into the drive. In a hurried attempt to look engrossed in her reading, she knocked the book off her lap.

'Damn, damn, damn,' she muttered through clenched teeth. 'Now she's going to think she shouldn't have left me.' Leaning over the side as far as she could, she was still nowhere near able to touch the book.

'Hi there! That's it, put your book away. I've got a proposition to put to you.'

'Quin! Jolly glad it's you. I wasn't putting it away, I dropped it. No, leave it, I don't want it anyway, I'd much rather hear your proposition.' This time the laugh in her voice was natural. 'That's a very military-looking affair you're driving. I'd take it to be a jeep except that it's the wrong colour.'

'That's exactly what it is. An ex-US Army jeep cheered up with a coat of fresh green paint. Now hear my suggestion. What do you say to coming for a ride in it?'

'You're kidding!' But he was in earnest. 'Quin, I'm such a useless hulk, you'd never be able to get me into a car.'

'Want to bet? Come on, Lydia. It's not like an ordinary saloon thing. I can lift you onto the front seat, then we'll dump the chair into the back. We'll have the freedom of the road. What do you say?'

Wordlessly she nodded, her strong white teeth clamping her bottom lip as if that way she'd contain her excitement. Her gingery brown eyes were shining. Pam Pepper normally helped her in and out of her chair with the knack that comes from training and experience. But Nurse Pepper was out and it was up to them to manage for themselves.

'Stand in front and bend over me so that I can put my arms round your neck,' she told him. As she said it she thought, as she had so often, how easy it was to be natural with Quintin. She felt herself pulled upwards, raised so that he bore her full weight even though she was in an upright position, her feet not quite touching the ground. Then with a deft movement he swung her gently into his arms, holding her as if she were a baby. Still her arms were around his neck.

Another car coming up the drive, and Grace was home.

'Guess what, Mum?' Lydia shouted. 'Quin's taking me out in his jeep.'

'That's wonderful! Can I give you a hand, Quintin?'

'No, we're managing beautifully. Don't worry if I keep her out a while, will you? Uncle Peter's getting the finish of the harvest in, we'll probably go back there to see the last load carried. They'll all be thrilled to see her.'

'Not so thrilled as I shall be to be there.' Lydia couldn't stop her face from smiling.

'I'll expect her when you bring her back.' Grace sounded as if it were the most ordinary thing to see them drive away together. She was glad to see Lydia distracted from whatever had been in the letter that had come for her that morning from Sebastian.

'Must we go straight to Rowans?' Lydia turned to Quintin with the trusting look that had always made him putty in her hands. 'I thought perhaps we could drive along to Whiteways. Will you take me there, Quin? I'd love to see it properly.'

'Of course we can go there. But Julie often walks that way with you, I've heard her say so.'

'That's different. I'm sitting much higher in here than I do in my hateful chair. It's almost like seeing it the way other people do.'

'We'll do better than that, Lydia. You shall be as tall as I am.'

Her first burst of excitement at the unexpected outing had evaporated. Just as it had raised her to the heights, now as the bubble burst she hurtled downwards. She'd schooled herself to skim the surface of her days: don't remember how things used to be; don't look ahead and see the hopelessness; never let yourself enjoy anything too much, that way could lead to tears. Quin's sudden offer to take her out had caught her off her guard, she hadn't been able to ward off more emotion than she could handle. He'd make her as tall as he was, he said. She bit her lip, this time not to hold back her excitement, but to fight down a wave of misery that threatened to swamp her. None of them could know what it was like to be *put* in a chair, to have to get used to seeing the world from the height of a six-year-old ... to know that nothing would ever be any different.

'Hold tight,' he said as they turned off the road and into the drive of Whiteways. 'It's full of ruts and potholes, but nothing a jeep can't take in its stride. I see there's a load of flintstone delivered – another day or so and your driveway will be level. Here we are. This, madame, is your home.'

The long, flat-roofed bungalow was as much a folly now as it had ever been. Its brilliant whiteness and ultramodern design would never blend into the background. It shrieked out to be noticed; this house must surely belong to someone rich and famous. And in that Lydia found comfort.

'You do like it, Quin? See, they've put in all new windows, much deeper ones. Sebastian must have realised how little I'd have been able to see from the old ones. From these I'll be able to look out even if I'm on the other side of the room. *He* arranged all that. He's wonderful, isn't he, Quin? Bet there aren't many men with enough imagination to arrange all the things he has. I've not been inside yet, but Julie has told me about what's being done. There'll be nowhere I can't go in my chair – ramps instead of steps, wide doorways. And he's had it all done just for me, because he wants to make it as perfect as he can for me.'

He heard the boast in her voice and ached with pity. That the ache held more than pity he wouldn't consider.

'Some of the gardeners are still here. Shall we see if the house is open? I'll get your chair down if you like.'

'Am I a ton weight, Quin? Instead of the chair, could you manage to carry me around? There must be something inside we could sit on for a rest if your arm goes numb.'

There was no sign of self-pity in her hopeful expression as she waited for his agreement. And of course he gave it. She never doubted that Quintin would agree to anything she wanted if it were within his power to give it to her; he always had. As he raised her into his arms for the second time that afternoon, it flashed through her mind just how tedious she used to find his adoration in those days when she'd hurtled headlong into love with Sebastian. Dear Quin, steadfast and unchanging. Now she could use him with an easy conscience; there was no disloyalty to Sebastian and it made her feel good to be giving such pleasure.

Whiteways proved much more attractive inside than out. The rooms were large, extra-wide sliding doors to each one, the windows almost to the ground and giving a beautiful view across the newly made terrace and down the sloping lawn to the beach. The feeling was of sunshine, the colours were yellows, golds, creams. Apart from those in the garden, two men were working in the interior, laying carpet, the same rich, deep gold throughout the house. This had been Lydia's choice, once Julie had told her that Sebastian wanted her to have a free hand. He must love her very much, of course he must. Looking around her, Lydia was comforted. That morning when she'd read the letter the disappointment had been too much to share with anyone, even Julie.

'I told the Squire I wasn't coming here until Sebastian carried me in,' she mused, looking around her new home. 'I said it just to be nasty. I wish I wasn't so beastly to him, Quin; can't stop myself, then afterwards I always feel sort of screwed up and − oh, I don't know, sort of spoiled. Mum doesn't make me want to be spiteful. Yet I don't think anything I said would hurt her like I know it does him. But I still do it, over and over I do it.'

'Yet you came with me, you didn't wait for Sebastian.' Quin ignored her outburst. He couldn't help turning the knife in the wound he wouldn't admit existed. 'You let me carry you over the threshold. This should be his privilege.'

'Oh, you're different. I thought Seb would have been here by the time the house was ready. But you can see, a few more days and I could move in. Julie has been shopping for furniture, using my ration of dockets, and Mum has been to auction sales, so there's everything we need all ready and waiting. A few more days and the drive will be done, everything finished. Seb will be in Hollywood for at least another month, I heard this morning. I was silly to expect he'd be free to come when the actual filming ended. Of course he'll need to be there for the premiere. He explained in his letter it's important he's there − the premiere of a big film like this has masses of publicity and without him it would go off like a damp squib.' Loyalty to him hid her disappointment.

'You could still wait where you are until he arrives, move from Delbridge House over here together.'

She shook her head. He felt the movement against his neck.

'No. He wants me to be here before he comes. And I expect he's right. He and the Squire are like a couple of dogs after the same bone.'

'And you're the bone.' Quintin's voice was soft, his laugh held affection but no humour. 'Poor Lydia, what it is to be loved too well!'

'So I thought if you brought me here it would be all right. The Squire's so jealous that he hates the thought of the place. Of course I could have persuaded him to bring me if I'd tried. He would have pushed the chair, making veiled remarks about Sebastian all the way. It would have cast a shadow long enough to be still dark when Seb gets here. That's why I thought it would be nice if you brought me.

I know it's only because he loves me, he's angry at what's happened to me and he's angry that Sebastian comes before he does. It's so much easier with you. You make me feel free.'

He wished he could hear it as a compliment.

When they heard the noisy engine of the nursery jeep coming up the track from the lane, Julie and Trudie were glad of an interruption. They'd been filling their basins in silence, the echo of their conversation all around them. Even Trudie knew she'd gone as far as either of them was ready. While they'd worked their thoughts had been busy, there was no way of stopping them. The arrival of a third person put them back on comfortable ground.

'Sounds like Quintin's jeep,' Trudie said, needlessly.

'And not just him! Do you see what I see?'

On the back seat of the open jeep was a wheelchair; in the passenger seat was Lydia. Quintin had pulled off the track to the edge of the field where they were and where already the stubble had been burned.

'Just look at her!' Julie's smile was radiant as she waved to Lydia. 'Trudie, imagine how thrilled she must be not to be pushed in that wretched chair. Come on, let's go and see them.' She started to run in the direction of the jeep.

'Surprise, surprise!' Lydia beamed with pleasure. 'I bet you didn't expect this, Julie! I was in the garden when Quin came. We've been to Whiteways, too. We've seen everything.'

'You girls take the chair.' Quintin was no Goliath, but with a superhuman effort he unloaded it. 'I'll carry her down to where you're working.'

That he meant to carry her didn't surprise Lydia. She'd been pushed over far rougher ground than the hard earth around the side of the field but this was their party piece, she was as ready as he was to show it off.

'Watch us.' That bragging note was back in her voice again. As he bent forward she gripped him tightly around the neck. 'We're getting this off to a fine art, aren't we, Quin? One, two and *up* she rises!' Determinedly she made a game of it; just as determinedly Quintin played his part. A stranger looking at them might have seen them as a normal young couple, happy in the antics of courtship: he, out to impress, showing off his strength; she, something of a coquette, laughing up into his face. For both of them it was an act. She'd never been more aware of the steel corset that supported her spine. Her legs had no feeling, but at least they looked normal, though her ankles would get puffy and ugly by bedtime. Her arms were her own, they still belonged to her. She held them tightly around his neck, turning her head against his chest, frightened of the all too familiar panic that hit her. She wouldn't be able to pick blackberries, a task she'd loved. She knew exactly how it felt to reach high into the brambles for the biggest fruit, feeling the prickles scratch her wrists and catch at the threads of her skirt. Now she'd sit where they put her, sit and watch. And not just *now* but *always*. The 'always' gave her a choking feeling of panic.

Don't think about it, don't imagine. Think of the house. Next week the furniture could go in, a week's time we could be living there. But, after all the excitement of moving in – what then? No, don't go down that road. Who would have expected the afternoon would have turned out like this? Quin must be stronger than he looks. I suppose if you stop to think about it he's quite good-looking. Is he doing this just to be kind? Once upon a time it wouldn't have been like that. Has he forgotten that he used to fancy himself in love with me? Perhaps he's relieved now that I pretended not to notice. No one could ever be in love with me now. Will Sebastian ever carry me like this?

Lydia kept her face turned away from Julie and Trudie while the unwanted thoughts chased through her mind.

'OK, Lydia?' Julie and Trudie were discussing the best place for the chair, but Quintin was more concerned with its reluctant occupant.

Vigorously she nodded her head, then raised her face and opened her mouth in a smile she was confident conveyed excitement at this unexpected treat.

'Quin Tarzan, me Jane!' she called as he carried her towards the others. Her fun-loving mask was firmly back in place.

'I can't believe what I'm hearing.' The Squire ran his hand through his wiry hair and looked at Grace as if she were some strange being from outer space. 'You stand there telling me you've let that child go rattling off in a jeep! Dear God, woman, you must have taken leave of your senses.'

She turned away. Reason told her that there were things better left unsaid. And so they might have remained, had he not grabbed her shoulder and pulled her to face him.

'No wonder you run away from what I'm saying. The first time for weeks I've taken an hour to go off and sketch, first time I've taken my eyes off her, tried to find an hour's escape from the nagging torment of watching over her. But what peace is there anywhere? All the time I see her, like a broken reed.'

'For God's sake pull yourself together before you drown in the tears of your self-pity!' There! She'd said it. Those words, and others like them, had festered in her mind all these weeks. It was as though something snapped in her, she could hold herself in check no longer.

In the same second his hand struck her cheek a stinging blow. Had Grace cared when Lydia had thought herself in love with Sebastian Sutcliffe? No. What would Grace know of the hell he'd endured imagining how the swine had taken her innocent young body. *His* darling child, *his* little girl, the whole purpose of his life. Had Grace even come near to knowing what it meant to him to see her sweet child-form swollen and mishapen with that fornicating devil's offspring? No, of course she hadn't. Hard as nails, nothing ever knocked Grace sideways. She'd always been the same, taking every setback as a challenge, never letting anything get beneath her thick skin. In venting his spite on her he could almost hide for a moment from the real reason of his anguish and misery. But only for a moment.

Her hand went up to her smarting face. They stared at each other in shocked silence.

Like a kaleidoscope a thousand memories filled her mind, encompassing her years with him and hitting her in a single flash. He's never looked beyond himself and Lydia. Because he wants to keep me on the outside, he's even jealous of *me*, her mother. Sometimes I hate him, *hate* him!

'Where's he taken her? Did you interest yourself enough to enquire? Once a week that battleaxe of a nurse goes out. If you had to go to the village, why in Christ's name couldn't you have walked and taken her with you?'

'Don't let's talk about it. You'll never understand. The only thing we can give Lydia is space, the chance to be herself. It did her far more good to know we were content to leave her − '

'We? I certainly would never leave her. As for letting her be jolted about the countryside, have you no imagination? Or is it that you don't care if it jars every nerve in her body? And Quintin, humping her about as if she were a sheaf of corn to throw into the cart.'

She viewed him with scorn. 'Quintin . . . even Quintin! Sometimes I think you're so obsessed that you mind is warped.'

This time when she turned her back on him he didn't stop her. The last minutes had taken them down an unfamiliar track, and both of them were more frightened than they were ready to face.

When a few minutes later she saw him walk down the drive she guessed he was going to Rowans, determined to make himself responsible for bringing Lydia home in her chair. What frightened her was that she should feel removed from what had happened, untouched by the things he'd said to her. The Squire had struck her. A red weal marked her cheek, and she could still feel the tingle; yet his words had had no power to hurt. The only emotion she felt now was anger, not for his attitude to her, but that he should assume the right to decide what Lydia could or couldn't do. Consciously Grace tried to hang on to the memory of how desperately she'd loved him, not just in the first months and years but through everything until this dreadful accident had happened. Even when he'd been spiteful and full of hatred for Sebastian she'd made allowances, she'd shared his unhappiness. Today, when honesty would let her have no secrets from herself, she admitted that she'd been glad when Lydia had married, confident that given time he'd come to accept that he couldn't always be first in her life, there was room for a husband and a father too.

From her bedroom window she could see him turn out of the gate and walk in the direction of Downing Wood just as she'd expected. And how would Lydia feel when she saw him arrive at Rowans? He had no right to intrude on her! Grace put more effort than she needed into brushing her steel-grey hair, then twisting it back into its customary bun. Somehow that set a seal on what had gone before, and she could turn her attention to the things waiting to be done downstairs. The children would be sure to come in hungry; then this evening there were five adults to be fed. Catering for a family didn't come easily to Grace, she'd never been a natural homemaker like Tess, but now she was glad to busy herself with her hands. That way she could pretend the dull ache of unhappiness didn't exist.

Trudie drove Julie and the children home.

'Come over again tomorrow, Julie. I could fetch you if you like, save you walking. It's Sunday, don't forget, so I have a free day.'

Not for the first time Julie panicked, feeling trapped. 'Leave tomorrow open, Trudie. There may be something else Lydia wants me to do with Merry.'

'Please come. We'll get the berries from around the top fields. It was a good afternoon, wasn't it?'

And so it had been. Yet Julie knew exactly how a fish must feel, the bait succulent in its mouth, and a landing net poised beneath it as it thrashed in the water. Yet why? She and Trudie got on well — look at the fun they'd had as she'd learned to drive. Even when they were almost strangers, Trudie thoughtfully used to wait outside the hospital until visiting time in the children's ward was over; sensitive to the fact that Anna would want her mother to herself, she'd never intruded.

'I expect I'll be able to come,' Julie told her now, bearing all these fleeting thoughts in mind and making sure her smile was warm. 'I

82

hope so. Merry and Anna had a marvellous time, didn't they? As your mother said, a day to remember.'

Content with the hope, Trudie turned the car and set off home.

'The Squire and Lydia are on their way?' Grace managed to ask the question casually, at the same time giving her attention to the children's garbled and noisy description of their afternoon.

'He came to fetch her – but no, when she's ready she wants to come back with Quintin. She was fine in the jeep.'

They concentrated on the children, Julie trying their bibs while Grace cut their sandwiches into manageable fingers.

Later the jeep arrived.

'Listen to Lydia.' Julie held her head still. 'When did we last hear her laughing like that?'

Grace was already on her way across the hall to hold the front door open. For a fleeting moment she thought of the Squire and was glad he wasn't there.

That was on Saturday. There was nothing Julie could do until Monday, but once the weekend was over she began to arrange for the move. Grace was interested, but didn't interfere. The Squire pretended he wasn't interested but interfered at every point. At Whiteways the flintstone drive was laid and rolled, the curtains were hung. All was ready.

It was Thursday when the furniture arrived, a day filled with more work than hours. What with two small children 'helping', and a wheelchair with its overexcited and determined occupant making her way from room to room, Whiteways was full of noise and activity. Quintin spent the day there. It was he who suggested to Lydia that she might usefully switch on the kettle for some tea; just as it had been he who'd made sure teapot, caddy, cups and saucers were all at her level. From there on it was up to her.

'Tea up!' They all heard the triumph in her shout. Lydia had made another step towards independence.

They'd been living at Whiteways for seven weeks when, towards the end of a grey, misty day, without warning Sebastian arrived. Whatever the spell he'd cast on Lydia from the silver screen, it had the same power now as when she'd been ten years younger and still at school. In those days, when one of his films had been showing at the Gaumont in Deremouth she'd always sat to see it round twice, then cycled home with stars in her eyes and dreams in her heart.

Now on his first evening at Whiteways he smiled just as charmingly at the unfortuantely plain Pamela Pepper as he did at Julie. She had written to him with regular reports on the alterations to the house, confident that she had a free hand to spend as much as it took; she'd never suggested to Lydia that full marks for thoughtfulness should go to her rather than him. And this evening she was glad the credit was laid at his door, seeing the look of adoration Lydia turned on him.

Julie went to bed early, glad to escape to the privacy of her own room. It was silly to feel let down because he had eyes for no one but his 'little honey'.

Next morning promptly at ten o'clock the photographers arrived. Now here was something that Sebastian had arranged. Pictures were taken of the two of them, Lydia in her wheelchair on the terrace, Sebastian by her side perched on the low white wall that surrounded it. The godlike hero of millions of female dreams on both sides of the Atlantic, yet see the look of loving solicitude he turns on his poor crippled wife. A hero indeed! Reporters were shown around the house, scribbling furiously as they noted the innovations that had been made in his determination to make her life as good as he could. And when the team was departing he pushed the wheelchair to the front of the house — was there one final picture?

'Did you see them, Julie?' Lydia called as she propelled herself indoors. 'Going to be in the nationals tomorrow. And the ginger-headed man was from the *Movie Times*.' It was months since her eyes had shone like that. The newsmen had never come to Grenville Place, there she'd been just Sebastian Sutcliffe's stay-at-home, boring wife. Today he'd given a long interview and welcomed the cameras to their home because he was proud for the world to see her. Lydia's heart sang joyfully.

When, just after lunch, Quin arrived in the jeep to collect her and take her to his nursery, he found her still wrapped in euphoria.

'Oh, Quin, I forgot all about it. I ought to have phoned you and stopped you coming. I'm sorry.'

His first reaction was alarm. Was something wrong? But her voice radiated happiness. With a sinking heart he understood why.

'Seb's back. He came last night. You should have seen us this morning, journalists and photographers all over the place.'

'I am glad, Lydia.' He didn't look directly at her, his attention was concentrated on polishing his glasses. Then he returned to the nursery.

In a fortnight Sebastian was due to start rehearsals in London. Two weeks is no time at all, yet it can take far less to change the course of a life. That was a lesson that had already been brought home to Lydia one stormy teatime in Downing Wood.

Chapter Six

The November afternoon was trying to beguile them into forgetting it was the vanguard of winter. The air was soft, the breeze too gentle to dislodge the last of the leaves that still clung to the trees in Downing Wood, fringing the hilltop to the north of Whiteways. Not that Lydia could see the wood from her position on the south-facing terrace. Wrapped in a warm coat, a blanket over her knees, she watched the four playing with a beach ball on the dark sands.

'All alone, Poppet? That's nice.' The Squire didn't disguise his pleasure. 'I've been out with my paintbrush for a few hours. Couldn't pass by without looking in. Let me move you over here by the bench, you'll soon lose the sun where you are. All very fine for them down there, running about and keeping warm. I'd have expected they could at least have seen you were left where you'd not get cold. It's November, you know, not mid-summer.'

'Squire, you're an old grouch.' It cost an effort to put that teasing note in her voice. 'Seen you were left' − as if she were a piece of furniture! 'I'm where I am because I can watch Merry and Seb from here. Anyway I don't need moving, I can do it myself. When I'm ready.'

The heavy wooden bench was some way from her, but as there was no other chair outside, if he intended to stay that was where he must sit.

'Getting very thick, aren't they, Sebastian and Mrs Freeman?'

'Mrs Freeman suddenly? She was always just Julie, what's she supposed to have done now to push her out of favour? I wish you wouldn't always try and cause trouble, always try and dig up something to turn into a suspicion.'

'Come over here, Poppet, come and sit by your old Squire. We don't want that know-it-all nurse to hear every word we say.'

'There you go again! She's super and I like her. As for Julie, she's my friend, the best friend I've ever had — except for Seb.'

She could tell from his expression that she'd stung him, and she was glad. Yet somehow the sunny afternoon had lost its wonder. Her anger vanished as quickly as it had come. She'd move over next to him, she couldn't bear to see him look like that. But as soon as she released the brake and gripped the wheels, he was on his feet.

'Don't you try and do that on your own. Let me. I'll move you.'

'Squire, I can go anywhere. Just let me do it by myself. Why do you think Sebastian had Mr Watts make all the alterations here? So that I can do things without help.'

'Humph!' A barely audible grunt. 'In one thing your mother is right, I suppose. We should be grateful you married someone who can *buy* the comforts you need; it would be a very different thing if you had to rely on the time he spends on you instead of the money.'

'Don't be mean. You'll end up making us quarrel. Is that what you came here for, to argue?' Then a change of mood, her frown vanished and a smile lit her face, the smile she knew he craved. 'I bet you didn't, not with me.'

'I drove out to Hay Tor, Poppet.' He caught on to her new mood. 'Remember how we used to go there, how you used to climb the crag?' Today, sitting in the lee of the great rocks, he had been alone and yet not alone, because her spirit had been all around him. Almost as clearly as if she'd been there he'd seen the little child who used to come with him, her gingery brown eyes bright with inner joy as she danced on the grassy slope, lost in a childish dream world of her own; he'd seen her again as she'd learned to walk on her hands, turn somersaults and cartwheels. Hay Tor had always been one of their special places. Today alone on the summit he had seen no need to hide his anguish, it had been part of the high solitude. When he felt the sting of tears he'd welcomed them. Loudly and unheard he'd cried, finding a strange comfort in the sound of his rasping sobs filling the silence. Afterwards he'd felt exhausted but cleansed, able to work. Then he'd come here, needing to be with her, to know that those happy memories mattered to her as much as to him. So why hadn't he been able to tell her so? When he'd found her alone near the edge of the terrace, why hadn't he sat down on the parapet close by her and pretended to enjoy the spectacle of Merry's efforts at football?

He squared his shoulders.

'Well done!' He applauded the deft way she handled her chair as she moved near to him, then set the brake again. He must train himself to be content with the crumbs she spared him. But how could he? The last thing he wanted was to watch that affected pimp down there on the sands. Wouldn't mind betting he was putting on the charm to attract Julie Freeman; second nature to him, all part of his profession.

'It must have been lovely up there today, Squire,' Lydia prompted him. 'Remember that day when you'd gone there painting on your own, I was so put out to think I'd been left behind that I cycled all the way out to join you. We brought my bike home on top of the car. Remember?'

'Of course I do. But today, you were there with me today, Poppet. Everywhere I looked you were there.' He heard the croak in his voice. She heard it too, and with all her might willed him not to give way. If he cried she couldn't bear it. Damn him! Her own battle was hard enough, he'd no right to expect her to fight his too. Anyway *he'd* got nothing to moan about, he could still climb the hill to Hay Tor, he could still do everything − today, tomorrow, next week, next year.

'What was Mum doing while you were gallivanting about the countryside?' To talk about her mother should put them on safer ground.

'Grace? Didn't ask her. She always finds plenty to do. I went up there to paint, but didn't get the paints out. Look, Poppet, look what I did up on the Tor. Only sketches, but I'll work from them. Didn't I say you were up there with me? You must have been about seven on that day. It was the first time you climbed to the top of the rock. Remember?'

His reward was the light in Lydia's eyes, the way she nodded her head, the smile he'd always seen as especially for him. The tension eased, and in her relief she held out her hand for the sketchpad.

'Let's see. Oh yes, of course I remember that day. You were busy, you had your easel somewhere over here − why didn't you put it in the sketch? I crept off, and by the time you saw me I was more than halfway to the top. "Come down from there", what a bossy old stick you sounded! I knew you meant it. But I wasn't going to get that far and then give in. I yelled for you to "Come and get me!" But you didn't. Now' − she held up the sketch − 'here I am at the top. You really ought to put yourself in too, hopping about like a scalded cat waiting to catch the pieces if I fell.'

'Don't! Don't say it, Poppet. Look at you now − and what am I able to do? Nothing. It hurts me as much as it does you, you know that.'

'Oh, for goodness sake! Oh, good, the others are coming back.'

Sebastian and Julie had abandoned the game of football and were turning back towards the house. The younger ones hesitated; the tide hadn't come in over the rocks yet. Determined not to miss an opportunity, Merry headed in that direction until Sebastian realised what he had in mind and chased after him in time to swoop him up just before the water went over the top of his red Wellington boots. Then he found himself hoisted high to sit astride his father's shoulders while Julie and Anna came behind carrying ball, towel, spades, buckets and shrimping net.

'Time I was getting home.' The Squire took his sketchpad and stood up. For those few moments she'd been *his* again, but already something was happening to them, driving them apart. 'Here they come, these friends of your bosom − they won't want to hear my reminiscences.'

'You might at least say hello to your grandson, Squire.'

'Nonsense. He's got eyes for only one person. Like his mother.'

By the time the noisy and sand-reddened party arrived on the terrace, the Squire's car could be heard reversing out of the drive.

Sebastian was only there for two weeks, and to Lydia their days together had an unreal quality, made worse by the strange relationship imposed on the couple. The start and finish of Lydia's days revolved around the attentions she received from Pam Pepper. Many women have been cared for by husbands and families, their very dependence bringing an intimacy that strengthens and deepens the roots of their love. But such a situation would never arise in Lydia's case; Sebastian could never be more than a visitor at Whiteways. His work would take him away for weeks and months at a time. She was determined he should see her as bright and lively, keen to push herself cheerfully to meet each challenge; he was determined that she should have the best care, that within its limitations her life should be as full and interesting as he could help to make it. Both of them played a part: while she defied sympathy, he acted the hardest role of his career, treating her as a pretty, petted and spoilt young sweetheart, just as he always had. Not to anyone would he admit how it tore his heart to see her gallant struggle.

Night after night, lying alone in his bedroom, Sebastian found it impossible to close his mind on the world and sleep. Between his rooms and hers was the bathroom he'd had adapted for her, and beyond that she would be lying just as Nurse Pepper put her. Could she even turn over? Dear God, how could she stand it? Was she awake? Was she miserable? Sometimes he went as far as getting out of bed to go and talk to her, to try and reassure her. But how could he reassure her, how could anyone? Moreover, he couldn't bear to strip her of the illusion that he believed her pretence of gaiety. For him to see her lying there helpless, surrounded by the trappings of the care Nurse Pepper gave her, would destroy the façade she fought so hard to hold in place. Poor darling little Lydia! When he closed his eyes the image of her was always there, a child on the brink of life, loving him and begging him to love her. Then his memory would go to the bedroom they had shared in London, times when he'd come home buoyed up after a specially successful performance, others when he'd been tense before a first night — whatever his mood, the one thing he'd known was that she'd be eager for him. There'd been plenty of women in his life, beautiful women, experienced women. What he'd loved in Lydia was her honesty; sex hadn't been a skill, it had been a joy. No, he couldn't go into her room now, for her sake he couldn't. And that was the sadness.

Those were the bad nights, when the only escape was to turn on the light and concentrate on rereading the play that was soon to go into rehearsal, pretending to learn the lines he already knew.

Before Sebastian went back to London to start rehearsals he bought a car for Julie's use. Everyone had expected him to see that, living more than a mile from the nearest shop and with two small children in her charge, Julie would need a car. But not for a moment had she expected him to arrive at Whiteways on the last day before the end of his stay, driving a brand-new Standard 14.

'The first day I was here I had a word with the chap at the garage in the village — what's his name, Matthew Ellis? I told him how necessary it was that you had transport before the winter came. Not just you, but the children too. I told him it was urgent, but gave him a free hand to get anything he could. Actually, we're in luck. It couldn't be more suitable, Julie. He took me to Exeter to pick it up and I drove it back. It handles well, you'll enjoy it.'

Black, streamlined and shiny, it stood in the front drive. For Julie and the children it would be perfect. No chance of getting the wheel-chair aboard, though. A van would have been the only way she could have done that, and a van would have been no use for everyone.

If Lydia had any reservations, she didn't say so. Wheeling herself outside, she joined the group who stood admiring its gleaming beauty. She laughed to see the way Merry jumped with excitement, and she drew strength and satisfaction from the appreciation she could read in Julie's expression and Pam's too. Her own eyes shone with triumph that it was Sebastian — *her* Sebastian — who had performed this miracle. Other people waited months for a new

89

car, but he was different. That Matthew Ellis had pulled strings on *her* account didn't enter her head – or Sebastian's either.

The next day he was gone. Pam Pepper was the only one to be unaffected, not having let his presence change the routine of the care she gave Lydia. To all the others, even Anna, there was a flatness about their days they'd not been aware of before he came. Fretful, Merry would cry for the least thing, blubbering that he wanted 'Seb come'. His moodiness rubbed off on Anna, and they quarrelled as they had never used to do. Lydia was quiet, riding along in a trough without any will to climb out of it.

And Julie? What possible difference could it make to her whether Lydia's husband was here or in London?

Pathetic! Silently she glowered at the girl reflected back at her from her wardrobe mirror. Of course you were with him a lot when he was here, you're paid to take care of his child, aren't you? Can't think what's come over you that you can be so selfish – so stupid. She stood a little taller, her straight, dark brows drawn into a frown. Julie Freeman, you ought to be ashamed. He doesn't even see you as a person, a woman; and a good thing too. You're meant to be a companion for Lydia, and a friend. Some friend!

From outside came the sound of the children racing up and down the terrace on their scooters.

'I's going to sand. C'mon, Anna, we go on rocks, like with Seb.'

A clatter as the scooters were unceremoniously abandoned. A quick look out of the window and she saw two small figures racing down the grassy slope. Before the escapees slithered down the final steep drop to the beach, Julie caught up with them.

Perched on a high wooden stool behind the bench he used as a desk, Peter Grant was doing paperwork. From the doorway Tess gazed out at the muddy farmyard, every dip so familiar that she knew exactly the shape and depth of each puddle.

'I wondered if that's where he'd gone.' She spoke more than half to herself.

'Who?' He responded automatically, but didn't wait for an answer. 'Agricultural Land Commission. Is this why we farm? Just look at this damned thing I'm having to fill in. All very well to tell us the Agricultural Bill gives us security of price for our produce, but who's master? Them or me? How much came out of each field last year, how much this year, project it forward and they tell me how much I must produce next. Damn it, you can't run a farm that way. It's not a factory with a production line. The land must be kept in good heart if it's to yield well.'

Leaving the open doorway, she came to his side. 'We managed all through the war, we even managed after the last one when things were really tough. We'll not be beaten by all these silly bits of paper, Peter love.'

'Silly bits of paper seem to be the order of the day.' He put an arm around her waist. 'Yes, you're right. We've got through worse times than these. Worse? They were good times, Tess.'

He didn't need to tell her what was behind his words. In the beginning it had been a battle to survive, but they'd been young and determined not to be beaten. And the birth of their son had given them a purpose. Right from when Paul as a toddler had first shadowed his father around the farm, he'd loved every inch of it. One day all this would have been his. Tess ran her fingers through Peter's wiry hair. Neither of them spoke; even now, years after he'd been killed, the pain was too deep.

'Quin wants to expand.' Peter's voice was firm as he pulled them away from the quicksands of misery. 'Trial grounds for his own seeds. And he has another scheme too, he was talking to me about it just before he went out. He knows just what he means to do, but he needs the land. He wants me to sell him Deans Meadow and the small field this side of the hill. What do you think, Tess?'

'Another scheme, you say? He can't want as much land as that for trial grounds.'

'No. This other is a long-term affair — very long-term. You know, Tess, it's good to hear him talking, planning and shaping the years ahead. He means to make a garden, design it, plant it. A showpiece for his nursery, you might say, but from the drawings he showed me, it'll be far more than that.'

Talking about Quin had lifted some of the gloom. There was no doubt of the affection in Tess's voice as she said, 'Always the per-fectionist, Quin never does things by halves. And this is where he wants to be.'

Peter nodded. It was important to both of them that Quintin, who was almost like a son, saw his future at Rowans.

'It was Quin I was watching just now,' Tess told him. 'Remember, you said "Who?" He's just come back in that jeep. Lydia's chair in the back; I saw him drive up the track to the nursery. He must have been off to Whiteways to get her.'

'He's very fond of Lydia — too fond. He always has been. There never was any future in it for him, even before she met Sebastian Sutcliffe. I'd be happier about him if he'd find himself a single girlfriend. As long as he hangs around Lydia that's not likely to happen.'

'Oh, Peter, no one can go out and find a girlfriend like buying a new suit, take one off the peg and hope it fits. When they were children she and Paul were always thick as thieves.' She had to say it, had to hear herself speak his name and bring him back into the circle — Paul, Trudie, Quintin and Lydia. 'They were two of a kind; what mischief one didn't think of the other one would.'

She was rewarded by Peter's reminiscent smile. 'Even then, though, Quin was her willing slave. And didn't the little monkey know how to make the most of it!' It was said without malice, all of it so long ago. 'But one thing's sure, she won't give him any encouragement now, she's too besotted with her Sebastian, poor little soul.'

The Grants were the nearest Quintin had ever known to relatives. Indeed, he'd grown up with more affection from them than many a child gets from its own family. As a six-year-old he'd been sent to board at nearby Merton House Preparatory School, in those days run by Dr Ewart Bradstock, a close friend of Peter. The youngest boarder, his solemn and frightened stare from behind those thick lenses earning him the nickname Owl, he'd become a solitary child. With no flair for sport, he'd taken refuge in reading and in making sure he did well at his work. He'd been sent to school because his father's regiment was going to India; he'd been conscious of his mother's excitement at the prospect and felt himself packed away just as surely as the furnishings of the house they were leaving behind. At the end of term he'd been put on the train in the charge of the guard and sent to his grandparents in Sussex. And so his school days might have gone on, but for the death of his grandfather just as term was coming to an end. Three days into the holiday, while Quintin roamed the grounds of Merton House on his own, Peter called to see Dr Bradstock. He noticed the solitary little boy and was told his story. Picturing his own family at home, he knew that Rowans had enough love to share with one extra. That was the beginning of Quintin spending his holidays with the Grants.

The next turn of fate happened thousands of miles away in India. Quin was ten when news came that his mother, the wife of a colonel, had gone off with a subaltern. The subaltern was cashiered. The colonel had no paternal feeling for Quintin; indeed, he'd often doubted that he could have sired a child he considered such a weakling. Now that his wife had left him it gave him a warped satisfaction to forsake her child. No longer did letters from India come to Merton House. But by this time Quin felt he belonged to Rowans.

92

Alice Ramsey, his grandmother in Sussex, made herself responsible for his education. Once or twice through the years she sent for him to visit her. He was shy and gauche, and she made no secret of the fact that she looked on inviting him as a duty. He was about eighteen when she died, making him her sole beneficiary, gaining a final satisfaction that whatever the boy's wayward mother might have hoped for by way of inheritance, the last point scored had been hers.

On the south-facing hillside the glass of the greenhouses had no sparkle on this grey early December day.

'You'll be warmer inside.' Quin lifted Lydia carefully from the jeep and lowered her to the waiting chair. 'I have to keep them at an even temperature.'

'It all looks so new and hopeful. That's how you must feel, Quin. Did you plan it all while you were in the army?'

'Every last pane of glass,' he said and laughed. 'Well, of course I started planning it years ago, before I went to the Horticultural College even. None of us expected we were going to have our lives disrupted by — ' He frowned. 'I should be the last one to complain. On the surface they never change, but, Lydia, it must have knocked the bottom out of their lives. They built that farm up, he was part of it, he was the future.'

For one second when he'd stopped mid-sentence she'd assumed that he must have been alluding to what had happened to her. But it was Paul he was talking about, talking to her as though she were the same person she'd been in the old days when they'd all been together. Her eyes smiled at him warmly; she held out her hand and felt it taken in his.

'Do you believe in things, Quin? You know what I mean? People dying, spirits, things that you can't find words to explain and yet you can feel?'

He pushed the chair into the greenhouse and closed the door behind them. Here the air was still and humid, heavy with a cocktail of smells she couldn't distinguish, a combination of damp earth, the heady perfume of flowers, even wet leaves.

'You can't do this sort of work if you doubt that there is a force much greater than ourselves. It's the same with farming. I'm sure it is, it has to be.'

'Did Paul ever talk about anything like that.'

'Now, would he?'

They looked at each other, remembering Paul. Both of them laughed.

93

'Come on, Quin' − she put her question behind them − 'I want you to show me everything. Just look along there, dozens and dozens of glorious plants. Are they being got ready for Christmas?'

It was the start of her inspection. The gangway was hardly wider than her chair, but everything was within touching distance. She listened to all he told her, she fingered the soil in the pots and learned how to know if they needed watering; she made a mental note of which were watered from the top and which ones must never get their leaves wet.

'Can I come again, Quin?' she asked, sure of the answer. The next request was less certain, but she knew exactly how much hope and trust to put in the look she turned on him. 'Wish I could learn to help. I know you couldn't be doing with my hateful chair underfoot when you're all busy, but sometimes, Quin, could you bring me up here and let me do a proper job, something useful?'

'You bet I will. Leave it to me, Lydia.'

And so she did. Quin never failed her.

Dusk was falling as they came out and he locked the doors. With a movement that became easier each time, he lifted her into the passenger seat, loaded the chair and got in by her side.

'What we were saying earlier,' she said as he started the engine, 'about whether people are still here even though they die. Uncle Peter must feel Paul's there on the farm. He is for me; I bet if I could run in Downing Wood like we used to, I'd know he was there.'

'He's here for me too, Lydia. I can say so to you. It's a private, personal sort of link. Downing Wood, you say. For me the first time I knew it was one evening when I was fishing off Deremouth Pier. We did it so often when we were kids. I wasn't even thinking of him especially − then suddenly he filled my whole mind. If I'd tried I couldn't have made it happen.'

At the bottom of the track Quintin didn't turn towards Rowans. This afternoon had been their own, he didn't want it to become a family teatime. He glanced at her, then braked to a halt. He didn't ask her why she was crying, but it tore his heart to see her face with its fading crisscross of scars puckering as she tried to control her tears.

'Sorry,' she gulped. 'It's all such a mess. Paul's gone, yet he seems to come close, probably he sees the real us clearer than he would if he were still here.'

'We must try and think that.' Lightly he touched her shoulder; anything more and she might pull away from him.

'Not really crying for Paul. Wish I was. That would be honest, good, sort of clean.'

94

This time Quin threw caution overboard and held his arms around her, nestling her wet face against his neck.

'This is honest and good too, Lydia. You're entitled to cry.'

'Not honest. Not honest at all. Can I borrow your hanky? Mine's with my things in the chair.' She pulled her shoulders free of his hold and mopped her face. 'Paul isn't part of our world and yet he's close, he knows all our sadnesses and all the laughs too − bet he does, he always saw jokes quicker than any of us. Sometimes people who are alive, always kind to you, do all the thoughtful things, yet you can't reach them, not really sort of be one with them, touch a real chord of understanding.' She sniffed. 'Because of being like this, I can't get near Seb at all. I'll never be part of his life, I'll never be a proper mother to Merry.'

Each time Quintin thought he was following the way her mind was working, the next sentence would throw him off beam again.

'That's nonsense. You'll always be the only mother Merry will want and you know it.' Here was something he understood, a chance for him to push her back onto the rails.

'Can't play with him. He's only a baby still, expect he thinks I don't want to play like we used to.'

'Lydia, you're just trying to hurt yourself. You're miserable − and God knows, I can understand that − and you're trying to latch on to anything but the real reason. Of course Merry wants you to play with him − the loss is his as well as yours. But as for him thinking you don't want to, that's nonsense and you know it.' With her chin in his hand he turned her face up to his. 'Don't run away, don't try and hide. You'll beat this thing − but not until you accept and build from there. Talk to Sebastian, say to him the things you've said to me − '

'Can't. It's different with you. I always tried to be pretty for him, better than my best. I'm not daft, I know I'm no beauty, but he used to make me feel − oh, just sort of bubbling with so much happiness. Now he's kind, he treats me carefully, as if he needs to spoil me. I think he's proud because I don't grizzle. Don't grizzle! He ought to ask *you,* you could tell him! Supposing he stops being in love with me? But of course he will, he must do. He can't be in love with someone who isn't a proper woman, can't share his life.'

'You don't give him credit for much sense, do you?'

'Can't expect you to understand.' She blew her nose and ran her fingers through her short curls. 'Will they see I've been crying? Do I look all right?'

He assured her she did, knowing that neither Julie nor Pam would comment on her puffy eyelids, then turned on the engine again. They were nearly back at Whiteways when she spoke again.

'Quin, I'm sorry about making a stupid scene like that. And we'd had such a good afternoon too, what did I have to go and spoil it all for? It's always to you I let off steam. Honestly, I'm quite cheery most of the time.'

'If I'm your whipping boy, then I'm grateful. That might mean that you'll let me be the one to give you the occasional kick in the pants when you need it, eh?'

'Fat lot of good that would do. Couldn't even feel it!' This was the old Lydia talking; she grinned at him proud that she'd managed to score a witty point at her own expense. She couldn't help believing that perhaps Paul had heard what she'd said and shared the joke.

Visits to the greenhouses became a regular occurrence as that winter went on. In the middle section of the longest Quintin took away the shelves on one side so that her chair wouldn't block the way, then he filled the remaining shelves with pots that he intended to put in her care. He'd oversee her, he'd teach her to take cuttings and grow them on, he'd teach her to prick out seedlings. His own salvation had always come from the miracle of growth: he'd help her, he'd show her a way forward.

Sebastian was playing to full houses. Greasepaint, footlights, the response of a live audience, even the harsh light of a naked bulb over the make-up table in the dressing room — these things were meat and drink to him. About twice a week he rang Whiteways. He said very little about his own life but he encouraged Lydia to tell him about hers. Some of the pleasure would have been lost to her if she could have seen the sympathy in his expression as he heard about Julie wheeling her to the village or to Rowans, or about how Quintin had given her jobs to do that were her very own.

'Merry keeps asking when you're coming. "When Seb come?" Every day he asks.' She couldn't bring herself to voice the real cry of her heart and say that she missed him just as much. Before the accident she could have put just the right warmth into her voice to encourage him to find the welcome waiting for him. But not now. Instead she said, 'I was thinking the other day, why don't you come one weekend? You don't have a performance on Mondays. It's a boring journey on your own, so you could bring some of the cast. We've spare rooms crying out to be used.'

'I'll come soon, Lydia. There's a week just before Easter when I'm free.' The repertory of plays, Shakespeare, Shaw, Wilde, changed week by week through the season, 'I'll come alone, I don't want to spend my time playing host to visitors. Tell Merry to get the shrimping net out ready.'

She ought to be glad he didn't want to fill the house with his stage friends, but his answer put the final nail in the coffin of that dream she'd had, herself as a sort of mother confessor, her inactivity endowing her with an understanding beyond that of ordinary people.

That conversation was on a Saturday morning in February, too cold yet for her to be given the freedom of the terrace. It was not too cold for the others, though. Down on the sands the children were clad in waterproofs, Wellingtons, leggings and mackintoshes, kneeling on the red sand building a mound that in their minds was a magic castle. Julie and Trudie sat smoking in companionable silence on a rock that jutted out from the final slope down from Whiteways' garden.

'Remember what you said to me once, Julie, about not living in the past, about looking to the future? Was it just idle words or did you mean it? You and me too, that's what you said.'

'Of course I meant it.'

'And you think that's what you're doing, wasting your time here like some domestic?'

'I hadn't really thought of it like that. When I applied for the job I suppose that's what it must have been, a live-in nursemaid. But that was a year ago. I wouldn't dream of leaving Lydia. I wouldn't want to. I don't think of myself as what you call a "domestic". Anyway, just look at those two. How could I think of taking a different sort of job, probably putting Anna into a day nursery back in London?'

'London? You'd not go back there if you left Lydia?'

'I told you, I'm not leaving Lydia.' Julie laughed. 'But if I did I'd go back where I belong, of course I would.'

'You belong here, Julie. I wish I hadn't brought the subject up. It's just that you could be making a proper career for yourself, women can do more with their lives than keep the home fires burning. Look at me!'

'I'm looking, Trudie.' Julie instilled affection and humour into her tone, even though something warned her to be wary. 'And I'm seeing a rare combination, a woman with brains and beauty. No wonder you have such sublime confidence in the possibilities.'

She wasn't sure whether it was pleasure or embarrassment that brought the colour to Trudie's cheeks.

'I don't know about brains — hard work and determination got me where I am. As for beauty, look in your own mirror.'

'No, Anna!' Julie was glad to run down the sand after her scarlet-clad daughter who, complete with bucket, was about to wade into the water to fill it. 'If you want water round your castle, this is the way to get it, don't you remember? Give me your spade.'

It took her five minutes to dig the trench and let the water through for their moat, too long to pick up the threads of a conversation she didn't want to analyse.

There was no putting it out of her mind entirely, though. In the watches of the night she'd think of Trudie's words and wonder. It was her responsibility to make a home for Anna. So what of the future? Anna wouldn't always be little, the time would come when she'd want a home to bring her friends to, and she deserved more than being the daughter of a live-in companion. Ambition fired Julie's imagination. During the year she'd been with Lydia she'd managed to save most of her salary. Perhaps by the time Merry was at school Lydia would have adjusted to her lifestyle; then Julie could become independent. She might rent an office where she and Anna could live upstairs. She imagined other women coming to fetch typing work just as she once had. When she'd been paid her few miserable shillings she'd always known that the agency was charging far more. If she could set herself up, it would be *she* who'd make the charge and pay the typists. Her mind filled with thoughts of Freeman's Secretarial Agency, as she grandly came to think of it. Everyone needs a dream.

The week before Easter, Sebastian came home. For a whole week Julie didn't give a thought to that dream of her distant tomorrow.

With natural ease he slipped into the routine of the house. Much of Lydia's morning was taken up with Nurse Pepper. The mysteries of care went on behind closed doors and it was customary for this to be the time when Julie took the children out. If the tide was low they might go no farther than the sands; if the tide was high or the wind too strong for the shore, she would sit them side by side in a cumbersome twin pushchair and set off for Downing Wood; sometimes to the village, calling at Delbridge House on the way; occasionally even as far as Rowans. The car was used only when the weather was bad or Lydia wanted something done in Deremouth, Newton Abbot or Exeter.

This week each morning they were joined by Sebastian, much to Merry's delight. Anna was less keen, with him there nothing was quite the same. She wasn't old enough to know exactly what it was that made her uncomfortable, but it had to do with Merry's Seb and her own mother. When either of them spoke, even to her or to

Merry, she felt they were really talking to each other. She scowled. Merry's Seb had been there before, she remembered it and the fun they'd had. Yet now it was different.

It was Thursday, his week already half over. No beach for the children today, the wind off the sea was colder than it had been at Christmas, blowing with a force that rekindled a night better forgotten, a night a year ago. So this morning Julie kept the children in the playroom painting, shrouded in long-sleeved overalls, elasticated at the wrists and tying at the back of their necks, overalls Tess had made years ago for Trudie and Paul and kept in the box of old treasures.

'I say, they looked dressed for the job.' Sebastian's voice surprised them, and had its effect on each one.

Merry flung himself round in his chair, all thought of the masterpiece he'd been creating forgotten. Julie's natural reaction wasn't so different, but to cover the excitement that seemed to flutter through her veins she made a show of holding on to his jam jar of water as if she expected his sudden movement to send it spinning. As for Anna, her glower encompassed them all; Sebastian for disturbing them, Merry for being so keen to abandon his painting, and, most of all, her mother without understanding the reason.

'I came to get you all, I thought we'd drive to Dartmoor. How say you, Julie?'

'How say I?' she mimicked. 'No, that's how. We can't go out like that and leave Lydia.' Julie frowned. 'Anyway, it would be blowing as cold as Siberia on Dartmoor today.'

'"Blow, blow, thou winter wind,"' he teased.

What was there about that beautiful speaking voice of his? She turned away from him, frightened that he'd read in her eyes how often it haunted her.

'Listen to it, look at it. New York was a long way away' – she tried to convey her meaning without making it too apparent to the children – 'but use your imagination. We'll stay here with Lydia.' But it wasn't her place to tell him what he couldn't do. If he wanted to go, if he wanted to take Merry –

His hand was warm as he turned her face to his and willed her to hold his gaze.

'What a nice woman you are, Julie Freeman.' That was all he said, his words engraving themselves indelibly on her mind. Even as she heard them she knew they would be recalled, hung on to, treasured.

'Did you see the paintings?' With forced brightness she changed the subject. Taking the cue from her, he admired what the children had done, then suggested that if they were staying at home to be with Lydia, then with Lydia they should be.

'Dumb charades, that's what we'll play. We'll practise in here while the nurse is putting her through her paces, then she can guess. Any suggestions?'

For a moment they both considered, while Merry and Anna gave up the pretence of painting and chased around the room, caught up with the excitement that something special was going to happen.

'What about "sandwich"? First syllable they could pretend to dig; second syllable a witch on a broomstick; whole word we could pretend to be having a picnic.'

'Not just a nice girl, but a bright one too.' The smile he threw at her hadn't altered since the days it had made Lydia's heart turn somersaults from the pages of her scrapbook. Julie looked away, reminding herself that outward charm was second nature to him, part of his stock in trade. 'And for a second word we'll do "hypnotise" – hip, no, ties. Hip's easy; for "no" you can check the children, ties is a simple tie-up job. For the whole word you can hypnotise me.'

He took hold of both her hands. 'Don't say a word, just look at me, Julie, at me, through me, into me.'

She pulled her hands away. What was he saying to her in the silence of that message?

'That's it then.' She stood up, her action bringing the children back into the scene. 'You're the actor, teach us what to do.'

Half an hour later, while the wind whistled down the chimney and rattled the huge windows of the sitting room, they did their performance for Lydia and Pam Pepper. The room came alive with laughter.

They'd finished 'sandwich' and were getting assembled for 'hypnotise' when Quin arrived.

'I had to go into the village and on the way home I thought I'd come this bit farther and say hello to Sebastian.'

He knew the warmth of Lydia's smile wasn't just because of his unexpected appearance. It was because he'd come to see Sebastian.

'Tell you what,' she interrupted with all the eagerness that had first attracted Sebastian to her, 'Pam and Quin and I will do one for you – a charade, I mean. You lot clear off in the other room while we choose a word. Dumb charades, Quin. Remember, we used to play at Christmas at Rowans?'

They acted out 'currant' – first 'cur', with Quin on all fours and Pam holding him on a lead improvised from a dressing-gown cord while the children fell about laughing, then 'rant', Lydia waving her arms about furiously making a silent speech worthy of Speakers' Corner. The whole word wasn't easy, so they cheated on the spelling and did a wild display of rowing against the tide and getting nowhere.

By this time the children were overexcited, but were rounded up to do their bit as rehearsed for 'hypnotise'. The five adults had become light-headed from playing a childish game in the middle of the morning, while outside the elements hammered at the house daring them to forget the heartbreak that was only just beneath the surface. To the children this was high sport, all the better because they hadn't been expecting to see the grown-ups suddenly not behaving like grown-ups.

Lydia snatched at her happiness too.

'Whole word,' she cried, her laugh defying anyone to stop playing and make the day normal again. 'Come on, three syllables. Aren't the children in it?'

'No. Just the two of us.' Was it Julie's imagination or was the room suddenly stilled at Sebastian's words, everyone as aware as she was of the feeling that gripped her? She tried to compose her face, but in her brain hammered what he'd said earlier: 'Look at me, Julie, at me, through me, into me.'

It was Quintin who guessed it, at least it was Quintin who called out the word. Looking at Lydia he thought she'd guessed too. She looked drained, the sparkle had gone. He stood up to leave.

'I know you won't want to come up to the nursery while Sebastian is here. I'll pick you up when you let me know you're ready,' he told her.

'I've been telling him all about what I do, that I'm more than just a pretty face. I'd like to have an hour or two up there — what about after lunch?' Her smile was back in place, defying any of them to suspect she wasn't happy. 'Please, Quin.'

'If he can spare you, I'll pick you up in the jeep. You'll be quite warm.'

She nodded. 'I shall like it — watching the storm, being shut in the greenhouses.'

Did the others know how slim the hold she had on her control? He hoped they didn't.

'About two o'clock then. There's a lot of work waiting.' Not expecting her this week, he'd taken care of the plants on her shelves. But before this afternoon he'd see to it there was what looked like a backlog waiting.

The children, with no understanding of the game they'd been playing, were pretending they were dogs as Quin had been and were tearing round the room on all fours. Sebastian went to see Quin out, but he didn't come back. Julie listened, wondering whether she'd missed the sound of the jeep leaving.

Seeing Lydia's sudden tiredness, Pam took her to her room, locking the door firmly behind them. What mysteries of care were to be undertaken Julie didn't know, but she imagined those trained hands would massage some sort of comfort back into her patient.

'Come on, you two' — she rounded up the children — 'you've some pictures waiting to be finished.' The playroom faced the front, and would enable her to look out of the window where Quintin would have parked. Surely he must have gone without her hearing.

But she was wrong. He and Sebastian were together in the jeep. Quin was talking, using his hands in an uncharacteristic way to emphasise his words. Sebastian was frowning, looking unsure. There was no reason for this feeling of guilt to grip her; if Sebastian knew the way her thoughts jumped at the sight of the two of them, he would laugh that a grown woman could be so naive. Again she looked out of the window, and her heart raced as she watched him, but there was no happiness.

Chapter Seven

The wind howling in the chimney was the only sound in the suddenly stilled dining room at Rowans. When a swirl of smoke belched back into the grate, movement broke the silence that followed Quintin's words.

'Damned wind!' The Squire's glower encompassed them all, the smoke-filled hearth and those around the table too. 'As if we needed a reminder of its devilishness. And *you* of all people, Quintin. I credited you with more sense. You've not told her?'

'It's not my place to tell her. Sebastian will do that. But, Squire, what better way is there to give her some modicum of independence?' Quintin felt all eyes on him as he spoke. He took off his glasses, cleaned them vigorously in his napkin, then put them on again as if he expected to find the Squire's accusing glare to have been polished away.

It was the evening of that same Thursday. The Harridays were visiting the Grants for the evening meal. Nothing unusual in that; their friendship had been firmly woven into the fabric of their lives for years.

'I agree with Quin.' Grace defied the Squire. 'Anything that can be done to give her self-reliance must be done. But it's not going to be easy. How Sebastian ever managed to pull strings to get that Standard for Julie so quickly I can't imagine. People wait months and months for a new car. What you're talking about now is a different thing altogether. Are there such vehicles? Not even a foot throttle?'

'Damn it, Grace!' The Squire's face was red with anger. 'Do you have to spell it out?' His outburst hardly dented the conversation.

'I hope Sebastian is sure of what he's telling her before he raises her hopes.' Peter too had his doubts.

'The whole idea is ridiculous — ridiculous and dangerous.' The

Squire wasn't to be silenced so easily. His voice rose in that way Grace knew all too well. 'I'll not have it, Quintin. You hear me? Isn't it enough to see how she is now, without throwing her out among the traffic, pitting this vehicle you're dreaming up against every powerful car on the road. Some puny motorised invalid carriage — yes, *invalid carriage*, and that for my Poppet!'

Grace closed her eyes. Dear God, please shut him up. Bad enough he makes a fool of himself at home. Make somebody say something before he goes right over the top. No use my trying. I only make things worse. Why can't he behave like other people? He's greedy, selfish — even the pain he wants all for himself.

In shutting her eyes she tried to escape a truth that filled her with guilt. In the beginning, if only he'd let it happen, they could have drawn strength from each other. But not any longer. If she let herself look at him now, she knew his face would be flushed, his mouth trembling, and she would feel nothing but shame and irritation. Which of them had changed? All their life together he'd turned to her for comfort and support. Willingly she'd been there for him. Was he different, or was she seeing him clearly for the first time?

' . . . give you my word.' Quin was talking and she had not even listened.

'Your word be buggered. She's not your daughter.'

'She's Sebastian's wife, Squire.' Tess's voice never lost its kindness. 'He'll make sure that whatever he buys, or has built, for her to learn to drive will be something that is solid and safe. He won't let her run any risks.'

'Huh! What difference would it make to him? Great ponce!' Screwing up his eyes, he dug to the depths, he needed to shock them with his hatred of Sebastian. 'More likely wants to be shot of her! Husband, some bloody husband! Swanning around first with one woman, then another. Any woman who'll flatter the conceited swine and give him his oats — '

Grace's patience snapped. 'Behave yourself!' So might she have spoken to any of the children in her schoolroom of long ago. The look she cast on him held no emotion. 'I for one think it's an excellent scheme, Quin my dear, and let's hope that whatever strings Sebastian found himself able to pull last time will fall into his hands again. And let's be thankful that money is no object, he can get her the very best there is, he always does in everything.' She didn't say it to support Quintin so much as to hurt the Squire.

Quin looked at her gratefully. 'That's what I've been telling myself. And he will. He was quite concerned when I suggested it to him, worried for her, I mean. But, Squire, I promised him I'd be responsible for teaching her and keeping an eye on her until she feels confident.'

'You did, did you? Who taught her to ride a bicycle? Who taught her to swim? Who taught her to drive her first car — my car?' He tapped his chest, his eyes half-closed as he glared first at Quin, then round the table defying anyone to argue. 'Me, that's who.'

'Won't be much teaching this time, Squire,' Peter put in. 'She knows as much about handling a vehicle as any of us. She'll soon get used to different controls.'

'I'll make the coffee.' Tess's words followed his before anyone had time to reply. 'All of you go into the sitting room where the air's clearer.' Then, realising her words might be misconstrued, 'it's only this chimney that's been smoking us out.'

'Lydia, my honey, how would you feel about getting yourself mobile again?' Sebastian gave her that smile that never failed.

'How mobile? I'm getting faster all the time propelling myself about.' Her laughing response may have been forced, but it defied pity and criticism too.

He rumpled her gingery brown curls. 'I mean on the roads. Listen, how's this for an idea?' Since the conversation in the jeep that morning he'd given the proposition so much thought that he'd almost forgotten Quintin's part in it.

Lydia's eyes shone with sudden hope. Her happiness stemmed from believing he'd been the one to help her towards independence. She was proud — and pride was something that had had no place in her recent days. She looked towards Julie and Pam to be sure they'd heard and realised how much Sebastian cared. She needed to bask in the glory of seeing their appreciation of him; she needed the world to realise how important she was to him. For months there had been nothing but a battle to accept; now Sebastian had given her something to look forward to.

Much later, when Pam Pepper had taken Lydia off to be settled in bed, Julie was in the kitchen banking up the boiler to ensure there'd be plenty of early morning hot water.

'I thought I heard you out here,' Sebastian said, joining her. 'I've poured a drink for us in the other room. No children, no nurses, no interruptions — don't rush away yet, Julie.'

She felt trapped by her own longing to be alone with him. She ought to say she was tired, to make an excuse that she had letters to write, anything rather than steal moments that would stay in her memory long after he'd gone back to London and forgotten them. She was ashamed of an emotion she couldn't control. Employee she might be, but she was Lydia's friend, he was Lydia's husband.

Instead, without looking at him, she answered, 'I must just see to the boiler.'

Most men would have offered to do it for her. Sebastian didn't and neither did she expect him to. Later she'd probably remember that, too.

'This car business — what do you think?' He stood watching her as she raked the ashes. 'Quintin Murray has given it a lot of thought, found out the possibilities.'

'Quintin has? So you talked to him about it when you were down here last time, got him to look into it?' She needed to keep the conversation moving, Quintin was a comfortably safe topic. 'That's why he came to see you this morning?'

'Yes, that's why he came. But this morning was the first I'd heard of it.'

'You mean it was Quintin's idea?'

Just for a second Sebastian hesistated. Into her mind flashed the memory of the first time she'd met him, her surprise that he was so ordinary, not the godlike creature she'd seen on the screen. And again now she was conscious of a moment of weakness in him: he knew that he'd taken credit that wasn't due to him.

'Was I wrong?' He didn't have to spell it out to her, she understood just what he meant.

'No, Sebastian, you were right. Quintin would say the same, especially if he could have seen her face when you told her. She loves you very much.' What was she doing talking to a man about his wife's feelings like that? Yet, she had to say it, it helped her to keep their own relationship on steady rails.

'Poor little honey. If that's what she wants to think, then I wish it were true, I wish it had been me. You know there's nothing I wouldn't give her if it would improve the quality of her life even one jot.'

In her heart she cried out that there was one way he could give meaning to Lydia's life, but she couldn't say the words. She'd seen enough in Grenville Place to know that the Sutcliffe's marriage had never held the sort of intimacy that would be bound closer by tragedy. He'd give everything money could buy, he'd still love her able-bodied or crippled, but his affection was detached. It always had been. Perhaps he was incapable of giving more of himself than he did to Lydia.

This time Julie did look at him. His omission to mention Quin's part ought to belittle him in her eyes but now she was aware only that they shared a secret and that he trusted her to be honest.

'That should keep burning till morning,' she said, changing the subject. 'I'll just empty the ashes.'

A minute ago she had not been surprised when he made no attempt to help her with the fire. Now he didn't say anything, just took the ash pan from her and carried it outside to the bin. Sebastian never usually noticed any domestic task that needed doing, so the trivial action somehow tightened their invisible bond. When he came back he replaced the tray under the closed fire and steered her towards the sitting room where the drinks were poured and ready. His hand barely touched her shoulder, yet she'd never been more aware of his nearness.

'I love her too, you know.' He picked up the conversation where she'd been glad to let it drop. 'In a strange way I believe I care for her more deeply now than before all this happened. Does that make any sense at all?'

'She needs you more now, too.'

'Perhaps I should never have married – not her, not anyone. I'm not much use as a husband.'

'I don't understand.' What was he hinting? She remembered the Lydia she'd first known: warm, loving, eager to be with Sebastian. A man who was 'not much use as a husband' couldn't have been so adored by his wife.

'Marriage never changed the way I lived.' Was he following her thoughts? 'She was such a child, generous, eager. I'm not proud of the way I've behaved. But, Julie' – he turned to look at her, sitting by his side on the sofa – 'Julie, whatever the special ingredient that makes a marriage complete, it was missing. The lack was surely for both of us.'

'You shouldn't be talking like this, not to me. Talk to *her* if there are things to be said. How do you think she must feel, lying there alone?'

He ran his hand through his hair. There was nothing of the debonair heart-throb of the masses in him now. For a long time fame and money had made his path easy – and still they must, Julie reminded herself. If his marriage had lacked that 'special ingredient' he talked about, it held a very real affection. He'd learn to build on that.

'Do you imagine I don't think about her lying there alone?' His voice held no hope. 'And if I went in to talk to her, would it make things any easier for her? You know it wouldn't. It would strip from her the last vestige of dignity. I've seen that room of hers – but never when she's in it. It's a sickroom, not a bedroom. She'd hate me to intrude. I couldn't do it to her. Poor little love, she has so little to cling on to. You've seen the act she puts up each day. This morning we all played charades like children. That's what her life is, one long charade.'

'One of you has to make the first move. If this has put a barrier between you, then, Sebastian, you have to be the one to let her see how fragile the barrier is. For her to reach out to you would be like asking for sympathy. That's something Lydia will never do.'

He leaned back in the sofa, his eyes closed. She let herself study him, willing her scrutiny to be dispassionate. He looked tired and careworn. It was almost as if it was he who carried the burden of Lydia's tragedy. Before she could stop herself she reached out her hand and let it rest on his. Still he didn't open his eyes, just turned his hand so that his fingers clung to hers.

'If our marriage had been different, I could have crossed that barrier, she would have wanted me to. Yet I truly love her. You do believe that, Julie?'

'Of course I know you love her. She knows it too.'

'I hope she does.' He opened his eyes, the familiar smile teasing the corner of his mouth. 'I've never been a saint, but nothing made any difference to how I felt for her. She knew that, I'm sure she did. And then there's Merry ...'

'Sebastian, you don't have to explain these things to me. She always knew — she still knows — that *this* part of your life belongs just to her and Merry.'

'Until now.' Taking her chin in his hand, he willed her to hold his gaze. Hip-no-ties. This was no game of charades.

'Don't. Please, don't. It's not fair. I'm her friend.'

'I know you are. And God knows she needs your friendship. Hear me, Julie, I have to say it. There have been other women — and there will always be Lydia. From the start she wasn't like any of the others, she was full of joy, she was untouched, I'd never known a girl so eager for living — and loving. Such a child, such a responsive, warm, passionate child. What would have happened had Merry not been on the way I don't know. Probably we would have married anyway. And then Merry came along.' He hesitated, seemed unsure how to go on. 'That put a seal on both our futures. I don't need to explain — you have a daughter.'

At some stage he'd relaxed his hold on her, and once more they were not quite looking at each other. He was saying things better left unsaid, and yet neither of them could put an end to these moments.

'Merry is a darling.' She clutched at the chance to steer them to calmer waters.

108

'Merry is my son, my beloved son.' How was it that he could speak the words without affectation, somehow making her throat tight with ushered tears? 'Lydia is my wife. Now and always that's how it will be.' He carried her hand and rested it against his cheek; with his eyes closed he held it to his lips.

'You're not being fair. Not to her – not to me ...' She heard herself stammer the words. If he guessed how he'd haunted her thoughts these last months, he'd never have used her as a safety valve like this.

'Not to any of us, Julie.'

What was he meaning? She tried not to think, yet her mind raced out of control. Had her feelings been so obvious? She ought to pull herself away from him, tell him he was mistaken, threaten to leave Whiteways. These were the thoughts chasing each other around her mind when, in barely more than a whisper, he spoke again.

'You loved your husband, you two must have found the key to the mystery of a proper marriage. Do you know how I'm so certain? It has left a mark on you, made you a richer person. Loving him, losing him, yet still loving him.'

She nodded. 'Of course I do. I always will.' This time it was her turn to will him to look at her. 'None of us knows what's in the future, but the past is safe. I'll always love Jeremy, nothing can take that away from me.'

'No one who cares for you would ever try. Loving him has made you the woman you are – the woman I love.'

'No, not that! It can never be like that. We mustn't let it. It would be playing with fire, Sebastian. We could so easily get burned – not just us ...'

'You're an extraordinarily nice woman. Was it only this morning I told you so? And you're right, there are too many people who would get hurt if we burn our fingers playing with fire. Just tell me one thing, tell me the honest truth just as I have you. How do you see me? Lydia's errant husband? Merry's doting father? A man you could learn to love? A man, perhaps, who touches your heart even though your mind warns you to beware?'

'All those things. And I don't want it to be like that. You've got a second compartment in your life, I haven't. I ought to find work somewhere else, make a career, look ahead. There's no future for us together, we both know that. And I'm not starting some illicit affair. Lydia may be my employer, but most of all she's my friend. I won't cheat her, Sebastian.'

They both knew that what she said was right. Into Julie's mind flashed a picture of Lydia as she'd first known her. Supposing there'd been no accident, supposing instead of living at Whiteways they'd now been in London . . . or all of them in New York or Hollywood. Where would *she* fit into the scene then? Merry's nursemaid, a background support. What was it Trudie had said? 'A domestic in someone else's home.' Sebastian would not even have noticed her.

'Don't say any more, Sebastian.' She snatched at the remnants of her pride. 'Coming here to Whiteways is like stepping out of reality for you, so different from the way things are in London.'

'You're wrong. This is reality. Sometimes it's easier to live in a world of make-believe. And that's what we have to learn to do.' Again that hint of a twinkle as he looked at her solemn face. 'Don't worry, my Julie. I shan't molest you. I had no right even to say what I have. Couldn't help myself. No more, though. Just promise me one thing: you won't go away. Promise me that when I come you'll be here.'

'I promised ages ago that I wouldn't leave Lydia. But she's not so dependent now − she's with Pam far more than she is with me. Then there's the nursery at Rowans, it's meant a lot to her to have a responsibility in the greenhouses. I know she'd be sorry if I left. But it's better than staying and giving her cause to believe you and I . . . we . . . we're . . . ' She left the sentence hanging in the air. 'Anyway,' she added, her eyes daring him to disagree, 'I'm not one of your extramarital pastimes. Even if loyalty to Lydia didn't come into it, I never would be.'

In answer he smiled at her − at her, through her, into her. She felt powerless to move away from him. And when she spoke again it was no more than voicing aloud something that wouldn't be silenced.

'Why couldn't you have let me go on to bed? None of this need have been said. Now nothing can be the same any more.'

As if to prove her wrong Sebastian took out his cigarette case, put one between his lips and lit it, then passed it to her before lighting another for himself. There was a new intimacy in the action and yet, at least superficially, the act of smoking relaxed them.

'We'll make a pact, Julie. You promise to be here when I come again, and I'll promise that by word or act I won't let anything be changed between us. Stay with Merry. Please, for his sake as well as for mine.'

'A pact.' Her little finger held tight to his. 'That's how we used to make binding promises when I was small − it's how I've taught Merry and Anna. If ever they squabble, when they make up they − '

Whatever it was the children said as they linked fingers and made

110

friends was forgotten. Her words died in the sudden stillness as he gently kissed her forehead.

At Rowans the lights were out. Only in Peter and Tess's room was there still the soft hum of conversation.

'I wish we could help them,' Tess was saying, the thought of Grace and the Squire emphasising by contrast her own sense of wellbeing as she snuggled close against Peter. 'You can feel he's knotted up with unhappiness. It blinds him to everyone else's feelings — even Grace's.'

'Particularly Grace's. He got better as the evening went on. Poor old Squire! I get the feeling that even Lydia tries to avoid him.'

Tess chuckled, but not unkindly. 'Can you blame her? Would you like some protector wanting to stand guard over you? This car business, that's going to cheer her up.'

'Umph.' Peter's mind was nearer home. He drew her closer.

'Wish they could all be like us,' she whispered against his chin. 'Suppose it had been us, the accident, I mean. Oh, Peter, it's awful to see the way they pull against each other. We've been so lucky, we're still so lucky.'

Neither of them said Paul's name, yet for both of them his memory was very close. Not just the agony of losing him, but the mischievous child he'd been, the companion he'd grown into. Sadness and joy were both part of it. Tightly she gripped Peter's hand. For both of them it was a thanksgiving for all they'd had, a pledge of trust that they could face anything the future brought to them. Wordlessly they caressed each other; there was no high adventure in their love-making. They both knew the exact moment when he'd move onto her, she'd hold him close. For them it was the natural expression of how completely they were bound, a giving and taking, a silent understanding of their need of each other.

At the other end of the corridor Trudie lay on her back staring up into the darkness. Her lovely face wore a half-smile of contentment. Although she'd talked to Julie about the way Jo had deceived her, she'd come to accept that her pride had been more hurt than her heart. It was a year since that evening when Quintin had brought Julie to Rowans. At the time she'd wondered whether this would be the woman to replace Lydia in his feelings. In the beginning she honestly hadn't cared. Ah, but that was before she and Julie had come to know each other. There would never be another man in Julie's life, her short time with Jeremy shone too bright for her to look for happiness with another husband. But life could be sweet without a man. Trudie was a bachelor girl and that was how she meant to stay. No man and woman could ever understand each other in the way two women could. Julie was her friend, she was her confidante. For the present Lydia needed her, but that wouldn't last for ever. Already Quintin was finding ways to put interest in her life, teaching her to find independence. Then Julie would be free, she would be ready to go back into the business world. In Trudie's imagination there was a home for the two of them and Anna. Two women making their way in the world, earning respect, proving that they needed no one but each other. Together they'd bring Anna up, she'd love them both.

Trudie put out her hand and switched on the bedside lamp. On the table was a photograph Lydia had taken one day last autumn of Trudie and Julie, arm in arm, on the terrace at Whiteways. Always it would be like that. The light off again, the smile still played around her mouth. With Julie she felt safe, complete. Her mind jumping ahead, she saw them middle-aged, she saw them elderly – still friends, still sharing, always caring.

The smile wouldn't have lasted if she could have followed Julie into her dark bedroom and known the thoughts that crowded in on her. In the sitting room the clock chimed midnight. Was he awake and hearing it too? And just as Trudie had, she reached out to turn on the light by her bed. The picture she looked at was of Jeremy. She tried to harness this aching need in her to her memories of him. But times leaves no one unchanged. The girl who had loved Jeremy loved him still. The woman she had become yearned for – no, she wouldn't say it, even silently she wouldn't admit to it. Switching off the light, she was isolated in the night. By daylight the world would take over. Here in the darkness she was his.

The tensions of the dinner table still cast a shadow as Grace and the Squire drove home. The Squire had relaxed as the evening went on, but once he was in the car the atmosphere of the Grants' home was lost.

'Bloody trees!' The Squire stared ahead of him as the car sped along the lane through Downing Wood. The wind whipped through the branches trying to tear them free to join the twigs and dead leaves that whirled and leaped in a wild dance in the lights of the headlamps.

Grace ignored him. He'd spoken more to himself than to her, but he was quick to take offence.

'You know, my dear' – he stressed the endearment, his tone heavy with dislike – 'I envy you. Nothing touches you, nothing wounds you.' He beat his clenched fists against his knee in a monotonous rhythm. Still she ignored him, though it took all her willpower not to take the bait he offered. He wanted to quarrel, it seemed to her that that was the way he drew strength. But she was drained, tired of the constant scenes, crushed by the hopelessness. She felt rather than saw the way he turned in his seat, peering at her in the darkness as she drove. 'What if it had been them it had happened to? Not that anyone could have compared Trudie and her father with Poppet and me. But do you think Tess would have been cold and uncaring? You, yes even *you* must have seen that she was troubled by my ... my sadness ...' His voice wavered.

The wood behind them, Grace turned the final corner on the road to Delbridge House. When she spoke her voice was cold with dislike. It frightened her to hear it.

'They lost their son. Or have you forgotten? At the time Paul was killed you were so eaten up with jealousy that another man was more important to Lydia than you were that you probably didn't notice.' Too fast she drove through the open gate, the tyres sending up a swirl of gravel, then just as violently she stopped in front of the house. 'Here.' She threw the keys onto his lap. 'Lock it if you want to. I'm going to bed.'

They shared a room, they didn't share a bed. As the minutes ticked by she courted sleep while all the time her mind became more wide awake. Waking or sleeping, her eyes would be closed when he came. But why was he so long? What could he be doing alone downstairs? Had she pushed him beyond the limit? Here her imagination dived onto a track she couldn't face. She even started to get out of bed to go and find him, to reassure him. Then she heard water running in the bathroom and noticed how loudly he slammed the doors, as if purposely to stop her from sleeping. Antagonism swamped her. By the time he came into their room − shutting the door noisily behind him − she feigned sleep; she even took comfort from the thought that she was depriving him of the satisfaction of imagining he'd succeeded in disturbing her. There had been a time when their days had ended in easy talk, companionship, friendliness. Other people still saw that side of him. It was only with *her* he was full of prickles.

Even Grace, practical, reliable Grace, didn't worry seriously about what he was doing to his relationship with Lydia.

Next morning Julie took the children into the village under the pretext of having heard that a crate of bananas was expected at the greengrocer's. A queue would form waiting for the door to open; only the first shoppers would get them. The bananas were a fact, but she had no need to be there early.

113

'I'll see to it that a nice bunch gets put aside for Lydia Harriday — well, that's how I always think o' her still. Always been a favourite of mine, since the Squire used to bring her in here no more than a mite,' Mr Hobson, the greengrocer, had told her yesterday. 'Had him round her little finger, wasn't a thing he could refuse her. Wouldn't mind betting he'll be in here in the morning if he gets wind that there's bananas to be had — not for himself, oh no, I'd put my money on him and his missus not getting a sniff. His Lydia, any treat he can find, be sure that's who'll get them. And why not, eh? Small comfort for what she has to put up with. You just get here when you can, be sure I'll not see you miss out.'

That had been the previous afternoon. With the gale at full force she'd left the children at home with Pam and driven to the village alone. By morning the storm had blown itself out, and the still air was full of the promise of spring. But what distanced her from the hours of yesterday was what had passed between Sebastian and her later. In the clear light of morning his words still echoed in Julie's mind. It was behind them now, neither of them would speak of it. And yet how could she be with him without remembering?

A brief word with Lydia, who was about to start her morning session with Pam, then Julie and the children set out. Merry and Anna needed to let off steam after forty-eight hours indoors. They galloped as far ahead of her as their reins would allow, believing themselves to be the pair of greys that pulled the baker's van. In the village she collected the bananas, with the added bonus of two oranges apiece on the children's ration books, then turned for home. By now the gallop of the 'greys' had slowed to a plod; a rest midway got rid of another quarter of an hour. Julie was glad to put off the moment when she and Sebastian would have to pretend that nothing had happened.

But she needn't have dallied. When they arrived at Whiteways there was no sign of Sebastian's car. Indoors she found Lydia dressed and prettied with extra care just as she had been each day he'd been there.

'You missed Seb,' she greeted Julie.

'How do you mean? Is he out for the day?'

'He's gone back.' But if he'd left for London, how was it Lydia looked so pleased with herself?

'You mean his holiday is over? But I thought — '

'He's doing it for *me*, silly. His life is so crowded, you know how little time he gets to himself, and I know he'd looked forward to this break. Yet he's giving up these few precious days so that he can see about what he calls "my ticket to ride". I don't know whether he will have something adapted, or perhaps even specially built.' With shining eyes she turned and gripped Julie's hand. 'Oh, Julie, don't you think he's just wonderful? Who else would think of a thing like that? And Seb will really get it done. It's because he's important, everyone knows his name, he's not just some ordinary person. Remember how quickly he got that car for you and the children? Of course, whatever make he decides I should have, it will be a terrific advertisement for the manufacturer. A model specially designed for Sebastian Sutcliffe's wife!'

'I don't think it'll be the publicity he's after, Lydia. He just likes doing things for you.'

'Yes, I know. Like the flowers he sends, the surprise presents.' Still she smiled. Yet, watching her, Julie remembered what Sebastian had said about her life being a charade.

'Is Quin coming for you again this afternoon?' She changed the subject.

'Yes, I rang him up after Seb left. Do you know what the Squire says? He was here just a bit before you got back.' She pouted. 'He had the cheek to say that it was Quin's idea about a special car, not Seb's at all. Frightfully stuffy about my being able to drive. He'd like to keep me wrapped in cotton wool somewhere where he can come and tell me how sad he is for me.' Her voice rising dangerously, she shut her eyes as if to blot out where her outburst was carrying her and bit hard on the corners of her mouth.

'Well, if he wants you to believe the idea was Quin's, then at least you can be sure of one thing: he must know in his heart that it's a jolly good idea. A bad one, and he'd be ready to let Sebastian take credit for it.' She laughed as she spoke, trying to will Lydia back on the rails.

She succeeded.

'Wish I wasn't always so nasty to him, Julie. Now he'll go home and be beastly to Mum, I expect. It's his own fault, though. Anyway, this afternoon I shall ask Quin.'

'No, don't do that. That's tantamount to saying you listen to the Squire instead of Sebastian. We both know it was he who thought of it. He talked about it to Quin, he told me so after you were in bed last night, but it was his idea to do it for you and it's he who'll have the influence to get what's needed.'

Lydia's smile was back in place.

'You're right. I'm glad Seb talked to Quin and he thought it was a good idea. He's sure to be the one to risk his neck when this legless wonder takes to the highway! He will, won't he, Julie? Squire talked about coming out with me, but once we get it into his stubborn head that it was Seb's brainchild he won't want anything to do with it.'

'Did he come because he'd heard about the car?'

Lydia shook her head. 'Wouldn't feel such a heel if he had. He'd queued up at Mr Hobson's, got a bunch of lovely speckly bananas just the way I like them. Brought them straight here, pleased as punch with himself. Then I let everything go sour. You know what I think? It's because deep down I'm spiteful. Yes, I do, honestly, Julie. I never knew I was such a rotten person till this happened to me, but inside that's how I must always have been. It's sort of punishment.' She made herself laugh as she said it, the sound told Julie how near the edge of her control she teetered.

'Can't have been all bad, Lydia Sutcliffe. Somewhere along the line there must have been something good for you to deserve Sebastian for a husband.'

'And you for a friend.' Lydia sniffed, tears safely averted. 'Expect I'm just hungry. Be a dear and fetch me a speckly banana from the bunch he brought me, will you? He put them in my room. I might even give you an inch to prove I'm not beyond redemption.'

After lunch Quin arrived. It might have been chance that sent Julie into the front garden at that moment to pick some daffodils.

'Hello, Quin, I think she's ready,' she called in greeting, her voice clearly audible from inside the house. 'Pretty soon she'll be making her own way.' As she spoke she came closer to him, nothing altering in her manner, only now her words were for him alone. 'She's over the moon that Sebastian thought of it. Proud, too. Please – '

It was all she had time for. Already Lydia was coming down the ramp from the house. If Julie expected Quintin to be slow to grasp her meaning, she was wrong.

'You approve?' He talked loudly too, his words addressed to Julie but aimed at Lydia. 'Sebastian told me about his ideas. He was worried that he can't be here often, so he asked if I'd go out with her till she got the hang of the controls – ah, here you are, Lydia.'

It occurred to Julie that if to deserve Sebastian Lydia had done something good, then she must indeed have a streak of saintliness to have earned the gentle humility of Quintin's friendship.

It was August by the time the transporter arrived delivering the new vehicle. Part saloon, part van, it had double doors at the back and a ramp that pulled down so that the wheelchair could be loaded; a wide, sliding door for the driver, and a normal door for the passenger. With two good arms there was nothing Lydia wouldn't be able to manage: hand throttle, hand gear change, everything at her fingertips. Not every car on the roads was black, but the majority were. With this in mind, Sebastian had chosen cherry red; he knew Lydia would want heads to turn as she sped through the village.

During the period between March and that August day, Sebastian had been to Whiteways for four or five weekends. True to his word he'd never referred to what had happened between Julie and him on that stormy evening. He'd been determined to build on their friendship, to restore her confidence. Often Trudie was with them; it didn't occur to her that Lydia's husband being home should change the pattern of their summer Sundays. Sand castles, shrimping, paddling, swimming, football on the sands ... only Lydia was left out. No one queried her pleasure when Quin would join her on the terrace. They assumed her interest in the land he'd bought from Peter was genuine. Perhaps it was. Playacting had become so much a part of her days that even she hardly knew where reality stopped.

By the time the new car — Ruby, as Lydia called it — arrived, Sebastian and his company were already en route for New York with their repertory of theatre. Dates were uncertain, but they were due to open in September and expected the season to carry through the winter months.

Lydia adapted naturally to her new mode of transport. Everyone thought that the freedom of the road was giving her back some of the happiness she'd lost. Only Quin, her ever faithful safety valve, knew it wasn't that simple.

'I'm giving a talk to the Roget Horticultural College tomorrow,' he told her one afternoon in November. 'Orchids. Would you find that interesting? We could take your car, if you like. Or would you rather we went in the jeep?'

The college was more than fifty miles away, so they both knew what he meant. Would she find it too tiring to drive? On this gloomy afternoon he'd felt that something was wrong ever since she arrived at the nursery in Ruby and he'd gone out to meet her and lift her into her chair.

'You'd be better on your own,' she growled, not meeting his eyes.

'I would not.'

'Sorry, Quin, I'm just being a grouch.' And that's just what she sounded. 'Go in Ruby if you like, what's the difference? Is it supposed to be a treat for me? Is that why you're suggesting I come? A nice long drive. Sure I can steer myself along the roads, I can even overtake, turn left, turn right, go anywhere I like. Yes, and you know what else I can do? Oh, but what a clever girl I am, I can put my hand out of the window and signal just as if I were a proper person.'

'It wasn't supposed to be a treat for you.' He ignored the other things she'd said. 'More likely it was meant as a treat for me to have you with me.'

'Now pull the other leg.' The unfortunate choice of words shocked them both. She looked at him, dry-eyed, frightened. 'Pull them both, see if I care.' This time he could hardly understand what she said, her words were stifled and her jaw stiff. 'Not even part of me any more. Look at them, Quin! Ugly! Did you ever see ankles so fat and ugly? 'Course you didn't.'

He dropped to his knees by the side of her chair. At the other end of the row of communicating glasshouses, a small group of people were working, all trained by Quin, all busy on the hundreds of pot plants that would be despatched in the next week or two ready for sale in the shops for Christmas. Quin gave them no thought, his concern was all for Lydia.

'No, you can't feel your legs, you can't make them walk. You can't feel your ankles. If some days they get swollen, to hell with it. Legs don't make a person, nor ankles either. We take walking for granted — you used to take it for granted — but it only gets a person from one place to another.'

'Only! You just don't understand.'

'No, of course, I don't. The only person who could truly understand is someone else who couldn't walk.' He took her hand in his. 'But it's the *person* that matters, *you*, Lydia, the same person now as you always were and always will be. Sebastian has wanted to make it easier for you, that's why you've got Ruby. Like you say, you can turn right, turn left, you can take yourself anywhere.'

'I know.' She was crying quietly. His hold on her hand tightened. 'I feel mean and rotten. You see, Quin, having Ruby is like a glimpse of proper living. Sort of jogs my memory. Before I had Ruby I just stayed where I was put, waited to be taken. Proper living didn't have anything to do with it. But now I still have to be lifted in and lifted out. Everyone thinks I have freedom.' Her voice rasped as she fought to get her breath. 'I haven't. Haven't anything.'

'Oh yes, you have, you've got steel in your backbone. Just temporarily you've mislaid it, and I'm grateful that I'm the one who you tell. But, Lydia, not many of us have your guts, most of us have jelly where the steel ought to be. You know what I think?'

Her answer was a snort, it might have meant anything. It might even have meant that she didn't care what he thought.

118

'I think there's a sort of justice. We all think we have troubles. You can handle yours because you're a fighter; some folk go to pieces for next to nothing – a spate of bills, a temporary patch of bad health, a few tiles blown off in a gale and that's as much as they can take.'

'What about you, Quin?' Apparently she must have been taking in what he'd been saying. She even gave him a watery smile. 'When your time comes, how will you stand up to the test?'

'Me? If I find myself quivering like a jelly I shall think of you, Lydia, you'll put the mettle into me. Now, about tomorrow. Your car or mine?'

It was January, nearly two years since they'd left Grenville Place and set out for Devon, and more than one since Sebastian had taken a small mews house near Hyde Park, something easy to shut up when he was away, as he so often was.

'I've been thinking' – despite the grey morning Lydia was in high spirits – 'perhaps only a few weeks now and Seb will be home from the States. I'm fed up with everything I've got to wear. I'm going to ring Suzanne O'Brien. You remember, Julie, that gorgeous little salon I used to go to? I got everything I have from Suzanne O'Brien, I haven't bought a thing since we've been down here. So I'll phone her, tell her that I've not used a single clothing coupon since we had our last issue – and I know the Squire and Mum would give me some if I needed them. I'm going to ask her to send me some things to try on. Blouses mostly, not a lot of good wasting coupons on anything else, anyway I've got masses of undies. But blouses, things that will make me look good for when Seb comes.'

'You sound like Merry. "When Seb come?" He never gets tired of asking.'

'Seb come soon, that's what we have to tell him. And, Julie, I want to look really good.'

Lydia tried to put through the call straight away, only to be told that the line was out of order. In the afternoon she tried again, and again the next morning. Impatiently, she wanted the latest fashion in blouses, and nothing Julie could buy for her in Exeter would do.

It was Tess who had the idea.

'Let Merry and Anna come to me for a couple of days, I'd enjoy having them. Then Julie could do your shopping. She'd jump at the chance of a day or two in London.'

She said it on the Wednesday. It was all so simple – and how true! London! Until Julie found herself on the train she'd never admitted how much she'd missed it all.

Chapter Eight

London didn't fail her. Perhaps no great city can ever fail a person brought up to be part of it. The red buses, the cheery voices of their Cockney conductors, the areas of emptiness where rubble had been cleared but nothing developed on the land to heal the scars of war, the stoicism of the people as they queued, all moved her equally. To wait in line had become a part of life — for a seat at the cinema, a bus that would arrive already full, off-the-ration sausages, pure silk stockings. In Julie's first hour she saw it all, and soaked up the atmosphere.

The longest queue was at a wool shop where a sign on the window advertised that a supply of a three-ply white wool would go on sale that afternoon; such a collection of smocked women, each bearing her special ration of clothing coupons, each letting her mind's eye jump ahead to the time the tiny garment she planned to make was finished and being worn. The afternoon was cold, and there was a dampness that couldn't quite bring itself to turn to rain. The women marked time as they waited in an effort to keep warm. They even talked to each other, the kind of talk that told nothing about themselves, probably about layettes, dates, knitting patterns; the next day they might pass each other by with no sign of recognition, yet the empty words united them in this moment.

Julie watched them from a Corner House restaurant opposite, where she was having tea and toast at a table bearing a sign that this section carried a table surcharge of sixpence. Except in the empty bomb sites, evidence of the war was fading. These were the wives of men who'd come home. Peace, hope for the future. If things had been different, if Jeremy had come back to her, perhaps she might have been one of them. She turned away from the window to the bright activity of the restaurant, the waitresses so trim in their navy and white uniforms. Might-have-beens would get her nowhere; they were chased away by other thoughts, can-never-be thoughts. And they, in turn, were stamped down by focusing her mind on her reason for being here. This evening was her own, she'd walk about, get her bearings again, gaze at the shop windows. Otterton St Giles might have belonged on another planet; this was home.

When the waitress brought Julie her bill, she opened her handbag to take out her purse. There among the coins was the key, the light glinting on it. Lydia had insisted she should use it.

'Why do you think he left a key here? Emergency, he said. Oh yes, and he suggested you might like to take the children up to see a pantomime. I'd forgotten all about that. Would it have been a good idea?'

'Next year, maybe. They're not quite old enough to enjoy the fun of a panto, all the shouting and joining in. But this time I could easily find a room somewhere, it'll only be one night and it's not as if I'm taking Merry. That's what Sebastian meant when he left the key.'

'Of course he didn't. He gave the key to *me*. If we still had the house in Grenville Place you'd go there, so what's the difference?'

What indeed? Yet Julie felt there was a difference. The mews house Sebastian had taken when he'd moved out of Grenville Place was his alone. Knowing she was to spend her night there, even though he was thousands of miles away, added an extra thrill to this unexpected trip. She tried not to acknowledge the feeling that to stay there in his absence was like reading his mail. Tonight she'd be surrounded by his things, take a book from his shelf, use his kitchen, his bath.

Across the road the queue was moving into the wool shop. Julie didn't even notice.

The house was smaller than she'd imagined, wooden steps from the street leading up to the front door. What had at one time been a carriage house was now the garage, his car would be in there. She liked to picture that, it was the one thing that was familiar in this strange setting. What had she expected? Something grander? Perhaps. Something more masculine? Certainly. This might have been the home of any single person, man or woman. He'd been away for more than four months, yet there was only one envelope on the mat. She put it on the mantelpiece, looking around her with a sense of disappointment. There was nothing here of the Sebastian she knew. Everywhere was scrupulously tidy, the surfaces shone, the fringes of the Chinese rugs had been combed so carefully that she found herself stepping over them to avoid scuffing them. Had those

121

elegant figurines been his choice? And so many pieces of beautiful antique silver in the cabinet. She supposed they must have been at Grenville Place, but of course the short time she'd lived there she'd spent in the nursery rooms.

Giving herself a mental shake, she picked up her small case to look for the room where she'd sleep. The first door she opened led to a small bedroom where the empty wardrobe told her this must be the spare. There was no need to go into the other bedroom; and yet there was every need. Somewhere there must be something of Sebastian, some lingering feeling of his presence. Like a thief she quietly opened his wardrobe, touched his suits that hung there. On the top of the chest of drawers was a silver-framed photograph of Merry, a smaller Merry than now.

It was that photograph that made her slam shut the wardrobe door. What a fool she was! In all the time he'd been away Sebastian hadn't written her one letter, he'd sent her no message. Cards came regularly for Merry, and a week never went by without a package of some sort arriving for Lydia. Not that anyone would expect he'd write to *her*, why should he? An evening's flirtation, a game he played so expertly that in her stupidity she'd hung on to every word, built her dreams around them even though she knew they could never be more than dreams. She felt alone; here in the place he made his home, she could find nothing of the man who'd spoken those words. If she'd gone to a guesthouse the pleasure of being in London would have held, yet now it had slipped out of her grasp. Going out of the room, she turned off the light with a sharp click and closed the door firmly behind her.

To sit in that living room was impossible. If he'd been a pipe smoker there might have been a rack of pipes; if he'd been a pianist there would have been a piano and a pile of music. Only the bookshelves gave any indication of his interests; plays ancient and modern, then, surprisingly, books on antiques, silver and glass from other centuries, other continents. She thought of Whiteways, Lydia's dockets used for modern furniture, even that from the auction rooms as up-to-date as Grace had been able to find. This discovery about him triggered her imagination, showed a side to him she had not known. Oh, but there must be many sides she did not know. Having taken a book from the bookcase she snapped it shut and pushed it back in place as if it had burned her fingers.

Minutes later she was curled up in the unaired single bed, clad in pyjamas and still wearing her prewar woollen dressing gown. The chill struck right through to her soul.

Even tucked away in the mews she could still hear the hum of life going on. Two years ago she wouldn't have noticed it. At Whiteways the only sounds that broke the stillness of night were the wind and the crashing waves. Julie lay with her eyes closed, unconsciously drawing comfort from the muffled symphony of life in the city. As carriage house or home, the building had stood many years; it creaked occasionally for no apparent reason as is the way with old buildings. It had survived through good times and bad. For a while it might house a famous actor, but he'd move on and who then? An artist? A market trader? A teacher? A go-ahead bachelor girl like Trudie — or one day like Julie herself? The steady purr of traffic never faltered; she knew that even in the depth of night there would be no real silence. Comforted, she slept.

What the sound was that woke her in the night she didn't know. Startled, she lay rigid until she remembered where she was. In seconds she'd dropped back into sleep.

At this time of year it was still dark when her day started, the habits of young children made sure of that. Routine held strong and that morning it was just after half past six when she turned on the bedside light to look at her watch. With no one to disturb her, nothing to take her from the warmth of her bed for at least an hour, she drifted luxuriously somewhere between waking and sleeping.

Then something happened that made her sit bolt upright, her heart pounding. The clatter of metal, something being dropped. Instantly she pulled her wits into place. Sebastian's cabinet of silverware! Someone must have broken in. She had not unbolted any window — but had she locked the door properly? Even while the unanswered questions were crowding in on her, she was out of bed looking around frantically for a weapon. The room revealed nothing. She grabbed one of her shoes. She'd creep in, quickly, quickly before he got away . . . she'd get him from behind, hit him with her heel . . . She was too frightened to admit that no grown man would fall under the sort of blow she'd give.

Silently she turned the handle of her door, barefoot she made no sound as she crossed the passage. But there was no one in the sitting room, and the cabinet hadn't been touched. Only now did her senses begin to function enough for her to be shocked that a burglar could have the cheek to switch on the lights. Lights in the empty sitting room and beyond in the kitchen too. Another rattle, this time from the kitchen. Not caring now about the fringes of the Chinese rugs, she tiptoed to the open doorway.

There kneeling to sweep scattered tea leaves into a dustpan, he saw her, her shoe poised for attack.

123

'Good God!'

'Sebastian!'

He started to laugh. 'Don't hit me, I'll come quietly.'

'I thought you were a burglar. I thought I'd not locked the door properly.' Then, needing to keep talking, 'I thought you were still in New York. Lydia said I must stay here, just for one night. I've come to do some shopping for her. The children – '

'We've both been here all night – '

'I'd have gone to a hotel if I'd known you were home.'

'Both of us here,' he went on as if she hadn't spoken. 'Fate pushed us together and we didn't even know it.'

'What a mess you've made!' Kneeling down she took the dustpan and brush out of his hands. 'That must have been the tea caddy I heard drop. I thought you were being robbed of your silver.' She ignored the implication of his remarks. He might be able to play games but she couldn't. Sweep the floor, turn off the boiling kettle, make the tea (unless he'd wasted it all).

'Julie?' He said it quizzically, asking so much in that one word. Was he laughing at her, at the situation? His right eyebrow was raised just that fraction higher than his left. She didn't want to look at him, knowing that expression was designed to make her pulses quicken – hers and millions more, she told herself.

'Good morning, my Julie. And what a good morning it is too, what a start for my first day in England.'

'I shouldn't call what you just did a good start.' Still she gripped the dustpan and brush, still she didn't quite look at him.

'And this?' Tilting her face he very lightly kissed the corners of her mouth, first one end, then the other.

Hanging on to her control, she knelt rigid as a statue.

'Well?' he prompted softly.

'No! I came here thinking you were away. Why can't you leave me alone? Aren't there enough women you can amuse yourself with, women who know the same games? I don't, Sebastian – and I don't want to learn. Keep away from me, let me alone.'

He stood up, switching off the kettle that was sending clouds of steam into the room.

'Can you honestly tell me that's what you want? Forget everything else, think just of us, you and me. Now can you still tell me to leave you alone? I don't believe you can be free of me any more easily than I can of you.'

'Your life is full, you always have a goal ahead of you. That's what I mean mine to be. Full of things I can achieve for myself.'

Furiously she swept the scattered tea leaves into the dustpan, even when there were none left she still kept sweeping.

'So it will be, if you do everything with the enthusiasm you're putting into that floor.' He laughed as he spoke, yet there was such affection in his tone that this time her defences went down and she looked directly at him as he put out his hands to raise her to her feet.

The dustpan remained on the floor and next to it her shoe, both of them forgotten. There was nothing except a great surge of joy as he held her close. This time he didn't kiss her, just held her, his unshaven chin moving against her bed-rumpled hair. She knew she was doing exactly as he'd said, thinking just of herself and him. She didn't fight the inevitable.

After a moment he whispered, 'Now, isn't this better? We'll start afresh. Good morning, Julie.'

She laughed. All her fears and reservations had gone; she'd look no further than this precious hour that had come to them both so unexpectedly.

'Go and get rid of that stubble,' she told him. 'You feel like a nutmeg grater. I suppose there's nothing to eat in the cupboard? No, of course there isn't, why would there be?'

'Not even any tea unless you spoon it out of the pan.'

'Perhaps there's coffee, black coffee. Nothing like it for putting life into one.' Even so she didn't pull away. How right it was to be standing here, propping each other up, no one within call.

'I've as much life in me as I know how to cope with.' He crushed her closer; there was no mistaking the meaning behind his words.

'And me,' she breathed. It would have been so easy to rush headlong down the path she wanted to take. What made her hold her head back from him, looking at him and trying to read deep into his mind? It wasn't Lydia; it was the thought of those women who were part of his other life, beautiful people in beautiful clothes. Awareness of her crumpled pyjamas and slept-in dressing gown suddenly planted her cold, bare feet firmly on the ground again.

'What is it?' He sensed her withdrawal. 'Come back to me, Julie. This hour is ours, some blessed deity must have brought us here together. Who could we hurt? No one. Unless we turn away from each other now. Then the hurt will be ours. It will be there between us, each time I'm at Whiteways we'll be reminded.'

'Just look at me . . .' And this time she moved out of his embrace, her hands falling to her sides as she glanced down at her shapeless, woollen dressing gown that had been with her since before clothes rationing.

'I'm looking at you. I'm loving you.' His fingers rang through her untidy hair.

Her answer was in the way she held out her arms. He was right. This short time together was a gift, it belonged neither to the past nor the future. If they denied what they felt, then like a wound it might fester, it might make it impossible for them to hold on to the friendship they shared at Whiteways. It was a naive belief, but with her need of his loving filling her whole mind she didn't question.

Lydia was forgotten, those nameless women were forgotten, the world held only this. She had not been prepared for the passion his touch aroused. Later, distanced from the carnal need that drove her, she'd look at herself as if at a stranger. But now there was only this. In their secret world no one could hear as she cried out, wondering at herself that this could be happening to her almost in their first moment. Reality hit her. They had this hour, but they had nothing else. He mustn't let it be over yet, she wanted to stay in the heights, to climb to the pinnacle again and again. There was no tenderness in her lovemaking, only in exhaustion could she be satisfied.

Afterwards they lay in each others arms, glad to pull the tent of bedding over their naked bodies on this cold January morning.

'I should have shaved.' Gently he touched his fingers on her red cheek.

'I'm not complaining.'

' ... was wonderful. You've haunted me for months. It had to happen.'

'I don't like "it".'

His left eyebrow shot towards his hairline. Clearly he thought she'd liked "it" very much.

'Don't mean that. "It" − as if what we did wasn't part of us being us.' She was out of her depth. Often enough she knew the need for love, she'd even come to believe that through these lonely years she'd been able to fulfil that need. This morning had proved her wrong. 'Sex starved,' she tried to make a joke of it, looking at him closely, trying to read his thoughts.

'Starved for each other.' He pulled her closer. 'One meal doesn't last a beggar for ever. And I'm a beggar, Julie, my darling.'

She didn't answer. Her heart cried out that he was right, that there could be no going back. They hadn't planned these few precious hours; they'd been a gift. To steal more would be to tempt fate. She wanted to hold back the day that waited. But the thought of it pressed on them. At home Lydia would be imagining her choosing blouses ...

126

The minutes melted so quickly. It must have been about half an hour later that he reached to open the drawer of the bedside table. She knew what he was getting. The first time she'd seen him take something from it she'd been filled with a mixture of emotions: disappointment that such a practical move destroyed the passion that was like a flowing tide, surprise that he kept such things by his bedside, relief that they could give themselves to each other safely with no one getting hurt. This time as he stretched his arm to open the drawer, she touched his shoulder with her lips, then almost reverently moved her hand down his body. They would love again; happiness surged through her veins. The urgency had been quenched, for her and for him too. Slowly, deeply, they relished each movement; they whispered words meant just for each other.

They wanted those moments to last, but time doesn't stand still.

'Make the coffee while I shave.' Still breathless, he knew the day couldn't be postponed. 'I'll run the water and we'll drink it in the bath.'

The prospect of this new intimacy made getting up bearable.

By one o'clock five Suzanne O'Brien bags were laid carefully on the back seat of his car, Julie's case and his stowed in the boot and they were heading out of London on the A4 road westward.

'I arrived this morning while you were shopping. You found me at the house when you came back to collect your overnight case.' He looked straight ahead of him as he spoke. 'We have to both be clear.'

'Both tell the same lie, you mean. I should have come back in the train, there would have been no need for lies at all.' How strange she could have felt no guilt in bed with Lydia's husband, yet now just those few words could tarnish something that had been pure.

'I telephoned Lydia while you were out, said I'd just arrived. She made me look in the bedroom to see if your case was still there. She was pleased to think we'd be driving back together.'

'I wish she wasn't. Makes us feel dirty about deceiving her.'

He let go of the steering wheel long enough to take her hand and carry it to his cheek.

'It doesn't — at least it doesn't as far as I'm concerned. I'd think myself a bastard if she showed any suspicions, she has problems enough without our adding that to them. But she likes us to get on well. She has a possessive feeling about you, since it was she who brought you into the home.'

'Next thing you'll be saying we've done her a favour.' Julie spoke with a pout, even though her face was devoid of expression.

'We've done her no harm, and we're not going to. Both of us care a great deal about her, we'll see to it that nothing we do ever makes her unhappy. Julie, I've never lived the life of a saint. Loving you, even over the months I was away, I've wanted just you. Yes, I think in a way we are doing her a favour.'

Their few short hours were behind them perfect and unchanging, safe in the past. The tyres drummed relentlessly on the road as they covered the miles. Soon they'd be back at Whiteways. That was the future, the only certainty.

It surprised her when he pulled off the road and stopped in front of a Georgian house that had recently been opened as a hotel.

'I told Lydia we'd not be home until late, I had people to see. I said we'd eat on the way. Dinner, Julie.'

'What's the point of delaying? We ought to get back, to pretend our horried lies are the truth.'

'We know the truth, the only truth that matters.' His voice was quiet, yet it seemed to put an end to all argument. Then, with a change of mood, 'Out you get, woman. We'll eat a huge dinner – and not before time. I'm ravenous, I don't know about you. And we'll talk.'

'We've said all there is to say.'

'Then, my Julie, that bodes ill for the years ahead.' Stationary outside the large country house, he didn't make any attempt to get out of the car. 'What do we know of each other? That we've been drawn together in a way that was too strong to be denied; that I have a wife who needs the support of my loyalty and yours too; that we have children who deserve and get our love; that – and I think this is the same for you as for me – what happened this morning was inevitable, inevitable and ... and beyond words, something I've never known.'

'Don't. You and your affairs! I told you, I'm not one of them. I won't be compared and – '

Her words were stifled as his mouth covered hers just at the very moment when her stomach rolled in a loud acclamation of hunger.

'I'll grant your pardon,' he said with a laugh. 'We're both famished, didn't I say so? Let's go in, sit across the table from each other, talk about all those things we don't know, the things that matter to us, that make us what we are. Where is your home? I don't even know where you come from. Have you a family? Tell me about Jeremy? And as for me, I'll tell you how I was drawn to the theatre, I'll make you feel the terror and the thrill of that first moment when the curtain rises.' Cupping her chin in his hand, he bent towards her. In the dim light that shone from the porch of the hotel, he peered close. 'We found a new heaven and a new earth, you and me. But there's more. Come, let's go inside. Between us there will be no hidden secrets.'

Not for the first time did it strike her that from anyone else his choice of words would have sounded affected. From him they didn't.

How easy it was to put the thought of Whiteways and Lydia out of her mind again. During that meal she didn't consider that anything she told him could have been of any importance, and she would have been surprised to know the pictures she created in his imagination of the orphaned child who'd been brought up by a loving aunt. But it wasn't about herself she wanted them to talk, it was about him. Almost shyly she asked him about his family.

'I loved my mother beyond all else. My father – yes, I can say it to you – fear was the only emotion I ever felt for him. Growing up, making my own life, the fear vanished. Then there was nothing. By his standards I'm sure he was an adequate parent, I lacked nothing except interest. But then by those same standards I must have been a great disappointment. My parents might have been closer to each other with no family. Even as a small boy I could feel the tension I caused between them.'

'Why? Was he jealous?'

'Of my mother's affection for me? Perhaps. You're asking me to understand from the viewpoint of an adult. As I saw it then he was someone who destroyed any warmth. Certainly he and I were poles apart. Mother died of tuberculosis when I was eight. I was sent off to school. You don't want to hear all this, Julie. Years ago, all of it. Except for the exchange of dutiful Christmas cards we've had no contact for ages, long before I met Lydia.'

'I do want to hear. Nothing grows out of nothing: what we are today came from our yesterdays. Go on. You went to school,' she prompted.

'I'd never had much to do with other children. Mother had had so much illness, none ever visited the house, neither was I invited into theirs. I can understand now how it was their parents kept them away from me, even though I showed no sign of the disease. The word "consumption" carried a ring of terror. That's why I'm so glad to see Merry with Anna. It's healthy. Most of my friends were made up, figments of my imagination. Looking back at myself now – and I must say it's not a thing I do as a rule, this is all your fault, my Julie – I must have been a queer sort of youngster. I felt that I was shunned, yet I hadn't understood the reason. So I built a protective barrier around myself. Even at school it was there. By that time it was of my own choice. Yes, I must have been an odd, uncomfortable sort of child. A loner, yet never shy. Probably too self-centred to care what anyone thought of me.'

'I don't believe it!' She laughed. 'No actor can honestly say he doesn't care what people think of him.'

He didn't answer straight away, he seemed to be turning over in his mind what she'd said. The waiter came and he gave their order, then studied the wine list. When they were alone again he answered her as though there had been no interruption.

'I care deeply what they think of my performances. I care deeply that any character I portray is whole, that in taking on his mantle I take the heart and soul of the man. I have made a few films, films that have been box-office successes, yet there I've felt myself to be a puppet. Sometimes I wish it were different; working in the cinema would be far less wearing, less of a strain. Take Richard the Second into your being for an evening and by the time the final curtain falls he leaves you completely drained, every emotion stretched beyond breaking point.'

'I saw your Richard the Second once. I'll never forget.'

He reached his hand across the small table and rested it on hers.

'And did you ache with pity for him?'

She nodded. 'Yes. I'd read it for School Certificate, that's why I went. I thought I knew Richard the Second. Yet seeing it I felt I'd never understood at all until then.'

'That's the nicest thing you've said to me.' Then, in the way his voice could change, lightening the mood, 'Well, not quite the nicest, if this is to be an evening of truth. Ah, I see food coming.'

Food, wine, truth and a new trust. So the evening set its seal. He talked a lot more about that other compartment of his life. He told her about Vincent de Ville, the director of the company, his good friend and someone he knew she'd get on well with; he talked about the other members of the cast, his colleagues, people who shared his interests, people who understood just as he did the moment of terror at the rise of the curtain. Then, as they sat over their coffee, he revealed his innermost and abiding ambition: the Sutcliffe Theatre, a theatre where his own vision would become reality. He meant to produce, direct and usually act as well.

'With an ambition like that you still make films?'

'A necessary evil. Films bring me a great deal of money; films, not theatre, make my name known. The true professional in me has no use for shooting a scene here, a scene there, often out of context for the convenience of the set. It's a craft and any actor worth his salt must have that skill. I need to have an established place in the public eye.'

That last statement surprised her. She'd always known how much his fame meant to Lydia, but it was out of character with the man she'd seen as being without conceit. Shying away from disappointment in him, she asked, 'Those other actors you work with in the theatre, do they feel the same?'

'I believe some may. I'm sure some don't. Confessions of truth like this seldom happen; I've never told my dreams to anyone until now.'

Silly that when she looked up, she saw him through a haze of tears. It was a moment of such joy, nothing must spoil it.

'Drink up your coffee,' she whispered. 'It's time we were on the road.'

'Not yet.'

'Yes. Because all this' − she spread her hands when she said it, somehow encompassing the two of them − 'has been important, meaningful. Let's stop now. Let's not let anything spoil it.'

She ought to have known that a man who could understand the complexities of personalities from Richard the Second to King Lear would be sensitive to the suspicion she was running away from.

'Misunderstanding is all that can spoil it. You think it's for myself I crave notoriety? Or even for Lydia?' His laugh was affectionate and natural as they both conjured up the picture of her longing to play the part of a film star's wife. 'It's for neither. I shall invest in something I feel important − theatre. The more my name is a household word, the better chance there is of initial success. My dream will take money. I mean to put on plays by new writers, new plays by established writers, not superficial floss that give no more than an evening's entertainment. What makes Will Shakespeare the greatest playwright ever known? What makes his work loved and acknowledged across the world? Love, hate, envy, jealousy, greed, fear, anguish − there is no emotion he doesn't reach. Four centuries ago or today, people never change.'

'Yet you say the Sutcliffe Theatre will put on new plays, new writers?'

'As part of the season, no more than that. It would be intellectual snobbery to assume that today's changed society won't bring forth writers who can encapsulate those same emotions against a setting familiar to our times. That's what I'm looking for. Theatre that will make our age live long after we've gone.'

Silently they looked at each other. She wished she could say something profound that would tell him how deeply his words had touched

131

her. But once more he was sensitive to what was unsaid. 'So there you are, my Julie,' he said, his tone putting all the soul-searching behind them. 'That's why I need to prostitute my art for filthy lucre and make every Tom, Dick and Harry know the name Sutcliffe.'

She nodded. 'Sebastian – thank you.'

For what? He didn't ask her. But then he seemed to have the gift of reading her mind.

'Here you are! Pam wanted to get me bedded down. As if I would when I knew you were on your way.' Lydia held her arms towards Sebastian. 'But didn't you bring Julie? Where is she?' She was disappointed that neither Julie nor Pam were here to see how Seb dropped to his knees by her side with such effortless grace.

'Yes, I drove her back. She's taking her things to her room. She'll come in soon, when we've had time to say hello.' He kissed her cheek, aware how carefully she had applied her make-up and feeling humbled that this could be for him.

'You know why she went to London, Seb? To buy me some pretty things to wear when you got back. Now, look at me! An old rag bag!' It had taken her half the day to choose between the cream blouse or the apricot, only to decide, having tried on both of them, that, after all, the gold was more flattering.

'You look lovely' – he laughed – 'and well you know it. Just as pretty as that day when you were given a part in the crowd on the beach. Remember?'

At his words she felt a moment of panic. It wasn't the first time he'd referred to that day, as if he did it out of kindness. For him it must have been a day like any other, even though he tried to make her think otherwise. She, of course, remembered every moment of it: the thrill of watching her idol, of hearing his voice over and over as he and some unknown who was playing a supporting role acted and re-enacted the same scene; and then the miracle of having him single her out from the crowd.

Only occasionally would her thoughts catch her off guard and let her see him as a mere mortal, the glamour stripped from him. Warding off the chance of one of those moments stealing up on her, she opened her mouth in a smile that dared him to patronise her.

'Thank you, kind sir. Oh, good, here comes Julie.' She swivelled her chair to greet her friend as she came in. 'Had Suzanne still got the most beautiful things? I used to spend hours in there, then come home to send out a cry for help to Mum and the Squire asking for some of their coupons. Let's have a look at it straight away. All these bags! It feels like Christmas, only better, because I'm sure I'm going to just love every one of them.'

'I hope you're not. I couldn't give her enough coupons for all of them – blouses, a cape, a jacket she was sure would be perfect. But she seemed to think you had ways. She said you should see them all, then ring her up.'

There was nothing forced about Lydia's pleasure now. Like a child she pulled each garment out of its tissue paper, held it up with squeaks of delight, then threw it onto the sofa as she held out her hands for the next. A pile of tissue one side of her chair, a pile of Suzanne O'Brien bags the other, and enthroned between them a girl with sandy brown hair and stars in her eyes.

Sebastian ruffled her curls.

'I ought to have brought you wearables from New York. Never mind, raid my ration book, there's nothing I'm needing.'

Her answer surprised him.

'No, you keep yours. The Squire was here this afternoon. He said the same thing to me. And, Seb, he'd be awfully hurt if I chose to use yours instead.' Then, fearful that a husband could be just as troublesome as a father, 'Anyway, clothes are necessary to you, it's important you're well dressed. The Squire never goes anywhere special. It always seems to me dreadfully unfair that young people don't get more than the oldies. Pretty new clothes are such *fun*. I'll tell Squire tomorrow I want to take him up on his offer – and if he gets stuck there's always Mum's he can use.'

For a second Julie was irritated. Then she looked at Lydia holding up one of the blouses, obviously imagining how she'd look in it. Turning to the sofa, she started to collect up the scattered garments. Torn between pity, guilt, affection and impatience, she kept her back to the wheelchair.

'I'll hang them in your cupboard.'

'No, not inside it,' Lydia shouted urgently. 'Julie, can you try and hang them along the outside, I want to be able to look at them.'

Pity and affection got the upper hand.

Looking back at them as she carried the pile of folded garments from the room, Julie saw that Sebastian was fastening a necklace of clear amber around Lydia's neck.

'A present for my good girl.' He lightly kissed the top of her head.

'Julie! Just throw the things on the bed and bring me a mirror first, will you? Look what Seb's given me! Amber, my favourite of all. Who'd have thought this morning that today was going to turn out so special?'

Who indeed! Purposely Julie avoided Sebastian's eyes.

Sebastian was scheduled to commence filming in the middle of the following week. Lydia was over the moon with excitement. Theatre removed him from her orbit; films were quite different. There'd be snippets of news about him, and often pictures of him too, in the movie magazines she knew most of the young girls in Otterton read. That gave her a special feeling of importance, albeit at second hand.

Before he left Whiteways there as one thing he took on himself to do: escort Merry to Deremouth for his first morning at school. It was his idea that at four Anna was old enough to start at the same time.

'If she's left behind she'll miss him dreadfully,' he persuaded.

'I know that. But they can't always be together. By September they'll take her in the village — '

'Julie, if they're both at school you'll be more company for Lydia. The bill for the fees will come to me. It'll be doing Lydia a favour.'

He'd put it badly, he could see that from Julie's closed-in expression.

'I don't want you to pay school fees for Anna, Sebastian. She's my responsibility and that's the way I like it. But if you think she'll be in Lydia's way, then it's time I found somewhere else for us.'

They were walking on the wintry shore, wrapped up against the easterly wind. The children raced far ahead, stopping to pick up dead crabs or throw stones into the water, yelling and whooping, quite oblivious that it was their future under discussion.

'You know that's not what I meant. Don't look for a fight just because there are hurts we can't escape.' He stopped walking and turned her to face him. 'Julie, my darling, of course you want to be responsible for Anna, but can't you let me have some share? Just as I want you to be responsible for Merry. Don't let pride make things harder for us than they need be. Look at them together — isn't that how you want them to be? I certainly do. Fees for one small person or two, what's the difference? It's such a small thing for me to do — please, let me at least do that.'

'We shouldn't make arrangements until you've talked to Lydia. That's important. If we break that promise we don't deserve any happiness.'

They walked on in silence, both of them mindful of Lydia in her wheelchair and their pledge that nothing must hurt her.

Later in the day Sebastian made the suggestion, saying it as though the thought had just come into his head. And later still it was Lydia herself who proposed to Julie that the children might both start Harbour House at the beginning of term.

'It'd be good for Merry to have her with him, and she's so bright, she's quite ready to start lessons.' Lydia was delighted at the prospect, because she and Julie would be able to go about together in Ruby. She felt a new freedom was almost within her grasp. 'And forget about the fees. I'll arrange for them both to be put on Seb's bill. That's right, isn't it, Seb?' She beamed at both of them. 'I'm the one to gain. There'll be no stopping us, Julie — you, me and Ruby.'

Except for their first morning when Sebastian and Julie went together to deliver the children into the hands of the kindergarten teacher, it fell to Julie to take them each day. He returned to London, to the mews house that was full of ghosts. His regular cleaning lady had kept it spic and span during his stay in New York; so she still did, hardly ever seeing her celebrated employer, who was on the road towards Buckinghamshire and the studio as each morning cast its first hint of light to the eastern sky. Hours of preparation — the wardrobe department, the make-up department — then hours of standing about, waiting, waiting, take one, take two, all of it another tedious step on the way towards his goal. Every few days he telephoned Lydia — always hoping that Julie would answer the phone. She seldom did; she hung back, letting either Lydia or Pam get there first.

For the next few weeks he didn't get down to Devon, but Lydia seemed remarkably satisfied with nothing more than those short phone calls. In the village she would take great delight in casually mentioning how busy he was at the film studio. There were moments when Julie was irritated by her childish boastfulness.

Sebastian usually made his phone call about eight o'clock in the evening. On this Thursday towards the end of February Lydia answered. She chattered about Merry, about what she'd been doing that afternoon in Quin's greenhouse, about some new exercises Pam was teaching her to do so that her shoulders wouldn't get stiff. He listened. Then it was his turn. From where Julie sat, making an effort to concentrate on the crossword puzzle in that morning's *Daily Telegraph*, she could hear the low murmur of his voice. She put down the paper and went out of the room.

A ting of the bell told her the call was over.

'Julie! Here, Julie come and listen.' Clearly Lydia had heard something that pleased her.

'Good news? You look pleased with yourself,' came Julie's smiling response as she came back into the room.

'He hopes to finish shooting in about two weeks. Then, guess what? We're going to hear him on the radio. He's signed to make a series of readings, about ten minutes each night on the week leading up to Easter. Holy Week, I think he called it, so they must be sort of religious readings. But it doesn't matter what it is he reads — just imagine having him on each evening. Do you think I ought to keep Merry up late to hear him? I think Seb said the broadcasts would be about eleven o'clock.' She didn't wait for Julie's answer; she was already dialling, making ready to spread the news among her friends. She couldn't quite see yet how she could alert the *Deremouth Post* and the *Western Evening Gazette*, but she was determined that publicity should be given.

It was much later, long after Pam had brought Lydia's day to an end, that the telephone rang. This time Julie answered it. She spoke the one word, 'Hello', then fell silent as she listened.

Chapter Nine

'Fancy you've never told me about her. You ought to have asked her here to stay or something. Julie, this is your home, I'd love to know your other friends. It must be ages since you saw her.'

'Yes, I suppose it is. Down here, our whole way of life is different. Bessie and I have a friendship that goes back too far for her to feel neglected because I don't see her for a while.'

Lydia was patently pleased to have a new factor introduced into their lives.

'You really are a dark horse,' she said with a laugh. 'How many other secrets have you got locked away?'

'I wouldn't call Bess a secret. If she'd stayed in Slough — that's where she lives — I wouldn't have expected to dash off to see her. It's only because for a while she'll be within easy driving distance.' Shame that she could lie to Lydia struggled with elation at the reason she was embarking on her tale.

'Well, go on, tell me the rest. Is she a friend from when you were children? And what's she doing in this place in Wiltshire? Westbury did you say? Oh, just listen to me! I sound like some old busybody. That's how Nosy Parkers come into being, living other people's lives at second-hand. I didn't mean to pry, it's just I like to know all about you.'

'And why not?' Julie laughed. 'No, I didn't know her as long ago as that. We joined the forces on the same day and did our initial training together. We always got on well; you know how easy it is with some people. It was the same with you and me, Lydia, right from the start. I remember coming for my interview, not expecting I could possibly get the job, no experience and Anna in tow. But you made it so easy.'

Julie had never felt so low. She'd felt the bond with Lydia from the first hour. And what had she done? She'd cheated, she'd seen

137

the danger of being with Sebastian and yet she'd done nothing to stop the inevitable happening. And now she was weaving a web of lies, making her story so intricate that she almost believed in it herself.

'Yes, but you hadn't seen the others! Stiff and starchy, I'm sure it was on purpose they made me feel inferior.' Lydia giggled. 'You don't know how relieved I was when you and Anna turned up. But about Bess: what's she doing in Westbury? And how did she know how to get you on the telephone?'

'Silly!' Julie laughed. 'Even darkest Devon has postboxes. I write to her occasionally, so she knew I was working for you. I suppose she must have asked directory enquiries for the number or something. She's staying with an aunt in Westbury. She's been quite ill. I didn't know at the time or I'd have tried to get up to Slough for a day to see her in hospital. She didn't go into details about her operation, but it must have been something nasty because now she's out she won't be working for some time. I'm invited for lunch there if that suits you. I'll drop the children off at school and be back in time to collect them.'

'No, don't feel you have to rush like that. Quin can get us in the jeep, he won't mind, he never minds. I shan't need my chair, so the children can drive home in the back. It'll be fun. But listen, Julie, why don't you ring her and suggest she comes back with you? We've got bags of space and I'd love to have a visitor. Don't you see, it would be much better for her to be here by the sea for her convalescence?'

'Lydia, you're a dear.' Oh, but don't be, don't be kind, don't be understanding. Julie felt sick with shame. 'Perhaps later on she might have a few days down here, but it's ages since we've even seen each other. Let's just see how it goes.'

'OK. You know best. But she's welcome.'

Julie had lain awake half the night wrestling with her conscience. Now more than anything she wished that Bess were real, that she was expected for lunch at an aunt's house, that she didn't feel guilt must be written like a sign on her forehead. And what a stupid name to give her: B-e-s(s). Turn it around and what have you?

Even Westbury was a lie. Westbury had been the first place that had come to mind, somewhere far enough away so that she'd need a full morning and afternoon. Did Sebastian feel as ashamed as she did as the miles behind him lengthened? He must have been well on his way by the time she set out, his journey was so much longer.

Exeter, Honiton, Ilminster, she couldn't have much farther to go.

She pulled up at a crossroads and read the signpost, peered at the Ordnance Survey map, then, as if to reassure herself, fingered the piece of paper in her pocket where she'd written down the address. By now guilt and shame had given way to wild excitement. Even the fact that no one knew where she was gave her a feeling of freedom. Rain that half an hour ago had started as a gentle warning had by now settled in for a wet day. She was bitterly cold, and the insides of the windows started to mist up again as soon as she wiped them. But none of that mattered. Yes, this was it, here was the camp site.

Turning through the open gate she went slowly up the track towards a field around which twenty or so caravans stood in winter desolation. She hardly glanced at them once she had spotted one, on the far side of the field, with light shining from the windows and his car parked alongside.

She parked her Standard close behind it. Rain, cold, what did it matter? He opened the car door for her and held his umbrella to protect her. Drawing her close he kissed her, out there in the February field, a trickle of rain falling from the tilted umbrella and finding a way down the back of her neck.

'Who wants moonlight and roses?' she chuckled as she nuzzled against him.

'Inside you go! It's not the Ritz but it's our own.'

The warmth met them as they went inside; the glowing bowl of a paraffin heater was designed for use in a room far larger than this eighteen-foot van. Sebastian had been there about an hour and already the windows were streaming with condensation.

'Did you hire it? I didn't know you could at this time of year.' Looking around her she took off her coat and hung it in the cupboard next to his.

'It's my own. I've had it since before the war. It's a bit rough — a far cry from today's models.'

'Lydia never mentioned you had a caravan. I suppose she used to come here to get Merry out of London in the summer?'

'This is my hide-out. I've never brought Lydia here.'

How quickly those old suspicions could be nudged into life! If not Lydia, how many others had he brought to his little love nest?

'How long is it going to be before you learn to trust me?' It wasn't the first time he'd read her thoughts. 'I told you it's my hide-out. I don't use it often, but sometimes I want just to get away, right away. And this is where I come. On my own, Julie. Until today, always on my own.'

'You've been married for six years and you've never told her.'

This time he laughed. 'Dear little honey, she'd have found it impossible not to drop a word to the *Somerset Gazette* or *Times* or *Echo* or whatever it calls itself. Once a year I call at the farm and pay the rent in notes for my humble plot. As far as old Mr Bowles, the farmer, is concerned I'm "that fella from Plot 11". And that's how I like it to be.'

She touched his cheek with her lips. 'You're an extraordinarily nice man, Sebastian Sutcliffe.' Purposely she mimicked the tone he'd used, but she was surprised that she should have remembered.

'Now that rings a bell. So, my Julie, here we are, two extra-ordinarily nice people, a pound of meatless-looking sausages and a French loaf for our lunch and an oasis of undisturbed peace ahead of us. Any suggestions?'

'Don't be so blatant.' She laughed. 'Oh, this is so good! It shouldn't be, we ought to be looking over our shoulders, full of guilt. I was, you know – full of guilt, I mean. Ever since you phoned and I started telling such dreadful garbled stories to Lydia. It would have been easier if she'd objected to my coming, but – Sebastian, I do hate it having to be like this. I made up this nonexistent wartime friend called Bess, said she'd had an operation and was convalescing in Westbury.'

His eyebrow climbed. 'You don't do things by halves.'

'Well, it had to be something plausible. By the time I finished I almost believed it myself. I wished it were the truth, too. I hate treating her like that. Do you know what she suggested?'

'My guess would be that she suggested you invited this Bess woman to stay at Whiteways.'

Julie nodded. 'She's so good – and we're rotten. Selfish and greedy.'

'Selfish, yes. Greedy, yes. But rotten, no. We are having to pay for our stolen hours; the only one who will not get hurt is Lydia. And that's right, that's the way it must always be.'

'I brought you some pictures Merry's done at school. His first week's work.'

'Tell me about him, about both of them.'

Her moment of self-abnegation was over. He lit the gas to reboil the kettle for coffee, and a feeling of domesticity enveloped them as the temperature in the little caravan rose and the rain beat on the roof.

Driving home she remembered all that was good: the shared pride in the children; the laughter as they'd played Lexicon, putting together words that were decidedly doubtful but earned good points; the satisfaction of sizzling their sausages to be eaten with an unbuttered French loaf, a meal equal to any nectar of the

140

gods; of sharing the secret of his hideaway; and above all else the joy of lying in his arms on that makeshift bed, finding in each other a crowning perfection that defied words. Ilminster, Honiton, Exeter, Deremouth, passing Rowans and on through Downing Wood . . . in a few minutes she'd be home. She must forget the blessed hours they'd shared, and conjure up instead the picture she'd created in her mind of Bess and the aunt, so that she would be ready to answer questions, to add to the story she'd made up. Quin would have brought the children home from school, so for the first hour she'd be able to busy herself seeing them off to bed. But the rest of the evening lay ahead. Lydia, who had to live at second-hand, would want a full description so that when Bess came she knew all about her.

Julie played her role. It occurred to her that her contact with an actor must be having an affect.

'Did you suggest she came to stay here? I was telling the Squire this afternoon I expected you'd arrange something.' Lydia was keen for a new face around the place.

'I think her aunt − Aunt Edith − would be disappointed if she rushed off too quickly. They say it'll be at least another six weeks before she goes back to her job in Slough −.'

'What was wrong with her?'

'Oh, er . . .' Julie dug into her mind for something that would fit the bill. 'She had a hysterectomy. Not nice even for a woman with a family, but tough luck for a single girl.' She marvelled at her inventiveness. The caravan was removed from all this, to Julie now it had no bearing on the story she made up. 'I told her I'd try and get up to see her again, but I didn't fix a date. She'll ring up some time, or perhaps I'll drop her a line.' Bess began to be more real than the hideaway at the back of the waterlogged field.

Julie went again to the caravan − and again after that. When Lydia told her that Sebastian had more or less finished at the studio she feigned surprise, just as she managed the right expression of pleasure that he meant to spend a few days at Whiteways before returning to London in time for the nightly readings he was to broadcast. In truth she was gripped by panic. It had been difficult last time he'd been there, those hours in his London house had been at the forefront of their minds. But since then they'd moved on, and nothing could ever be as it had been before he'd shared with her the secret of that elderly caravan at the far side of a field in the middle of nowhere.

She needn't have worried; Lydia suspected nothing, she noticed nothing. And surprisingly it was because they'd had those hours

141

together, because they'd kept no secrets from each other, that they were able to act out the roles expected of them. For both of them Lydia was the central figure of his four days' stay. Like a child showing off a new toy, she took him driving with her in Ruby. One of those outings was aimed especially at a visit to the greenhouses so that he could admire the niche she was making for herself.

'Don't you lift me!' Her beaming smile took the sting out of her words. 'Quin's served his apprenticeship, he knows just how to do it without putting his back out when he heaves me up.'

Sebastian didn't argue; imagining the feelings of a husband who resented another man usurping his place, he stood back with an expression somewhere between hurt and smouldering jealousy. It wasn't lost on Lydia. Holding her arms towards Quin, she, too, played a role. Two men vying for her favours — for her it was a rare moment of triumph.

There was one morning that would boost her in the days ahead: Sebastian took her in her chair to the village. She swelled with pride. It was a sunny morning, the village street was busy. Her cup of happiness was full and overflowing as people called their greetings and noted his devotion.

'Do you want to call and see your people?' he asked her as they approached the gate of Delbridge House on the way home.

'No. I spoke to Mum on the phone, she'll probably come over. The Squire's got the grumps. I could tell he had even though she didn't actually say so. I'm not having him spoiling our morning by being rude and horrid like he can be when I'm with you. It's not fair, Seb, I don't see why I have to be the buffer for his jealousy.'

'If there's a buffer I'd say it's Grace.'

'Mum? Oh, she can cope. She's tough as anything. Anyway, she's not likely to make him jealous, she's always doted on him. It's just me. He can't bear me to be important to any man but him. Best we just go straight by the house. You mustn't worry about the way he treats you, Seb.'

Sebastian didn't, but somehow the fact that she thought he might was added evidence that he wasn't failing her. His only answer now was to rumple her short curls as he walked behind her.

All too soon he was gone. His nightly readings on the radio were to go on the air live. His days were free, but Julie's weren't, for this was Easter and the children had broken up for their first school holiday. There could be no clandestine meetings. Each night she and Lydia, usually with Pam too, gathered in front of the radio to hear him.

'I'm surprised he's doing this sort of thing.' Lydia's proprietorial way of talking about him touched Julie on a raw nerve, especially as she cut in during the reading. 'I bet half the people who queue up to see his films won't even listen. Any old actor could have done this, it's a waste of talent.'

'He reads so well,' Pam Pepper whispered, something in her stillness silencing Lydia.

Julie listened to each beautifully modulated word. 'Any old actor' Lydia had said. But no, there wasn't another voice like his; speaking softly, every syllable clear in that distinctive way that made poetry of common language, every word spoken as if from his heart. She was carried back to the evening he'd told her his dreams. This was the real Sebastian, the artist, the lover of the beauty of language. Through the ether her spirit reached out to his. The emotion that held her went deeper than thought, she could feel it as a physical power in her. Let Lydia try and impose the image of the screen hero, let Pam defend his art; only *she* could listen and understand, not just the words or their message, but the man, the yearning in him to be the medium that would reach out and transmit the spirit.

Trudie was ready to follow any lead that would take her to the root of her unease. Lately she'd felt a new aloofness in Julie. It wasn't that she was less friendly, yet Trudie was sensitive to the fact that something was withheld. It must have to do with this wartime colleague she went off to see. That Julie had given her love to Jeremy was acceptable. He was safely in the past, he was no threat. But Bess was a different matter; Julie's friendship with her was rooted in days before Jeremy had come on the scene, and had withstood years with no contact.

'Julie must be missing her visits to Westbury.' Consciously she made her voice casual as she sat on the stone wall of the terrace near Lydia.

'Next week the children go back to school. She's sure to have a day with her friend then. I wanted her to have her to stay — after all, this is her home. Anyway, I could do with some fresh company.'

'So why didn't she? Even if Bess isn't fit enough to dash about, I should have thought a break by the sea would have been just the thing.'

'Don't ask me why, ask Julie. She makes excuses. It's as if she's frightened of what we'll think of Bess. But if she's Julie's friend that's good enough for me.'

'Perhaps I can persuade her.'

Trudie resented the thought of the unknown Bess. But one thing was certain, she wanted to know her; only then could she loosen the tie that held Julie to her. There must be some reason why she was kept hidden and Julie was withdrawn. Not that she was quiet, if anything she talked more, laughed a little too brightly; yet she was guarded, never quite relaxed.

Trudie's persuasions got no further than Lydia's.

'No, she feels she shouldn't run out on her aunt as soon as she can. She's a great-aunt really, quite elderly, but she's been so kind.'

It was some sort of consolation to count how the weeks were passing. Even convalescence from a major operation couldn't spin out much longer, then Bess would go back to her job in Slough. Trudie told herself that all she had to do was bide her time and Julie would be hers again.

The one person who had no idea that her manner had given rise to conjecture was Julie herself. With the children back at school she again started visiting Bess. But of course it couldn't go on, she had to think of a sequel to the story she'd invented. Lying was easy, she discovered. Once you set the characters in place you could play God with them. She gave Bess's elderly Aunt Edith failing sight, explained that Bess felt she ought to stay nearby. Providentially she'd heard of a live-in job not far from Westbury, housekeeper to a widower with two teenage children. The story snowballed all by itself. A live-in housekeeper responsible for a family would have no chance to come visiting, yet she must get a few hours off each week to spare for a friend.

Julie's moods seesawed between times of joy and certainty that what she and Sebastian had was precious beyond belief and times filled with self-hatred.

Lydia encouraged her to talk about Bess and her new 'family'. Remembering how sure Sebastian had been that they were doing her no harm, Julie added colour and interest to the story. Of course he was right, Lydia enjoyed hearing all about the Merediths (the name Julie had given Bess's new employer). Like some ongoing serial, week by week she related the latest happenings when she came back from her visits. In her mind she likened herself to Scheherazade: as long as the story continued she earned her hours with Sebastian. With each visit she grew closer to him.

Lydia's life was so narrow, no wonder she looked for colour in other people's doings. At least once a week a large bouquet of flowers would be delivered from Sebastian; sometimes, if anything took his eye that she might like, the postman would bring a package. The pride she'd felt in arranging his gift of flowers herself, or the excitement of tearing open a surprise parcel, had waned. As that spring gave way to summer Lydia was bored. It was all very fine to go up to the nursery, she honestly did take a pride in the jobs she considered to be her own. But she was twenty-five years old, and ahead of her there stretched perhaps more than twice as long. She would never be the centre of anyone's existence. Not that she ever had — except the Squire's and he was her father so that didn't count. There was only one centre to Seb's existence and that was himself. Perhaps Merry came a close second, but women were there for his gratification when the mood was right. That was something she'd always known, although it had never altered how wonderful everything had been. Was he being kind and tactful, was that why he never hinted how he longed for it to be like that again, the way it had been when she was a proper woman? Mr Bonham-Miles must have talked to him just as he had to her. She couldn't bear it if he saw her body as it was now — yet she couldn't bear him not caring. Lydia was out of step with life.

'Look, Mum, I did my shoes; no one helped, not even Julie.' Merry marched into the room and stood in front of her chair, one foot held high for her admiration.

'Good, that was clever,' she answered.

He looked crestfallen. She had not really looked, and the child realised that she had not even listened.

Joining them, Julie was in time to sense his hurt.

'When's Seb coming?' Nearly two terms at school had taught Merry the joy of finding new skills. He could write the words MERRY SUTCLIFFE in misshapen capitals. There was so much he wanted to show his idol.

'You'll just have to make do with me, Merry,' Lydia told him. 'Seb's too busy to have time to waste coming to see *us*.'

'Not waste.' Merry glared at her. 'Seb wants to come and see me. Anyway I need to show him my name.'

'Why don't you get your Mummy to write a letter for you, Merry, then you could sign your name on it for him?' Julie had seen the fear behind the glower.

'Shall we do that, Mum?'

'Perhaps, some time.'

Merry looked down at his shoes. The bows he'd been so proud of looked uneven and one of them was coming undone already. He wouldn't cry. He wouldn't.

'Merry, can you go and help Anna for me, love?' Julie pretended not to have seen the danger sign. 'She's changing out of her uniform still and the buttons take her ages.'

It gave him an excuse to get out of the room. She doubted if he'd get as far as Anna's room before he found some valid excuse for

145

tears. Children laughed together, cried together, picked each other up when they fell down. But Merry's quivering lips came from the fear of something he couldn't understand. Sebastian hadn't been home for more than a month; Lydia was isolated by a depression that was deeper than anything she'd felt in the early days after her accident.

Julie knew that only one person could help. So that night she wrote to Sebastian.

The children were about to break up for their summer holidays, so this week she wouldn't be 'meeting Bess for lunch'. This week, too, Sebastian's short season was ending. Normally Lydia would have been overjoyed that his next major undertaking was a film to be made by a Hollywood company on location in the Middle East. But now the very thought of it annoyed her. She couldn't understand why he was turning himself into what, in her present mood, she considered a 'stodgy sobersides'. Did he purposely want to destroy the image of the idol whose photographs had filled the scrapbooks of her adolescence? Stage productions of Shakespeare, Easter readings on the radio, and slotted into the short time between finishing at the theatre and embarking for location he was what he called 'indulging' himself with a few evenings of poetry readings. And the film itself, of epic grandeur, in Technicolor, with a dazzling, star-studded cast, was based on the Old Testament. Not likely his adoring fans would queue to see him! And if they did they would barely recognise him, costumed, bearded, the contours of his face moulded and reshaped by the make-up department. Why couldn't he see that a role like that appealed to the wrong sort of people? No dreamy young girls would pin a picture of him looking like that on their bedroom wall!

Lydia's ability to accept her own restricted horizons depended on everything staying as she'd known it. Sebastian could live two separate lives, as long as the one she had no part in was coloured with fame and glamour; she liked to imagine the Squire and her mother unchanging, their lives moving along on level, parallel lines; she needed the assurance of Quin's devotion and Julie's friendship. When any of these things showed signs of altering, it terrified her. In the first months after her accident, despite the moments of anguish she'd shared just with Quin, hers had been the major role. She'd played it with courage knowing that in all their lives she held a place of paramount importance. Boosted by their admiration she'd made sure her face was ready to wear a smile and her low moments kept private (unless she counted Quin).

It was a visit from Grace the afternoon after the shoelace incident that left Lydia with no escape from the truth. How was it she had

146

taken them all for granted, never considered that they might hide from her an altering climate?

'I didn't really expect to find you here,' Grace said as she came round the side path to the terrace. 'I almost didn't stop, you're usually at the nursery.'

'I told Squire this morning that Quin had gone off lecturing somewhere in Somerset. Don't remember where.' She felt her mother's scrutiny, but today she didn't trouble to force her face into a smile or to disguise her boredom.

'The Squire's been to see you?'

'Comes most mornings, you know he does.'

'I didn't know, but then he's never been in the habit of telling me where he goes.' It was a simple statement of fact, he had always found his own freedom.

'Probably knows you wouldn't be interested.'

Grace could feel the tension. Was it to do with the Squire? At lunchtime he'd barely spoken a word, then gone off into the room he liked to call his studio and closed the door firmly.

'What's up, Lydia? You say he comes every morning? Is it too often?'

Into Lydia's guilt-laden mind sprang the trapped feeling the sound of his car turning in at the gate always aroused. But for that she might have managed to force some laughing rejoinder. Instead she turned angrily on her mother.

'That's a hateful thing to say! If that's the way you think about him I'm not surprised he's glad to come over here. Like he says, he and I have always been buddies. It's hard for him to see me like this and not be able to help. I'd have expected you to understand.'

Grace was tired, tired to death of the Squire's moods, the tension of never knowing whether he'd be so withdrawn she couldn't speak to him – didn't want to speak to him, honesty prompted her – whether self-pity would be making him look for a reason to take offence, whether he'd use her as a whipping boy simply because he was angry with life or whether, as seldom happened these days, he'd show an inkling of interest in anything except himself or Lydia. At Whiteways she could usually recharge her batteries, see Lydia's acceptance and be grateful.

'It might be better for him if he took an interest in someone other than himself for a change,' she snapped before she could put a brake on her words. Then, with a sweep of her hand as if to rub out what she'd said, 'That was mean. I've got no business coming here grouching to you. As long as that's not what he does, if you say he comes nearly every day.'

147

'You never liked me and the Squire doing things together. But I don't want to talk about it, not about him at all, with you being so beastly about him. Merry breaks up this afternoon, Julie's driven in to collect them from school now.'

'Talking of schools' — gratefully Grace pulled a new topic out of the air — 'do you remember my friend Evelyn Keeble?'

'Sort of. Battleaxe of a school mistress.' Lydia had to wound.

'She's no such thing.' Grace was quick to her friend's defence, yet it wasn't like Lydia to look for a fight. 'Not a battleaxe, but a schoolteacher, yes.'

'I remember her. She used to come and stay. Squire and I used to hop off as soon as breakfast was done. He was such fun, Mum, we used to escape like a pair of truants.'

'A pity he didn't have any normal man's courtesy for his wife's friends. I had a letter from Evelyn this morning, she's been given the post of deputy head of Trewarin Abbey, a girls' boarding school in Cornwall. Battleaxe she may be to you and your father; to me she's a dear friend, someone with interests that go beyond herself, someone who reads the papers and cares what's happening in this dreadful torn world.'

'Good for her! Personally it doesn't make much difference to me what happens in the big world, I seem to have fallen off the edge of it.'

'That's not true! Anyway, instead of doing nothing it might be to your own advantage to read things that matter. Or what about painting? Your father would guide you. If you've this wonderful affinity, perhaps you've inherited the artistic ability he's managed to fill his years with.'

Lydia wasn't listening. She was looking at her mother with a new curiosity.

'I never thought about it until now, but you don't even like him. He's had me, but nothing else. When I was young I just accepted how things were at home. Naturally I loved you both, children take grown-ups for granted, don't think about relationships. But why can't you see, Mum, things are easier for you than for him? You don't bruise.'

'And that, my dear, is the best protection against the knocks. Don't pretend you haven't learned it already.'

'Not talking about me, I'm talking about Squire. He never comes here running you down like you have been him.'

'And you know why?' Grace asked, with a wry laugh. 'Because he doesn't talk about me at all. Am I not right?'

'Please don't fight him. Why can't things just go on the way they always have?' It was a cry from her heart. 'You don't have to be wonderful buddies, but you might at least not pull different ways.'

Long after her mother had gone, Lydia remembered and sunk deeper into her depression. The trouble was everyone except her had moved on, yet to protect her they pretended nothing had changed. One by one she thought of those around her. Sebastian treated her with kind consideration, but even that hurt; she would rather he shouted at her sometimes, argued, anything to show that he saw her as a normal person. The Squire dithered around her as if she were some priceless and breakable possession. She remembered the contempt in her mother's tone as she'd talked about the Squire. It was cruel, disloyal and horrid. Mum didn't love him at all and he didn't even know it.

Lydia pulled her mind away from them and thought of Quin instead. His kindness didn't hurt her in the way that Sebastian's did. She wondered why. It must be because she wasn't in love with Quin. There had been a time when she had believed – no, that was wrong, she'd been absolutely certain – that he had been in love with her. For a while she'd enjoyed encouraging him. But that had been before she met Seb. Imagine if one day Quintin fell in love with some other girl, someone who was free and who loved him too. She looked down at her useless legs, the ankles swelling. Bet it would be someone pretty, someone who could run up the hill to the greenhouses, someone who . . . She bit hard on the corners of her mouth. It took all her determination to pull her thoughts to the safe ground of Julie – the one person who never changed. If only her knees were her own to bend, she ought to go down on them and say thank you for sending Julie to her. It was as if fate had known what was ahead of her and had brought Julie and Anna. Think how different it would have been for Merry without them. They were closer than a family.

Lydia almost pulled herself out of her low trough.

When the telephone rang at exactly five o'clock on Friday, they knew it would be Sebastian. Three times a week he spoke to Lydia, and the times seldom varied; in this way he knew she'd be ready to get to the phone. By now he would have received Julie's letter. He wouldn't mention it, but he might say something to cheer Lydia and reassure her.

From the hall outside the sitting-room door came the distant hum of conversation, Lydia saying very little, his voice for her ears alone. Julie leaned forward and turned the knob of the radio.

'*Children's Hour*'. Her voice was bright with anticipation. 'Pull

149

your chairs near so you won't miss anything.' That way she tried to cut herself off from the thought that only yards away from her his voice could be heard.

The door slid open and Lydia propelled herself back.

'Seb's going to Salisbury on Monday, I forget where on Tuesday — Oxford, I think it was — then Bath on Wednesday. After that he has nothing until Friday. He'll come down here from Bath and stay until Friday morning.'

'Yippee!' *Children's Hour* had lost Merry. He need to run wild with excitement and Anna never took much encouragement.

'Come on, you two. Get the quoit, we'll have half an hour on the sand before the tide comes up. You don't mind, Lydia? I think they need to let off steam.'

'Don't we all?' The blues might have lightened but they'd certainly not cleared.

At this time of year and on such a glorious day as this, the beaches of Devon thronged with holidaymakers. Whiteways, however, was too far from habitation and there was no public track from the road. The occasional stalwarts came by walking their dogs, but today there was no one. It was possible to reach this stretch of sand only by climbing over the rocks when the tide was low, and already the rising water had cut off the access.

'Don't hurl it too far, Merry, you monster!' Julie laughed, rushing along the sand to retrieve the quoit. She envied him his unchecked exuberance; when he turned a somersault and covered his hair with sand, how could she grumble at him? She knew exactly the feeling. There was no sane way to express the happiness that consumed him.

'Look, Merry's mummy's coming down too!' This time it was Anna.

'Let's go and help them.'

Quin stood there with Lydia in his arms. He had carried her to sit at the end of the garden where sloping grass gave way to the short drop of even steeper red rocks like a miniature cliff face. Then, having reached the sand himself, he held his arms to where she was perched on the edge.

'Wait, I'll help,' Julie yelled. 'I thought you were away lecturing.'

'I've just got back. Looked in as I came by. No, don't worry, Julie.' He wanted to do this himself. 'We can manage, we're an invincible team.' It put Julie in mind of that first time she'd seen him carrying Lydia, 'Him Tarzan, me Jane.' This time, though, Lydia looked uncertain as she sat with her legs dangling over the edge of the grassy bank. Turning to her, he spoke gently, his steady

150

voice giving her courage. 'Just lean right forward, let yourself fall on me. Trust me, Lydia.'

For a second she hesitated; she'd never been more conscious of her helplessness.

'Trust me,' he repeated.

Of course she trusted him. When had he ever failed her? With her eyes tightly closed she let herself fall and felt his arms around her. In that upright position he held her, just as he had the first day he'd lifted her from her chair, making her as tall as he was. Opening her eyes, she saw Merry and Anna at waist level, jumping around her with excitement.

'I want to feel the sand.' Her face was pulled into a grimace that wanted to laugh and wanted to cry. 'Never thought . . . expected . . . oh, Quin!'

'This rock looks about right.' His matter-of-fact manner helped her to get a grip on the jumble of emotions that were running away with her. 'You sit here while I take my shoes off; then, Lydia, you and I are going for a paddle.'

From the low rock where he'd put her she could reach forward to take off her own shoes.

'I won,' she giggled, 'I'm ready first.'

'Ah, but you didn't have socks.'

The children were watching fascinated, and Julie felt humble. They all went out of their way to make life easy for Lydia, yet only Quin treated her as an equal.

'Here we go then. And if you don't behave, I'll dunk you.'

'Is it cold?' she asked him as he waded in, the water covering her ankles.

'Have you ever known it not to be? Remember how we used to swim just round the other side of these rocks, how you used to watch for some sign of life from Whiteways? Never thought then that you'd live there and have a more or less private beach.'

'Never thought a lot of things.' Her arms gripped him tightly round the neck, he held her close. 'Paul used to swim right round Hunters Rock, remember?'

He was glad she talked of Paul. For her to speak of the happy, carefree days of her childhood seemed to him to be a sign that she was learning to merge past and present. This must surely be an important day, another large step forward.

The weather held through the weekend and into next week. Locals tapped their barometers expecting each day to hear the announcement that garden hosepipes were banned; holidaymakers looked at the high, clear sky and accepted it without question as the fulfilment of their workday dreams.

By Wednesday there was an air of expectancy at Whiteways.

'Is it today Seb's coming?' Merry was sure it was, he'd heard them say Wednesday. And this was Wednesday. He only asked for the thrill of having it confirmed. So he was disappointed at Lydia's reply.

'Not until after bedtime. We shan't see him until morning. But he'll be here all day tomorrow.'

That was worse than not having expected him. Merry's bottom lip pouted and he kicked his foot disconsolately against the table leg.

'If you don't pick that lip up, you'll step on it!' she teased. 'And Merry, don't kick the table leg.'

His lip slipped even further, but he turned his back on her so that she wouldn't see. Going off into the garden, he picked up stones and hurled them at the sumach tree. When the occasional one hit the bark he got satisfaction from its resounding thud.

'A day's a long time when you're only five years old,' Julie sympathised, watching him. 'Go and cheer him up, Anna. But mind you keep out of the way of the stones.'

''Spect he's fed up,' she observed sagely. 'House filled up just with girls. I'll tell him I'll go to bed early tonight if he likes. If we do that it'll soon be next morning.'

The day was all set to drag along at a snail's pace. Even Anna's patience with Merry showed signs of wearing thin by midday and Julie wasn't looking forward to an afternoon on the sands with two cantankerous children – or, nearer the truth, one cantankerous and the other reaching the point where she'd show him that even a worm can turn.

'Here's Quin come,' Merry announced, the look he turned on Lydia telling her quite clearly that he wasn't pleased. 'S'pose that means you're going to that nursery.' Nearly every day that's what she did. He'd thought today was going to be different. He'd pictured all of them watching out of the window, waiting for Seb's car to come. But it was the same as any other day, not special at all.

' ... if they squeeze in with the chair.'

He'd been too full of resentment to look at Quin and he'd purposely shut his mind to what the grown-ups were saying. Then he heard those last few words and for a second forgot he was cross. Quin must be going to take Anna and him up to the nursery. Stupid nursery, he didn't want to go there. But he liked it at the farm, Aunt Tess was nice, Uncle Peter might let them help feed the animals ...

He listened; already he had decided to fight for his rights if his mother refused.

'I haven't seen the procession for years. You can't manage all of us, they're happy on the beach.'

'Rubbish! They'll love the procession. It starts at two thirty. We have to take the youngsters, Lydia, they give us a good excuse for pushing to the front and enjoying ourselves.'

She knew, and he knew, that a wheelchair would never be left at the back of the crowd. But she clutched at the thought that a pathway would be made for the sake of the children.

'Turn out your small change, Julie,' she said, laughing. 'And you, Pam. We have to have lots of pennies to throw in the buckets.'

Merry had no idea what they were talking about, but the ring of excitement in his mother's voice chased away the blues.

'Me and Anna coming with you?'

'You certainly are,' Quin told him. 'Tradition demands it.'

Merry still didn't understand. Only later, as they watched the procession, would a shadowy memory tease the back of his mind. Something his mother had told him about a long time ago when she was young and she'd worn a crown and been driven in a coach all along the road by the sea.

Once a year Deremouth held its carnival. It raised money from the holidaymakers for local charities. It was hard to say who got the most pleasure from it, those who spent weeks beforehand making their floats and sewing their costumes or those who lined the pavements throwing their money into the collectors' buckets. On this particular afternoon Lydia's memories were bittersweet: herself, queen for a day, surrounded by girls from Otterton who'd been her attendants. Her own life was very different now – but she wasn't the only one who'd had to face troubles. Emmie Brown, the prettiest of them all, had married a worker from Rowans and had a daughter who looked as lovely as herself but now, at four years old, showed no dawning intelligence; another's husband had been killed in the war. Today's queen passed by, her coach drawn by two dappled greys, her four attentants standing behind her chair looking self-conscious in their finery. What would life do to them? Involuntarily, Lydia shivered. On the kerbside, the brake of her chair keeping her firmly in place, she looked at Merry and Anna, and at Quin handing out pennies to them. Dear Quin, her one unchanging rock! She hardly glanced at Deremouth's newest dancing group, majorettes of various shapes and sizes who were leaping their way forward with more hope than expertise. Her mind was on Quin. He was becoming successful, already establishing a reputation. As a young child he'd hidden his loneliness and insecurity behind a protection of learning, it was something that had become part of his character. So at horticultural college he'd made a blueprint for his future and, Quin being Quin, he would work at it until he reached his goal and even further. Again she shivered, despite the heatwave and the crush of people.

The tide was rising, already the rocks were covered. It was not an ideal time for bathing, in another hour it would be better, but Julie meant to make the most of this unexpected afternoon of complete freedom. She carried her beach towel and book along the gritty sand to a place just beyond the land belonging to Whiteways. Here the cliffs behind were taller and steeper, their protection gave her an added privacy, yet she would see anyone coming. Not that anyone was likely to. Pam had decided to borrow the Standard and go to Newton Abbot market; unless something went wrong, Lydia and the children wouldn't be back for a couple of hours.

Even here on the beach there was scarcely a movement in the air. Julie took a dip into the cool water and stretched out in the sunshine to dry. She was still lying there, the straps of her two-piece swimsuit pulled from her shoulders, her face raised to the sun, her eyes closed, the water glistening on her summer-brown body, when she felt rather than heard someone approaching.

'Sebastian! But you're in Bath.'

'Correction: I *was* in Bath. This morning. Are you here on your own?'

She made the explanations, he listened to them, but to both of them this was another gift from that benign deity. He stripped to the waist, took off shoes and socks. For a long time they lay side by side, fingers linked, talking – sharing the summer afternoon as holidaymaking couples must have been in every quiet stretch of the beach. But this one was cut off from the rest by the incoming tide.

'You're salty,' he murmured presently, his mouth against her shoulder, his tongue exploring the unfamiliar taste of her skin. 'Like a mermaid.'

'It wasn't deep enough for a mermaid. We'll go in again when the water comes up a bit more, that's when it's best to swim.'

'I've no trunks. Will it offend your maidenly conventions?'

'What maidenly conventions?'

For almost an hour they'd been content to lie scarcely touching each other, hearing the gentle lapping of the water as it crept nearer, revelling in the warmth of the sun. Now when he touched her naked waist she felt a tingle of excitement. Soon they would swim. Soon, but not yet.

They'd made love in the comfort of his bedroom in London, many times in the less than luxurious caravan, and every time the wonder seemed more intense. Today there was nothing beyond themselves, the sun beating on their nakedness, the firm sand beneath them, the ripples breaking only feet away as the sea crept nearer.

The swim was less tempting; they would rather have lain close in each other's arms. But life pressed in on them, the others would be coming home from Deremouth. It must have been those thoughts that prompted Julie to replace her two-piece costume and Sebastian to improvise with his new-style Y-fronts. Neither put into words why they covered their nakedness, that would somehow have cast a shadow on something too precious to spoil.

It was as they waded into the water, catching their breath in the sudden coldness, that they became aware someone was coming down the grassy slope from the house.

Trudie was disappointed. She'd hurried there expecting to find Julie alone.

Chapter Ten

They came out of the water just in time to rescue the towel, Sebastian's clothes and Julie's book from the incoming tide. Sebastian took the towel and wrapped it around his waist. It might shock Trudie's sense of decorum to see him wandering about in his soaking-wet underpants.

'Nice to see you, Trudie. You should have brought your swimsuit.' His smile gave no hint of how ill-timed her appearance had been. 'Forgive me if I go on in, I'd like to get this salt off me and be dressed when Lydia gets home.'

'I only looked in because I knew Quintin talked of taking the others to the carnival procession. I thought Julie might like some company.'

'And I'm sure she would. Do you want me to throw you another towel, Julie?'

'No, I like the sun to dry me. We'll stay out here on the lawn and talk.'

Trudie's disappointment had vanished. Watching Sebastian walk towards the house, she dropped to the parched grass and tapped the space next to her.

'He loves her an awful lot, doesn't he.' It wasn't a question. 'I remember when Lydia first met him, she seemed to sweep him off his feet. And as for her, when news got around that he was to be down here with the film crew, you'd think heaven had dropped into her lap. No wonder he noticed her. Could there ever have been a girl so starry-eyed?' Trudie stretched full length on the grass, content to speak her thoughts aloud in this easy friendship she enjoyed with Julie. 'When the accident happened I was frightened for her. In my profession I hear of plenty of divorce cases that come about because one of the partners goes bed-hopping. In his case, with Lydia like she is now, he'd be a pretty remarkable man if he suddenly became celibate. He never has been from what one hears from the Squire, always was a rake.'

'Rubbish, he's no such thing. He's here to see Lydia at every possible opportunity, you know he is. The Squire is warped, he can't bear Lydia to look at any man but him.'

'He never seems to worry that Quintin is always at her beck and call.'

'Didn't I just say he's warped? Of course he delights in her being with Quintin, he sees that as a smack in the eye for Sebastian. He knows Quin is the nearest she's known to a brother.' The sun was still as warm, yet for Julie the glory of the afternoon was dimmed.

But Trudie hadn't come here to discuss Lydia's affections. 'How's your friend in Wiltshire?'

'Bess? Settling in, I think. What with Merry and Anna being on holiday and the two children where she lives, too, I shan't be going up there for a while.' She tried to sound bright and matter-of-fact. Early next week Sebastian would be flying out to join the crew who were already building their set on location. Though set against the biblical background of the Middle East, the film was to be shot in southern Spain, such was the wonder of cinema. Next time she met him at their secret hide-out the summer would be over, the caravans closed up and battened down for winter.

Less than an hour ago her world had been filled with a joy almost too intense to bear. In body and in soul she had felt them to be at one with each other and at one with the beauty of the universe. Of course Lydia was to be protected, *her* friend, *his* wife, his poor little honey. Trudie talked of marriages ending in divorce, but they could never let that happen to Lydia. Julie shivered.

'You're getting cold. Perhaps you ought to go and get dressed.'

'No, its just what my aunt used to call a "goose walking over my grave".'

'So what do you think about Sunday? Shall we go? The children would enjoy it.' Trudie was waiting for an answer; Julie hated having to tell her she hadn't heard a word.

'I'm sorry, Trudie, I wasn't concentrating. I was thinking about Lydia, they've been gone more than two hours. I do hope it hasn't been too much for her.' To lie to Trudie made her feel mean, and to pretend it was concern for Lydia that had been on her mind told her just how low she'd sunk.

At that moment they heard the jeep on the gravel path.

'Seb's here! Look, Mum, that's Seb's car. Me out quickly, want to find Seb.' As the engine stopped, Merry's shriek of excitement could be heard from the bottom of the garden.

'I'd better dress. Don't run away, Trudie.' Julie wanted to escape from the reunion. Indoors she dressed quickly, but spent longer than usual on making up her face and brushing her hair. She tried to believe it was to put off hurrying out to join the party now assembled on the terrace where Sebastian was putting a tray of drinks on the table. But she knew that, tanned by the sun, compared with office-bound Trudie and chair-bound Lydia, she was a picture of health and vitality. She wanted him to notice and be proud.

It wasn't for Lydia's sake that Julie made her suggestion next morning.

'I thought this would be an ideal opportunity for me to go in to Exeter,' she said. 'You and Sebastian and Merry deserve a day on your own and there are quite a few things written on the "memory board" in the kitchen, things we can't get in Otterton. I'll take Anna, of course. Is that all right with you, Lydia?'

Purposely she didn't look at Sebastian. He must know why she was running away. This charade was getting progressively more difficult to make convincing. If she stayed at home today she knew what would happen: the children would want to go to the beach, she and Sebastian would take them. And it would be no use telling him that Lydia could come too if he carried her. Sebastian saw his poor honey as an invalid; his heart ached with pity for her, but he would not attempt to involve her in their outings. A silent voice told her that he had every bit as much strength as Quintin, what he lacked was imagination and courage. So today she was determined to stay out of their way, let Lydia have him to herself for these last few hours. For herself it was the coward's way out too, for how could she bear to watch him *en famille*?

A day in Exeter, meeting Trudie for lunch, helped to keep her mind occupied.

'You must get fed up sometimes, Julie, living such a restricted life. When did you last have a whole day in the city? You're not a country girl. Don't you ever yearn to have a deadline, to pit yourself against a task that stretches you? It makes your adrenaline flow faster. My work's a bit different, but I get that same feeling. See a case to a satisfactory conclusion and the reward is far greater than the fee. I feel it adds to my personal stature. Can you understand that? Working at Whiteways you never get the chance to test yourself against competitiion. Pack it in, Julie, you're worth so much more. Lydia's a dear but, don't kid yourself, she'd have no qualms if your positions were reversed. She and Pam are good friends. Merry's at school now, Lydia could easily get a girl from the village to keep an eye on him during the holidays. Anna's at school, that gives you freedom, and if you were working freelance you could organise something to cover the holiday periods for her. Even that would be a challenge, a hurdle to get over. You need more than the sort of drab existence you get at Whiteways.'

'Here endeth the first lesson,' Julie teased. 'Trudie, I know there's a lot of truth in what you say. But no, I'm not going to leave Lydia. All very fine for us to talk about challenges, but if any of us has a challenge then it's her. Doubt if it does much to make her adrenaline quicken its flow, though.'

Trudie sighed. 'No, I expect you're right. Lydia of all people, she was never still a second.'

Trudie had sown a seed in Julie's mind. How much easier it would be for Sebastian and her to make something of those meagre crumbs of time together if she had a place in London again, even took in work from some secretarial bureau. Then she looked at Anna and saw what a different life she had here from anything they'd been able to make in their attic bed-sitter. Finding housing was very little easier now than it had been two years ago. And in Julie was a stubborn streak: whatever home they had it would be the reward of her own labour, she wouldn't let Sebastian meet her bills.

'They make lovely pink ice cream here, Anna,' Trudie said encouragingly. 'Let's all three of us have one, shall we?'

'You and Mum too? Yes, let's all have one, Mum, shall we do that?'

Her eyes were likes saucers, probably bigger than her appetite. She hadn't understood what Aunt Trudie was talking about, but she'd felt uncomfortable. All three of them waiting expectantly for their ice cream put her mind at rest. She beamed at them both, showing two rows of small, even teeth; she swung her legs and hummed out of tune. All was well with Anna's world and she was having a splendid day out; it was like being a grown-up lady.

The next morning Sebastian left. Julie stood back as Lydia wheeled herself to his car to see him on his way.

'I'll be in touch.' He must have been talking to her, because it was her short gingery brown curls he kissed as he said it. Yet his gaze was on Julie. This was her farewell. And when he spoke again it was to her: 'Look after them for me, Lydia and Merry too. Promise me.'

'You know I already have.'

So that was the end. Work on a studio-based film, expected to run for perhaps an hour and a half, might have taken only two or three months. But this was an epic of gigantic proportions. Tonight he was due in Malvern for his final session of readings, then tomorrow returning to London in readiness for his flight to Spain. None of them knew when he'd be back.

That was on the Friday morning. It was very late Sunday evening, so late that there was no chance of anyone being up. When the shrill bell of the telephone rent the stillness it was Pam who answered it,. then came to bang on Julie's door.

Already sitting up in bed, filled with some unaccountable foreboding, Julie called for her to come in.

'It's for you.'

'At this time of night? Whoever is it?'

'Think it's your friend Bess. Started crying soon as she spoke, I couldn't take in what she was saying. Better come quickly.'

'But of course you must go.' Still in bed, waiting for the daily routine of Pam's ministrations that ended with a bath, massage and finally getting her dressed, made up and ready to face the world, Lydia's freckled face was full of concern. 'Pam said she sounded in a dreadful state. I thought she was recovered, I thought she'd settled in her job. Look, Julie, I've told you lots of times, we've masses of space. Bring her down here. Bother the job, she can get another when she's quite fit. Must be awful to get so low that she phones like that.'

Lydia's answer filled Julie with shame, but something stronger than herself made her colour her story. Nothing would stop her snatching these last few hours with Sebastian. 'I've told her I'll see if I can get away for a few hours,' she said. 'It's nothing to do with the operation. I've known her like this before. During the war, when the station was bombed she was buried under the rubble. Only the way a filing cabinet fell against the desk saved her life at all. It was a single-thickness brick-walled building, you know what those wartime buildings were like, it just collapsed. A pocket of air saved her life. Through it all she never lost consciousness but she was pretty badly hurt. Ever since then she gets these fits of terror. Of course she turned to me, she knew I'd understand. If she's as unhinged as she was last night I'd rather the children weren't there, it wouldn't be good for them. Pam has said she'd keep an eye on them for a while — I wondered if perhaps your mother would collect them?' She had to be free, she had to see him.

'I won't ask Mum, the Squire hasn't a lot of patience with the children.' They both knew she meant 'with Merry'. 'I'll phone Aunt Tess. If she's free she'll willingly have them. They like going to Rowans, there's lots to do. And if she can't have them, then

160

I'll get Quin to pick me up and them too. *He'll* find them something to keep them occupied. You just forget about them and get on your way.'

A quarter of an hour later, while the children were still spooning up their cornflakes, Julie set off. Her mind raced ahead of her. The roads were a little more crowded than they had been when she'd first learned to drive. Occasionally she glanced in her driving mirror, occasionally a motorcycle sped past her. Whether the car behind her was the same one as ten minutes ago she didn't consider; like the Standard 14 she drove it was a black saloon, but then so were most cars on the road. She knew the route so well she had no need to look at the signposts. Off the road and onto the lane, a quick glance in the mirror not expecting to see, and not seeing, anything behind her. As always, this was the moment when she felt she'd left the world behind. From then on she didn't even glance.

Since last she'd been there the schools had broken up; this was halfway through July. For a second as she turned into the field she felt cheated. This was *their* place, they'd seldom seen more than one or two caravans in use. Now the field had become a playground for children, doors of the caravans were open, washing was strung up to dry. A few had cars parked near them, but not many. Most people who rented a caravan took a train to the nearest railway station, a bus to the end of the long lane, then carried their suitcases for the last mile. Julie felt like a stranger; the bustle of activity bore no resemblance to the oasis of peace they'd made their own.

Then she saw his car already parked.

Trudie was about to leave the house when Lydia phoned her mother. That afternoon she had an appointment that must be kept; that morning she'd meant to work in the office. But she wouldn't. She knew exactly what she meant to do.

She drove towards Exeter, then reversed into a lane where she could see what traffic went by. This far there was no doubt which road Julie would take on her way to Westbury. From there it had been easy. What was there between Julie and this friend Bess that she would drop everything at the merest phone call? Trudie didn't know exactly why she was concerned; perhaps it was plain jealousy. Today Trudie meant to find out about Bess. At the final turning into the lane she hung back, giving Julie a chance to pull away. Among other traffic she might not be noticed, but here a following car would be conspicuous.

Wherever she'd expected the trail to lead, it certainly wasn't a

161

caravan site. But there could be no mistake, for beyond that point the narrow lane became no more than a farm track. She stopped the car about ten yards before she reached the open gate of the field and walked the rest of the way. Yes, there was Julie's car, just pulling to a standstill on the far side next to another, one that in any other circumstances Trudie would have instantly recognized. Now, though, she focused on the open caravan door. In a second Bess would come down the step and probably hurl her arms around her friend. With her fists clenched tight, Trudie waited.

Then she saw him.

Realising they'd have no eyes for her, she drew quite openly off the lane into the field, turned the car and set off back towards Exeter.

'How was she?' Lydia asked when Julie reached home, having collected the children from Rowans on the way.

'I needn't have got in such a panic about her. By this morning she was herself again. I was going to say she was ashamed of having made such a scene on the phone, but I'm not sure how much of it she even remembered.' The longer the make-believe went on, the easier it was becoming. The fabrication offered her shelter from reality. 'They're nice people she's with, I don't think I need worry about her too much. There's Mr Meredith — Donald, Bess calls him, she's really been taken into the family — then Susan, who's fifteen, and Desmond, thirteen.'

'If they're so wonderful, why was she in such a hysterical state last night? Perhaps they aren't always as nice to her as they'd like you to believe.' Lydia's life had become unbearably dull, she needed to give it a dash of extra colour.

Julie's answer did just that. 'I'm sure it's not that. Poor Mr Meredith must have been out of his depth. I'm glad I went today, it gave me a chance to talk to him and help him understand.' The picture she created took on a new vividness; it was easier to dwell on the fiction than the fact, the certainty that Sebastian would be gone from her life for many months. 'He told me that there had been a storm, sudden thunder. That's what seemed to unsettle her. Of course he didn't know anything about what had happened to her during the bombing. No wonder it left her mind scarred; it's hard to imagine how terrifying it must have been, not knowing if they'd ever get to her. Her nerves were in shreds. Afterwards she had a breakdown and was discharged from the service.'

Lydia wanted the story to go on. What a relief to be talked to about something outside her own narrow existence!

162

'Last night when they could hear the storm getting closer, the noise must have triggered off her old fears. And she'd been so much better recently too. I half guessed at the truth when I found everything so normal this morning. She wasn't just hysterical, Lydia, she was drunk.' Julie added another colourful strand to the story she wove. 'I could hear it in her voice. It's her refuge, she can't face the devils that get at her.'

Listening to the story she told, Julie felt she stood outside herself. Clearly Lydia was intrigued by Bess's sad tale; her eyes were full of sympathy. If only Julie could have told her the truth, swept away the lies and deceit.

The yarn she weaved helped her over the next few hours. By now he'd be on his way to the airport. Somehow the coming months had to be lived through. She knew she would have no letters from him, any news could only come second-hand. It wasn't fair on her, or on him either. He'd never talked to Lydia of his ambitions for the Sutcliffe Theatre; he'd never told *her* about the caravan where he escaped the world; *they'd* never sat with rain beating on the metal roof while they laughed uproariously over a game of Lexicon; *they'd* never cooked a feast of sausages together on that temperamental little stove; *they'd* never discussed the tragedy of the thousands of displaced persons who, four years after the end of the war in Europe, were still trying to build their lives out of the wreckage, nor yet the hopes of the welfare state that was reshaping Britain. Lydia was his little honey, to be loved, cosseted and protected.

She was glad to escape early to her room, put all the lies and deceits out of her mind and think only of him. They shared so much; they could talk for hours and still have more to say; they played at the water's edge with gusto as great as the children's ('Ah,' came a silent reminder, 'but is that cause for pride or for gratitude? What about Lydia sitting watching? Remember the way she used to romp with Merry?'); and surely when they made love they touched the heavens. And Lydia? Had it been like that for her too? Forget her, think just of him. He loves you, you know he does. And you love him. But none of that counts for anything compared with Lydia. He'll never let anything hurt Lydia.

'What's the matter with my Poppet? Aren't you pleased to see your old Squire?'

She wasn't. This morning she wouldn't have bothered to raise a welcoming smile for the angel Gabriel himself.

'What do you expect me to do' — she pouted — 'throw my hat in the air with excitement? I see you most mornings.'

'Are you saying your mother's right, that I come too often? Is that it? She says I've no business to inflict – '

'Oh, stop it, Squire.' She reached both hands towards him. 'Of course I want you to come, of course I'm always glad when you're here. I'm just in a foul mood. I'm sorry.'

'You've every right to be in a foul mood, child. Tell me what I can do to make you feel better. What about pushing you out for half an hour, eh?'

'No!' she snapped. Then, seeing his crestfallen expression, 'No, let's just stay here. It's grey and horrid, I expect that's why I've got the miseries. Summer's well and truly over. Aunt Grace's witches will soon be spitting on the blackberries – and it's not even nice enough to tempt anyone to get the last of them in. Not that *I'd* be any help.'

'Anyway it's nice and quiet with the children out of the way at school. Where's Julie? Gone off to see this friend you told me about? I see her car's not there.'

'No, she took the children to school, then went on to Exeter for a few things.'

'Wonder you keep her, she's not much of a companion if you ask me.'

'I didn't ask y – oh, sorry, Squire, there I go again. How's Mum? I haven't seen her lately, is she busy?'

'Got that hatchet-faced Evelyn Keeble coming for the weekend. Expect she told you, the venerable Miss Keeble is assistant head at Trewarin Abbey – very "jolly hockey sticks", you may be sure. Remember how we used to make our escape when she visited, Poppet? Reckon I'll be asking for a place at your table for my Sunday dinner.'

'She's Mum's friend, you just behave yourself and put on the charm for her. You can when you like.' Then, with a giggle that made conspirators of them, 'You don't often like, that's your downfall. Come to dinner by all means but, if you do, make sure you bring the others with you.'

'Not bloody likely! If I can't take refuge here I'll go off with my paints. Not that they'd want to come anyway, talk about a pair of bluestockings! Politics, bloody trade unions, the economic state of the country – anything that has more than one point of view they thrive on. Useless bloody lot of nonsense, pontificating as if the way they think'll make a jot of difference. Leave it to those who under-stand, that's what I say. I tell you, Poppet, I'm just in their way, I can feel it. That's why I thought I might come here. Like it used to be when we'd slip off out of their way, eh?' He looked at her

164

thoughtfully, his hand rubbing his clipped beard as he did when he was agitated. He'd come to Whiteways to be cheered up, but it was as if Lydia's mind was somewhere else. 'I suppose you're worried because you don't hear from the saintly Sebastian?'

'Don't hear? Of course I do, so does Merry.' And timed to perfection there came a ring at the doorbell. A minute later Pam brought in a bouquet of expensive hothouse flowers.

'That van from the florist will soon know its own way from Deremouth,' she said laughing. 'Every week, regular as clockwork. Shall I bring you the vase and put it on the little table for you?'

'No, I won't bother. You do them, will you, Pam?'

'Sends regularly, does he?' the Squire probed.

Lydia shrugged. 'He always has, usually phoned the shop when he was in London. Now they come just the same.'

'Plenty of money and there's nothing you can't do. He must have left a standing order when he went away.'

Again Lydia shrugged. 'He could hardly telephone from location in Spain. Not that I'd expect you to give him credit for thoughtfulness.'

'Seems I can't do much right for anyone today. Your mother's got a tongue like a viper, I thought at least I'd get a welcome from you. If it's not the devoted Sebastian's fault, then it must be this bloody chair. And I don't blame you. How you stand it I don't know. I tell you, Poppet, it's never out of my mind. It's a cruel injustice, it's — '

'Oh, stop it, for heaven's sake. Just leave me alone. I don't need you telling me what it's like to be a useless hulk. Shut up about it.'

The Squire unfolded a clean handkerchief and made a great show of sniffing into it, then mopping his face.

'I'm sorry, I never learn. It's just that I can't bear to see you unhappy. Shall I go? Is that what you want?'

'I'm sorry too.' Just as she had before, she reached out to take his hands. 'Let's say "pax" and start again, shall we.'

He settled himself more comfortably. This looked more promising.

'Have you been to Rowans lately, Squire? Quin has been so busy getting the trial ground prepared I've not see him for a day or two. Perhaps he'll ring me presently and tell me if he's going to be in the glasshouses this afternoon. I don't want to drive over and find he isn't there. It's only Quin who'll carry me through to my "place of work". He's promised me that when I can't get there he sees someone else looks after my things, but I do miss going.'

'Full of big ideas is Quintin. I did catch a glimpse of him as I drove by his new ground yesterday. That young girl from Deans Farm is starting to work for him, I hear. He was pointing out the lie of the land to her. About time that young man found himself a bird, if you ask me.'

She hadn't asked him, but this time she refrained from saying so.

After he'd gone the conversation echoed and re-echoed. She suspected the Squire's sentiments were much the same as Peter and Tess Grant's. But what did they know about Quin? None of them knew him the way *she* did. She tried to remember what she could of Olive Sharp from Deans Farm. She was about Lydia's age, and had never left the local gymkhanas without a rosette or two; as for boyfriends, Lydia had no idea; her war work had been on her father's farm. Plump, healthy-looking, jolly, an outdoor girl, that was all Lydia really knew about her. When they'd been young their interests had been different. Olive Sharp preferred mucking out the stables to queuing for the pictures; *she* would never have stuck pictures of Sebastian Sutcliffe in a scrapbook.

'There, I've done my best.' Pam came in proudly bearing her handiwork. 'Haven't your knack, Lydia, but they're such gorgeous blooms that even I couldn't make too much of a disaster of them. Where shall I put them?'

'Just stick them down anywhere.' Lydia really didn't care, these routine offerings had ceased to interest her ages ago. But seeing Pam's pride she added, 'You've done them beautifully, Pam. I'll let you have the job permanently if you like.'

'I wonder how much Julie will remember to get. Mrs Briggs says she went without the list from the memory board.'

Each morning Mrs Briggs cycled out to Whiteways from Otterton St Giles. Rain or shine, they could set their clock by her arrival at half past eight. In the village she spoke of herself as 'the housekeeper', and it was she who saw they were all fed and watered, the windows sparkling, the floors and drains kept clean. Mrs Briggs took pride in all she did; her cheerful motto was: 'No job above me, no job beneath me.' Her standards were high and she expected everyone to be as conscientious as she was herself. This morning she'd written a shopping list and put it on the table for Julie; this evening when her husband took her for her nightly stout in the Pig and Whistle her friends would be told how the 'silly girl went off without m'list, head stuffed with some nonsense or other, you know what the young ones are these days. Although, fair to say, she's usually reliable.'

But for Julie nothing was usual any more. She'd promised

Sebastian she'd take care of Merry, she'd given her word that she'd stay with Lydia. He'd been gone nearly two months, and she still had no idea when he'd be back. Her mind flitted from him to Lydia, to Merry, to a future that was frightening in its uncertainty, to that attic bed-sitter in Finchley, to her reason for resurrecting Bess, whom she was supposed to be meeting today in Exeter. She drove automatically; it wasn't until the driver of an oncoming lorry hooted furiously that she realised she'd drifted to the middle of the road. As he passed he shouted just what he thought of women drivers. Pulling herself together, she concentrated. Ahead of her she could see the city, the great cathedral standing sentinel, a symbol of survival. Think of *that*, look hard at it, think of the centuries it has endured, the people who've come and gone. How many generations have been dwarfed by its magnificence? When she was old it would be unchanged, when she was dead it would still stand guard as people around it strived for earthly happiness ... Julie shivered.

There was always plenty of room to park at the kerbside. She left the car on the southern side of the city. Having nearly an hour before the time of her appointment, she'd boost her confidence with a cup of coffee and a cigarette. Ten minutes later she was sitting in a small café when her attention was taken by an empty building opposite, an agent's sign in the window proclaiming it a 'Vacant Business Premise − Leasehold'. It nudged at an old dream.

Julie crushed out her second cigarette with a hand that was less than steady, took a last sip of cold coffee and went to the ladies' room. A little extra lipstick, a touch of powder and a dab of perfume helped her to clutch at her flagging confidence. Then, with a last glance at her reflection she was ready, 'Please, please,' she whispered. Would that benign deity help her? Could she expect Him to? She'd lied, she'd deceived, she'd taken what wasn't hers (oh, but that wasn't true, he loved Lydia as much now as he had before), what sort of a deity was it who would listen to her cries for help?

Five minutes to eleven. She'd killed so much time that now she was late. Half running and half walking she took a short cut across the grass in front of the cathedral, then turned left down the road beyond.

'Mrs Howard. Come in and take a seat.'

It was reassuring to Julie that the doctor could accept her name so trustingly. Under the new National Health scheme she could have visited the doctor she'd registered with in Deremouth. Instead she'd picked a physician from the telephone directory, and to be doubly sure of not being identified she'd used her maiden name.

167

'I understand you aren't one of my patients — a visitor, I believe? If you care to give my receptionist details of your own doctor, arrangements can be made that my treatment is covered by the Health Service.'

'I'll speak to her on my way out. I come from London.'

'Now, what seems to be your trouble?'

'I feel perfectly well, none of the normal symptoms. But I've missed two periods. I thought perhaps there might be some other reason. I don't see that I can be pregnant.'

She felt like an ostrich burying her head in the sand. Sebastian had always been so careful. Ah, not just for your sake, a voice whispered, but for Lydia's.

The doctor made a note, the scratch of his nib the only sound.

'If you'd like to go behind the screen and get undressed, I'll examine you. You say you're feeling well?'

'Yes, perfectly. I have a daughter, you see, so I know what to expect.'

'Pregnancies can vary. But I'll check you over, make sure that's all it is.'

Julie undressed except for her slip and lay down on the hard couch. Just as she did when she talked about Bess, she felt she was acting a part. Even the name wasn't her own. This morning she tried to believe she had a husband and a home somewhere in London, the illusion helping to hold her away from a truth she might have to face.

'Dr Pym' — the words tumbled out as the elderly doctor pushed her straps from her shoulders and examined her breasts — 'you see, my husband was wounded, I have to care for him. I have a young daughter already. I don't see how I could manage if I'm to have another.' She heard her voice as a cry for help.

He heard it too. He listened to her heart, he took her blood pressure, he pummelled her stomach.

'Far better to tell you it's another child than that there is something more alarming wrong with you. Nature will help you, my dear. Your husband is a war casualty? Dear, dear, dear.' He shook his balding head as if man's folly was beyond his understanding.

'I have to do everything for him. Don't you see, I *can't* have another child.'

'There is no doubt. I would recommend that you book into a nursing home as soon as possible. Never have there been so many babies as there are these days; leave it beyond three months or so and you'll get in nowhere.'

She wasn't listening. She lay quite still, her eyes closed. In her heart of course she'd known, only her conscious mind hadn't let her accept, because before she could come to the joy of acceptance she had to face what this must mean to Lydia. Lydia, who was even at this moment still sitting in that chair she so hated, watching life going on all around her and having no part in it. Whatever we do, we must never hurt Lydia. That had been the rule; as long as they'd kept to it they'd earned the right to love. But how could they not hurt her now?

'Dr Pym, can't you help me? Isn't there *something* I could take, someone I could go to? Not just for my sake, but for my husband's too.' Lies! Lies! But what other way could there be? 'How will he feel when he realises I've been with another man? And is it such a crime? I tell you, I'm more like a nurse than a wife. Please help me.' With her eyes still closed she talked, it was easier to cut herself off. Only now did she open them, not knowing what she expected by way of response.

The doctor's face showed no expression.

'You may get your clothes on, Mrs Howard. The war was responsible for a great deal of unhappiness. As for what you ask, you know it's impossible. I prefer to forget you said it. I'm in the business of helping the sick, but one thing I've found through my long years of dealing with people: honesty isn't always easy, but it's the surest rock to build on. Talk to your husband. You've faced problems together before and with truth, trust and understanding I hope you will again.'

He finished speaking as she came out from behind the screen.

'I shouldn't have asked you.' The unexpected kindness in his smile and his talk of honesty made her suddenly ready to face whatever life hurled at her. 'You see, the truth is I'm glad about the baby. I know I oughtn't to be. I've no right.' Her mind was clear now. Glad! As if the word could even begin to express the great surge of joy that filled her. She was carrying his child, his and hers. Until this moment she'd shied from looking that far into the future, but now she imagined a baby − boy? Girl? With his features? With her colouring? A new person, part of each of them, someone both of them would love. Then back came the image of Lydia, a kaleidoscope of pictures crowding her mind: Lydia driving towards Devon, so sure of the future, childishly proud that she was Sebastian Sutcliffe's wife; today's Lydia turning her head away so that no one would guess how hard her battle; the look of pathetic hope when Sebastian was expected; Lydia, her friend, with a generosity of spirit that never varied.

These days so much of Julie's life was a web of deceit, it came

169

easily to tell the receptionist that her own doctor was in London and she wanted to settle straight away for this visit to Dr Pym.

She'd gone to his surgery unable to see through the fog into the future; she came away with a new inner calm. To tell Lydia the truth would be impossible; she had no choice but to leave Whiteways. Later, she would be dragged down into a mire of shame and wretchedness. But walking back across the grass in the shadow of the great cathedral she felt one with the rhythm of time. She and Sebastian were to share the parenthood of a child, a living symbol of their unity.

When, the previous day, Trudie had heard Grace talking to Tess about Julie's friend Bess she'd pretended to concentrate on the newspaper but in fact she'd listened. What possible reason could Julie have for inventing a meeting with the imaginary Bess? With Sebastian gone it made no sense. If only she could ask, tell her that she knew there was no such person. But she was frightened of Julie's reaction. Instead she waited, always ready to listen, hoping to be confided in. After Grace had left she phoned Julie and suggested they might all three meet for lunch. Now, surely Julie would tell her.

'All on your own? Has Bess Gone?' She now greeted Julie, innocently.

'Bess? Oh, yes. Trudie, I want to talk to you.'

Trudie smiled. At last Julie was going to tell her about those meetings with Sebastian. For weeks she'd been waiting for this moment. The day when she'd seen them together at that dreadful caravan field her reaction had been hurt that Julie could have lied to her. Her initial relief that Bess had no reality and was no rival had soon been overtaken by desolation that Julie hadn't felt she could trust her with the truth. For a few minutes she had pulled off the road wanting to let her thoughts centre just on their friendship. To her it mattered so much; had it never meant the same to Julie? Even today, from this distance, she shied from the memory of her empty despair. But it hadn't lasted: another angle had nudged at her with new hope. Bess had been a threat. That was something Sebastian never could be. Julie might fancy herself in love with him — and if she did, she was only one of many if one could believe the stories — but Lydia was his real love.

Now leaning towards Julie, her smile encouraged the confidence she was sure would follow.

Instead, Julie said, 'It's about something you've often suggested to me. Now that Merry's settled well at school, I'm hardly needed

170

as a nursemaid; Lydia depends on Pam, not on me. It's time Anna and I moved on.'

'Not back to London? Please, Julie, don't run away back to London.'

'Run away! Who said anything about running away?' Immediately Julie was on the defensive. 'Trudie, I may not have your professional qualification, but I'm not stupid and I mean to use the only talent I have. I've stood on my own feet before and so I can again.' She'd make a home and when Sebastian came back there would be a place where they could be together.

'You can't take Anna to the sort of life you had in London. She was just a baby in those days, she needs a proper home now.'

Julie crumbled her bread roll. Silently she vowed she would not let herself be beaten, she would not fail. If it were just herself, she'd manage somehow. But there was Anna, and later on there would be another. Trudie was right, Anna couldn't be taken back to London to hunt for a room to live in.

'I've told you for ages that this is the decision you should make. You have to think of yourself, Julie, yourself and Anna. What's made you suddenly decide?'

Perhaps now the confidence would come. If only Julie would tell her, trust her with her secret, then she'd be able to show understanding. After all, the same thing happened to her when Jo had 'used' her and then gone back to his wife. She'd show that she understood, they'd find their way forward together.

Yet still Julie hid behind the barrier of lies.

'I've been coming to the decision for weeks. Perhaps it was seeing Bess this morning, so wrapped up in a family that's not her own.' She'd built such a tale around Bess, she could almost believe in her; she drew confidence from the thought of the fictitious friend who looked to her for support. 'We had coffee at the Tudor Tea Room and right opposite there's an empty property. The lease is for sale, I'm sure I haven't enough money for it, but it was seeing it that finally made up my mind for me. I'm going to start looking. Trudie, I'm telling you all this in confidence. Promise me, swear to me, you won't tell a soul. I don't want Lydia to hear about it until I know exactly what I'm doing. London is where I belong, that's where I ought to be. But London will be even more expensive, and I can't possibly take Anna away from Whiteways without finding a home for her first.'

'Of course I promise you, swear to you, of course I won't tell anyone what you plan. And you're right to do it.' For a moment Trudie hesitated, uncertain of whether she was going too far. But it had to be said, 'There's no future for you going on the way you have been. He's married to Lydia and, even if he's the roué the Squire believes, he'll never forsake her, not as she is now.'

Trudie knew! But how could she? And if she'd guessed, what about Lydia? Was that why she'd been in such a black mood recently? Even when she was cheerful it seemed forced, her old merry twinkle was gone. Was that what she and Sebastian had done to her?

'I don't know what you're talking about,' she said, defying Trudie.

'Yes, you do, Julie. Why can't you trust me? How do I know? I know because I understand you and I care about you.' Trudie didn't see it as a lie, just as an exaggeration of the truth.

Julie's fingers had been nervously tearing at her bread roll; hardly aware of what she was doing she'd pummelled it, squeezed and shaped it into pellets as if she'd been preparing them for a fish hook.

'He's always said he'll never leave her, and if he did it would give us both so much guilt that everything would be spoilt. Of course he loves her. So do I. So do you, Trudie. She's just that sort of person. But you're wrong if you think all I am to him is a woman to go to bed with. I promised him I'd never leave her. Now I'm breaking my word. Oh, Trudie' − her voice was hardly audible − 'don't know what to do.'

'Then I'll tell you.' Trudie's tone was matter-of-fact, yet warm. 'Eat your lunch, that's the first thing to do. Nothing looks so bleak on a full stomach.'

Julie laughed at the unexpected change of mood. Nothing was ever so bad that it couldn't be faced. Again memory jumped backwards: the evening of the day the telegram had come from the War Office, her misery a physical thing, making her nauseous and aching in every joint; as if it transmitted itself to Anna, she'd screamed, her face red, her knees drawn up. Julie hadn't been able to stop her screaming. She remembered all that, but most of all she felt again the panic. She was alone, she had to be well, she had to be strong; for Anna there was no one else. Well, she'd been strong, she'd overcome those early difficulties. And she would overcome this one too.

'Stay in Devon, Julie. In London rents will be higher, property harder to find. I do know a lot of people in the business world around here. Lady solicitors are few and far between.' She laughed, but Julie didn't miss the ring of pride and envied her for it. 'I'm something of a novelty. I'll use my womanly wiles and see what there is in the offing, shall I?'

Already Julie's spirits were reviving. There would be hurdles, any goal worth striving for set hurdles that had to be overcome. The thought both terrified and excited her. 'The Lord helps those who helps themselves.' She wouldn't be found wanting. And when Sebastian came home he'd know she'd had no choice, it would have been impossible for her to stay at Whiteways.

Her first and worst hurdle would be telling Lydia she was leaving her. She dreaded it. She felt sick with shame. Easier to look beyond that, to let herself feel the stirring of excitement in imagining her own business, herself actually doing the things she had half dreamed, putting up a painted sign − or even a brass plate − bearing the words 'Freeman's Secretarial Agency'. Not yet could she bring herself to picture the day Sebastian heard from Lydia that she'd broken her promise to him and gone. It was surprisingly easy to push that to the back of her mind, confident in the knowledge that when he knew everything he would understand.

Exeter wasn't much more than twenty miles from Otterton St Giles. Reason told her she ought to move far away, make a home for herself and Anna where no gossip could be carried back to Lydia . . . to Sebastian. No wonder she wouldn't listen to the silent voice of reason. Time enough to invent some imaginary lover when she had to, for the present it was enough to know that word would reach him. She thought of all the years he'd had his caravan retreat, unsuspected by anyone. So, somewhere, they would find a place where they could be together.

173

Chapter Eleven

Trudie took the arrangements into her own hands, negotiating a short lease of only two years on the empty property Julie had seen. It was settled remarkably quickly, a sure proof that she wasn't without influence.

'And I can move in by the middle of the month? Oh, Trudie, you don't know ... I can't tell you ...'

'Then I'll tell you something. Julie, nothing has meant as much to me as us doing this together. I've used every bit of my knowledge and all my girlish charms too, not just for you but for me as well. Because it means so much to me that you'll be here.'

'I'm grateful,' Julie told her. So she was, the gratitude weighing against her natural instinct to withhold something of herself. 'Trudie, you haven't told anyone, have you? Not your parents, especially not Quintin?'

'Of course I haven't. Until you're ready to speak to Lydia, it's our secret. Julie, it's going to be so good. You'll forget all the things that have made you miserable, you'll learn what real friendship can be. Honestly, don't forget I do know how you must have been suffering, that dreadful let-down feeling. I told you about Jo.'

Jo! Julie felt the all too familiar threat of nausea. Jo! What had Jo to do with what she and Sebastian shared? One day she'd have to face the next hurdle, but not yet. One step at a time, and the next step was to tell Lydia she and Anna were leaving her. She had hated living a lie over these weeks but until everything was settled she had had no alternative. If only she could explain to Lydia why she must go away, yet not mention Sebastian. Her fertile imagination had got to work on some unnamed man. But no, she couldn't do that. Lydia would want to be involved, to support her, to thrive on a new element in life, even at second-hand. There was no way but to slip right out of her life and make

174

a new start, let everyone believe she was tired of a job that had no future.

She expected Lydia to try to persuade her to change her mind. Had she put herself in the position of the bored and frustrated occupant of a wheelchair snatching at any chance to add drama to her days, she might have been more prepared for Lydia's reaction.

'You say you're fed up! Well, I don't blame you. I'm fed up too! Fed up with everyone pandering to me, fed up with sitting like a fat slug.' If it weren't so pathetic the description would have been funny. 'I'm glad you've got the guts to tell me you've had enough. More than Seb has! See those damned flowers − Tuesday morning, day for flowers.'

'That's a wicked thing to say. Of course he hasn't had enough, he'd never want to leave you.'

'Might as well for all the difference it would make.' She needed to make a scene, she was excited by her own shrill voice. Day after day she lived as the recipient of kindness and consideration, now here was someone to vent her pent-up anger on. 'Treats me like a child, or a maiden aunt he owes loyalty to. Loyalty! Well, I don't want that sort of loyalty, handed out like charity to the poor. Not his and not yours. Go and make this fine career for yourself.'

'Lydia, that was a rotten thing to say about Sebastian. Self-pity doesn't suit you.' Julie wanted to halt Lydia's tirade before she reached the point of no return.

'Bollocks!' The expletive filled the room, a word quite out of character. Lydia heard it, pleased with the shock waves it generated, exhilarated by the fast beating of her heart.

'Lydia, you engaged me to look after Merry. He was a baby then. Now that he's at school you don't need me −!' How weak it sounded! No mention of good times and bad they'd shared.

'Of course I don't need you, I don't need anyone fawning round me. I wonder you've put up with being here for so long. You with your fine ambition. There's a whole big world out there waiting for Julie Freeman to conquer it. Bet you didn't even mean it when you promised Seb you'd stay. Nice as pie you told him you'd "stay with Lydia", "stay with Merry". I don't care, I don't give a damn where you go. Doesn't matter to you about Merry. He's too little to understand about careers, work satisfaction, all that other squit you want to fill your life with. Suppose he's not important −'

'Lydia, don't −'

'Don't what? Don't say I can manage without you? Clear off soon as you like − just see if I care!' Lydia's gingery eyes flashed fire. She ran her fingers through her sandy curls. She was caught in the torrent, she couldn't stop her flow of words, she wanted to wound as she'd been wounded. Not yet could she look ahead to the days when there would be no Julie, when Merry would be without Anna. The moment was enough and into that moment she put all the frustration and anger that had lain dormant in her. 'Go off and find your brave new world, see if I care.' It was as if a cork had blown.

Julie knew the outburst was bravado, she could see beyond it to the hurt and puzzlement.

'Lydia, I hate it being like this. We've always been friends.'

'Friends?' Lydia reached to pick up the newspaper that she had let slip from her lap. It was a mistake, she couldn't reach it. Julie passed it to her, the action a bigger reminder than any words. Normally Lydia could have said, 'Thanks'; now she couldn't. 'Don't want it!' She glared defiantly. 'That's why I chucked it down. You'd better tell Mrs Briggs when you're leaving, she'll need extra help. She might know of someone from the village to take your place.' Her only salve came from having the power to slight their friendship.

Julie had never felt more compassion towards her than she did at that remark. Lydia was born to be happy, to love and be loved. What was it Trudie had said in describing the satisfaction she found in her work, something about it making her adrenaline flow faster? No doubt that was what these minutes had done for Lydia. But later there would come a time of reckoning; from the exhilaration of the heights she would be cast into black despair. And who was there to share it with her? No one. It was that knowledge that hurt Julie, not the cutting words.

'Take care of Merry,' Sebastian had told her, sure in the knowledge that the little boy's days would be filled with happiness, with no more than the occasional 'When's Seb coming again?' to show that his Utopia wasn't quite complete. That was how it had been in those first weeks after Sebastian left for Spain. Then the first inkling of change put him on his guard. There was something different about his mother. For a long time she hadn't laughed the way she used to but lately she looked really cross. Then there was Julie, she was different; she'd talk to him and to Anna yet he was sure she was thinking about something else. He was worried. He wished Seb would come home. Everything was always happy when he was there.

He and Anna weren't finally told about the move until a few days before it hapoened. They knew they were being pushed into something they didn't want, that they would be living in separate houses and they wouldn't be together; but neither of them had the

176

experience of loneliness to imagine what life would be like without the other.

It was almost the end of October, ten weeks after Sebastian had gone away, their lives changed. Someone from the village called Marie Dale used the Standard 14 now; she cycled from the village with Mrs Briggs in time to take Merry to Deremouth to school and she never failed to be waiting outside when it was time to come home. A pleasant young woman, she'd learned to drive in the ATS. It wasn't in Merry's nature to be churlish but he couldn't help resenting her. In his child's mind he blamed her for Julie's absence. He looked dolefully at Marie, his gruff voice answering her overtures of friendship; he took an unkind delight in watching how the dark clump of hair that grew out of a mole on her upper lip moved as she talked. Marie was no beauty; her eyebrows met over the bridge of her nose, her complexion was greasy and her enlarged pores given to blackheads. That was another of his games, 'hunt the black dots'. He drew a certain comfort from her imperfections. But had she possessed all the charm of Aphrodite, he would still have found faults.

When Julie and Anna had left Whiteways, driven to Exeter by Trudie, Merry had been cantankerous and grizzly all day but cheered himself up with the thought that he'd see Anna again the next day at school. But of course he didn't. Day followed day, he was taken to school, brought home, given his tea, left to his own devices.

'Shall we play a game, Mum? Charades or something. You against me.'

'It takes more than two people, Merry. Anyway, games aren't fun with just us.'

He pouted, glaring at her as if all his misery was laid at her doorstep. 'Nothing's fun with only us. I wish Seb would come home. Don't know why Anna and Julie had to go away. Why did they, Mum?'

'I suppose because Julie thought the same as you do that things aren't much fun here.'

'Was fun before Anna went.' He was determined to fight down the threat of tears, but they were so near the surface he couldn't swallow them. Well, he wouldn't let her see how miserable he was, he'd give himself a proper hurt to cry for. With his back to Lydia he picked up the poker and started to stir the fire; a burning coal fell out and he took the tongs. He'd burn himself, then she'd be sorry she didn't care about him.

'Merry! Drop those tongs. Stupid idiot! Come away from the fire.' With surprising speed she wheeled herself towards him and yanked him back from the grate. 'You know you're not to touch the fire!'

177

It wasn't the excuse he was looking for but he was crying anyway. He saw no further than his own unhappiness and, probably, she saw no further than hers.

'My back hurts,' she said, like him looking for a peg to hang her misery on. 'Stop grizzling and go and tell Pam I need her. Oh, Merry, surely there's *something* you can find to do? What about a puzzle, or haven't you any colouring? You used to paint for hours.'

'That was Anna and me both doing it. What did you have to go and send them away for?'

'Just go and get Pam.' Then, as an afterthought, 'There's a good chap.' She tried to instil warmth into those last words, but her tone was forced, and both of them knew it. They couldn't help each other.

He went off in search of Pam, then to the empty playroom.

Already Lydia's thoughts had moved to the real reason for her wretchedness. No wonder she needed aching shoulders to blame for her mood. That afternoon she had driven Ruby to the nursery. Quin had been watching out for her, and her spirit had risen when he opened the door and bent to lift her out. Wheeling her way through the greenhouses she'd even forgotten about Julie and the changed atmosphere at Whiteways.

'I'll come back in an hour or so,' he'd told her, his words casting her back into the gloom. 'We're working outside. I'm lucky to have taken Olive on. Her experience has been on the farm, but she's very keen to learn − and a real worker. I'm thinking of suggesting I send her on a course, twelve months' horticultural work, coming back to the nursery here in the breaks between term. She's quick to learn, she's going to be invaluable.'

Lydia forced her face into a smile. 'That's good, Quin. That sounds as though you anticipate her staying permanently?'

'I don't see her as the rolling-stone type; anyway, I hope not. Gardening is a long-term project and, of course, seeing the development of the trial grounds from the very start must give her an extra interest. Are you all right, Lydia? Got everything you'll need? I'll put the bell here close to hand, give it a clang if you want anything, one of the chaps will hear you. I'll be back presently.'

She'd needed all her flagging willpower to concentrate on her plants. She'd nurtured them from seeds, now they were growing sturdy and strong; before long the first buds would be formed, then the flowers ready for the Christmas sales. Christmas − no, she wouldn't think of it, just a day like any other, followed by New Year and then the whole round over again.

*

Trudie had arranged the lease, she'd 'happened to know' where to lay her hands on excellent, almost new equipment and, although Julie didn't know it, she canvassed her associates for work to be entrusted to Freeman's Secretarial Agency in its first days.

A regular advertisement in the local papers was an outlay Julie had to be prepared to meet. She was in competition with the Labour Exchange, she wanted businesses to come to her for staff, she wanted women with secretarial skills to register with her. Because she dealt with no other type of employee, and because in-house work was undertaken − in truth it was much the same as the typing she'd done in that bed-sitter in Finchley, but how different to know that she was the captain at the bridge of her own ship − the professional world soon felt it could deal confidently with Freeman's.

The ground floor was given over to business use, a front office with two desks. These had been procured by Trudie, as had the two silent typewriters and the duplicating machine which was housed in the small back room. The purchase of all these items had been arranged by Trudie at a price less reasonable than Julie had been told, but that was Trudie's secret. A visit to the local saleroom had been the basis for the upstairs furnishings, although Tess had found some surplus oddments − 'Tell her they're just to give it a homely touch until she wants to throw them out and choose things for herself,' she'd told Trudie as she loaded the car − a bookshelf, two vases, various pairs of discarded curtains, cushions and one or two useless ornaments. Even Anna forgot how miserable she was not to be at Whiteways as she helped turn the upstairs rooms into their new home.

'Isn't this fun?' Trudie said it so often that neither Julie nor Anna answered. 'Let me get up the steps, Julie, you take the weight of the curtain while I hang it.'

'And me!' Anna wasn't going to be left out. 'I'll hold it up with Mum.'

'No, you hold it up with Trudie. I'm taller and the rail is high, I'll climb up. Anyway, I want to be the one to hang them; hanging curtains is like unveiling a plaque. I hereby declare this home is ours, that sort of thing.'

'OK. Here's the top, the hooks are all in. "This home is ours," you say. I wish that were true for all of us, Julie, I wish it were mine too. I work in Exeter, drive back and forth each day. There's an empty room here. We could make it such a happy place, three girls together.'

Julie kept her back to her friend. She felt as if the doors of a cage were closing on her. Her fingers fumbled with the hooks; it

179

was hard to focus when the ceiling wouldn't keep still. She mustn't stop now, she mustn't let Trudie see anything was wrong. All her concentration was on that next hook, the others hadn't been this much trouble. Get beyond that and she'd be over the hurdle.

The first she knew that Trudie had dragged a chair near and climbed up was when she felt the gentle touch of her supporting arm.

'Are you all right?'

'Just a crick in my neck. Be OK if I hold my head down for a second.'

Until that moment Trudie's touch had been so light it was no more than a support held in readiness. Something in Julie's tone alerted her. Both of them knew it. Her hand pressed gently against Julie's side, moved to her stomach. Over these last weeks, how was it she'd had no suspicion?

'Let me move in, we're friends, friends should share.'

Julie knew it was more than the home she was talking about. Leaning against the half-hung curtain, she submitted.

'Just these last few hooks and I've finished. Then it's bedtime for you, Anna, my love.'

Trudie could see her dreams coming to fruition.

Soon, Julie and Trudie were sitting on the edge of Anna's bath. All three of them felt the atmosphere of harmony in the steamy room. It prepared Anna to go contentedly to bed, her self-importance boosted by Trudie's reference to them as 'three girls together'; it filled Trudie with hope that they'd be a family, loving each other, wanting no one else; it frightened Julie, conscious that it would have been easy to submit to Trudie's genuine affection. But she wouldn't; this was *her* home. One day he'd be here with her; their stolen hours in that ramshackle caravan would be replaced by time together here.

'He's hoodwinked you,' Trudie told her later. 'You've always stood up for him, now look at the mess he's got you into.'

'You don't understand.'

'At least Jo took care! But listen, Julie, forget about Sebastian Sutcliffe, forget everything about him except that he's Lydia's husband and Merry's father. As far as you're concerned, let's both of us look on this as a symbol of something – someone – we share in the future.'

'Stop it, Trudie. The baby is Sebastian's, his and mine. As if I could say, "Oh yes, come and share Sebastian's child." Once he knows, he'll sort out the best thing to do.'

'And all this – the business you were so keen to set up? Are you just using this – using me, for that matter – to help you over a brief difficult period? Is that all our friendship means to you? It can't be. Think how good it was this evening, you, me and Anna. And when there's another we could both be there to love it.' Dropping to her knees, Trudie put her hands on Julie's waist, moving them to press gently but firmly against her belly that was a little rounder, a lot firmer, than a few months ago. 'We can do without men, we can be a proper family, the four of us, two adults, two children.'

'What are you saying?' Julie drew back.

'I'm not trying to force myself on you, not in the way you mean. But no man can ever understand a woman's needs, the way a woman's body and mind work in unison. Probably we don't understand men either — '

'Trudie, stop it. We're friends, I've never had a friend as close as you.'

'Not even Bess?'

Silence. The tick of the clock was the only sound.

'I made her up.'

A great joy enveloped Trudie. Leaning forward she put her arms around Julie and laid her head against her. 'I know you did.'

'You know? You couldn't possibly know.'

'I know because I followed you to that caravan — '

Something snapped in Julie. It was as if all the shame she'd felt in creating her web of deceit had found an outlet.

'Friend? I said you were my *friend*. Spying on me, following me, pretending you didn't know — '

'I had to find out about her, Julie.' Trudie was frightened by Julie's anger.

'And why? What had it to do with you? You had no right. Damn you, Trudie! You're trying to make it sordid.'

'Yes, I am. That's how you must see it too. He's had women galore, Lydia knows he has. But she's always been the one who matters, the only one he loves as a person and not just an object to take to bed.' Her voice was running away with her. She had to make Julie see him for what he was. 'He used you, Julie, got all he wanted knowing that you'd never upset the applecart by telling Lydia. Please, don't let us quarrel. Now we both know the truth — I followed you, but you can't turn round and blame me! Who was it telling the lies, me or you?

'You don't understand anything about it. You wouldn't recognise the sort of love Sebastian and I have even if you tripped over it.'

'There was Jo. He left me — ' Jo! As if that could be compared! Yet something in her expression touched Julie.

'I won't listen. All you'll do is make us quarrel. Listen to me.'

181

She raised Trudie's shoulders, forcing her to meet her eyes. 'I loved Jeremy. I always will. But then I was young, full of hope. He was taken away from me. Sebastian is quite different. Whatever I am — and heaven knows I'm not much — I am his. Yes, and he's mine too. He'll never leave Lydia and I don't think I could bear to think I'd done that to her. But I know him as she never has, as no woman ever has. Now I'm having his child. People will gossip, they'll probably think the worst when they see a woman who's been a widow all this time is pregnant. But I'm proud. If ever I've had anything to thank God for it's that I have something of his, something that no one can take from me. And when he knows about it he'll be proud too.'

Trudie's clear blue eyes were swimming with tears; her mouth trembled as the first rolled unchecked down her face.

'Even if he loves you as much as you say — and the Squire says, oh well, you know what the Squire says — but even if he does, there's no future for you. You loved your Jeremy and yet you made a life without him. Do it again. Julie . . . please want me.' Trudie sobbed.

'Of course I want you.' Cradling her close, Julie rubbed her face against the smooth, fair hair. 'And I'm grateful —'

'Don't want you to be. Just want us to be together. I want to take care of you.' Trudie was blessed with such a lovely face, yet now her eyelids were badly swollen from crying and her face drenched in tears. But she didn't care. 'When Jo went I thought I knew about being unhappy. But, Julie, never felt like this. Don't understand it, just can't bear it . . . ' Her voice was lost in a breathless croak. 'Please want me, be everything to each other, Anna needs two, the new baby . . . ' She buried her face against Julie's lap, the wet of her tears seeping through her skirt.

'Can't go home looking like this. Let me stay, Julie. I'll sleep on the sofa. Can't go home like this.'

By contrast Julie sounded composed. 'Yes, you'd better stay tonight. I'll phone your mother and tell her you're busy helping me. I want to thank her for the things she sent.'

Having asked for the number, she heard the operator pass the call to the exchange in Deremouth, and when she heard the phone ringing she started to count. She'd reached twenty-four rings and was about to hang up when the girl on the Deremouth switchboard told her, 'Sorry, caller, I'm getting no reply. Can I try again for you later?'

That was at about nine o'clock. It was after midnight when the call came through.

'I tried earlier,' Julie told her. 'Have I got you out of bed, trying at this time of night?'

'No, we've been out.' She was surprised when Tess gave no reason. At Rowans they went to bed early and got up early.

'I wanted to thank you for the things, you really are a dear. And to say that Trudie has been helping me until so late that she's going to doss down on the sofa for a night.'

'Don't work too hard.' It wasn't like Tess to sound so distant. But had anything been wrong, she surely would have wanted to talk to Trudie. Julie told herself she was being imaginative, it was stupid to be uneasy.

That was the Friday when Merry started his half-term break. From that day he had no school until Thursday of the following week. As if to tantalise him with reminders of how things used to be, the morning mist gave way to sun that shone almost brightly enough to make them believe winter wasn't waiting just beyond the horizon.

The previous night through his bedroom window when he'd seen the new moon, he'd closed his eyes tight and wished with all his might that he could find out where Anna had gone. Sometimes he suspected his mother knew; more than once she broke off in the middle of a sentence when he came into the room.

'Mum, when the rocks show can I go shrimping?'

'On your own? Of course you can't. Why don't you see if Mrs Briggs has any jobs she wants you to do?'

He heard the answer as 'Go away and don't pester'. Then, as if that weren't bad enough, here was Grandma parking in the drive. Mum would have time for her. There would be grown-up talk, they'd tell him to run away and amuse himself.

He retreated to the kitchen.

'Any jobs for me, Mrs Briggs?' He tried to sound big and capable.

'Bless me, let's think now. Pity Marie didn't take you off with her to the village, that would have been better for you than hanging around here. Take the mat and give it a good shake if you like.'

He did, and not a fleck of dust came off it. His lips wanted to quiver, it took all his determination to stop them. He wasn't even useful, 'hanging around', Mrs Briggs had said. He didn't bother to take the mat back indoors — let her come and fetch it, that would tell her what he thought of being treated like a baby! Turning his back on the house he went into the garden and kicked a ball. The only game he could play was to kick it across the garden, then run as fast as he could to get to the other side first. The ball always won.

'Be careful, Merry,' Grace called. 'The ball is knocking into the rose bushes. The flowers will be gone soon enough without that.'

Disconsolately he bounced his ball. He'd inherited his looks from his father, but his optimism came from Lydia. It wasn't in his nature to mope. If he went indoors quietly perhaps he could be in the room with Mum and Grandma; probably they wouldn't be talking about anything he could join in, but he'd feel part of it. Anyway, it must soon be time for Mrs Briggs to take Mum her coffee, then there might be some biscuits or a piece of cake. Considerably cheered, he kicked his ball one last time, gave a quick look over his shoulder to make sure no one had seen the shower of rose petals, then sedately went in, being sure to wipe his shoes. He wasn't risking another wigging from Granda.

They didn't hear him coming and for a moment he hovered just inside the half-open sliding door of the sitting room.

' . . . idea if you ask me. She's a strange girl. Plenty of them have crushes when they're young, I saw enough of it when I was teaching. But it doesn't make any sense. I would have staked my last penny that Julie would have stayed here. She was on an easy number, and it was a good home for Anna — that, plus her school fees.'

'Julie wants a career. And maybe Trudie did influence her, I wouldn't know.'

'This place she's taken in Exeter, you may be sure Trudie had something to do with that. I was at Rowans yesterday morning and there was Tess making a pile of things for Trudie to take when she went today. Little things to make it more like a home, she said. Vases, curtains, cushions — you know what a dear Tess is, she'd give away her coat is she thought someone was cold.'

'Did you see how Quin's getting on preparing the ground he bought from Uncle Peter?' That wasn't the question Lydia wanted to ask, and perhaps Grace realised it.

'It's all been ploughed and broken up with the harrow. I could see that girl from Deans Farm on the hill there, and two or three men digging now that the first of the preparation is done. Not Quin, though, he wasn't there.'

'Mum, he's very impressed with her.' It was said timidly, giving Grace the choice of taking it at face value or hearing the ripples below the surface.

'If he is, then, Lydia, you ought to be glad. There's no use being dog in the manger, that way will bring no happiness for you or for him either. There was a time when Quintin Murray would have been yours for the taking. But you fell for Sebastian and I'm thankful it's worked well. I know he's away a lot, but not as much as if he were in the navy, just tell yourself that. Good, I hear the rattle of cups. Mrs Briggs must be making coffee. May I invite myself?'

184

'Silly, of course you'll stay.'

A day seldom went by when the Squire didn't come, but Grace was a less frequent visitor. Whenever she came it struck Lydia afresh how aged she was. Her face had character and strength, but recently it had become gaunt, and dark shadows around her eyes gave the impression that they were sunk in their sockets.

'Mum, why don't you and the Squire go away for a holiday? Is it because of me? I shan't run away, you know. No, that was a bad joke, sorry. You look as though you could do with a break.'

Grace sat back in her chair, her eyes closed. The suggestion seemed to have fallen on stony ground.

'He wouldn't come.' Her eyes shot open, their expression hard and full of dislike. 'And if he did it would be no holiday, not for him and not for me.'

'You don't mean that. If you went away without him you'd worry all the time, you know you would. Why, Mum, without you the Squire would be lost.'

Grace laughed, a laugh full of misery.

'Please, please, Mum, don't you two quarrel. He comes here full of self-pity with a stock of snide remarks about Seb. Now there's you trying to make me think you're badly used by *him*. Well, I don't want to hear about it, not from either of you. I may be stuck here to be talked at, but I'm not some agony aunt.' Just as when she'd tried to quarrel with Julie, a demon was egging her on. She heard her voice grow louder and couldn't stop herself; she revelled in its shrill tone. 'I bet when they knew Paul wasn't coming home Aunt Tess and Uncle Peter never expected the rest of the family to have to listen to their woes. I bet they cried together. But you two are so self-centred, all you think of is your own feelings.' If she could have used up some of her emotional energy in movement the demon would have stood no chance, but all she could do was drum her fingers on the metal wheels of her chair while she dug into her mind for barbs that would wound. 'And he was *dead*, they'd never see him again. Not like *me*, I'm not dead. I'm alive, sitting here where I can't escape from all your selfish grizzling. All right, I can't walk, but I'm still a person, I still have a life to live.'

Merry heard her voice break. He bit hard on his knucles, silently retreating back into the corridor.

'You've come in from the garden then, Merry?' He was still hovering when Mrs Briggs came from the kitchen with her tray. She must have heard his mother shouting just as he had, but she gave no sign of it. 'I've brought you a glass of lemonade. Are you coming to have it with your mother, or in the kitchen with me?'

185

'He'll have it with us, won't you, Merry?' Grace decided for him.

The day hadn't done with him yet. After he waved Grace on her way from the gate, he decided he'd go back into the sitting room. His mother had sounded different when she was shouting, and he was sure she'd been almost crying. That made him uncomfortable. Yet while they were drinking their coffee she hadn't looked a bit cross, in fact there had been a sort of excitement about her. He didn't understand it at all. If only Julie were here − or Seb, that would be even better − then she would be happy.

He'd better take a colouring book with him; if she was still cross with him as she had been earlier, then he'd sit very quietly with his crayons.

But she wasn't cross. She was on the telephone and she was smiling. Whom could she be talking to? She never sounded like that when she talked to him or Pam. He knew nothing of coquetry and to see her made him uneasy. He supposed she must be talking to someone she didn't know very well, someone she wanted to believe she was pretty; it was a pretty sort of voice she was using. But of course Mum was pretty. He wished he hadn't come in with his book, he would rather not have been listening.

'I won't bring Ruby then, if you're sure you don't mind coming for me? Not too busy on the outside work? . . . So Mum told me. Yes, she was here earlier. . . . I wish I could too . . . I believe you really mean it! You do me so much good. . . . I wasn't very nice to Mum. . . . I hope she does. . . . Yes, I'll be ready. And, Quin − oh, nothing really, just what I said before, you do me so much good, make me feel like me again . . . Kind sir, you say the nicest things. . . . Two o'clock then.'

Merry didn't look up from his colouring when he heard her ring off. When Quin came for Lydia at two o'clock the little boy made sure he was out of the way.

The Squire usually visited in the morning. Indeed, he had walked along the clifftop intended to come to Whiteways today only to find the Delbridge House car in the driveway. What he wanted was Poppet's undivided attention, he certainly didn't want Grace hearing everything he said.

'Where's your mother?' He came down the terrace steps to the grass where Merry was turning somersaults. 'Why isn't she in the sitting room?'

'Because she's out.'

'I didn't think she'd be hiding in a cupboard. And don't I get the courtesy of a name?' He sounded as angry as everyone else today.

'Squire,' Merry mumbled, not looking at him.

'Just you watch your manners.' With Lydia out of the way he could vent all his dislike on the child. 'It's quite time someone took you in hand. You'll end up with all the arrogance of that ponce of a father.'

Merry had no idea what a ponce was, but clearly it wasn't meant kindly.

'I want to be what you called him, I'm going to be just as ponce as Seb.' Lydia being out must have had an effect on him too. Starting at the ground somewhere between himself and his grandfather he mumbled, 'Better be like Seb than like you, grumpy and horrid.'

There, he'd said it, been as rude as he'd always wanted to be. He felt exhilarated, but not brave enough to raise his eyes and meet the Squire's fury. For one bad moment he considered the possibility that a ponce was just another way of saying actor or film man. No, no, Squire hadn't said it in a nice way. Being young meant that you didn't really count, that was why the Squire had said bad things that he wouldn't have the courage to say to Seb's face. A bit like Grandma this morning, she said bad things that she wouldn't have said to the Squire's face. Merry dug the heel of his shoe into the grass, making a hole. If only Anna and Julie hadn't gone away! Fed up with being here, Mum had said. But it wasn't true, they'd been happy, there had been lots of laughter. Not like now.

He felt his small shoulders taken in his grandfather's hands. 'Insolent young pup! You'd not speak to me in that tone if your mother could hear you.'

Merry scowled. He knew it was true.

'Where is she? At the nursery, I suppose? That precious Seb of yours wants to watch her, she and Quintin have always been very thick, you know.' He spoke in a man-to-man tone that threw Merry off his guard. 'There was a time when I thought she'd marry Quintin. Likes him coming here, doesn't she? Spends a lot of time with him? The great Sebastian had better look to his laurels and stop chasing after other women. He does, you know. We've got a tom cat always chasing after the lady cats. Serve him right if she told him she'd had enough of him. You and your everlasting "When's Seb coming?" He wouldn't be coming at all then.'

''Course she wouldn't.' This time his heel managed to dislodge a chunk of turf.

'Strikes me she spends a good deal of time at that nursery. Now you just think about it.'

Merry scowled at the ground. In any mood he never felt comfortable with his grandfather; in this one he was frightened. He wished his mother would hurry up and come home.

'Think she's going to be out a long time.' That was his only answer. It had the desired effect and without another word the Squire left.

The afternoon dragged on. The rocks looked tempting, and Merry got as far as getting his shrimping net ready, only natural obedience to his mother stopped him going further. When she came home he'd ask her again; perhaps if she wasn't still cross she might say yes.

When they arrived he watched Quin lift her out of the jeep and wished she wouldn't smile up at him like that; it was that silly face he'd noticed when she was on the telephone.

When they came into the house, Quin's 'Hello there, Merry. You ought to have come too. Perhaps tomorrow? I can find you plenty to do' was reassuringly normal. Merry almost forgot how miserable he was. But as soon as Lydia was put in her chair, Quin went and his memories tumbled back. It wasn't that his mother looked cross, yet she was no easier to talk to. She seemed to be living in a world of her own.

'Mum?' Then again, 'Mum? I don't see why you won't let me go on the beach. Seb always comes shrimping with me and the tide is still quite low. It's 'cos of the moon, you see, Seb told me.'

'And I told you no. The rocks aren't safe for you to clamber about on your own.'

'I know which are the flat ones. And I know which ones have the green slime on them.'

'*No.* Don't you listen? Here's tea. You pour, Pam, will you? I worked hard this afternoon, I deserve to be waited on.'

No one asked him how his afternoon had been. Well, he'd show them. It was just stupid to say that he couldn't look after himself on the rocks. He'd go anyway. Not that she'd notice, she was too busy thinking about other people, never about him.

Tea over. Pam took Lydia to the bedroom to massage her shoulders. This was his opportunity. A scheme was brewing in his brain. There was still a big lump of cake left on the table, so he cut it in half — to take more would be too obvious — made a sandwich of bread and meat paste, then carried his spoils to his bedroom. In the wardrobe he had his school satchel, that would do beautifully. A pity he couldn't ask Mrs Briggs for a paper bag, but she might wonder why he wanted it. He imagined the scare he was going to give them; that would make them sorry you hadn't cared that he was miserable without Anna.

It was already dusk, the tide was washing in over the rocks, and the sitting-room curtains were drawn to shut out the time of day Lydia hated. He put on his blue gaberdine mackintosh, then, with his satchel firmly on his back and his shrimping net in his hand, he crept out through the side door and down the sloping path to the shore.

'Has Merry gone on to bed, Lydia? I was just going to chase him off for a bath, I thought he was in here with you.' Pam slid the sitting-room door closed behind her, quite glad that he was already out of the way. There was a good play on the radio this evening, and with him in bed early she and Lydia could get comfortable by the fire and enjoy it.

'I've not seen him since tea. If he's not in the playroom he must be messing about in his bedroom. Who ever heard of Merry going to bed without being chased there!'

Pam put a brave face on it and went to find him. There was no school tomorrow, it wouldn't hurt him to miss his bath tonight.

'Merry! Merry! Come on now, don't play the silly goat, it's bedtime. Wherever you're hiding, out you come.' Silence. 'Merry! Do as you're told. Come along. I'll count five and if you're not here by then, then woe betide you when I do find you.' Again silence. 'Merry!'

By then Lydia came to add her voice.

'Oh, no . . .' Pam's voice was suddenly quiet. 'He wouldn't do a thing like that.'

'Like what? Come on out, you rascal. Game over.'

'His shrimping net. It was here, just inside his bedroom door.' Pam was a practical, unimaginative woman, so the premonition of disaster frightened her.

'He wanted to take it on the rocks, that's why he got it out ready. I wouldn't let him. He was still pestering when I came back with Quin. Don't fuss, Pam. Like you say, he wouldn't. If he'd meant to get up to those tricks then he would have done it this afternoon when I was out and there were rocks to climb on.'

'It was here. I brought his clean washing in and put it away just before I did your shoulders. It was here, I saw it.'

'It's not dark yet, not quite. Go and look on the beach, Pam. Tell him he's in for it when *I* get at him.'

'He's only a little lad, Lydia. Don't be too hard on him. Half-term and no one to play with.'

'Well, I can't help it if I'm no company for him. Instead of trying

189

to scare me he should be blaming Julie, it's her fault he hasn't got Anna.'

'I'll go and get him back. He knows better than to go in the water. He's probably got himself wet and is ashamed to show his face. We've got to be gentle with him, Lydia.'

'Buck up, it's getting darker every minute.'

Pam hurried, she didn't even stop to put on a coat. The children had always played on this stretch of the beach, he knew every inch of it and wouldn't want to stray. She'd warn him that he was in for trouble, but in the few minutes it took to bring him back she had to make him understand that his mother's anger was because she was worried and frightened.

Indoors Lydia wheeled herself to the window, expecting that Pam would already be marching the culprit back up the path. Five minutes later she'd dragged open the glass door and was shivering on the terrace. In the distance she could hear Pam calling ... calling.

Perhaps he'd gone to Delbridge House. No, of course he hadn't. Listen, was that him answering Pam? No. 'Merry!' Nothing but silence. She'd never been more aware of her helplessness. To sit and do nothing was impossible, so she wheeled herself back inside, then one by one to each of the rooms, turning on the lights. He must be somewhere nearby, so the lights would be a beacon to draw him come; he'd realise when he saw them just how worried she was.

Pam was coming back up the path alone.

'I've been from end to end, I've called and called. We've got to tell *someone*. Ought we to phone your parents?'

'I'll ring Rowans.'

'But he wouldn't have gone there. Why would he take his shrimping net to Rowans?' Or to Delbridge House either for that matter.

'Quin'll know what to do.'

From there on everything moved fast. In less than ten minutes Quin was with them, while at Rowans Peter phoned Delbridge House before he and Tess followed the jeep on that road through Downing Wood. They brought lanterns, for by now it was practically dark, and the new moon would be hidden by mist rolling in from the sea.

'We ought to tell the police.' Grace rested a hand on Lydia's knee.

'Not the police!' The police to look for Merry! It couldn't be happening. 'How can the police see further than anyone else?'

'Perhaps he didn't go to the beach at all. Oh, God, surely no one would have talked to him and encouraged him away, would they? Would they?'

'I'll phone them, shall I?' This was Tess. 'We ought to tell them, Lydia. They're here to help — we all are. Perhaps he's hurt himself. They'll help us find him. Let me ask them to come, Lydia.'

With her arms held tight across her chest, Lydia was rocking backwards and forwards as if her misery was too much to bear. Seeing it Grace was reminded of the Squire, all too often she'd seen him do exactly the same. There was no despair in him this evening though, out there with Peter and Quin calling and searching for the missing child. In a moment of clarity she knew it without doubt: it wasn't just that he had no love for Merry, he disliked him. She felt sick with shame for him that an innocent child should be no more than a permanent reminder that Lydia loved another man.

Minutes later they heard a car pull into the drive. The police had arrived from Deremouth.

Never had an evening been so long. On the beach they spread out, two policemen, Peter, the Squire and Quintin, each covering a section so that as each wave broke on the tideline nothing could be washed in without one of them seeing. They stayed there until finally the water reached the sloping garden and the cliffs on either side of it. By the time the search party came back up the path it was almost eleven o'clock. There was nothing but blackness and the sound of waves rushing in against the cliff. None of them could see the shrimping net that had been carried westward by the current and was being washed to and fro on the surf.

'No sign of the lad down there, Mrs Sutcliffe,' the police sergeant announced as they were ushered into the sitting room. 'No sign he's been there even. If children go on the beach you'd expect there to be some sign, a bucket, for instance. If he'd intended finding shrimps — and this is what we suppose, seeing as 'ow he took his net when he went out — wouldn't there have been a pail to bring them home in? That's the sort of question springs to mind.'

Crime in Deremouth was restricted to the occasional petty pilfering or minor road incident. Sergeant Towley wished his inspector could have been there to appreciate his professional approach to what looked like being the beginning of a case to make local history. Ah, and it might well get his name into the London papers too: child of famous film star abducted, cases like that weren't two a penny. The more Sergeant Towley thought of it, the more his imagination romped into play. 'Now, work it out for yourselves; some no-good blaggard comes to hear that Sebastian Sutcliffe owns this house, and that he has a young son. Now, where does that take

191

us? Easy as anything he could walk round those rocks at low tide — and this time o'year when the moon is new like it is, tides are at their longest. All he's got to do is wait, then, when the lad goes to the beach, have a nice friendly chat with him, tempt him away like. Friendly with folk, is he? Wouldn't wonder he wasn't called Merry for nothing.'

No one interrupted him. He felt himself to be a sleuth *extraordinaire*. If he got it right, he'd be inspector before you could say 'knife'.

'Bunkum!' It was the Squire who finally broke the silence. 'Plenty of children about with better chance of a ransom than the son of some actor chap. If you want my opinion he's hiding within half a mile of this house. When did you last check his room, Pam? It wouldn't surprise me if he was in bed and enjoying being the centre of all the fuss.'

Grace watched him with silent contempt. In that moment she hated him.

'Lydia, I think we ought to get a message to Sebastian.' Quin's quiet voice filled the silence.

'Oh, no!' Lydia grabbed his hand. 'We've got to find him. Quin, we've got to do it ourselves. It would be like admitting something had happened.' Her voice rasped and she tightened her grip on his hand.

'Perhaps he tried to get to Delbridge House,' Grace suggested. 'But it's an easy road, how could he have got lost?'

'Or Rowans.' Peter thought that more likely, Merry always enjoyed being at the farm. 'But why? He'd had his tea, it was starting to get dark. Why should he go anywhere?'

Silence filled every corner of the room. To Lydia more than to anyone the reason was clear.

'Because he was miserable. He was fed up. He'd got no one to play with. He wanted Anna but she'd gone away.' Her eyes met Quin's. 'He must be trying to get to Anna! But I've never told him where she is. And even if he knew, he wouldn't find his way to Exeter. He's only a baby.' But she clung to the hope. Let it be that. Don't let some dreadful man have stolen him. Don't let him be — but in her silent prayer she hadn't the courage to find words for the real terror, that somewhere trapped under the water among the rocks his little body was lying.

Everyone was suddenly talking at once. Grace had thought this morning that he'd heard them mention Julie being in Exeter; Tess was equally sure that even though Merry wouldn't know the way to Exeter, he would know that you started off by going past Rowans.

Silently she reminded herself that had he been on that lane, surely they would have seen him as they'd driven through the woods on the way here. Under the volume of voices Quin whispered something to Pam, who went out of the room; when she returned with a folded piece of paper he put it in his pocket, and in the confusion no one noticed.

The police left, taking with them Merry's latest photograph from the mantelpiece so that a poster could be made: "Have you seen this child?" Tess drove their own car back to Rowans, Peter took the jeep. Quin walked, carrying a lantern, calling Merry's name, searching among the trees near the sides of the lane as he went through Downing Wood.

When he got home it was nearly one o'clock. Every hour was precious. He unfolded the piece of paper Pam had given him and put through a call to Sebastian's agent's home.

193

Chapter Twelve

Julie had opened her business with no staff to help her. Her advertisement in the paper had brought one or two young women to register with her and in her first few days she'd had one enquiry from a firm of accountants wanting a skilled shorthand typist. Enough work had been put her way — thanks to Trudie, but Julie didn't know that — to keep a home typist busy for a few hours each day. She'd taken in a badly scrawled and difficult-to-read manuscript for typing, a job she was undertaking herself; it looked better to be busy as she sat in the front office waiting for clients. Before long she hoped to be able to employ a permanent member of staff, either to work with her or fill temporary posts as required. Mrs Arkwright, the home typist, might be ideal for this when there was enough work coming in to merit it.

'You can come downstairs with me and sit at the second desk,' she told Anna, 'but as soon as anyone comes in the rule is that you take yourself off to the back room. We must be firm about that, Anna. Keep a colouring book or something on the back-room desk and when we see someone coming in you pop straight in there until I'm on my own again.'

Julie expected a protest or at least a sulky glare. But this morning Anna was keen to be seen as one of the 'three girls together', a useful member of the team.

At not yet five years old, she was lucky the headmistress of the local school had been prepared to take her in, particularly at mid-term. What had tipped the scales was the fact that Julie was a war widow, whose future depended on the success of Freeman's Secretarial Agency. At the moment it was half-term, there was no more school until Thursday. Anna might be full of enthusiasm and team spirit on Monday morning, but Julie had no illusions; by Tuesday the gilt would have worn thin. Four hours of crayoning can be a great test of stamina. Anna was at the wriggling stage, kicking her toes against the underside of the desk, when Trudie rushed in bearing an appetisingly pungent bundle wrapped in newspaper.

'Come on, girls, two minutes to one, time to bolt the door for lunch. Sniff! Now don't tell me you're not hungry. I'll take them straight up, shall I? We can't have it smelling like a fish-and-chip shop in here.'

Anna liked the smell, but even more she liked the 'come on, girls'. Resolutions were restored.

Never before had she had crispy golden batter special to the fish-and-chip shop, all puffed up and covered with grease that made her lips feel shiny. As for the chips, they were thick and long, yet so soggy that they bent when she picked them up on her fork. She'd never eaten chips that tasted as scrumptious. She sat taller, smiling at her partners. Downstairs, trying to look busy with her crayoning book, as the morning had crept by at snail's pace, it had been impossible not to think about Merry and imagine the games they could have been having if they'd still been living together. But she had to remember that her mother depended on her. She'd been given her own jobs to do, like laying the table, drying the dishes and taking the rubbish down to the bin in the yard. She was so busy munching her fish and chips and priding herself on her usefulness that she missed the beginning of the conversation.

'But won't she be in the way? You say you have to drive out there to see a client.' That was her mother speaking. Who was 'she'? Anna pricked up her ears, suspecting it was her they were talking about. A drive . . .? She looked from one to the other expectantly.

'I shan't be in the house many minutes, I have to go over a document with the old lady and get her signature, that's all. Anna will be fine in the car, I'll park it up the drive right by the house.' Then, to Anna, 'You'd like to come, wouldn't you? You've kept your mother company all the morning, what about keeping me company this afternoon?'

Anna beamed. 'I'd like to go with Trudie, Mum. Will you be all right without me?'

Julie didn't try to hide her pride. 'I'll miss you, but I'll manage. When you come home you can tell me all about it.'

Anna pushed the last, long chip into her wide-open mouth. There was a lot to be said for this growing-up business.

By the time they returned, Julie was ready to bolt the door. A full day of deciphering handwriting that was barely legible and putting right incorrect spelling wasn't her idea of fun at any time, and this afternoon the dull ache in the small of her back was a constant reminder that the months ahead would be an ever-increasing challenge.

Anna was carrying a bunch of chrysanthemums.

'Look, Mum, look what Trudie bought. I'll do them for us, shall I? There's that vase Auntie Tess sent us. Shall I do that?'

'Can you reach?' Julie called after the retreating figure, but her words were wasted. If Anna couldn't reach to get the vase or to turn on the tap, then she'd stand on a chair. That was what having responsibilities was all about.

'Are you staying for tea?' she suggested to Trudie. 'No, cake, but we're going to make toast.'

'No, Mum will have a meal ready. Anyway, I'd rather leave you wishing I was going to be here than stay and have you wish I'd gone.'

Julie reached to take her hand. She never meant to hurt Trudie, she had to make her understand.

It seemed Trudie understood without being told. She took the hand and held it to her cheek. 'I'm not pushing you. Anna was super this afternoon, we had a lovely time together, sang songs as we bumped along the lanes. I'm not sure what's in my diary, but if I can I'll pick her up again. I must go, I want to look in at the office before I go home.' Then a light kiss on Julie's cheek, a shouted goodbye to Anna, and she was gone.

It must have been about an hour and a half later when there was an urgent hammering on the outside door.

'I'll come with you.' Anna slid off her chair.

'No, it'll only be Mrs Arkwright bringing her typing back. You start dealing the cards, Anna, I won't be a minute. Half the pack each, then we'll play Snap.'

'You'd better be ready to lose tonight, Mum. I'm going to win all your cards.'

'A likely thing!' Julie laughed. 'I'm back in a jiffy.'

Down the stairs, through the front office, then Julie pulled back the bolt of the door to the street, ready to take in the completed work and hurry back to Anna. But instead of Mrs Arkwright she found Trudie waiting for her.

'I thought you were going home. Is something wrong?'

'I don't want Anna to hear, I won't come in. Julie, Merry's gone missing. You've not seen the evening paper? No, you can't have. He's not been seen since yesterday evening.'

'But he can't be missing! Have they searched, *really* searched? Oh, but they wouldn't know his faviourite places.' Julie backed into the office and flopped into a typing chair. 'He wouldn't wander off. Trudie, he can't be lost!'

'I wasn't home for many minutes, but Mum told me what she knew. They've searched the shore, every inch of it, and, Julie' — she hated saying it, she couldn't bear to look at Julie — 'a shrimping net has been found in Cockerton Bay. He'd taken his with him.'

'But they can't have let him go alone on those rocks!'

'What they're saying — I mean what they're suggesting in the paper — is that he's been kidnapped because of who he is. They're watching out for a ransom note. But of course they won't get one, whoever has taken him will know it's too dangerous while the police are on the alert.'

'I've got to look for him. Trudie, I must.' As she stood up she felt as if her legs would crumple under her.

'There's another theory. Lydia had told me he was lonely and fed up, he blamed her for sending you and Anna away. Yesterday morning he heard that you were in Exeter, so they think he may be trying to get to you.'

'He doesn't know where Exeter is. Anyhow he's only little, how could he walk to Exeter?'

'He's driven there lots of times, he probably imagines it's not far. And he'll know that you have to go past Rowans and on to Deremouth. It's my belief that's what he meant to do. Poor little boy.'

Julie cried so seldom that the rare occasions left scars on her memory. Now, though, it would have been no use to try to hold back the tears; silently they spilled down her cheeks, her face contorted, her eyes bloodshot. She cried for a long time.

'Merry, my little Merry, somewhere all by himself! And it's my fault. I promised to stay with him,' she sobbed. 'Merry . . .'

'Wipe your face and things will look better. I don't believe he would have gone on the rocks. Lydia said he'd asked her in the morning and again later, and each time she'd said no. Merry wouldn't have wilfully disobeyed. Would he?'

'I'm sure he wouldn't. He must be somewhere!' The face-wiping had helped; Julie's resolve was strengthening.

'Take my car,' Trudie told her. 'Forget all about Anna and me, we'll look after each other.'

'Trudie.' Still sitting, Julie put her arms around her friend's waist and felt herself drawn close. Shock tingled in her veins as her head was cushioned against Trudie's soft breast. Drawing away she looked up, knowing they'd both been startled by the contact.

'I'll go upstairs and get your coat, Anna will be worried if she thinks something's wrong. I'll tell her Lydia wants to see you, she'll believe that.'

'And you'll stay? I don't know what I'd do without you, Trudie.'

Coming back with the coat, Trudie bundled her out of the door, but not before Anna could be heard on her way down the straight flight of stairs.

'I won't be long, love.' Julie forced her voice to sound normal, but she was thankful that they were in the shadow between two street-lights. 'If I'm not back, go to bed when Trudie says. She's good at Snap, you'd better look out!' How easy it was to act a part.

'But Mum —'

'There's a big torch on the back seat.' Trudie opened the car door for her. 'And, Julie, don't talk about being without me. Friends are for always.' Then, more loudly and holding out her hand to draw Anna outside to wave her mother off, 'Don't bother to hurry. We can take care of each other, can't we, Anna?'

As she was driving towards Otterton St Giles, the possibilities were going round and round in Julie's brain. She couldn't bear to think about the shrimping net. All day the search had continued along the coast, just remember that. No, Merry must have gone some-where else. Had they searched properly in all the barns at Rowans? Oh, but they must have. And the village? Word spreads quickly, even before the evening paper came out there wouldn't have been a person in Otterton who hadn't heard. Bicycle sheds, coal houses, garages, all of them would have been checked.

She'd had very little experience of driving after dark, but with her foot hard on the accelerator, she sped on. With the coming of evening the clouds had built up, the wind changed direction. Now, as she drove, the first heavy spots of rain hit the windscreen. Lights from oncoming cars shone on the wet ground and dazzled her. She must marshal her thoughts, before she reached Otterton she must be sure what she meant to do. Supposing Merry hadn't wanted to be seen, would he have gone along the roads at all? Somewhere far into the wood there was a clearing, a favourite place with the children, the Fairy Glen they all called it. As she pictured the two of them there together she became more certain what she had to do.

The windscreen wipers swishing backwards and forwards, she peered through the small section of glass that was cleared. How far could he have walked? Every shadow became for her a little boy, lost and frightened. Through Deremouth, past Rowans, then she turned right into the road where in the beam from the car lights the branches of the tall trees seemed to reach out and make a tunnel. Then out into the open again and to the edge of the village where she turned right again, past Delbridge House and on along the cliff road. Before she reached Whiteways she drew onto the grass verge and stopped. The torch was powerful, she needed it to see her way across the uneven ground as she climbed the long hill towards Downing Wood. Here near the coast the wind was gusting, the rain hitting hard against her face. How much worse it would be for him, and by now he'd be so hungry and frightened. Perhaps he was somewhere deep in the wood, lost and alone.

'Merry!' She was no more than halfway up the long grassy climb and knew it was useless to shout from there, but just calling his name made him seem nearer, gave her hope.

The only wide tracks were those leading from the lane where Lydia had parked on that fateful night. Even without well-defined paths Julie could find her way by daylight, guided by the slant of sunlight through the branches and using familiar clumps of bushes as trig points. By night there was nothing to guide her. Was she going round in circles? Was she anywhere near the Fairy Glen? It was as if she were cut off from the real world, a captive in some sort of hell. Not hell, please let it be no more than purgatory. It's *me* You want to punish, not Merry. I broke all the rules; I was Lydia's friend, yet I took her husband away from her. Can anything be lower than that? Yes, it can, and I stooped to that too: I told myself that I wasn't hurting her.

Standing still she was suddenly frightened, though not by the dense wood nor yet by the darkness as the torch gave its first flickering warning. Surely the battery wasn't failing already? Time had ceased to have any meaning; until now she hadn't held the light to the face of her wristwatch. Ten past one. No wonder the torch was dying.

'Merry! Merry!' she yelled. 'Shout for me, I'll come and find you.'

The only sound that broke the silence was the whistle of the wind as it forced its way through the tree-tops, bringing down leaves so water-laden that they fell straight to the ground. The night was chill, full of the smell of rotting leaves and wet timber; in the shaft of light from her torch she saw a small animal scurrying to shelter. Field mouse? Vole? It was then that she caught the sight of something else, something that made her forget everything but the wild joy that surged through her. How many times had she held that satchel while he slipped his arms through the straps?

'Merry!' No answering call. Taking the sodden leather satchel, she looked inside as if she expected to find a clue. It was empty but, when she looked closer, there were crumbs and a currant from a cake. Her eyes filled with tears. So he'd planned his escape, it was true that he'd been miserable enough to do that.

With no path it was impossible to know which way he might have gone. Still she went on, but by now she felt her way, reaching out from one tree to the next rather than use up her battery. At intervals she put on the torch, scanning as far as its feeble beam radiated. The first euphoria of knowing he'd been in the wood was fading, and she could no longer ignore her own weariness. She'd been walking for hours and the wet had seeped right through her clothes; when she pressed her hands to her aching groin she could feel the cold dampness against her. For a minute she leaned back against the bark of a tree, letting the drips trickle down her face. How far into the wood was she? For one mad moment she imagined that she'd never find her way out. She shuddered, ashamed that she could care about herself when it must be worse for Merry. In that moment of finding his satchel she'd believed he must be close by, but perhaps it had already been there last night while the police had been searching the beach.

With her torch switched off the darkness closed around her. Then she thought she could see a light moving, a lantern held high. Someone was coming towards her. Perhaps it was the police; perhaps it was a vagrant. Either way there was no reason for the wild beating of her heart, the sudden panic that gripped her.

'Merry!' She heard the shout. In purgatory, in hell even, she would recognise the voice.

'Sebastian!' Tiredness fell from her. There was no need now to conserve the battery of her torch, and she let its feeble beam light her way as she ran towards him. Now they'd search together, they'd find Merry; now that Sebastian was here the nightmare would be over.

It must have been the angle of the light that turned him into a stranger as he looked at her.

'This is *your* fault.' She read hate in his eyes, she heard it in his voice. 'You and your fine promises!' There was mockery in his mimicry of her words: '"I'll look after Lydia, I'll take care of Merry". No, don't do that' As if her touch scorched his skin, he pulled his hand away from her. 'Get away from me!'

She couldn't believe what she was hearing. 'Sebastian, there was no other way. I had to break my word. I wouldn't have left them —'

'Now look what you've done. Oh God, God, where is he?'

She heard his voice break and wanted to hold him, to comfort him just as she'd been imagining herself finding and comforting Merry. Surely he would trust her once she had told him about the baby. They were only a step away from understanding.

'Go home, damn you! Go to wherever you've set up your fine business. Don't pretend you're here out of love for him. You left him, if you'd stayed he would have been safe. You knew Lydia couldn't watch over him. But did you care?' He ranted as if he'd lost his reason. 'Go and make a life for yourself, if that's what you want. And when you're banging your typewriter keys, sing, "Alleluia, this is freedom". You won't be bored, hampered by a cripple and a child – '

'Stop it, Sebastian! You don't understand.'

'Only one thing I understand, only one thing I care about.' His voice broke, his face contorted. 'Merry, oh, please God, Merry, answer me.'

Already he was walking away from her, his lantern bright and high, while her torch flickered into its final minutes. She heard his shouts grow faint until they were swallowed up in the sound of the wind and the rain.

Half an hour or so later she was still groping her way between the trees. If she kept a straight course she must come to a break in the trees, the road perhaps, Rowans, or the long slope that led down towards the car. She hadn't found Merry, but Sebastian wouldn't stop looking until he had his son in his arms. She'd go home, she must go home. Sebastian's words were still hammering through her brain, yet they were but part of the agony. She shuffled her feet through the fallen leaves, every now and then kicking an exposed tree root. So tired ... just keep walking ... so tired ... wet ... just keep going. Concentrating on putting one foot in front of the other, she was unprepared to kick against something large enough to throw her balance. There was nothing to stop her falling.

For a second it was a relief not to be walking. Then something else forced into her consciousness: it wasn't a tree root that had tripped her. Struggling to her knees she felt the ground where she'd fallen. Cloth, wet cloth. Her hands explored, she heard herself whimpering, crying with relief: bare knees, little legs. She put her face close to his. Merry.

She'd found Merry. But his face was cold as she rubbed hers against it. Please, please, don't let him be – she couldn't bring herself to say it even in her silent plea. It took all her strength, more strength than she knew she had left, to lift him into her arms.

201

Just keep walking ... one foot in front of the other ... soon you'll see the open sky ... She babbled; it didn't matter what she said, but she had to keep talking, hoping to elicit some sign that he heard her voice.

Then like a miracle she saw the paler darkness ahead of her; she was coming out of the wood.

'When Seb come? Find Anna ...'

'Seb's coming soon, darling. Very soon. Thank you, thank you more than any words.'

'I hurt. Julie, I hurt.'

'Nearly home, love. Pam will make you better.'

'Want *you*.' He was crying now. 'Want Seb. Want my dinner.' He mumbled, his head flopped. Asleep? Unconscious? He was safe, soon he would be warm and fed.

The way out of the wood proved to be on that same road where the tree had fallen. She had a mile and a half to go, perhaps two miles, but at least the road was flat. Like a robot she moved forwards. Her eyes used to the darkness, she could see the shape of a parked car.

''Evening, ma'am.' His flashing torchlight revealed a dark-blue uniform.

'Constable! Are you with the car? Thank goodness!'

The ordeal was over. Only now, as the little boy was taken in his strong arms, did she realise how exhausted she was.

'So this is Merrick Sutcliffe? And who might you be, out this time o'night?'

'Julie Freeman, I used to look after him. I've been looking for him in the wood.'

To a police sergeant full of expectations of promotion, it seemed a rum affair that this one-time nursemaid had known where to find the lad — and without a light to help her as far as he could make out. At the house he'd heard that the child had missed this Julie woman. What was to say she hadn't been down there on the beach when he'd gone with his net, and enticed him away? Could be that she was making back towards that other car he'd seen parked, thinking she'd get away with it at dead of night, no one the wiser. His imagination was in full spate.

'I think he's hurt. Carry him carefully, it's his leg, I think.'

'Hey, George, we got a couple of passengers. First stop the hospital with the lad.'

'You found the boy! Hadn't we best go to the house, report he's been picked up?'

202

Julie thought of Lydia, helpless and waiting. 'I'll do that. I'm parked not far from Whiteways.'

''Fraid we can't let you do that, ma'am. You'll need to come along to the station, we'll need a statement.'

At the hospital the sergeant, seven foot tall with self-importance, alerted the night porter to the identity of their passenger and told him to arrange for him to be taken in. In no time two men appeared with a trolley and Merry was laid on it. He whimpered and muttered, but he was beyond knowing what was happening to him.

'Now, ma'am, if you'll come along with us to the station.'

'Will someone ring Whiteways? That's the most important.'

'That'll be done, never you fear. That poor little lady must be half out of her mind.'

At the police station she was ushered into an interview room. None of it seemed real, it was like a scene from a second-rate movie. There was no sane reason why they should question her searching for Merry. She felt confused and desperately tired, and now that Merry was safe she was haunted by that scene with Sebastian.

The sergeant made notes of all she told him. It wasn't often he had the chance to bring a 'suspect' into this stark cubicle, and he wasn't prepared to cut his hour of glory a moment shorter than he need. But after a while his colleague from the reception desk came to the door saying that there was a gentleman come who would vouch for Mrs Freeman's story. Then, with a secretive look in her direction, he whispered something in the overzealous sleuth's ear.

Julie's heart was banging wildly: it must be Sebastian. He hadn't meant those things he'd said, he'd been upset, he'd needed to lash out. 'You always hurt the one you love', how often had she heard that said? Tiredness fell from her.

They led her out. And there, waiting for her, was Quintin.

As he drove her back to where she'd left Trudie's car by the hillside, he explained the things she'd not yet come to question. Twenty-four hours ago he'd woken Sebastian's agent with his telephone call, insisting that Sebastian must be sent a message straight away. Sebastian had come on the first possible flight, landed during the afternoon and been driven straight to Whiteways. Quintin had been there when he arrived, but he'd kept out of their way; this was something for Sebastian and Lydia.

Sebastian had been in the house only long enough to hear the bare facts, then he'd set off with a lantern.

'Where he went I don't know, but not to the beach. Poor devil, he looked awful — Julie, you've no idea. I waited with Lydia.' By this

203

time they had almost reached the place where Julie had parked.

'You were still at Whiteways when the police phoned? You mean he wasn't back?'

'I waited until he came. Thank God, the telephone rang just as he arrived. I'd no excuse to stay with Lydia once he was there – but I don't think I could have left her. He looked wild, crazed. I answered the phone. When I called out that Merry was safe, that you'd found him, it was as if a spring in him snapped. That boy's his whole world. The Squire says he's a selfish swine, and perhaps he is. He didn't so much as look at Lydia. She'd cared, too, but you wouldn't think so, you'd think it was just him.'

'But they're together now.'

Now he knew that it had been she who had found Merry, Julie told herself, he'd be rational again. Soon he'd find out where she was and come to see her and then he'd understand.

'Together?' Quintin answered. 'Lydia is exhausted, Pam will have her in bed and asleep by now. As for him, where would you expect him to be? At the hospital, of course.'

'And so he should be. Poor Sebastian!'

'Poor Lydia.' By now he was pulling up beside Trudie's waiting car. 'Poor all of us, Julie.'

'We don't deal the cards, we have to play our hand with what we're given. But that doesn't have to make losers of us. Quin, thank you for rescuing me.' Tired though she was, she was struck by the humour of the situation. 'I reckon our gallant sergeant saw me as just the card he needed to set him on his way up the ladder of success.'

It was still the middle of the night as she drove back, and the roads were as empty as her mind. Her one thought was that she must get home, she could no longer fight off the pain that enveloped her in waves. Of course she was cold, she told herself, her wet clothes were drying on her. That's all it was, that and natural tiredness. Once she was in bed, warmth and comfort would lull her to sleep. The pain would be gone by morning. It must. If it went on like this she couldn't stand it.

The streetlights were off now, so when she finally arrived she had to feel for the keyhole. At last she was indoors and heaved a great sigh: the agony was over, Merry was safe. Taking off her shoes at the foot of the stairs, she crept up. Dear Trudie had put a hot-water bottle in her bed. By now it was cold – 'like a dead dog in the bed', her aunt used to say.

Sitting on the side of the bed she started to undress, letting her damp clothes drop to the floor.

'I'm boiling a kettle.' Trudie's whisper startled her.

'He's found. Sebastian came home.' Nothing ever woke Anna once she was asleep, but instinctively they were quiet.

'Thank God he's found! And you? You look dreadful.'

'Thanks' − a brave attempt to joke. Undoing her suspenders, Julie peeled off her wet stockings, Trudie kneeling to help her. 'Trudie, I feel awful.'

'You need to be warm in bed. I'll refill your bottle and get you a warm drink.'

'Glad you're here,' Julie breathed, trying without much success to find a smile. She was sitting on the edge of the bed, sagging like an old rag doll.

'Get your nightie on. By the way, I borrowed one from your drawer. You don't mind?'

Just to shake her head was more effort than Julie wanted to make. The pain had gone beyond being a dull ache in her back to a cramp in her groin, and now the agony enveloped her, making everything outside it distant.

'I'll get you a hot drink.' Trudie retrieved the cold rubber bottle from between the sheets.

In less than five minutes she was back, a cup of steaming cocoa in one hand, a comforting hot-water bottle in the other.

'Trudie.' Julie looked beseechingly at her. 'Such an awful hurt.' She clenched her teeth hard together, sitting as still as if all movement were beyond her.

'Come on, I'll help you into your nightie.' Trudie tried to sound confident, because she mustn't let Julie guess how frightened she was. Being overtired and rain-drenched couldn't account for the glazed look of pain in her friend's drawn face. 'Now, into bed with you. Cuddle the hot bottle, you'll be asleep in no time.'

Like a dummy, Julie let Trudie help her, lifting her aching legs and swinging them onto the bed, then putting the water bottle into her arms.

'Such a pain . . .' Julie was still gripping her teeth together so that the words were barely audible.

'Have you anything to take with your drink?'

When Julie didn't answer, Trudie went to the bathroom cupboard to look, coming back with a bottle of aspirin. She put her arm around Julie's shoulders to raise her and kept a steadying hold on the cup.

'Thankful you're here,' Julie breathed in between sips.

'You're entitled to a bit of fussing after the night you've had. But you found him. Just hang on to that, Julie. In a few minutes the aspirin will ease your pain.'

'It's a bit easier already. Was frightened; wasn't an ordinary pain. He was unconscious, you see. Seemed like hours I carried him.'

'Strained your back, I expect. You'll be off to sleep in no time now.'

Julie lay down obediently. In her relief that the pain was lifting she smiled gratefully at her friend.

'And you. I've messed your night up properly. It wasn't my back, Trudie − well, partly it was, but that wasn't what frightened me. So scared I'd hurt my baby. But it's lifting. Think it's going. Was so frightened.' She tried to get a grip on herself, her voice stronger now.

'I'll put out your light. Shall I leave your door open in case you call?'

'No. I'll be better now.'

When Trudie bent to brush her forehead lightly and murmur 'Sleep tight', Julie's eyes were already closing.

It must have been an hour or so later that Trudie woke with a start. She was conscious that she'd heard something, yet had no idea what. Sitting up in bed she listened. Her own door was open, but there was no sign of any lights on. Hark! There it was again. A whimper, a moan, high-pitched and unnatural. Out of bed in a second, Trudie ran barefoot into Julie's room.

'Is it the pain again?' she asked as she flooded the room with the hard glare of electric light. There was no need to ask.

'Never felt like this,' Julie panted. 'Don't let me lose my baby. Trudie, help me.' Beads of sweat glistened on her forehead. 'Sebastian ...'

'Of course you won't. You'll feel better after a day in bed.' Whose confidence was she trying to boost? she asked herself.

She saw Julie's expression change, pain giving way to a fear that was worse; she saw the way she moved her hand that had been gripping the bedspread and reached down the bed; she saw − they both saw − the hand reappear, the fingers red with blood.

'Knew I was. Told you.'

Trudie pulled the covers back as if to disprove what they'd seen.

'It's hardly anything. I know what I have to do, I have to raise the bottom of the bed, keep your legs high. But you'd better wear something. Have you any −'

''Course I haven't.' Julie's face crumpled. 'Our baby.' She found a comfort in her tears, just as she did in the weak, helpless tone of her voice. It was nature's way of holding her from the stark misery of what was happening.

For the next quarter of an hour she gave herself wordlessly into Trudie's care. The pain put a barrier between her and what went on around her as Trudie took the rug off the floor, rolled it up and pushed it under the mattress at the foot of the bed. Towels were brought from the bathroom to soak up the sudden gushing of blood.

'It's only blood. Surely if you were losing the baby it wouldn't be only blood.'

She tried to believe.

Don't let it happen, Julie begged silently. I'll stand all the pain; please, if you want to punish me, do it with the pain. Don't take his baby away from me. Make the bleeding stop, don't let me lose his baby, our baby. Oh God, it's getting worse. Don't let . . .

But there was no holding nature. The pain tore her as her body gave up its slim hold on that new life.

'Fancy disturbing us at this time of night.' The Squire had listened from the upstairs landing as Grace had taken Pam's message.

'I dare say she expected even *you* might be interested to hear that your grandson is found.'

'Well? Was our imaginative bobby right? Was there some evil kidnapper at the back of it?'

'Julie found him. He was in Downing Wood. He's been taken to Deremouth Hospital, it seems he has a broken ankle.'

'Downing Wood! What have I been telling you all? Of course he hadn't been kidnapped. A born play-actor − anything to make himself the centre of attention. Ought to be given the hiding he deserves. There's his poor mother scared half to death and all because he can't be trusted to behave himself. Probably watched from the wood, glorying in the fuss of police cars coming to the house.'

His words hammered at Grace, who tried to close off her mind and her ears. Halfway up the stairs she sat down. She couldn't come nearer to him, she couldn't make herself look at him.

'Sebastian searched for hours. It was Julie who found him.' Two items of fact, said with no emotion.

'What have I always said? While my Poppet sits helplessly by, what's he doing? Out there in the wood looking for *her* son, our grandson, and with his bit on the side to help him.'

'You talk like a fool,' she told him, her voice flat. 'A pathetic jealous old fool.' Sitting on the stair, she rested her face in her hands, feeling old and weary.

'Are you going to sit there all night? I'm tired even if you're not. There was no need to startle us with a phone call at this hour.' He turned back towards the room they still shared.

Single beds, single lives. But he was her husband, her first loyalty must be to him. And wasn't it? There was no one else in her life. She talked to Lydia, sometimes she felt she was close to Lydia; but one word of criticism of *him* and she knew she would never be part of their magic circle. So what had she? Nothing, no one. Tess had been her friend for years, but as long as Tess had Peter her world was complete. Thank God Merry was safe. Oughtn't that to be enough?

At Whiteways Lydia tried to stay awake and listen for Sebastian returning from the hospital. She was filled with joy and unfamiliar excitement: Merry was safe and Sebastian had rushed to her the moment he knew she wanted him. The anguish of sitting helplessly by while the search for Merry went on had dragged her down to the very pit of misery. Then Sebastian had come. In the years since her accident she'd been determined never to let him see her cry. Yet this evening when he'd come so unexpectedly into the room, she had taken one look at his haggard face and held out her arms to him, and there had been relief in her tears.

She'd stay awake until he was home from seeing Merry, she had so much to think about. She'd relive those moments when he'd knelt by her chair, his arms around her as she'd sobbed out her story. Of course he'd known already from her letters that Julie had gone, but how good it had been to say it again, to paint the picture of Merry lonely without Anna, of how let down she'd felt that life here had been too dull for Julie to stand, a career had been more important than friendship. Quick to stress that she didn't blame Julie, who could wonder that she'd been bored with life at Whiteways? It had given her pleasure to see his expression harden as he listened. Not that she'd ever taken the Squire's insinuations seriously; Seb and Julie had naturally spent time together but they'd always been with the children.

He'd only been with her a few minutes, then, wearing a mackintosh and Wellington boots, he'd lit a lantern and gone out. Seb would find Merry, Lydia had told herself, and all the agony would be over. Quin had insisted that if she was going to wait up for Sebastian to get home, then he'd wait with her. The long evening had stretched far into the night. Then, in a few packed moments, it had all been over. Sebastian had come home alone and at that exact second the telephone bell had shattered the silence.

No wonder she wanted to lie awake; her heart was full of relief, thankfulness and something else. She didn't examine what gave her this rebirth of romance, but it was like falling in love with him all over again. It was so long since there had been any adventure in her life, yet tonight their relationship had held drama, passion, despair, all the rich emotions that had been denied to her. Her heavy lids were closing, exhaustion was winning. Her last thought as she drifted into sleep was to remember that reporter who came when they first moved in. Imagine how much more interest there was in *this* story! She hoped all that crying hadn't spoiled her face. It would be good if Seb looked haggard and unshaven, his night had been long as he'd combed Downing Wood. They'd pose for photographs in the front of the house, the wood would be the background ... Lydia slept.

Chapter Thirteen

Next morning Trudie told Anna as much of the story as she thought good for her. Merry had been lost in Downing Wood; her mother had gone to look for him because she knew the wood so well and it had been she who found him and carried him home. By the time she arrived back it had been late and after so long in the rain she was cold and wet. That was why they had to be very quiet and not wake her.

'Would you like to spend the day at Rowans? Mum — Auntie Tess — says she'll drive straight over and fetch you if you'd like to.'

'But what about Mum? I could look after Mum.'

'Honestly, Anna, the best thing we can do is just let her have a good long sleep. I'm going to the office, you go to Rowans. She'll get better quicker if we leave her warm and sleeping.'

That seemed to placate Anna. For a minute she'd suspected that she was being shipped off out of the way because she was little, but she trusted Trudie to tell her the truth, because she always treated her like a grown-up.

'I'll go to Auntie Tess then, it's good fun at Rowans. But Trudie, why didn't Merry say he wanted me to go there and play? Is he having to sleep all day too?'

Trudie explained about his fall — but not how long he'd lain in the wood waiting to be found.

'They may keep him in hospital a day or two, I don't know. But his father is with him.'

'Oh, that's all right them. Don't 'spect he'd even want me if he's got Seb with him.'

The previous night's storm had moved eastwards. London and the Home Counties had woken to a dull, damp morning, but in Exeter the sun was drying away the traces of the night. Julie opened her eyes to find the sun streaming through the window. What time could it be? That was her first thought, before memory brought her face to face with events. Quarter to eleven! The rooms were full of silence.

'Anna! Trudie!' No sound. Then she saw a package left on the bedside table. Before Trudie left for the office she must have gone to the chemist. And by the side of the package was a note.

Don't worry about Anna. Don't worry about anything. I thought you'd be out late last night so when Mrs Arkwright brought back her typing I arranged with her that today she'd work here. She seemed glad to do it, so everything will be under control downstairs.

Mum came over very early and fetched Anna. For the day, we told her. But see how you are. They'll give her a good time at Rowans, I promise, so good that if you'd like her to stay the night she'll fall for the temptation!

Mum says Merry is OK except for a broken ankle.

I'll come in at midday — looks like being fish and chips again! Pity Anna will miss them!

Rest and keep warm.

Trudie.

Gratefully Julie did just that. She closed her mind to Sebastian and what his outburst meant. This morning the physical pain had eased, and last night's haemorrhage had become today's normal menstruation. She got out of bed, tidied herself up, made a cup of coffee. Not yet could her mind face what would have to be faced. It was easier to crawl back into bed, pull up the bedclothes and shut out the world.

'I really could get used to this — coming here for lunch, I mean,' Trudie said as she tucked into cod and chips.

Julie wasn't ready to go along that track. She ate in silence, surprising herself with the appetite that took possession of her with the first mouthful.

'It's good to see you're truly feeling better.'

'Truly,' Julie confirmed between mouthfuls, 'I slept all the morning, you know. Tomorrow I'll be normal again.'

'Mrs Arkwright likes being here. And Sebastian is sure to come once Merry's home. He won't go straight back to Spain.'

'I can't afford yet to employ her here full time. But perhaps just this next day or two . . .' She couldn't bring herself to recount the scene in the wood, and perhaps Trudie was right.

211

Julie stayed in bed all the afternoon. She couldn't muster up the energy to dress and make herself look attractive in case he turned up. And perhaps she wanted him to see her while she was still weak, to feel the grip of his hand on hers and know that the loss was his as well as hers.

Anna fell for temptation; on the telephone she told Julie that Uncle Peter had promised her if she stayed the night he'd call her really early so that she could watch him do the milking.

'Are you really all right, Mum? You're not fibbing?'

'No, darling, I'm truly quite better now I've had a sleep. You stay with Auntie Tess if you like. And aren't you lucky, being able to see the cows being milked? I've never done that. You'll have to tell me all about it when you come home.'

Again that night Trudie stayed with her. The gas fire turned up high, the yellow flame giving a good warmth but no real comfort. With a blanket folded into four thickenesses on the end of the table, Trudie insisted on doing the ironing. An ironing board was still on Julie's list of needs.

'Trudie, do you believe in God?'

'Why, yes, of course I do. I can't say I know much about theology, but you can't grow up on a farm and not believe there's a God. Don't you?'

'I suppose so. There must be something. A sort of judge on high, do you think? Weighing up what we do that's good and bad making sure we get our just deserts. And if that's what He does, we oughtn't to grumble. But where does love come into it? I thought that's what He was all about. You'd think He'd take it into account when He's dishing out the penalties, wouldn't you?'

'I don't follow where you're leading me.'

'I'm not so sure I know the way well enough to lead you anywhere. I'm so confused, Trudie. All of it with Sebastian – it was all because I love him. Sometimes I'm frightened how much I love him. You see, he never pretended there could be a way of our being together, always he'd be Lydia's husband. Tell me I'm a fool if you like, but it won't make any difference.'

'I didn't tell you any such thing. If he really loves you, then the only loser is Lydia. But he wouldn't suddenly feel differently about her if he hadn't got you.' Trudie didn't look up from her ironing. She knew there was more on Julie's mind than she'd heard yet.

'No. Oh no, nothing changes what he feels for Lydia. He honestly does love her, and I couldn't bear him not to. If he hadn't got me he'd replace me with one of his many affairs.'

'You don't believe that. You're just feeling low. Stick with it,

212

Julie, take what gets thrown at you. One of these days you'll look back and see there was a purpose.'

'For losing my baby?' Julie's grief was too new, she was frightened at the sound of her own voice. 'Now I'll have nothing of him.'

'It's the baby you lost, Julie, not Sebastian. All right, he'll always be Lydia's husband. But that hasn't come between you.'

'I thought he'd come to see me. All afternoon I listened for him. He could have found out my phone number, he could have spoken to me. I saw him in Downing Wood − ' And then she told Trudie all about it, repeating it word for word the things he'd said. She didn't notice the iron being switched off so that Trudie could put her arm around her shoulder, her hand gripping her tight.

'Damn him! Julie, there's not a whisker of difference between any of them. Men! They want one thing, that plus their freedom. He's probably no worse than any other. Except for when he was hampered by the children being with you, I bet every time you were together he got you to bed.'

'What if he did? I wanted him to.'

'And now? If he came now, could you talk to him, tell him what's in your heart and mind? Or would you be content just to make love to him?'

'Wouldn't be much good to him at the moment.' Julie tried to make a joke, but her misery was too great.

'You would be if he loved you or if you honestly loved him. You say he truly cares for Lydia but if he did, would he behave like he does? Flowers, presents, a kind pat on her head! No, he'd want to make her feel whole, he'd hold her in his arms. But does he? You know he doesn't. He gets a nurse to look after her and takes you to bed. Men! I hate the lot of them.'

This time Julie did laugh. Trudie's outburst was so out of character that for a moment it made her forget her troubles.

'This God business,' Trudie was saying, 'why did you ask?'

'I suppose this has made me think, real deep-down thinking, sort of take stock of what happened and how much of it was *my* fault. It was my fault, Trudie. Not in the way Sebastian believed − that I'd got bored and wanted a career − but my fault just the same.'

Listening, Trudie still couldn't see this as an answer to her question.

'When Merry was missing they said he'd been lost off the rocks; I know when I conceived my baby, it was there on the sands by those rocks. I prayed as hard as I knew how, I didn't care who this God was, I just prayed with all my heart that Merry would be safe. He was given back and my baby was taken in exchange. It was

213

like telling me that I'd sinned, warning me that the power belonged to this all-seeing judge.' Once started, Julie's words rushed out; she found relief in acknowledging her guilt. 'I know just how often I've tried to make myself look more attractive than Lydia; I've longed to hear Sebastian say that he wanted to leave her and come to me. I wouldn't have let him, but I wanted to hear it. I wanted to be the one to deny us the right to be together. There! I've confessed. But this deity who sees everything and reads our hearts, He knew about my wickedness. He knew how to mete out justice.'

'If there was wrong done, it was no more you than Sebastian. Now it's over, Julie. Let it go, don't hang on to something that will make you bitter. Remember Jeremy and the happiness you had with him. That's something that's pure and good.'

'You say that, yet he was taken away. Was that a punishment too?' Julie wasn't ready to find comfort, her hurt was too new.

'That was different. Jeremy died — like thousands of others — for freedom for the rest of us. Remember him and think of Anna. You have Anna, she loves you and she trusts you.'

'Trudie, you make me so ashamed. I just feel so lost. Of course I think of Jeremy, I'll always love the memories that are left to me. They ought to be enough, but I'm mortal, I've had to build a life without him. Sometimes I think I've grown into a different person. But Anna, yes, Anna is my reason for everything I do.'

There was so much Trudie wanted to say, but a warning voice told her it was too soon. Instead she went back to the ironing. Later she put a hot-water bottle in Julie's bed and one in her own.

Trudie's undemanding loyalty comforted Julie more than she realised. Earlier, as she'd unburdened herself of the guilt that had been tormenting her, she had felt cleansed. In truth the result might have been the same had she confessed aloud to an empty room. But she had told Trudie and had let her in to the inner sanctum of her soul.

The bed was warm. Along the passage in Anna's vacant bed Trudie was still making shift with a borrowed nightgown.

'Trudie! Trudie, are you awake?'

She was. In a second she burst into the room. 'Is something wrong?' Last night was still so clear in her mind.

'I've been thinking.' Julie held out her hand to her. 'Why don't we ring your mother in the morning and say you'll go over to fetch Anna when you finish work? You could get your things. We'll make up the other bedroom.'

214

Trudie nodded. Her dark-blue eyes shone with happiness. It was all happening just as she had dreamed.

'We'll make it good, Julie. You, Anna and me.' With a light kiss on Julie's brow she left her. If we only get what we're entitled to in this world, then somewhere along the line she must have done something good.

In the morning Julie insisted she was fit enough to work. Mrs Arkwright (who, before the morning was over, had become Cecily) was torn between wanting to make a good impression on her employer by keeping the typewriter keys rattling and her desire to hear about Julie's search for the Sutcliffe boy. The papers had been full of it and, this morning, some of the national press had a picture of poor Sebastian Sutcliffe, so handsome and yet looking quite ill, as he arrived at the hospital. At mid-morning she went to the back room to make their coffee and while they were drinking it she had her opportunity. Out came the morning paper.

After the coffee break and the conversation Julie hadn't been able to sidetrack, she felt the night's brave resolutions slipping away. Every sound of a car slowing down made her look up; every ring of the telephone set her heart pounding. Surely today he'd come. Yesterday he must have been with Merry, of course that was why she hadn't heard from him. Today he'd want to find out the real reason why she'd broken her promise to him and left Whiteways, he must realise there was some other reason apart from what Lydia had told him. Today he'd come back to her, he must.

By mid-afternoon she had found every possible excuse, making the way clear for what she knew she had to do.

'You can cope if I go upstairs for a few minutes, Cecily?'

'Of course. You mustn't overdo it. Miss Grant explained to me how poorly you were yesterday.'

'I won't be more than a few minutes.'

She shut the door at the foot of the long, straight flight of stairs; she shut the door at the top, too. The telephone was fixed to the wall in the passage. Taking up the receiver she dialled 0 and waited for the operator, then gave the number she wanted.

'The number is ex-directory. Will you tell them it's Julie Freeman calling.'

A delay, then, 'Putting you through, caller.' A few clicks, which she hoped meant the operator wouldn't be listening.

'Julie, you'll be wanting to speak to Lydia.' She recognised Pam's voice.

'Or Sebastian. He'll be the one who's seen Merry. Is Merry all right?'

'Yes, he's coming home tomorrow. Lydia isn't here, she's taken Sebastian out in Ruby. You should have seen her face, pleased as Punch she was to be driving and having him as a passenger.'

'I bet.'

'He won't be staying – well, of course he won't. As it is, they must be champing at the bit to get him back there on this location in Spain. He just pulled up sticks and came, you know, the moment he got the call about Merry. If Lydia were able to be like an ordinary mum, then it wouldn't have been so dreadful. He must have been as worried about her as he was about poor little Merry. Julie, I know it's not our business, we ought not to be chatting about them, but you'll understand what I'm saying. It's Lydia. Before Merry disappeared, before you went away even, you know how down in the dumps she'd been. I suppose it was the thought that Sebastian would be gone so long. You should just see her now, looking as if a lamp's been lit in her.'

'That's splendid. But what about Merry? He's all right? You promise me he is?'

'A plastered ankle. From what I've seen of children with broken bones, in no time he'll be scooting around on his crutches, proud as a peacock of his new importance. Julie, it's none of my business, but you must care for that lad or you wouldn't have been out there on a night like that, searching for him. It was because you left him, that's why he ran away, you know. He needed you, same as he needed Anna. I have to say it, you let them down – Lydia, Merry and even Sebastian, although he's not often here. Everyone trusted you. And all the time you must have been waiting for your moment to drop everything and snatch your opportunity.'

'Pam –'

'Well, to each his own. Job satisfaction has to be important, it must be or we couldn't do the best that's in us. I'm lucky, I love what I do. For me job satisfaction is trying to make a patient as happy as circumstances allow. For you it's the challenge of proving yourself. No one can say which of us is right.'

'It wasn't like that.'

'Come on, ducky, of course it was. And no crime in that. Listen, Julie, I'm not saying you made the wrong choice. You have Anna to think of, she's got to be first priority. You can't spend your life being a companion to Lydia, taking and fetching Merry from school until he's old enough to be sent off to board and have other boys to mix with. Where would that have left you? No proper home for Anna. No, you were right to do what you did. Let them say what they may.'

Julie wanted to ring off, but Pam had always been friendly, she couldn't cut her short.

'I bet Lydia was pleased with herself, playing chauffeur to Sebastian?' She managed just the right bright interest.

Pam laughed. 'Oh, but wasn't she just! These last days, since he's been home she's been like a new woman. Wish I could say the same for him — well, not a new man, but the man we'd come to be used to. It must have given him such a fright being called home like that, then the business with the net in the sea. Young rascal! Merry, I mean. It seems he told his dad that he went down to the rocks before he made off to the woods, and threw his net as far as he could into the sea because he wanted to let them see how much he'd wanted to go shrimping. Would never have believed it, young monkey. Don't expect for a moment he's big enough to know the mischief he was making.'

'Poor little Merry.'

'Not what Squire said. You should have heard him ranting and carrying on. Dreadful thing to say, but I reckon he hates that boy. He looks on him as a burden on Lydia. I say I get my job satisfaction from people — tell you one thing, he's about the most mixed up I've hit on.'

'Tell Lydia and Sebastian I phoned. Say I wanted to know.'

'I will, Julie. Did I tell you where they've gone? No, I hadn't got round to that yet. They've gone to Plymouth, or somewhere that way. They've made enquiries from an agency and it seems there's a girl there likely to just fit the bill. To look after Merry, I mean, and be a bit of company for Lydia when I'm busy.'

'I thought Lydia had found someone to replace me?' She wanted to know, yet she couldn't bear to hear.

'A girl from the village, Marie Dale. Oh, Marie's a great help. Drives the Standard, takes Merry to school.' All that was spoken in a loud voice. Then, in a conspiratorial whisper, 'Good worker in the kitchen, but wouldn't be on the same wavelength as Lydia, nor would she want to get too friendly. That wasn't what she came for. And you know Sebastian' — again her tone said more than her actual words — 'very fussy is Sebastian about who's responsible for Merry. Between ourselves, Julie, I heard him carrying on alarmingly about you going. Always put great faith in you.'

'I must go. I have a business to run.'

'Very quiet yet a while, I expect? Well, it must be, that you can sit and chat like this.'

'I'm upstairs at the moment. So far I've engaged one full-time member of staff to actually work here with me.' She kept her fingers crossed, she didn't intend to tempt fate. 'Work has been coming in much more quickly than I'd expected. I suspect Trudie spread the word. She's thinking of moving in with Anna and me, we really are a good team. Must go. Give my love to Lydia — and Merry when he comes home.'

She rang off. The passageway seemed quiet, empty and lifeless. He and Lydia were out together choosing staff. And wasn't that how it should be? 'Of course we're a good team, Anna, Trudie and me,' she said aloud. Then she flopped to lean against the wall.

He wasn't coming. How many times had she looked up expectantly when she'd heard a car? But he'd been with Lydia, lighting a lamp in her eyes. They'd believed they'd lost Merry, then he'd been restored to them. What more natural than that they should see each other afresh, realise they needed each other? His poor little honey. Oh, but there had been a time when Lydia had swept him off his feet. If this was a second beginning for them, she should be happy.

Happy or otherwise, she had to accept.

'Cecily, I've been thinking.' She came back into the office where the keys of the so-called silent typewriter continued unfalteringly, like someone tap-dancing in carpet slippers.

'Yes?' Cecily Arkwright needed this job; her husband Jack's salary was low, the rent on their flat was high. 'Is there something you want me to do? I could make time for an hour or two's work this evening if there's something.'

Last night Trudie's kindness had bolstered Julie. But it was Cecily's expression, part hope and part fear, that did more than anything to put the mettle back into her. She offered Cecily a permanent job in the office as long as she was prepared to take temporary work as necessary.

Cecily's thanks were profuse, and with new determination, Julie went back to the ill-spelled manuscript. 'Sing alleluia as you type,' Sebastian had sneered at her. She'd sing alleluia for her independence, for a road ahead of her that was well defined, for a challenge that would give her no time for remorse. Hope, fear and ultimately relief on Cecily's face had pointed the way for her. She meant to aim high, she meant to steer her own course. Even when she'd willingly let her heart and head be full of Sebastian, she'd never pictured herself with the years passing and her life stagnating. So what had she imagined? Here she came against a wall of fog; there could have been no future for them.

Forty-eight hours ago her greatest joy had been to be carrying his child; twenty-four hours ago she had been torn with grief, yet even then she'd believed that his anger had been a safety valve for his fears. Now she knew that in leaving Lydia and Merry she had removed herself from his life.

Her mouth set in a hard line. The time would come when he'd be reminded of her, he'd see hoardings advertising Freeman's Secretarial Agency and know that she wasn't the woman to sing alleluia as she typed at someone else's bidding. She might be starting in Exeter, but she wouldn't stop until she was established in London. For good measure she threw in extra branches in the provinces too. That would show him there was more to her than a woman to take to bed!

The following morning, Anna had been deposited safely in the school playground. In the office of Freeman's Agency the shrill ring of the telephone bell swamped the muffled background noise of the typewriters.

'Freeman's Secretarial Agency. How can I help you?' Cecily's voice was clear and helpful, she was the model of efficiency. She took a quick glance at Julie, hoping her telephone manner had been noted. 'If you hold, I'll see if she's free. Who is it calling?' Then, 'Oh, I'm so sorry, I didn't realise it was personal. I'll get her for you.'

'I'll take it upstairs. Put it through for me, will you, Cecily?'

With exaggerated professionalism, Cecily pressed down a key on the small switchboard and turned a handle to ring the bell upstairs.

All Julie's hard-won resolve was gone by the time she reached the corridor at the top of the stairs. How could she have doubted him? Excitement and nerves combined to make her clammy hand shake as she lifted the receiver.

'Julie? Is it you this time?' Lydia! Julie leaned against the wall. She'd been so sure, so ready to hear his voice. 'Julie?'

'Sorry, I ran up the stairs. Must be out of condition.' She forced a breathless laugh. 'Lydia, is everything all right?'

'Yes. Now I've phoned you everything's fine. These weeks since you've been gone I've missed you like anything, Julie. But pig-headed pride wouldn't let me phone. I just hoped *you* would.'

Disappointment at not hearing Sebastian was a physical ache, but it couldn't detract from the relief Julie felt that between her and Lydia peace was to be made. Until now she'd never let herself admit to the shame she'd felt that she had deserted Lydia, hiding behind a pretence of lies; in truth her mind had been so taken up with her own affairs that she had given no thought to the hurt she'd caused. Now a hand of friendship was being held out to her.

219

'Lydia, I truly am sorry. I behaved badly running out on you like that. It all came up in such a rush – this place, the chance to do what I'd always planned. I expect I was a bit ashamed of what I was doing. Shame makes cowards of us all. I don't think I realised how badly I felt about it until now, hearing you again.'

'If you hadn't found Merry – oh, I don't want to think of what might have happened. But when you found him, why didn't you bring him back here! Why did you take him to the police? That's what's been worrying me. It was as if you felt we couldn't be friends again.'

'Me take him to the police? There's a likely story!' Exaggerating the episode, Julie tried to instil humour into her tale. It was so far from the reality of that night that it helped to keep her memories at bay. 'I was arrested! Sergeant Whatever-his-name-is was on top of himself with importance. A fair cop it was, I was coming down the lane with Merry in my arms and walked right into our Policeman Plod. I got the full treatment, taken into a sort of cell place, notebook out, my statement heard. Quin must have told you how he came to the police station and vouched for my character.'

'That's dreadful, Julie, after all you'd done! I've not seen Quin since. It seems a lifetime ago, but it's not even two whole days. Julie, listen, I just have to say this. I have to tell someone, and I could always talk to you. Sounds like sentimental slush, but you know I'm not that sort of person. I've never seen Sebastian in the state he was in when he came home. It was like seeing him afresh, like seeing both of us afresh.'

'What are you telling me?' The way her heart was pounding had nothing to do with running up the stairs. It must be that Sebastian had told Lydia about *her*. It was as if a great weight was lifted. Lydia wasn't hurt, her voice was buoyant; but then, how often Julie had seen the bored way she looked at his cards, disregarded his gifts. All that flashed through her mind. The things he'd said in the wood suddenly counted for nothing.

Lydia laughed, a laugh that seemed to bubble up from the depth of her. 'It sounds crazy. Can you fall in love with someone you've been married to for six years? It was because of Merry, both of us so frightened for Merry. We found each other all over again. I had to tell you, Julie. I knew you'd be happy for me – for us – you must have seen I'd been in the dumps. But I needn't have been. Even now, the way I am, he's still in love with me. I know he is, I can tell.'

'I often thought you'd got tired of him. But as for Sebastian, you know he always loved you.'

220

'It's so hard though, I'm something and nothing of a wife, aren't I? You know the way the gossip columnists always try and make out he's with other women − well, they used to − and anyway, with me so useless, who could blame him if he'd got a mistress? He's human. That's what I've always told myself.'

'Lydia, nothing will make Sebastian feel differently about you, I'm sure it won't.'

'No, I know. But women are more necessary to some men that to others. Seb's one of those, I've always known it, that's why making love with him was so wonderful − '

'No. You shouldn't tell me. That's between you and him.'

'You mean it *used* to be. It ought not to matter to me, but it does. It matters to me more than any of the rest − I can remember the feel of his touch, I want to feel it again. But I never will. Frightens me. It's so final. But I know you're right, I know he loves me.'

'Did you tell him you were phoning me?' Any question to stop Lydia's confidences.

'He's not in. He's gone to fetch Merry home. We went together yesterday to interview the girl who's going to look after him. She's nice. Not a bit like you.' Then, with that familiar chuckle, 'I didn't mean that the way it hopped out. But it's true, she's quite different from you and she is nice, although I don't see her and me ever getting to be real close buddies. She's about twenty but seems much younger, like a podgy schoolgirl. She'll be good with Merry, that's what matters. He was so lonely. And, Julie, I'm ashamed, but I wasn't a bit nice to him. Just couldn't seem to be bothered. Oh, here's the car turning in. I must ring off. Poor little love. Seb's out of the car ... opening the back door to get him ... lifting him ... yes, I can see his plastered ankle. Julie' − her words tumbled out at a great rate as she watched the others coming towards the house − 'we *are* friends still, aren't we? That's what I wanted to say, that and to tell you about Seb, about it all being so thrilling again.' Her excited laugh might have come from the eighteen-year-old who'd first come face to face with her idol. 'Honestly, just looking at him makes my heart dance a jig.'

'I'm glad for you, Lydia. And of course we're friends.'

'Have to go, they're coming in. Bye.' A click and the dialling tone buzzed in Julie's ear.

She must go back downstairs to the office, she must fix her face in a smile and say to Cecily that Merry had been sent home from the hospital. Bracing herself, Julie went down the stairs.

Once more she forced herself to concentrate on the manuscript she was copying. It wouldn't always be like this; each day her small empire would grow. She must keep her goal in sight. Men! Who needs them? That was Trudie's view. And so it would be hers. She must rebuild the resolve that had dissolved as she'd rushed up those stairs.

The girl Sebastian and Lydia had engaged to share Merry's out-of-school hours was a far cry from both Marie Dale and Julie. Polly Sinclair was fun-loving, unsophisticated and without a thought of hero worship in her ex-public-school mind. Just as she had in her years at school, she still loved games: netball, lacrosse, hockey, tennis; given the opportunity she played all of them with more enthusiasm than skill. Her muscles were as tough as many a young man's despite her stocky build. Little did they know in Deremouth the new competition that would take to the sea in next year's regatta, pulling on the oars and leaving every other young woman behind. To Sebastian, Polly was a relief; she'd never seen him on the screen, theatres were of no interest to her, in fact he was simply Merry's father. As for Merry, he took to her immediately, seeing her as a playmate. He planned that they'd go to the village together and both buy shrimping nets, maybe hooks and lines too; there were lots of things he could teach her about the marine life they found in the rock pools, things Seb had told him. His optimistic spirits revived.

With Merry in safe and understanding hands, Sebastian was glad to return to Spain. His confused anger against Julie had struck him like a physical blow when he'd first received Lydia's letter telling him that she had gone. He needed the anger; in that he could hide from the hurt. In Downing Wood, bedraggled, weary and soaked from hours in the rain, she had found him unprepared. He hated her for the obsessive hold she'd had on him. Animal instinct had made him want to abuse her physically, to destroy the vision of her that haunted him. Something in her appearance had shocked him; in his bitter resentment, as never before, he'd seen her as plain. But for her, Merry would have been safely at home. Sebastian's slim hold on control had come from his disparagement of her. Turning his back on her in the wood had for him been symbolic, it had rung down the curtain on something he meant to erase from his mind.

Back in Spain he gave himself wholeheartedly to his work. Here it was easier for the wound to heal. And if there was a scar, then let it be a reminder to him that he wouldn't be such a fool again. How many women would be able to take what had happened to Lydia and never complain? And wasn't it enough to remember the way she had turned to him in her helpless isolation while Merry was lost? She and Merry were

222

his world — his domestic world, came the half-acknowledged truth.

He spent long days on the set, bearded, the contours of his face altered almost beyond recognition by the make-up artist. But even if he weren't free himself there was often someone with time for a day's trip to Toledo or a weekend in Madrid, willing to keep an eye open for any unusual little gift for him to send to Lydia. He liked to think of her excitement as she tore open the package.

For a while after she'd been lifted out of her low rut by what she liked to think was, for both of them, a reawakening of romance, his gifts added colour to her days. But it couldn't last. It had all happened before: picture postcards, parcels, flowers every Tuesday. She sank back into despondency, sank even lower than before. There was the nursery to go to, but more often than not, once he had seen her settled, Quin would work in another glasshouse or outside where Olive was overseeing the preparation of the trial ground. Polly Sinclair was a jolly youngster, and even though she didn't suit Lydia's present mood it was a relief to see that scowl gone from Merry's countenance. Since she had been with him he never came to Lydia with his draught board and a look of hope.

'I've been listening to Merry reading,' Polly told her. 'He's brought his book so that you can hear him. He's coming on wonderfully.'

He stood in front of her with his book of easy reading. His voice was clear, his confidence enormous. Only occasionally he frowned in annoyance at himself that he had to take a word letter by letter phonetically before in triumph he conquered. He held her attention, or at least two eyes and half an ear of it. How like Seb he was! The set of his straight shoulders, the quick irritation when he failed himself, but most of all the confident ring of his tone.

'Jolly good,' she interrupted when he was at the end of a sentence.

'But there's more. Don't you want to hear what happens?'

'Let's keep some back for tomorrow. If you've been reading to Polly and now to me, I think you deserve a break. Don't you and Polly usually play a game — ludo, draughts, something like that?'

He shut his book, feeling his face getting warm with embarrassment. It had been an interesting story, but Mum hadn't cared about what happened. That meant he hadn't done it well enough. Tomorrow he'd read just to Polly.

'Isn't he reading well? Hardly stumbles at all.' Polly was as proud as if she'd taught him herself.

'Yes. I shall look forward to hearing the rest, Merry.'

223

'No, you won't, you're only *saying* that.' His voice had always been deep, and now it growled. 'Shan't do it again, not till I do it better.'

He stomped out of the room; with a laugh and a shrug, Polly followed him. Lydia was ashamed. Sebastian would have listened, he would have been proud.

'Here I am.' Pam bounced into the room bearing her routine tray. 'Tonic wine. There's the second instalment of *Queen Eleanor* starting on the wireless in ten minutes. Remember we heard the beginning last week? Have you ever thought of getting a television set? You ought to, you know. I was looking at one working in a shop window when I went to Newton Abbot. It wasn't nearly as flickery as I'd expected. It would be wonderful company for you.'

Lydia took her glass, swallowed a large gulp of tonic wine and blinked back the misery that flooded over her.

'When Seb comes next we'll talk to him about it,' she promised.

If at the back of her mind Lydia knew why she decided to go out on a cold December morning, she didn't let herself admit to it. She understood how much the Squire looked forward to coming to see her; she ought to be there for him. As Pam helped her pull herself from the chair to the driving seat of Ruby, her mind was on him far more than it was on the shopping list that was in her pocket.

'Now, you're sure you can manage? What if they don't hear the horn and don't come out to serve you?'

Lydia flashed her the confident smile she expected to see. 'What do you think I have a pair of lungs for? I'll yell. Don't you worry, Pam. It's time I did something useful instead of killing time cruising round the roads. Oh, by the way, if the Squire comes − and of course there's nothing to say that he will − '

'Except that he always does.' Pam laughed. 'Go on, if he comes ...? Do I hang on to him here or send him to find you in Otterton?'

'Pam, would you mind awfully telling a white lie? Just say you don't know where I am. Well, not really a lie, because by that time you won't know where I am. Maybe I'll take off somewhere exciting; I've got the freedom of the road, me and my friend Ruby.'

'Don't worry, I'll say the last I saw of you, you went *that* way.' She pointed in the opposite direction from the village.

'And that's no lie; I'll have to go that way and all the way round the lane to come out on the Deremouth road, then back through the wood. If I don't I'll have to pass Delbridge House. Oh, Pam, I feel such a heel! Bet at this very moment he's tarting himself up with an extra dab of aftershave, making sure his bow tie's right. He does it all for me, I know he does – and I love him dearly. It's just that ...' She closed her eyes. 'I ought not to go. He needs to feel I depend on him.'

'Off you buzz. I'll make him welcome, give him an extra top-up of sherry and tell him he smells nice. Poor old lad, all he wants is a bit of appreciation.'

Lydia took Pam so much for granted, it had never entered her head that the homely nurse might be forming opinions of her own.

'I'm off then.' She put the car into reverse as she spoke, backing out through the gate, taking a quick glance in the direction of Delbridge House and the village before she accelerated as hard as Ruby knew how and sped off in the opposite direction. She felt uneasy. He came every day and when she heard him open the door her heart always fell. If she weren't so wrapped up in herself she would be able to chase away his gloom, instead of letting it overshadow both of them. It was her mother's fault! She'd changed, she'd grown hard. As a child Lydia had come to expect that her mother's greatest joy was to see the Squire happy. But not now. And her mother couldn't pretend it was the accident that had changed *her*, because she was much too stoical to challenge what fate had meted out. Poor Squire, all he asked was a chance to be happy.

So thought Lydia as she sped off in the opposite direction to avoid him!

She'd turned into the lane that in a mile or so would take her to the Deremouth road, when she realised something was wrong with the car; with no warning all power would be gone, then in seconds power was restored to normal. The first time she told herself she'd imagined it, but it happened again. This time she was ready and pulled hard on the accelerator, only to find her speed dropped. Then, just as last time, the car sped on. This erratic progress continued until she was at the top of the lane at its junction with the Deremouth road. She slowed down to see that the way was clear to turn right, then pulled on the throttle control and moved into the road. There the car stopped dead, refusing all her efforts to restart it.

It was never a busy road, and now there was no traffic. The minutes seemed like hours as she sat there flattening her battery trying to put Ruby into action. At last help came in the form of a young man in a green sports car with its canvas top open despite the season.

'What's the trouble?' He came over to her side.

'If I knew I'd – ' She stopped herself. Once upon a time she could have said it, but not now. If she knew she'd be able to do nothing.

'Have never yet met a pretty girl who knew what went on under the bonnet of a motorcar. I'll take a look, shall I? But first hop out and I'll push it to the side of the road.'

'I'll steer, you push.' She gave him her most beguiling smile. He'd called her pretty, something no one had done for so long. She felt pretty.

She steered, he pushed, and a minute later he was hidden behind the open bonnet.

'I see what the trouble is. You'd better hop out and take a look in case it plays you up again. You really ought to get a garage to check the carburettor. I can only do a get-you-home de-gunge. Come and have a look.'

Her prettiness forsook her. 'Would if I could, but I can't.' She made a gallant effort to put a sparkle in her voice.

'Can't? How do you mean? You needn't touch anything and dirty yourself.'

'As if I'd care about that! Can't get out, I mean.'

He wiped his hands on his handkerchief, looked at the oil-blackened linen, then again at her, pulling his face into the expression of a naughty child.

'Mummy slap my bottom for that.'

How easy it was to laugh! She forgot she'd lost her prettiness.

'You tell Mummy you saved a lady in distress. All mummies like their little boys to do that.'

'What's this about can't get out?' Coming to her side he put his head through the open window, expecting to see a bandaged leg.

'Can't walk. Oh, I used to be able to. But' – like him she pulled a face, overacting the playfulness but finding it the only way to tell him – 'I got in the way of a falling beech tree. So here I am and here I stay till I get hauled out when Ruby decides to stop playing the fool and take me home.'

He made no sympathetic noises and for that she was grateful.

'Have you by chance a needle on you?'

'Not a thing I carry on a shopping trip. You don't look to me like a sewing man?' Lydia was having more fun than she had had for a long time and her gingery eyes shone with merriment. Just to talk to a stranger, to be treated like a whole human being, was doing her more good than all the tonic wine Pam made her pour down her throat each evening.

'It's not me who needs it, it's Ruby. I have to perform a minor operation if she's to get going. Once done I have every faith that she'll be your obedient slave again. Even so, Mrs ...?' He hesitated, waiting.

'Sutcliffe. Lydia Sutcliffe. My husband is Sebastian Sutcliffe.'
She couldn't resist saying it, it never failed to impress.

'Mrs Sutcliffe. Lydia, you say. If I'm allowed to be on Christian name terms with Ruby, then surely Lydia will be in order?'

She chuckled. 'And you? A knight errant who is to perform surgery on Ruby, I ought to know who you are.'

'Terry O'Hara.'

'From Ireland. Of course, I can hear it now you've told me.'

'Not me, not even my father. 'Twas my grandfather came to seek his fortune. Didn't have a lot of luck in that direction, but − ' he lowered his voice, leaning through the window again to guard his secret − 'but what would a leprechaun have been wanting with wealth even if it had dropped into his lap?'

It was so long since Lydia had felt such youthful light-heartedness. Who Terry was or where he came from she had no idea, indeed she could almost believe there was something of a leprechaun in him, with his curly auburn hair, his manner of having all the time in the world to spare, and the teasing laughter in his brown eyes.

'All well-trained ladies carry a needle and thread, even a safety pin in cases of emergency − or so I've been led to believe. I can see you were never a Girl Guide, prepared for any contingency.'

'You can't mend a motorcar with a needle and thread. What do you want it for?'

'I told you, Ruby requires surgery. More exactly there's a wee jet, part of the carburettor. Seems to me it's blocked; the needle would be to shove through it.'

'Well now, why didn't you say so?' She unclipped the brooch from the lapel of her coat, seed pearls clustered round a large, dark piece of amber. Sebastian had given it to her a long time ago, the magic summer when she first met him. He'd told her the amber was the colour of her beautiful eyes. She remembered it clearly as she passed the jewel to Terry.

'Sure it's OK to use this? Are they proper stones?'

She shrugged. 'Sebastian gave it to me so they must be, I suppose.' Sebastian would never buy anything that was less than the best. Nonsense packages to give her pleasure when he was away fell into a different category.

'Your husband, Sebastian Sutcliffe − some sort of film idol, isn't he?'

'That's the one. He'd not thank you for calling him that, though. A Thespian, pure and traditional.'

It was Terry's turn to shrug. 'I'm not a theatre man myself. Now, a few jars and a good singsong, bit of poetry when you're just oiled enough to shed your inhibitions, that's more my line of country. Sitting there in rows, clapping at the end, ach, no, that's not for the sons of leprechauns.' Then, moving back to the open bonnet, 'Now, Ruby, you've had your fun, we want no more temperamental nonsense out of you.'

In no time the bonnet was down, the brooch wiped in his oily handkerchief and returned to her.

'Try starting her up, then I'll follow behind you. By the way, where are you heading?'

'Only into Otterton and then home. But you were going the other way.'

'No panic. What calls I don't make this morning, I'll make this afternoon; what doesn't get done today will get done tomorrow — or the day after. Would you be thinking that that's the sort of reasoning stopped my grandfather being another Dick Whittington? And what if it was? There's more to life than rushing around earning a bob. If we don't give ourselves time to stand and stare — ' then, raising his hands, palms upwards, and nodding his head in her direction — 'stand and stare or sit and stare, what difference? Anyone can beaver about fancying what they do is important, but if you ask me that's the way to miss out on the things that matter most. Start her up, and I'll be right behind you.'

So they drove towards the village. 'Right behind you,' he'd said and so he was. Not as though he were there to protect her, but enjoying himself, liking the way the morning had shaped. When she waved at him in the driving mirror he replied with a jaunty thumbs up. She'd almost forgotten this feeling of joy in simply being alive.

We have only one life to live and in Lydia a new resolution was born. Perhaps Terry had more to do with it than she realised.

Chapter Fourteen

The friendship that developed between Lydia and Terry was an easy-going affair, it made no demands on either of them. His carefree air might so easily have made her resentful, emphasising as it did the difference between his life and her own. Instead, some of his delight in living seemed to rub off on her. When he came to Whiteways his presence sharpened her vitality.

He earned a meagre living — which was all he needed — collecting weekly insurance premiums, sixpence at one house, half a crown at another, perhaps as little as fourpence for a month at the next. Somehow he managed to do that, have a friendly chat in each doorway, and still look on himself as a free soul with no one to watch his every movement. He enjoyed the fun of a mild flirtation as well as any young man, but he looked for nothing more permanent. For him Lydia held two attractions: she was no threat to his freedom, since she was tied not only to a wheelchair but also to a husband most girls would give their eyeteeth for; and her sense of humour matched his own. The thought of a girlfriend expecting him to make love to her put more fear than ardour into Terry; that would be only one stage away from captivity and he had a suspicion the game wouldn't be worth the candle. His path didn't cross Trudie's or he would have been an education to her, sure as she was that men wanted of a woman just one thing; Terry's goal was to extract the last ounce of pleasure out of living in other ways. Perhaps that's the way with leprechauns! Asked to describe the ideal girlfriend, he would surely have come up with Lydia.

They'd met at the beginning of December, and from that first day he made a habit of looking in at Whiteways whenever he was over that way, sometimes for no more than ten minutes, sometimes much longer. If he found her at home he was pleased; if he didn't, well, that was fine, he'd spend a while with Jolly Polly, as he called her, then go on his way. Terry's breezy visits never failed to lift Lydia from the doldrums.

She wasn't falling in love with him, of course she wasn't; why, it was only a few weeks since she'd confided in Julie the rebirth of her feelings for Sebastian. As the weeks of winter went by, though, and filming on location drew towards a close, she found remarkably little thrill in the thought of her husband coming back to England.

Sebastian arrived at Whiteways towards the end of February, stayed for four or five days during which most of his time was spent with Merry, then moved on to London. He was determined to have a full schedule. Ambition had always been his driving force, and never more so than now; his goals were the same as they had been the night he and Julie had broken their drive to Otterton St Giles and, over dinner, he had shared with her his aspirations. If he had been sure then of the way he planned his life, now he was doubly sure. In his profession neither success nor failure go unpublicised, only mediocrity. At the back of his mind and never fully acknowledged was an added reason why he filled his life with the theate he loved. Julie: she would see the reviews, she would remember the night he'd confided his dreams to her; soon she would read about the formation of the Sutcliffe Theatre. He knew now that her word to him had meant nothing, she had broken it at a whim just for the sake of earning an independent living. But she would learn that his own course remained set, it would take more power than her to move him from it.

'I see your young admirer has been visiting again. Just driving off as I came up the road.' The Squire forced a smile to his face, but he couldn't disguise the pout in his voice.

'Think it's me who does the admiring, Squire. There's nothing complicated about Terry, just plain, honest appreciation of the simple things.'

'Humph. Knows he's on to a good thing, in and out here as if he's part of the establishment. Anyway, never mind your Irish Mick, let's talk about you. How's my Poppet this morning? Warm enough for me to push you out to the terrace? Springtime again, let's see if we can get some colour in your cheeks.'

'Squire, if I want to go on the terrace — ' Then she stopped herself. 'Come on then, I'll sit back and be waited on. Put me where the sun shines, then bring your chair over.'

She was rewarded by his changed expression. Had he been a dog his tail would have been wagging. He honestly believed that it took so little to make him happy, he had no idea how his need of her crushed the vitality from her. A few months ago his clinging dependence had been more than she could endure, and she had wanted to show him she could manage without him. Time and time again she'd watched the dejected droop of his shoulders as he'd left her, and when it was too late, she had been filled with remorse. Lately she'd gained patience and learned to hold back the wounding words and let his possessiveness wash over her.

She didn't ask herself who had taught her to see beyond herself and had anyone suggested that Terry had been her mentor she would have scoffed.

'What's the attraction for him? You? A married woman?'

'Of course not, not the way you mean. Terry's not hurting anyone. Don't harp on things that make us quarrel, Squire. Look at the sunshine, let's forget our troubles.'

But the Squire wasn't to be sidetracked so easily. 'Tell you what I think he's after. Who, not what. That little rubber ball of a nursemaid. Two of a kind, those two, both think life's nothing but fun and games.'

'Come on, grouch, I thought you were here to cheer me up. How's Mum? She's not been in for a while. What's she up to?' They should be on safe ground there.

But she was wrong.

'I'll tell you why she hasn't been here. It's her conscience. She'd be ashamed for you to see how little she cares about me, Poppet. What's changed her? Or didn't she ever care? Was I always no more than her bread ticket?'

Lydia laughed, a laugh as forced as her father's smile had been when they'd talked about Terry. Suddenly she was frightened. More than once her mother had used her as a safety valve, but this was different. Things between them must be badly wrong for the Squire to have noticed. That was something she couldn't face. Her parents had never shown signs of any romantic feelings towards each other, but she wouldn't have wanted them to, it would have made her uncomfortable. She needed to take their presence and their personalities for granted.

'My word, but you are in a bad way today! Did you get sent out of the way with a flea in your ear this morning?' She made light of his remark, she had to; somehow he had to be stopped, before he said things that would for ever cast a shadow.

'Poppet, if I hadn't got you I'd have nothing. She's cold as ice. Have you seen the way she looks at me? No, of course you haven't,

231

she avoids being here when we're together. She knows that you and I —'

'Stop it! I'm not going to listen. It's not fair that you expect me to.' She turned her face away from him, but he could tell from her voice and from the way she pressed her knuckles against the corners of her mouth that it was too late to hold back her tears.

'Poppet, you mustn't be upset. Please, Poppet.' He wasn't prepared for her loud, harsh sobs; he didn't know how to cope.

Indeed, even Lydia was unprepared. Her uphill battle was suddenly more than she could bear, yet she couldn't run away from any of it. It was only her legs that didn't work, her spirit was still the same. But was that enough? The Squire had found an unexpected crack in her armour. She listened to her own sobbing, her shaking hands pressed against her face.

In all this time her father had never seen her cry. He felt helpless. 'Listen, child, stop crying and listen to me. I was wrong to talk to you. But we've never kept our troubles from each other.'

Turning to him, Lydia's brimming eyes were full of accusation. How could he say that? When had she ever felt she could rest her burden on his shoulders? Perhaps long ago when she'd been a child, but not now, not since he'd been warped with jealousy for Sebastian.

'It's not fair of you. To me you're just Mum and the Squire; haven't I the right to keep even *you* unchanged? It's probably all her fault, I don't care which one of you is wrong, but Squire, go and be nice to her, make things right. For *me*, Squire. I can't bear it if you two quarrel.'

'There now, love, dry your eyes. I ought to have realised. Of course I can't expect you to add to your own troubles by worrying about mine. It's done me good to talk, all the same. There's no one but you, Poppet, no one to care, no one to listen. But I've upset you, I shouldn't have. Here, dry your eyes and say you forgive your old Squire. After thirty-odd years together your mother and I aren't going to rock your foundations now. Bread ticket may be all I am, but she's not stupid enough to think she can manage without one.'

'Hate crying,' Lydia burbled. 'Lend me your hanky, Squire. Let's forget it all.'

From his top pocket he produced a large, red silk handkerchief and she wiped her face and made a gallant attempt to put the scene behind her.

'Anyway —' She hiccoughed as she found her control. 'I want to tell you about Saturday. I'm running the raffle at the Village

Hall bazaar. I expect you to contribute a prize and to buy lots of tickets. It's for the fund for a new roof.'

'You! But you can't possibly run a raffle. I wouldn't mind betting that Irish Mick of yours is behind this nonsense!'

'Then you'd bet wrong. It was Mrs Briggs told me about the bazaar — her husband's the caretaker of the hall. I offered.' Then, knowing she said it to score a point and yet ashamed that she should want to, 'They're putting a write-up in Friday's local paper, saying that Sebastian Sutcliffe's wife is selling the draw tickets. They're sure that will bring people from outside the village — probably hoping Seb might be here.'

'Humph!' was all the answer she got.

'I'm looking forward to it. And, if the winners aren't still there when the draw is called, then I can deliver the prizes in Ruby.'

'They've no business to expect it of you. I'd better come and help.'

'No. No, Squire. I don't want help, can't you understand?' Her gingery eyes were full of rebellion.

They could hear Pam coming towards them carrying a tray with three glasses of sherry, part of the morning routine.

'Ah, there's a sight to gladden the eye.' Collecting together what he liked to think of as his debonair charm, the Squire aimed his remark at Pam, but his smile encompassed nurse and tray alike. With a perception that had grown out of the years she'd spent considering her patients, Pam remembered that Marie was waiting for her in the kitchen.

'You're lucky having Pam, she's the pivot this house revolves on.'

Lydia nodded, not quite trusting her voice but glad of a change of subject.

'That other girl, can't think of her name, Rubber Ball — '

'You can't think what she's called because you don't try.'

'Polly something or other, that's it isn't it? I give her another six months here, she'll leave you in the lurch same as that other one did. Freeman's Secretarial Agency. I went by her so-called office the other day — looks more like a shop with a big window like that. Outside the sun was shining, you could feel spring in the air. And there she sat, clicking away at her damned typewriter. Ought to be ashamed of herself. To think I gave her hospitality in my house, treated her like one of the family. You speak for yourself, but I for one will never forgive her. And this other one, Miss Rubber Ball, she'll have no more consideration when the precious Terry snaps her fingers. I've seen the

233

way they play together, showing off to each other and pretending it's all for Merry's sake.'

This time Lydia's laugh was genuine.

'Sometimes I wonder I love you at all.' She leaned towards him and brushed his beard with her lips. 'You're a disagreeable old grouch, you think the world exists just for you and me.'

'Ah but that it did, Poppet.'

'Off you go home to Mum and give her a bit of attention. We all need to feel we're loved, not just you and me.'

He put down his empty glass and prepared to leave.

'Young Quintin's nursery's looking good. He and the Sharp girl make a good pair. With Paul gone and Trudie a rum egg if you ask me, for Peter and Tess's sake let's hope Quin gets young Olive Sharp up the aisle and let's them see a new generation coming along. Broad hips, generous mouth, she's the kind for easy breeding. I suppose you're going up there this afternoon? You must be getting useful after all this time.' Then, with a laugh that showed his previous moans and groans were behind him, 'Always thought young Quintin Murray was a bit of a dreamer, but damn me if he hasn't got his head screwed. *You* work for the love of it; put a ring on Olive Sharp's finger and she'll dig and hoe out there in all weather with no pay packet. Damn me if he hasn't got the right idea! Well, I'm off. I won't forget, I'll treat her with kid gloves.' He kissed the top of Lydia's head, then gave her a saucy wink. 'First I've got to see whether I'm to be allowed out of the doghouse. I expect you'll be here in the morning if I look in, will you?' He didn't expect an answer.

He hung on to his resolutions most of the way back to Delbridge House.

'I'm home!' he shouted, having slammed the heavy front door and aimed his green soft felt hat accurately to land on the hallstand.

'So I hear.' Her voice held no interest. 'I'm just finishing a letter so that I catch the one-o'clock collection.'

'What's so urgent?' he asked, coming to read over her shoulder. 'Who are you writing to?'

'I had a telephone call from Evelyn this morning. Squire, I'm going away for a while.'

'With Evelyn? No accounting for taste.'

Her lips tightened. 'Your stupid remarks about my friends ceased to be funny long ago.'

'How is it that the estimable Miss Keeble is holidaying during termtime? Have they decided to dispense with her services at this "jolly hockey sticks" school of hers?'

234

'The lower-school maths mistress has been rushed into hospital. She'll be off school at least until the end of term. Miss Watley-Jones, the headmistress, phoned me this morning.'

'Where's this rigmarole leading? What did Miss What's-it want with you?'

'I've just told you. Someone has suddenly gone sick. Don't forget my degree was in mathematics.'

'How many years ago? Good God, woman, your brain is as rusty as the hinge on the potting-house door. Anyhow, surely they could find a younger woman? Girls need teachers they can look up to and admire.'

She kept her back to him as she sealed the envelope and stamped it.

'Brains go rusty only if you don't use them. You of all people ought to be an authority on *that*. I taught for too many years to have forgotten. Philip' − the use of his proper name put a distance between them and emphasised the importance of what she said − 'a little while apart won't do us any harm. We can't go on like this, picking at each other, looking for slights −'

'Nonsense. You imagine things. The trouble is you don't look outside yourself. With a daughter in her state, any mother not entirely self-centred would want to be with her. Her whole life is ruined −'

Grace had gone, hurrying down the drive to the postbox built into the stone wall of Delbridge House in the days of Queen Victoria for the convenience of the few houses nearby.

'I told Mrs Randlesome we were ready.' When she came back the Squire indicated the open door of the dining room where the daily cook-cum-general-help was putting some sort of a corned-beef hash in front of Grace's place to be served. It wasn't until they were alone again that he picked up the previous conversation. 'Anyway, why does teaching a class of thirteen-year-olds their theorems, always assuming you remember them yourself, make it so vital that a letter goes to Evelyn Keeble? No doubt Miss Double-Barrel will tell her you've snatched at the excuse to get away.'

'It matters because I shall be staying with her, she has a flat in the grounds. Of course she'll already know I've accepted, but − oh, Squire, you can be so beastly sometimes. If it's true and I do want to get away, who can blame me?'

He shrugged his shoulders. 'Not I, my dear. I don't blame you. I don't begin to understand you. Women get difficult in middle age, so I've read. But you can hardly still be hanging on to that for an excuse!'

Grace kept her head down, as if the food on her plate held enormous interest. She felt old, tired, plain, all the things he implied. The offer had come from out of the blue, and she saw it as her salvation. Let him say what he liked, but she had never let her brain go rusty. Faced with a classroom of senior students she could still teach them and prepare them for their examinations; but hers would be thirteens and fourteens, some of them keen, some of them looking on mathematics as something to be endured. She had to open their eyes to the excitement of it. When she was young it had been a rare subject for a girl to want to take up. But times were changing, the war had opened new doors. The Squire had told her − even if not in so many words − that she was drab, that the girls would find her dull. She would do her damnedest to prove him wrong and to fire them with her own enthusiasm.

That afternoon she went to Rowans with her news. Just as she'd known, Tess was delighted for her. Next, she climbed up the hill to the greenhouses to tell Lydia.

'Without the Squire? Mum, you can't just cruise off and leave him in the house on his own. Think how lonely he'll be, you know how down in the dumps he gets. Instead of staying with Miss Keeble you could put up at a local inn or something − you and the Squire together. A change of scene would be good for him, get him away from worrying about me. Mum' − she changed the subject ' − did he tell you about the raffle? I'm organising it. I've collected prizes from the shops in the village −'

'I'm glad you're starting to do things. I know Quintin finds you jobs to do here, but I'm glad you're sorting things out for yourself.' Lydia wished she hadn't said it like that, as if the work at the greenhouses was contrived out of Quin's kindness. 'But for myself, my mind is made up. I shall stay with Evelyn. I need to be at the Abbey, there's more to boarding-school life than teaching in a classroom a few hours a day. If I have him to worry about I shan't do a good job.'

Lydia pouted. 'Should have thought a husband was more important than a classroom of twittering girls. They won't want to learn maths anyway. *I* never did, and with you for a mother you'd think I might have been interested.'

They held each other's gaze, like fencers with swords crossed waiting for the first to move. It was Grace who turned away. 'With the Squire for a father I should think it highly unlikely.' She longed for tomorrow, to be enveloped in the atmosphere of Trewarin Abbey and the companionship she and Evelyn shared.

'Mum, if you knew how I envy you!'

'I thought you condemned what I'm doing?'

'For you, I do. You and the Squire ought to be together. You're my mum and dad, it's all wrong trying to chase a career at your age.'

Grace didn't argue. She assumed she was responsible for Lydia's mood. She couldn't know the confusion in the girl's heart as she worked her way along the shelves of 'her' greenhouse, checking the seedlings.

'I rang Mum today. She tells me that Aunt Grace — Grace Harriday, I mean, how silly it is to bring children up to say Aunt to friends — has taken a temporary job at Trewarin Abbey in Cornwall.' Trudie was washing the dishes from their evening meal, eaten early enough for Anna to join them. Washing up was a necessary chore to the two grown-ups, only Anna was still keen enough on this team business to enjoy the responsibility of putting the dried crockery away.

'I call you Aunt Trudie,' she observed. 'That's not silly.'

'But that's different. We all live together. You're my chosen niece, someone special.'

'I don't blame her.' The last plate dried, Julie hung up the tea towel. 'She needs something, everyone needs something. She loved teaching; when I lived there she used to talk about her teaching days occasionally, and she seemed to come alive.'

'He's enough to crush the joy out of anyone. Been spoiled rotten, that's his trouble — and her fault. Are you going to read to us, Anna? We got to page fourteen in your reader last night. Let's see if you can finish the story for us.'

Trudie had never known such happiness as over the months she'd lived here. Each day her friendship with Julie seemed more firmly cemented, their unspoken understanding stronger. She knew something of Julie's ambitions; the office in Exeter was simply the beginning. But wherever they went, they'd go together. They were a family, Julie, Anna and she.

Three years at university, a year at law school and five years in practice had not taken away Trudie's naive ability to hope that her friend would not one day fall in love with some man. Sometimes memories of Jo and what she'd believed to be love would wake a hungry yearning in her. And if *she* felt like that, then surely Julie must too. Neither of them ever talked about it. One day everything would fall naturally into place. First of all the base had to be firm, they'd build their lives together on it. And from that everything would follow. What sin could there be in that? Even the word 'sin'

237

conjured up pictures veiled in mystery. She mustn't rush; when the time was right the last veil would fall.

When the schools broke up for the Easter holiday news filtered through that Grace was back at Delbridge House, but only until next term. Like everyone else they supposed that the permanent junior maths mistress was still convalescing and Grace would stay at Trewarin Abbey until she was fit.

One day towards the end of April Julie saw a car draw up to the kerb in front of her window. She recognised it as belonging to the Squire and Grace, so why should her heart do a double somersault? After all these months, was she still listening, watching and expecting him? In any case he'd never borrow the Delbridge House car. She gathered her composure and even felt pleasure when she saw Grace get out.

'How nice!' Julie voiced her first reaction. 'Cecily, you can manage for a while, can't you?'

'Of course I can. Is it a visitor for you – or a client?' It was the nearest she could come to asking who the austere-looking woman was.

Julie took pity on her. 'It's Mrs Harriday, Lydia Sutcliffe's mother.'

'Fancy! Oh, dear, I do hope that doesn't mean there's something wrong with poor Mrs Sutcliffe.'

Grace strode in, her long hand held out to find it taken firmly in both of Julie's.

'I saw you draw up. What a lovely surprise! I'm so glad you're not going back to the Abbey without coming to tell me all the news. I speak to Lydia on the phone sometimes, but except for once at Rowan's I've not seen her. I've purposely not taken Anna back to Whiteways, it might be unsettling for her – and for Merry. A few hours together on the shore and they'd remember how much they enjoyed each other. Come upstairs.'

'I certainly will. Since you left Otterton I've missed our talks. But first I want to see what you're doing here. Are things going well – with the business, I mean?'

'Yes, I've been lucky. It was surprising how many people put work my way. Of course, we've been going more than six months, so by this time the work that comes in must be on our own merit. But to start with I know I had Trudie to thank for so much. We're up and flying now, though, we've quite a number of temporary secretaries and typists out, and our register is growing. As for Cecily and me, we're never idle. This is Mrs Arkwright, Cecily Arkwright. Lydia's mother, Mrs Harriday.'

'Grace Harriday.' Grace's voice was as firm as the handshake she gave Cecily. It was important that she should be seen as her own self, not simply Mrs Harriday, Lydia's mother. 'I find this really exciting.' She looked around both offices admiringly. 'The beginning of great things. We were given two feet to stand on, and once we've got our balance it's a mighty satisfying feeling. Upstairs, did you say? I want to see everything. You lead the way.'

Julie was sure the reason for this visit was deeper than to see the offices or the rooms above it. She and Grace had always been able to talk frankly with each other, so she was prepared to hear a confidence about Lydia or the Squire, perhaps even Sebastian. At this last possibility her hard-won composure threatened to desert her.

But Grace insisted on being shown round. 'Good big rooms, Julie.'

'A bit spartan, but it's all our own, and I know you can understand how important this is. We're not beholden to anyone, no one can tell us to up sticks and go. It's early days, but you just watch. Freeman's Secretarial Agency won't always be a couple of rooms in a side road of Exeter. Women will never be content to be slaves to a home like they were when I was growing up. I mean the average woman, the average married woman. From part-time jobs, even temporary work covering for holidays, they get a taste for earning a few pounds they can call their own.'

'Is that the way you see it, you with a home to run and a child to care for? Hardly money to call your own.'

Julie laughed. She enjoyed Grace, she always had. 'I put it badly if I implied that they all want to earn money to go out and spend on themselves. That's the last thing – for me and for most of them. I remember when Anna and I lived in Finchley and I took in typing, I got a real kick out of those extra shillings, the difference my efforts made to what Jeremy's pension paid for. But rich or poor, the pride would have been the same. And don't try and pretend you don't understand; you're not the sort to be able to get your fulfilment in plumping up the cushions so that the Squire sits more comfortably.' Had she overstepped the privilege of friendship? Grace was more than old enough to be her mother.

Apparently she hadn't. 'Oh, I understand, believe me.' Grace slumped into an easy chair, or came as near to slumping as such a ramrod back ever could. 'I've seen Trudie once or twice over the holiday when she's been over to Rowans. Never seen her so ... so complete. I'm not prying, please don't think I am. I've known her since she was a child; she always seemed aloof from the others, and to me she was an enigma. She came from a home so full of love, yet she seemed to hold herself back. Now she's blossomed.'

Julie sat on the humpty. Conversation with Grace never stuck long on trivia, and their understanding of each other put a natural bridge across the age gap.

'Julie, you are I have always been on the same wavelength. I have to talk to someone, someone who cares about Lydia.'

'Is something wrong? Well, of course it is, she can't always wave that banner of courage. I felt dreadful about leaving her, you do believe that?'

'I never doubted it. I'm not asking you why you did it − I don't want to be fobbed off with stories about this having always been your ambition. And when you talk about waving a banner of courage, I think you did just that and you did it for *her* sake.'

'What are you saying?'

'My dear, I'm not blind. I've seen you and Sebastian together. What was it I said just now about Trudie? She is complete. I could feel the same with you and him.'

Julie couldn't look at her. If she'd seen, then so must Lydia.

Reading her thoughts, Grace answered what she couldn't bring herself to ask. 'No, Lydia had no idea, and the Squire certainly didn't or he would have relished the fresh accusations he could have hurled at Sebastian − out of earshot, of course, only for my hearing. But whatever the Squire says about him − and some of it may be true, marriage to Lydia didn't alter his ways − he is devoted to Lydia and as for Merry I think he worships the boy. However hard it was for you, you made the right decision. And, Julie, my dear, you have your reward in all this.'

'You mustn't put too much faith in intuition,' Julie forced a laugh. If only she could have confided the whole miserable story to Grace! 'But I'm glad you approve of our home. I expect you recognise some of the things that came from Rowans; Mrs Grant was so helpful even before Trudie moved in.'

These were words to cover the confusion of the moment and somehow, through the sort of small talk they usually bypassed, they got back to a topic that was relevant and yet safe. 'You were going to tell me something about Lydia − you had to talk to someone who cares, you said.'

'Yes, and someone who is fond of her, someone her own age. She has so much to bear, and I've hurt her beyond words.'

'As if you would! I don't believe it. She's probably using you as a whipping boy, she won't mean to but sometimes she just has to let off steam. We all do, don't we?'

'Tomorrow I'm going back to the Abbey. I've been offered the post as a permanency. I'd told them I'd give them my decision when I returned from the holiday but in any case I'd agreed to be there until the end of next term. For nearly a month I've been home. Home? Well, at Delbridge House. I've put off saying anything, I've mulled it over and over in my mind. My conscience tells me I have responsibilities. But aren't we entitled to expect more from life than duty?' She fidgeted her long fingers, her self-assurance having deserted her.

Julie reached out and took hold of her hand. 'Of course we are. But it's so easy to resent being tied, believe that it's duty. Surely if your conscience is speaking to you it's because you love what you'd be leaving? The Squire, Lydia and Merry, your place in the community, your easy friendship with the Grants. But, Mrs Harriday — '

'Grace. Let me just be Grace, we're friends enough for that, surely? He's always been the same, you know. All my adult life Evelyn Keeble has been my friend. Whenever she's visited me he's been, oh, hateful, full of sneer. And don't tell me he was jealous, that's one thing he never was, not of *me*. Oh, he's jealous of Lydia, that's why he hates Sebastian, even Quintin or that young man she's made friends with, Terry someone or other.'

'Who's that? I don't know him.'

'He's not important. I've met him once or twice, I've seen Lydia with him. He's just someone who cheers her up, her leprechaun, she calls him. But the Squire's so terrified she might cast a smile in someone else's direction that he's withered up with hate. It's eaten into his soul, Julie, I can't take it any more.' Her thin face was contorted, her long nose red with the first tear. 'Lydia has always been everything to him. I remember when she was born, when he came to the hospital. It was as if a miracle had dropped into his arms. I was proud, I thought I was part of the miracle. But of course I wasn't. But it never mattered, I was content to care for them both and see them sharing something that I could never be part of. He was happy, not just placidly content but actively happy, and the house took its mood from him. It was like that until she met Sebastian. Hate is like a canker, it feeds on itself, it destroys. He had to vent his spite on someone — me! His strength came from wearing me down, trying to make me *nothing*. Until that's what I was.'

'No, Grace, that's not true. If anyone else said a word against him you'd be the first to defend him.'

'I used to love him. I must have done. Can't even remember now.'

'You're upset because he's trying to make you change your mind and not go back next term? Isn't that the truth?'

Grace snorted, an ugly sound in keeping with her haggard, tear-stained face. 'Doesn't want me to go, wants me to be there — to plump up his cushions, wasn't that what you said? When did we stop having a proper marriage? Don't even know if we ever had one at all. Sometimes I've thought he wanted a mother, not a wife.' She wiped the backs of her shaking hands across her cheeks, tried unsuccessfully to sniff the dewdrop that glistened on the end of her nose, then dug in her pocket for a man-size paper tissue and blew furiously. 'Oh, dear, shouldn't behave like this.'

'Yes, you should. Don't hold back, Grace, you'll think all the clearer.'

For a few seconds she was silent, hesitating. Then the words poured out, cleansing her mind of something that had haunted her through the winter months. 'He's demented with hate − hate even for an innocent child. Julie, when Merry disappeared he pretended to help in the search on the beach, but I could feel a sort of triumph in him. That evening I was too frightened and worried to care. It was later, at home, when he talked about Merry, I sensed − I was going to say jubilation. To feel like that about the disappearance of any child would be inhuman, but this was his own grandchild. He told me that he'd called at Whiteways in the afternoon when Lydia had been out. He'd just seen Merry. A sad and lonely little boy, and he, a grown man, boasted of the things he'd said to frighten him, wicked things about Sebastian. "When's Seb coming?" You remember how it was Merry's constant question. Squire told him things a child couldn't understand about other women in his life, that Lydia could divorce him and then he would never come at all. That was the afternoon that Merry ran away. There, now I've told someone. How long I've hated him I've no idea, but from that night I never blamed myself for how I felt. It's all he deserves.'

'If I hadn't run away −'

'No. Such consuming hatred will find a way to surface somewhere.'

'Poor Lydia! You may be able to walk away from it, Grace, but she's the object of his love, she's the one with the responsibility.'

'Lydia can handle him. She always could.' The storm had left her drained, even her voice had lost its usual vibrance. 'I'm leaving him. I told Lydia this morning. That's what I meant when I said I'd hurt her. Seemed to knock the chocks from under her. She sees me as selfish, says that I don't care about anyone else so long as I can bolster my own newfound importance. I knew that's how she would see it. She has a right to two parents, to Delbridge House always being there. Am I wicked? Am I obsessed with self? Julie, I had to talk to you. You're young, as she is. Do you see me as a woman frightened of growing old, chasing opportunities that are gone? It's not like that. Philip − the Squire' − more than anything she'd said before, it was the way she used his chosen name that told Julie her scorn, her anger and hurt — 'he says it is, he says we're a joke, Evelyn and me, he says ...' Whatever he had said was lost in the depth of a second man-size tissue.

'It's an enormous step, actually leaving him and Delbridge House for good. Why don't you take the job but come home sometimes at weekends? Then there are half-terms, holidays. Grace, do you have to be so final? You say Lydia's hurt — and he must be too, that's why he's saying the things he is.'

'If he's hurt he'll thrive on it. He makes a profession of self-pity, Lydia knows that as well as I do. You lived there long enough to have seen how he wears her down. Yet she'll not hear a word against him. Even knowing how he feels about Sebastian, she still loves him.' The screwed-up tissue was put back in Grace's pocket and she spoke with cold calm. 'I don't. I've tried, but I can't. He's put me down too often, now I'm not even interested. It's years, more years than I can tell you, since he's touched me, you know. It was as if once I'd given him his precious Poppet he didn't need me. Strange, isn't it, a man so natty in his appearance, you'd think women were important to him, but they never have been. In the beginning he needed me to love him, to take care of him. And I did, fool that I was; I built my life around him. He hadn't any driving need for physical love, so I learned to pretend that I hadn't either. But it's not true.'

'Tell me about your life at the Abbey. Maybe that will help you be sure whether what you're doing is right. Do you get on well with the girls? Is teaching as good as you remembered?'

Grace leaned back in her chair, her eyes closed.

'Teaching, trying to help them see there's a thrill in logical reasoning and getting things right, oh yes, there's enormous satisfaction in it. And, you know, I think they quite like me.' Julie was touched to hear the way she said it. 'Then at the end of the school day I go back to the flat with Evelyn. Such contentment, such completeness! We sit there marking our books — how Squire would jeer, a couple of elderly women feeling they have the answer to the mystery of life. But we do. I'm like a coin that's been spinning and has come to rest, the right side up. He'll weep and moan, gather sympathy and draw strength from it. Just now you talked about my place in Otterton; by the time he's spread his tale of woe my reputation will be in shreds. Doesn't matter. Tess will understand. I shan't tell her the things I've said to you. It wouldn't be fair to burden her, she and Peter have been our friends for too long. But I know without being told that she will understand. She's the most truly good person I've ever known.'

'Goodness is easier if you're happy.'

Grace digested the idea, then laughed wryly. 'That must tell us something. But it's true. So where does happiness stem from? They've lost a beloved son, I saw them go through that dreadful period — I dare say it never gets less dreadful, although the numbness of shock wears off — but there's a deep abiding peace in them.' She shook herself. 'I must go, I must let you get back to building your new empire. Feel so much better than I did when I came. Thank you, Julie.'

'Promise me you'll come to talk to me again. Trewarin Abbey isn't too far away for that.'

'Can I give my face a cold splash before we go downstairs?'

A cold splash did little to get rid of the ravages, but Julie managed to whisk her visitor through the office with no more than a cheery goodbye to Cecily in passing, then she was outside in the car.

It was then that she gripped Julie's hand as if that way she'd drive her words home.

'It was seeing Trudie that made me so sure you'd understand about Evelyn and me,' she said. 'What you've found together is good, Julie; don't look back over your shoulder, take your happiness. I know the truth of what I say. Lydia is my daughter so I don't count her in the equation, any more than you would Anna. But this is what I want you to remember: the deepest, most profound love I have found is what I share with Evelyn. It's based on understanding that needs no words. Dependence on each other is there, it must be, and yet we're two independent people, proud of each other's successes, sharing each other's sadnesses. It must be like that for you and Trudie. How near you are to finding the ultimate joy in each other I don't know — no, don't tell me. But feel no shame. Let the world think what it likes of you, love is the greatest power on this earth.'

Julie's instinct was to pull away, yet she was too fond of Grace to do it.

After she'd watched the car disappear she went back into the office.

'What a nice lady!' Cecily served the first ball, hoping to hear more when it was returned.

'She is. We've always been friends. Shall we check over those figures for the McIntyre and Radley work?'

Cecily knew when she was beaten.

That evening passed much as every other, but Grace's words echoed in Julie's head. 'The greatest power on this earth is love.'

Bedtime came. Just as they did each night, Trudie put out the milk bottles, Julie set the table for breakfast. Nothing varied, not even who took first turn for the bathroom. Then, goodnights said, they went to their separate rooms.

Julie tossed and turned. Far away a clock struck three loud, clear clangs. She'd heard it chime one o'clock, then two, now three, and felt there was something symbolic in the sound. One, two, three . . . Jeremy, Sebastian, her brave new venture. Before long the minute hand would move full circle again, four chimes would mark the progress of the night. 'Never look back over your shoulder', Grace had said. But today could never be independent of yesterday. Soon it would be tomorrow. Jeremy, Sebastian, ambition shared with Trudie . . . Julie's lids were closing. 'The greatest power on this earth is love.'

Drifting at last into sleep she couldn't see the shape of the road she had to take, but she knew where it had to carry her.

Chapter Fifteen

'It's the Deremouth they show on the picture postcards.' Lydia's voice was flat. A week ago the coast of Devon had been shrouded in mist, a week hence it might well be again. But on this day what she said was true. Mid-May was masquerading as mid-summer: the sky was unbelievably blue and the far horizon lost in a haze of heat. It was Saturday afternoon and on the gritty sand children built castles, one family played cricket, in the sea the more stalwart were braving the first chilly swim of the season. Near to where Quin had parked the jeep was a row of deck chairs where the elderly were taking their pleasure with less energy but just as much appreciation. Lydia wished she hadn't let him bring her. Her bare legs were stuck out in front of her, the straps of her sandal tight now because her feet and ankles were puffy. She turned her face away from him so that he wouldn't see how much she cared.

Put some sparkle into your voice, she told herself, he mustn't guess how hopeless everything is. 'Saturday afternoon − if Olive isn't working, you ought to be out there together having fun.'

Lydia had never felt so alone as lately. She made sure her days were busy − the carnival committee, for example, had welcomed her (Sebastian Sutcliffe's wife!) − but nothing filled the emptiness that came from the Squire's oft-repeated certainty that Quin and Olive were perfectly suited and heading towards marriage. And that was good, she told herself. Perhaps if Quin had confided in her himself she wouldn't have felt so cut off, so frighteningly isolated in her unhappiness. Because he said nothing it put an insurmountable barrier between them. Why couldn't he talk to her just as she always had to him? More than anything that was what hurt − or so she believed. Olive was always friendly to her, she never seemed to be pushing her out. In her present mood, that hurt too; it was proof that she couldn't think of Lydia as a rival.

246

She felt her hand taken in Quin's, then very gently he turned her face back towards his.

'Olive not working? No, it's her Saturday off, but young Jim Clegg is there, we don't need to worry about the nursery.' His manner implied that the nursery was what had concerned her. 'Fun? Would I prefer to be out there on the beach? Is that what you think?'

She nodded, biting hard on the corners of her mouth. ''Course you would. So would I.'

It wasn't easy to hear what she said, but he knew exactly what she meant.

'I know you would.' For a second he hesitated, but he couldn't hold back the words. 'If you could run on the sand, then I'd rather be there too. But, Lydia, you can't and we have to accept.' His hands cradled her scarred face. His tone, his words, his expression, all these things stirred feelings that frightened and excited her. 'If this is where you are, then it's where I want to be. I've no right to say it – but I can't help it. You must think me an awful weak fool that all these years I've never seen anyone but you, never want to see anyone but you. If you can't walk, then I want to be the one to carry you, to sit with you. There's only ever been you, for me there only ever could be.'

He turned away from her, resting his hands on the steering wheel and staring unseeingly at the Saturday afternoon sun worshippers. Her own fears were nothing compared to his. Had he destroyed her trust? Would even that be lost?

Over the past few years she'd known frustration, loneliness, despair; she'd had the only firm foundation knocked away when her parents had separated. For one brief spell she'd believed romance was still alive but once Merry was safe, Sebastian had gone away and she recognised it for what it had been – a dream built on her need to put colour into the greyness of her life. But for Terry O'Hara the winter would have held no ray of light, for the outlook had been flatter and emptier than she'd ever known it. In the past Julie had been there – and Grace, too. And Olive had not.

Now suddenly here was Quin talking to her as though she were the same as the girl he'd loved when she'd been whole. There was no way of holding back the tears, they were the only outlet for the emotions that set the blood pulsing through her veins. Joy fought with desolation, desire with disbelief, some half-recognised anticipation with her all too familiar hopelessness.

Without a word he started the engine and drove slowly along the front and up the slope to the grassy cliff. Here it was quiet, away from the shore that drew the people. He pulled off the road and parked the jeep facing the open sea.

'Tell me, Lydia,' he prompted gently. 'Is it seeing people playing on the sands? Or is it because of what I said? I'm a fool, I shouldn't have let myself say things that upset you. I'm sorry. If it's that, then let's pretend it didn't happen. Just couldn't help it.'

'No. It's not that.' She gripped his hands, her nails were sharp on his palms. Not asking himself why, he knew he wanted to feel the pain, and clenched his fingers over hers so that they dug more deeply. 'It's everything. Such a mess! Look at my ankles.' They were the least of her problems, yet this afternoon it had been the ugliness of her swollen ankles more even than her paralysis that had symbolised the woman she had become.

'I know. For your sake I wish they were slim and pretty like nature meant them to be.'

'Oh, Quin!' She buffeted her head against his shoulder. 'Don't be too nice to me.'

'Now we've dispensed with your ankles, tell me what the real trouble is. And don't say, "Look at me, I can't walk", because I know that already.'

This was the Quin she was familiar with, ready to give support but never useless words of sympathy. As usual it was the way he pulled off his glasses and concentrated on polishing the lenses in his handkerchief that told her he wasn't as calm as he tried to appear.

'Don't know why I'm crying,' she snorted, 'can't seem to stop. Turning into a wet wimp.' She pulled her hands away from his and rubbed the backs of them vigorously on her blotchy face. 'Why did you say those things, Quin? I thought you and Olive were expecting to' — she hiccoughed on a sob she tried to hold back — 'get married. She's so right for the nursery. The Squire talks to Aunt Tess and Uncle Peter, they must think so too. She's keen and interested, she's got bags of energy, could have your children —'

'Indeed she is interested in the nursery. She's a nice girl, you know that as well as I do, and I'm lucky she cares as much as she does for what we're going to do there. She's also got a life away from it, perhaps a boyfriend too for all I know.' He looked at her so seriously that she knew he'd expect a truthful answer to whatever question she was about to hear. 'Could your tears have anything to do with these tales the Squire tells you?'

'I don't know. No, of course not. I want you to be happy and the Squire says —'

'It's *you* I want to talk about. Lydia, maybe I oughtn't to have told you how I feel about you, you're Sebastian's wife. I can't remember a time when you weren't the centre of my world. You hardly noticed me because of Paul. Ever since then you've been the only girl I've cared about. You were so young when you met Sebastian, you probably never dreamed how I felt. And anyway' — again he pulled off his glasses, realised what he was doing and rammed them back on — 'anyway, what chance would I have had once he came along? So all these years I've kept quiet, I've tried to let it be enough to be your friend. Please don't look so sad, Lydia, darling Lydia.'

'Not sad,' she gulped. 'It's not that. I'm so happy. Even if I'm married to Sebastian, that can't stop us loving each other.'

He was in love with her! Just as if she were a whole, proper woman. Her arms reached out to him and she felt him kiss her stinging eyelids, so gently, first one and then the other. Then his lips covered hers. As far as she was able she turned towards him, her mouth moved against his. Hungrily she kissed him.

'Been such a fool,' she whispered, her face against his. 'Quin, why didn't you stop me? What were you waiting for? I was grown-up enough to want romance. I thought I'd found it, I thought what Seb and I had was what marriages are made of.'

'What are you telling me? Are you saying you love me too?'

'I wouldn't be any use, Quin. No more to you than I am to Sebastian. Don't you understand how I am?' She blurted it out in the only way she knew how. 'No one could ever want me like I am. Don't you understand? Since the accident I've never been any use.'

'Do you want me to say I don't mind? Of course I mind. And of course you do too.'

'Rum sort of mistress.' Her voice was her own again, she even found enough bravado to attempt a laugh.

He moved away from her, his action surprising her and, for a second, halting the flow of adrenaline that even the truth of what she was saying hadn't been able to slow.

'You see, I'm right aren't I?' But she couldn't bring herself to look at him for fear that his expression might tell her that he agreed.

'We're wasting good sunshine sitting in here. I'm coming round to get you out.'

He came to her side of the jeep, opened the door and bent to unfasten her restricting sandals. 'You won't be needing those.' Then, just as he told her so often, 'Arms around my neck.' But never had it been like this. She gripped him around the neck, he lifted her from her seat. Once she was safe in his hold, he looked down at her.

'Is a mistress just someone to make love to? Is ending each day with someone you love no more than that?' He stood still, looking down at her. 'It's more. Just as marriage is more. You are mistress of my soul, you always will be. Please God you could be my wife.'

Lying back in his arms she looked up at the high blue sky. There was no name for the emotion that held her, it had to do with the eternity above, the aching need in her to be all that he wanted, a wild and strange feeling that nothing mattered but that she was held like this and loved like this.

As he carried her along the sloping grass of the clifftop, she noticed another young couple lying in a sheltered spot protected by wild bramble bushes. She laughed up at Quin, proud of the image they gave: a young lover with his lady, proving his strength as he carried her. He too had seen the other couple. He raised Lydia to hold her closer, to touch her forehead with his lips. To Quin no one except themselves mattered, but he was sensitive enough to Lydia's feelings to know how important it was to her that she should be seen as the same as every other girl. The same? Not to him. Mistress of his soul, he'd told her, and so she always would be. No moment in his life had held the aching joy of this.

Just as the other couple lay in shade of the bramble bushes so, a hundred yards or so further along, did they. The sun beat down on them, there was no breeze here in the shelter of the bushes. She wanted to lie close in his arms. She drew him nearer, she fumbled with the buttons of his open-neck shirt and moved her hand on his naked chest.

'Want to touch you,' she whispered, 'nothing between us, warm, close. Take off your shirt.' Her hand caressed him, to the waist his flesh was warm. On the outside of his linen trousers her flat palm wandered further, exalting with joyous pride in the certain knowledge that he wanted her, just as if she were whole, he wanted her. She wasn't a blob, a thing, a sexless hulk, or any of the things she called herself when she bumped along the bottom of her trough of misery; she was a woman. 'Say something, Quin.' Perhaps even now she needed reassurance.

'I love you.' He bent above her. 'Love you, love you. Now you – you say something.'

'I want just to be yours. If I were whole I'd prove to you how much I need to be yours. Undo me, Quin.' She'd pulled her blouse loose from the anchorage of the waistband of her skirt. 'My bra. Undo me.'

He did. He unbuttoned her blouse. His beautiful Lydia! He feasted his eyes on her pale flesh. When she drew his hand to her breast, he felt the warm softness, he was excited by the hard, protruding nipples.

'Look at me, Quin, that's all there is. Not much of a mistress. You want more, of course you do.'

It would have been useless to deny. 'I want you. Yes, I want it to be the same for us as every couple who love.' He lay down at her side, his hand warm against her. 'You're so lovely, you're just as I've dreamed. Sometimes I lie in bed at night imagining the feel of you in my arms, the rightness of ending each day holding you, waking to – '

'Stop it, Quin. I want it too.' The afternoon was destroying all the barriers, making her face things she'd never talked about even to Sebastian – perhaps especially to Sebastian. Dry sobs racked her. 'Mr Bonham-Miles talked tripe about adjusting, about conceiving. As if I could! Told you I'm no use. Don't work the same way as other people. Not just my legs. Beastly bag thing and a catheter. Worse than a baby. Only Pam knows the secrets of this ugly lump of flesh that's me.'

'Hush, sweetheart. *You*, the real you, have nothing to do with those things, any more than if you lost your teeth or your hair. Things like that can't make us into different people.' He leaned up on his elbow watching her. Her outburst was over as suddenly as, driven by fear, it had started.

She didn't answer, but her smile told him more than all the words. This time there was none of the usual bravado, no overexcitement, no challenge for anyone to doubt her command of the situation. It held tenderness, it held relief.

'None of this can be more than a pipe dream,' she told him, holding her arms around him and cradling his head to her breast, 'so I'm not being selfish, am I?'

'I can feel your heart beating,' he muttered.

'Can you hear what it's saying?'

He didn't answer, but he believed he could. Knowing Lydia as well as he did, he ought to have realised that a new hope had been born in her and, with it, determination to shape her own destiny.

'Trudie, will you be here at the weekend?' Julie tried to make her question casual.

'I'd expected to be. Why, have you got something planned?'

'In a way, I have. Can you and Anna look after each other if I'm away on Saturday night? I want to go to London on Saturday and it would be less of a rush if I caught the Sunday-morning train home. I might meet an old friend and I know she enjoys going to the theatre. I don't fancy travelling back so late.'

Trudie looked at her thoughtfully. 'It wouldn't be Bessie, by any chance?'

Julie turned to look out of the window, taking an exaggerated interest in a young lad on a bicycle racing as fast as he could and leaving behind him a trail of small pieces of torn-up paper.

'There's the makings of a game of paper chase out here,' she said. 'Another minute or two and the pack of hunters will be on his trail.'

'Aren't you going to tell me?' Trudie ignored the red herring.

'You might say I want to see Bessie.' The made-up name made it easier to speak of what was still a sensitive subject for both of them.

'Have you heard from him?'

'No. And I shan't. Trudie, I can't let it all end like that with him thinking I'd walked out on him and all he cared about. I've thought and thought about it.'

Trudie flopped down onto a dining chair, her hands clasped between her knees. All these months when she'd believed they were moving towards being a proper family unit, had Julie been thinking of Sebastian?

'Trudie, I'll be back by lunchtime Sunday.'

'It's not that. Anna and I are fine together, you know that. It's just that I'd imagined you'd put it all behind you. No good can come of it, you'll only get hurt.'

'Here come the chasers.' Julie was still at the window. 'Do come and see them, heads down, tearing along.' But it was no use, there was no ducking the issue. 'Perhaps you're right and I shall get hurt — I'm not expecting it to be easy. But it's like lancing a septic wound, healing can't begin until it's done. He thinks I let him down, so it's not just my life that's being soured, it's his too. He doesn't know about the baby. I've got to tell him, make him see that I did what I had to do, and that I did it for Lydia's sake. I'm not going to let you dissuade me. We have to live by our beliefs — and it was something Grace Harriday said that made me suddenly see this as my only way to be free.'

'Aunt Grace? Did she know?'

Julie shrugged. 'She wasn't talking about Sebastian. "The greatest power on earth is love", that's what she told me. And she's right. What Sebastian and I had is being tainted, poisoned; I'm not going to let that happen. Like a canker it will destroy something that was pure and good. I can't forget him, yet I can't bear to remember. I

252

have to see him, get rid of all the lies and deceptions, then at least we'll be left with memories that are clean. Then I shall be free, able to concentrate on what I mean to make of the future.'

Trudie frowned. 'You're playing with fire. Anyhow, it's weeks since you saw Aunt Grace. If you were so sure, why didn't you do it before? Don't go, Julie. Put the idea out of your head, use your willpower. By next week you'll be proud that you've overcome the temptation. We don't want men cluttering up our lives.'

'Trudie, the only thing that clutters my life is the tangles that *have* to be straightened. I almost wrote to him, but the company's been touring in the north. I thought a letter might not catch up with him and it's not the sort of thing I want to get into strange hands, so I waited. This week he's in London. What about Anna? I can ask your mother – I could even ask Lydia, she'd understand if I told her I was seeing Bessie.'

'Bessie! As soon as you mention Sebastian, out come the lies. And you say you want to set the record straight!' Trudie remembered something else Julie had said, something that to her was more important than Sebastian. 'That thing Aunt Grace said, about love being the most important thing, was she talking about herself and Miss Keeble?'

'What if she was? People will whisper and gossip and wonder at the menage they have. But it's no one's business. "This above all; to thine own self be true", that's what she was meaning. After all those years she was married to the Squire, she has found herself, for the first time really found herself, in that tiny flat with Evelyn.'

'It's like that for us, Julie. Don't go chasing after Sebastian. What can he give you that we can't build together, except babies – and heartache?' As she spoke she crossed to stand behind Julie, putting her arms around her waist. 'Don't go, Julie,' she whispered, 'please stay with me. We've got so much going for us, no man can ever understand us as we understand each other.'

Julie felt herself stiffen. 'Oh, come on.' She tried to laugh the situation away. 'Whatever is between Grace and Evelyn I've no idea – probably nothing more than undemanding, harmonious companionship; that's something Grace's life has been short of. If that's what you have in mind, then, yes, we have a lot going for us. Don't let's build false castles, either of us. One of these days you'll really fall in love – not a wartime infatuation but the sort of love that is this greatest power we're talking about –'

'Don't talk down to me!' It wasn't like Trudie to raise her voice, but now she shouted to cover her humiliation. Rebuffed by Julie's frigid withdrawal, she felt anger was her only defence. 'You needn't

253

be so high and mighty about the affair with Lydia Sutcliffe's rake of a husband. Did he even pretend that you came before Lydia? No, he didn't. You and your power of love – power of lust, more likely. I don't want to fall in love again; you know what I think about the lot of them.'

It took all Julie's willpower not to take up the cudgels. But Trudie had said they understood each other and perhaps she'd been right.

'What about Saturday? Shall I give your mother a ring? I could take her by train to Deremouth – '

'Don't be so beastly. Of course I'll look after Anna.'

Instinct made Julie want to reach out and hug poor, hurt Trudie. Reason told her this wasn't the moment, and some inner voice warned of a danger she'd never considered.

It was nearly one o'clock when Julie's train pulled to a smoky halt under the arched glass roof of Paddington Station. Saturday was early closing day for many of the West End shops, but she had not come to shop. She knew exactly where she was going.

She had enough money in her purse to take a taxi, but the red buses gave her confidence. She was back in her own environment. The bus ride was short, and soon she was walking down the mews and up the steps to his front door. When she pressed the electric bell she felt its shrill buzz must have wakened the neighbourhood. In a second he'd come to the door, she'd see him face to face. Yes, there was a movement, he was coming. No, oh no! This was something she'd never anticipated. As she heard the clip-clop of high heels she turned and ran down the steps. She must hide, she must get under the cover of the landing outside the door.

'No one here.' The voice was young, the diction clear. 'Probably children playing a prank.' Then a click as the door was closed.

Julie stayed in her hiding place; her legs seemed to have lost their power. Into her mind flashed the memory of a conversation she'd had with Grace the day she'd gone for the first time to Delbridge House: something to do with how one's life can change in a second, an abyss come between the present and what used to be. She looked around her at the quiet mews and heard the steady drone of the traffic just beyond it. Giving herself a mental shake, she gripped her small overnight case and forced her mind into action.

She did not look back as she walked to the end of the mews. Not that he'd be at the window. Her mind balked at imagining what was happening in the rooms she remembered so clearly.

When the West Country express pulled out of Paddington Station at half past two she was on it. Less than two hours ago she'd arrived,

254

full of hope — for what? She leaned back and closed her eyes. As the train pulled out of the station, it seemed to shriek at her, 'Now we leave him, now we leave him ... now leave him, now leave him ...', all the time gathering speed until it was no more than 'leave him, leave him, leave him ...'

At ten minutes to five the train hissed and whistled itself to a standstill at Exeter St David's Station. It would have been easy to allow herself to wallow in misery and disappointment, but Julie's natural will to survive was asserting itself. No man was worth ruining her life for — unconsciously she hung on to Trudie's words. The rooms over her offices were empty and as immaculately tidy as she would expect Trudie to leave them. The car was kept just inside the back gates. The gates were open, the car gone.

Downstairs in the office there was work to be done. 'And when you're banging your typewriter keys, sing, "Alleluia, this is freedom."' The echo of his voice mocked her. She'd show him! What a fool she'd been, racing to London to talk to him, expecting it to be as important to him as it was to her that between them there was only truth. It had opened her eyes to what he really was, made her face what she'd refused to see. Rake, roué, philanderer, he was all those things. She immersed herself in work, Trudie must have taken Anna out somewhere special, they were usually back earlier than this. Julie didn't worry, she was glad to have the place to herself and not to have questions fired at her.

When a green sports car pulled up outside she barely glanced up from what she was doing. Then she recognised Anna's voice, high-pitched with excitement.

'Look, the light's on. Mum must be home. Mum! Mum!' Small palms drummed against the window. 'Look out of the window, Mum! Terry brought us home. Look what we came home in, all windy and out of doors it was, Mum.'

Terry O'Hara accepted their invitation to come in, even to stay for supper. Anna was beside herself with the responsibility of being a full partner in a household where the guest was hers as much as anyone else's. Julie was thankful that in front of a visitor she was free from the cross-examination she'd expected.

'What happened?' Trudie whispered as Anna carted Terry off to see her room and her new desk.

'A fool's errand. He wasn't home and I decided not to wait and try again. I caught the next train back.'

Trudie was satisfied. Her own day had turned out much better than she had dared to hope. She changed the subject. 'Terry's nice, isn't he? Jolly, doesn't put one on one's guard as most young men

255

do. I think he's having just as much fun with Anna as with a grown-up.'

'I'm sure he's nice, but what have you done with your own car? You must have left here in it.'

On the coast road and near to Whiteways the back tyre had had a puncture. With her usual independence Trudie had meant to change the wheel, and it seemed convenient to take Anna along to Whiteways, meaning to leave her there while she did it.

'She'd not been there since we left. How were they together?' Of course Julie referred to Anna and Merry.

'How do you think?' Trudie laughed. 'I wish you could have been there for the excitement. I didn't see Lydia, she was with Quinn. Usually is, if you ask me.'

'Go on. So where did Terry O'Hara come into the picture?'

'Oh, he was at Whiteways. The Squire spreads the word that he has a fanciful eye on Polly, but he's wrong. Terry hasn't an eye on anyone. I left Anna with Merry and Polly while he and I went back to change the wheel. He's a thoroughly nice guy, Julie.'

'You said.' Julie laughed. 'So where's your car?'

'Ah, well, you see, I'm ashamed to admit this, but we found the spare was flat as a pancake, the valve had perished or something. He said he'd see to it for me and come and fetch me on Monday to bring it home. We couldn't do anything in Otterton on Saturday afternoon.'

At supper Trudie was relaxed, viewing Terry with none of the suspicion she reserved for most new acquaintances of his sex.

'Don't you think Terry is 'tremely nice, Mum?' Anna asked as she was bundled into bed. 'Aunt Trudie and I do. Well, she hasn't said she does, but I know she must do. We sang songs and played "first one to see a brown horse" and "first one to see a black cat" games in the car coming home. This afternoon there wasn't any sand 'cos the tide was in, so we all went to Downing Wood, me, Merry, Aunt Trudie, Polly and Terry. We arranged to go again tomorrow morning, we thought you'd be in London with your friend Bessie, you see. Terry said he'd come and fetch us.'

Julie's instinct was to find some reason why Anna shouldn't go to Whiteways. In the train coming home she had vowed to herself that she would keep right away from all of them, even Lydia.

'You could come too, I expect, Mum. You did like him, didn't you?'

'Terry? Yes, of course I did. And I'm glad you had a good time. Tomorrow I'm going to be busy; being out so long today I've things to catch up on.'

256

'But I can go?' Her big blue eyes looked expectantly at her mother.

And how could Julie refuse her?

Never had Julie seen Trudie so happy in a friendship, except their own. Yet even theirs had had an underlying sense of possessivenes, threatening to her, necessary to Trudie. As far as she could see, Trudie and Terry made no demands on each other, simply enjoyed each other's company.

During the daytime, out on his collection rounds, he'd often call at Whiteways. Occasionally, too, if he found himself in Exeter during the daytime he'd put his cheery face around the door of Freeman's Secretarial Agency, hinder the progress of work for a few minutes and breeze on his way. More often his visits would be in the evening, but his manner never varied. Even Julie, watching from an adult viewpoint, decided there was no budding romance between him and Trudie; as for Anna, she was convinced that his evening calls were on *her* account as much as anyone's. And perhaps she was right.

It was a few weeks later, Saturday again, and Trudie had taken Anna to Whiteways.

'Aunt Trudie says there'll be sand this afternoon,' Anna had told her mother. 'We'll be able to play on the rocks. Why don't you come, Mum? Remember what a good time we used to have — and Terry plays even better than Merry's dad used to.'

'I want to finish some work. Don't look so worried, sweetheart, I'll be very happy. I like the things I do.'

'Well, that's all right then.'

And it was true. It had to be true.

They'd been gone half an hour or so when the continuous sound of a car horn brought Julie to her office window. Outside was a red car. Ruby! Her mind flew from one calamity to another: something must have happened to Trudie and Anna; Grace's leaving the Squire had driven him to do something desperate; Sebastian, could it be? No, why should Lydia come here to talk about Sebastian? Whatever brought her, it couldn't be anything good.

'I thought you'd never hear me!' From the driver's seat Lydia turned to her with a beaming smile. 'Just had to talk to you, Julie. Can I come in? Not upstairs, but we could talk in your office place, couldn't we? Get my chair and I'll show you how clever I've got at putting myself into it. Quin taught me. See, he had this handle thing put above the door, I can heave myself across.' Julie opened the back doors and pulled out the ramp, then wheeled the chair down it. Lydia didn't wait for an answer, she was racing on. 'I can do lots of things

257

now, I'm not going to sit like a useless lump all my days. Julie, I just had to come, we never had any secrets, I have to tell you. But first watch, see how I do it. One, two, three!' She gripped the bar, pulled herself up and with one deft movement swung herself to sit in the chair. 'What do you think?' She exuded pride.

Julie pinned a smile on her face. Whatever she was about to hear, she was determined to keep it there.

'That's a very clever feat! I'll hold the door wide. Just inside, then turn right into the front office. No one will interrupt us, we're closed on Saturday. What made Quin think up that bar for you to pull on? I wonder it wasn't on the car when you had it.'

'Quin has more imagination than Sebastian. I'm not criticising, Sebastian has always been generous.'

'I don't see it as generosity, trying to do things for someone you love.' Julie rose to his defence.

'No, that's true. Especially when you're loaded with money anyway. But he must think my brain's out of action as well as my legs. I know he leaves a regular order for those wretched flowers, and when he's in London my "little surprises" always come from the same shop, packed by the shop and everything. Useless trinkets, novelties, smellies to put in with my clothes. I'd rather he didn't do it at all. I bet some gormless shop assistant chooses what she thinks I ought to appreciate.'

'That's not fair, Lydia. Doesn't it show he thinks of you?'

'A standing order, I expect, like the flowers, then once a month or so they send him a bill. I may be wrong.' Then the smile Julie had noticed before, a smile that lit lamps behind her eyes. 'But it doesn't matter one way or the other. Julie, this is what I came to tell you. Quin has gone up to London today, he's gone to see Seb.'

'Quin has? Is it about the work you do at the nursery?'

'Oh, what a dumbo you are! I want Seb to divorce me. We'll give him grounds — we'll go to a hotel, book a double room. And anyone at home would be able to give evidence how often he's there with me, each day really.'

'You can't mean it, Lydia. Why? Sebastian was the beginning and end of everything for you. And he truly loves you. Don't be hurt by the order with the florists —'

'I'm not hurt. I used to be, as least my pride used to be. Julie' — she held out her hands and Julie found herself reaching to take them in her own — 'it was like a miracle. I knew Quin used to fancy himself in love with me when I was just a kid. I'd known him so long that I hardly noticed him; I wanted romance with a capital R, and in Sebastian I found it. The Squire was hateful about him and

258

that made me even more keen. At that age, of course it did. But never mind Seb, I was telling you about Quin. It sort of burst on me. All these years he's never wanted any girl but me. Don't you see, for Quin I'm not a lump in a wheelchair with swollen ankles and a scarred face. I'm *me*.'

Julie's grip on her hands was tight. 'And you truly love him? It's not just hurt pride? He's too good to be used, Lydia.'

'I've used him for years, at least that's what I thought I was doing; only now I see that I've done it because he's like a part of me. Squire doesn't know which side of the fence to jump, poor old darling. He wants me to turn against Seb, then he finds he has to get used to the idea of hating Quin.' She chuckled, enjoying her own new role. 'Poor old love, it's hard for him. He can't be too beastly to Quin, you see, because Aunt Tess and Uncle Peter are his closest friends.'

'What if Sebastian won't do as you say? There's Merry to think of. He'll never do anything that will upset Merry.'

The lights went out behind Lydia's eyes. 'I know. I've been over and over it. What ought I to do, Julie? I know the court usually says a mother should have custody, but I'm not an ordinary mother. If only you hadn't gone – he was happy with you and Anna. I'd have had a much better case for keeping him then. If I'm the adulteress' – said with a swagger in her voice – 'then the court might give him custody. Sebastian can afford to give Merry everything he needs.'

'Afford! What's money got to do with what he needs?' Julie pulled her hands away. How dare Lydia suggest that what Sebastian gave to Merry could be bought? 'He needs love, and that's what Sebastian gives him. "When's Seb coming?" How often have you heard him say it? Poor little boy! He needs love and pride, someone to praise him when he does well, someone to be interested. He knows you can't play games, but there's more to being a mother than physically looking after a child. You're there for him to tell his secrets and bring his worries to.'

'I'm not much good at listening. I do love him, honestly I do. And I'll fight Seb every inch of the way. I've lost enough without having my son stripped from me.'

'What does Quin say?'

'He says if we were married, living like an ordinary couple, then Merry wouldn't need a nursemaid, he'd be part of a proper family. Quin would make a splendid father for him.'

'He'd never look on anyone but Sebastian as his father. He never must. If you married the angel Gabriel himself, he wouldn't be a good enough father to take Sebastian's place in Merry's life.'

'I know. I'm not going to worry about it, not yet. I'll worry if I have to. Of course, if Seb won't divorce me, then I'll have a better chance of keeping Merry.'

'Poor little boy,' Julie said again. But Lydia's mind had moved on.

'There's only one thing about it all that bothers me. It's hard to say it so that you'll understand, perhaps you never can understand. I love Quin, it's as if I'm part of him and he's part of me. Not a bit like when I fell in love with Sebastian, all the whirlwind excitement. And because it's like that with Quin, I'll never again say I can't do this or I can't do that. But, Julie, to get over all the hurdles, to be a person who counts and does something useful instead of an invalid who sits like a dummy in the midst of other people's activities, is going to take every bit of my strength, mentally and physically. It won't cut me off from Quin, without him I'd not get anywhere, but will there be anything over for anyone else, even Merry? Whatever Sebastian says, nothing will change my mind. If he won't divorce me, then Quin and I will live together. He's my strength.'

'I can't see him divorcing you, Lydia. My bet would be he'll refuse point-blank. Because of Merry he'll fight to hold on to your marriage.'

Lydia laughed. 'Well, if he takes that attidude, then it's up to me. Get *him* trailed by a private eye for a week or two and he'd soon be caught with his pants down!'

It was the crudeness of her expression that left Julie in no doubt: Lydia might have had a wild, passionate infatuation for her hero Sebastian Sutcliffe, but she had had no deep and meaningful love for him. Memories crowded Julie's mind, but not of her fruitless trip to London; suddenly none of that was important. A great wave of joy swamped her. Sebastian my darling Sebastian, for the sake of your 'poor little honey' we denied ourselves a love that was real and whole.

Lydia was still talking, something about not wanting to stay at Whiteways, something about Quin and a bungalow they'd build near the nursery.

Julie got up and walked to the window, one ear on Lydia's words, her heart and mind far away. Love had no room for pride. She'd make him listen to her, make him hear the whole story. Now she did not tell herself that her future depended on making a clean sweep, that once she'd told him the truth her mind would be free of him.

'Lydia,' she interrupted, 'Trudie has taken Anna to Whiteways.

When you get home, will you give her a message? Tell her I'm going to London, and I shan't be home until tomorrow.'

'You hadn't said you were going out. Why so suddenly? Is it something to do with the divorce?' Lydia looked puzzled.

'You've made me think, made me see things in perspective.'

'I don't see what I could have said to make you want to dash off. Is there some man? I've told you all about us' — Lydia pouted teasingly — 'and you still keep secrets.'

'I will tell you, Lydia, but not now. I want to get ready.'

This time Lydia's pout held disappointment. 'What rotten luck! The first time I've driven Ruby right over here and I thought we'd have a real heart-to-heart. Anyway' — she cheered up — 'at least you've been able to see how well I'm doing in my fight for independence.'

A returned ticket gave Julie a seat in the stalls. The Sutcliffe Theatre presentation on that Saturday evening was *King Lear*. Today Sebastian had learned that his world was being torn apart, threatened by the loss of his beloved son. How could he put all that out of his mind and take on the mantle of Lear? Watching him, she marvelled. Tonight she understood Lear the king and Sebastian the professional, and she had never loved him more.

This afternoon Lydia came to see me. *Please*, Sebastian, I must talk to you. There is so much to be explained.

Julie.

As the final curtain fell she elbowed her way out of the theatre, down a neighbouring alleyway to the stage door, where she handed in her note. Waiting for the stage doorkeeper to return with the answer, she knew that explanations were only an excuse for her burning need to be with him, to help him.

'He says for you to go in. Last door on the left, can't miss it, got his name on it.'

It was actually happening. Whatever the future held might depend on the next few minutes; she was crossing the divide between those two closely guarded compartments of his life, he was inviting her in. She felt she was living a familiar dream. All coherent thought seemed to have forsaken her, and all that mattered was that in seconds she would see him face to face. Halfway down the long corridor she stopped to send up a silent and garbled prayer.

Then his door opened. Except for the beard he was still in costume and make-up. She saw it as symbolic: Sebastian the actor, Sebastian the man.

261

'Julie?' He spoke hesitantly. In that one word she heard fear, loneliness, distress, but clearer than any she heard hope. She forgot her own feelings and cared only for his.

Her mind had never gone beyond the moment of being with him again; even on the train today she'd been frightened to let herself imagine further. Old misgivings, mistrust, hurt, there had been so much that stood in the way. She had been certain of only one thing: she had to be with him.

Now suddenly the veil lifted. She hurried down the passage, her hands outstretched to be gripped in his.

Epilogue

Press photographers vied for place with newsreel camera crews. Posing outside Buckingham Palace was the icing on the cake for many of those who had been to the investiture, for not all of them were used to being in the public eye. Awards for service to the community, awards for outstanding contributions to medicine or industry; there were politicians, athletes, civil servants and entertainers, but on this day there was none better known in all strata of British society than Sir Sebastian Sutcliffe. From those who still hero-worshipped him much the same as star-struck Lydia had more than twenty years before, to the serious theatregoers, the lovers of Shakespeare and the aspiring Thespians who trod the boards of their local halls, Sebastian's name was a household word, with or without the appendage of his knighthood.

Turning off the lane, Lydia pulled hard on the throttle control; it always gave her a feeling of power to race as fast as the car would go up the track to the nursery. Once there, she braked so abruptly that she jolted to standstill, then, independent of all assistance, opened the door, slid her folded chair forward and out. Deftly she opened it, then, with a deep breath, got ready for the next stage before she swung herself into it.

'Quin!' she yelled. 'Quin, look at this! Oh, damn, I've left it in the car.'

Miraculously he appeared. Always when she was out in the car he had one eye on the track waiting for her to arrive safely back. But that was *his* secret. He'd taught her how to be independent, he didn't mean to spoil it for her.

'What's the Squire doing, gracing the nursery with a visit?' She saw her father's brand-new 1965 model parked just beyond the first glasshouse.

'Remember the newspaper was late this morning — '

'Yes, I collected one in town. That's what I want to show you.'

'Too late.' He laughed. 'That's what sent the Squire up here with his feathers ruffled.'

She pouted. 'I wanted to be the one to show you. Still' — her good humour bounced back — 'I didn't get our usual paper, that never has many photos. They were much better in the *Mail*. Look, isn't Julie gorgeous, so poised and elegant?'

Quin rumpled her short curls, his teasing action a caress. 'Not like some of us, eh?'

'Other pictures on page 4, it says. Here they are back home, still decked in their glad rags, but see, there's Merry — it says about him being with the Cranborne Players — and Anna and the twins. Oh, Quin!' She rubbed her already untidy hair against his waist. 'Aren't you proud of them? I am.' There followed a chortle that made her sound like the jolly eighteen-year-old who'd temporarily swept Sir Sebastian off his feet. 'Bet the Squire isn't proud, poor old darling.'

Coming out of the long shed that was known as 'the flower room', he hobbled across to join them. These days the Squire used a walking stick, a slim silver-topped affair and, when he remembered, he had a limp to go with it.

'I see you've bought a paper in town, Poppet. You ought not to put up with it, Quintin, that's twice this week that lad from the shop hasn't delivered until after you've gone out in the morning. It's not good enough. There was a time when young people could be relied — '

'Let's see that one, Squire,' Lydia cut in. 'How many pictures do they give? The *Mail* does them proud.'

'*Sir* Sebastian and her, a girl who came to work as staff in my house, *Lady*. Fine lady she turned out to be, couldn't keep her hands off someone else's husband.'

'Come on, Squire.' Quin put an arm around his father-in-law's unnecessarily bent shoulders. 'However it all came about, I for one am grateful.'

'Humph. Yes, well . . .' His mind didn't work as quickly as it used to, he couldn't pull a scathing retort out of the air. So he resorted to the only excuse he could find for his cantankerous ways: 'All very well for you two, you've got each other. Since your mother died . . . ah, well . . .' And he limped away towards his car before Lydia had time to remind him that Grace had reached breaking point with him ten years before the onset of the short illness that had ended her life. Lydia

264

might have been tempted to point it out to him; Quin never would.

The Squire meant to drive away without another glance. But how could he? As he went past he looked at his Poppet — to him that's what she would always be even though she'd celebrated her fortieth birthday — so happy, so confident too. To watch the way she enjoyed that swimming pool Quintin had had built he could almost forget the tragedy that had shadowed his years. He thought of Sylvia, nine years old now, as pretty as a picture with her red-gold curls and big blue eyes; already she could twist him around her little finger, which was just the way he liked it. He remembered his terrified fury when he'd heard that his precious Poppet was pregnant, he'd hated Quin with all the venom he used to feel for Sebastian. But not now. He knew he ought to be grateful; he *was* grateful. But there was no need to make a dog's dinner out of his gratitude. He'd been at a low ebb when they'd suggested he should make his home with them in the bungalow Quin had had built close to Rowans. They made him very welcome, gave him a bedroom and a sitting room of his own. He smiled as he drove back down the hill, picturing his room, himself working at his easel and often his little Sylvia at hers. What a thrill it had been to take her to buy it, helping her develop what he was sure was a very real talent. And where else would she have inherited it but from him? And he had to admit, too, it was pleasant to know that with Delbridge House sold he had a handsome sum in the bank.

A few minutes later Lydia was working in her flower shed. She considered that this was a side of the business that had sprung from her own ideas; which all goes to show the tact and understanding Quin used. After her first amateurish effort at drying flowers he'd occasionally 'just happened' to put his hand on a book that she might find interesting, or a little later on 'wondered whether it was worth turning a section over to growing flowers for drying — if, of course, he could get hold of any staff with the skill and patience'; it was just an idea, he wondered what she thought. Once the seed was sown, time and encouragement nurtured it. She learnt to preserve flowers without losing the lustre of their colour, and it developed into a sideline for the nursery. The Squire took some of the credit for her skill in making the arrangements; after all, he'd always been artistic, no doubt it was in her genes! From that stage it had flourished, the wooden flower house had been built where she reigned supreme over a staff of two young women from Otterton. Advertising in local papers had led to advertising in glossy magazines. The flower house was part of Rowans Nursery, that was where the flowers were grown, but the business was Lydia's separate empire. The arrangements went out bearing a simple white tag on which was printed in gold lettering:

Lydia's
Flowers for All Seasons
from
Beyond Downing Wood

On this day she was determined to make up a basket of flowers more beautiful than anything she'd ever done. Into it she would put all her own personal gratitude that her life was so good. Reading about Julie and Seb sent her mind back through the years as she selected the flowers she meant to use. There's poor old Pam, she thought, still looking after me. Not much of a life for her, I reckon she deserves a medal! She's like family to all of us. Then her thoughts turned to Julie. Even if what the Squire says is true and she was cheating me with Sebastian, if he'd loved me and if I'd loved him he wouldn't even have noticed her. So there you are, it worked out the way it should. Poor old Squire, I know he's a pest sometimes, but it's hard for a show-off like him to grow old. Quin's so good with him, never bites his head off. Then she chuckled to herself, wondering if perhaps the Squire found patience more irritating than a good argument.

When she was satisfied with her flower basket and had it safely boxed, she would take it to the station herself. And on the way back she'd call at the farm and talk to Aunt Tess for a while. There couldn't have been any news of Trudie yet or someone would have come up to let them know. Fancy having her first baby at more than forty! Lydia stopped working and crossed her fingers, her eyes tightly closed. The trouble had been that Trudie and Terry had messed about for years being 'just good friends' before they decided to get married at all.

The arrangement had to be perfect, nothing less would do. But at last it was done. She took a card to fix in the usual way, then hesitated and trundled into the tiny office to get her pen. There was a smile of satisfaction on her face as she wrote her message on the back of the card.

For Sebastian's career to be followed by the press was something he was too used to to be anxious to scan to the newspapers. As for Julie, the morning after the investiture she was away from the house before nine o'clock to attend a board meeting arranged for eleven. The traffic going into London made progress

266

frustratingly slow and, Lady Julie or no, she had a business to run.

She must have been coming towards journey's end by the time Sebastian emerged for breakfast, showered, shaved, immaculately groomed, and clad in a richly coloured heavy silk robe.

'Here comes Sir.' Anna dropped an affectionate kiss on his greying temple as he took his seat at the table for his customary ten-o'clock breakfast. 'You've missed all the fun, slacking there in bed. Merry and I have played two sets of tennis, *and* done twenty lengths each.'

The indoor pool had been built as an extension to the house during the last winter. Sebastian swam every day, with Julie if she was at home, alone if she wasn't, but he had no intention of competing with the youthful stamina of Merry and Anna. Swimming, like slow, deep breathing, was necessary exercise, it helped keep him in the shape his profession demanded.

'Anna and I are going to drive in to Guildford for the papers. Anything you want, Dad?' With a week 'resting' between engagements, Merry was enjoying his newly acquired sports car.

'All that way to read something you already know?' Sebastian raised his brows.

'You can be as blasé as you like, but I bet Mum will want to read every single word. And it's not every day even you get to see the Queen.' Anna had no time for humbug. 'Bet you when we get home with our pile of papers you'll pore over them just the same as we shall.'

Despite his dignity and graceful bearing, something boyish remained in Sebastian's grin. 'Shouldn't wonder you're right. It was quite a day, and tonight will be quite a night. Are you two coming up to town with Julie for the party? Nothing grand, don't dress up, just a few bottles of fizz for the folk at the theatre, but you might enjoy it.'

Later that morning while she was at her board meeting, Julie would have delighted in the sight of Sebastian, Merry and Anna, together in the dining room of their Surrey home, surrounded by newspapers.

'Here, listen to what this one says, picture what a feather this'll be in Mum's cap.' Anna marked a cross in the margin to make sure Julie would notice this was worthy of her attention. '"Leaving Buckingham Palace yesterday after receiving his Knighthood was Sir Sebastian Sutcliffe with his beautiful wife. Lady Julie Sutcliffe has a successful career in her own right. She is the founder and director of Freeman's Secretarial Agency, one of the foremost bureaux of its kind with branches in London and many towns in the south of England." Mum'll be chuffed about that!'

From the way Sebastian took the paper from her and reread it, clearly so was he.

By the next day, 'Investiture Plus Two' as Anna called it, some of the euphoria was fading and normality taking over. Julie and Sebastian were having a late breakfast when they saw the railway van come up the drive then Yvette — whose real name was Gwen, but she kept that to herself — came in bearing a large box.

'This just been brought. For you, m'lady.' She'd practised saying 'M'lady' in front of her mirror, but even so she coloured with embarrassment when she put her skill into operation.

'Shall I open it, Mum?' Anna already had her knife ready.

All of them were curious enough to stop eating and watch as she cut the string, as if they knew this was no ordinary delivery. Merry made a space on the table for the box: Julius and Juliet — known even at school as Lius and Etta — stood up so that they could see what was about to be revealed.

Merry held the box while Anna lifted out the basket, the flower display looking as beautiful as when Lydia had attached her card.

'They'll be from Mum.' There was a ring of pride in his voice.

'They're exquisite,' Julie said, taking the card and turning it over to read what Lydia had written on the back.

"It couldn't have happened to nicer people. Congratulations from Lydia, Quin and Sylvia." Then on the front "Lydia's Flowers for All Seasons from Beyond Downing Wood."

She passed the card to Sebastian. He read it, turned it over, read the other side, then back again.

'Yes,' he agreed, 'as you say, they are exquisite. And to think I used to call her "poor little honey".'

His gaze held Julie's. Poor little honey — what memories it conjured up! Julie's eyes smiled into his, and silently she sent up a thank you to that benign deity who had led them all to this moment.

268